THE PEOPLE OF THE COVENANT

THE EXILES

Robert L. Wise

A
JANET
THOMA
BOOK

THOMAS NELSON PUBLISHERS
NASHVILLE

Other Books by the Author
When the Night Is Too Long
THE PEOPLE OF THE COVENANT
The Dawning

Published in Nashville, Tennessee, by Thomas Nelson, Inc., and distributed in Canada by Lawson Falle, Ltd., Cambridge, Ontario.

Scripture quotations are from the NEW KING JAMES VERSION of the Bible. Copyright © 1979, 1980, 1982, Thomas Nelson, Inc., Publishers.

ISBN: 0-8407-7495-8

Library of Congress

92–050832
Printed in the United States of America

1 2 3 4 5 6—98 97 96 95 94 93

Contents

To
Margueritte
who ended my exile
by
walking with me

———————

THE STORY OF the raising of Jarius' daughter is
found in the New Testament in Matthew 9:23–26,
Mark 5:35–43, and Luke 8:49–56. The setting for
the continuing story of the Ben Aaron family is
taken from the ancient writers of the Judeo-Roman
world including Tacitus, *Annals;* Sulipicius
Serverus, *Chronicle;* and Josephus Flavius,
Antiques of the Jews.
Descriptions of Rome are drawn from the
archaeological reconstructions of Leonardo B. Del
Maso's *Rome of the Caesars.*

Once again I am indebted to Bernice McShane for
advice and assistance and to Janet Thoma for
editorial guidance! I also deeply appreciate my
secretary, Kristin Jacobs, for her assistance in
bringing the manuscript into its final form.

Robert L. Wise
LENT 1992

PART ONE

A.D. 60

In this you greatly rejoice, though
now for a little
while, if need be, you have been
grieved by various trials.

1 Peter 1:6

I

THE MEDITERRANEAN A.D. 60

Each time the Roman trading ship pitched forward in the violent storm, sea water poured through the small porthole. The heat of summer had not warmed the Mare Internum sufficiently to keep the salty spray from chilling the Ben Aarons to the bone. The narrow bottom of the boat was slowly sinking in the rising water.

Mariam breathed deeply and tried to smile bravely at her son, but she was forced to clench her teeth and grab for a timber as the brine from the porthole exploded in her face. Courage was not the issue. Leaving family, friends, and all security behind was bold enough, but neither she nor any of the family had ever been on the sea. Never. Never again.

Stephanos reached for his mother but disappeared in an explosion of sea water. He coughed violently. "W—a—t—ch o—u—t!" The storm swallowed his words.

To drown anonymously and ignobly mocked everything Mariam believed and held to be true. Pointlessly sinking into a watery grave scrambled her convictions. Mariam felt sick and confused.

A gigantic wave lifted the galley completely out of

the water and effortlessly dropped the craft the way a child discards a toy. The huge single mast groaned and strained at its moorings as if it might snap at any moment, smashing the huge sail onto the deck. Jarius went straight up in the air, cracking his head against the floor joist that ran the length of the boat.

Fortunately, the old man fell back into the arms of his son-in-law, Philip. Any warning or inquiry about injury was impossible over the roar of the storm. Philip only had a moment to grab the frail patriarch.

Even though Mariam braced herself against the heavy rib of the hull of the ship, the enormous swell of the ocean had shaken her violently. She kept her balance only by quickly clutching Stephanos. Although he had done little heavy manual labor during his twenty-four years, Stephanos had the unusual natural strength of the Ben Aaron family. He had been able to work his fingers under the huge red wood rib and to pull himself next to the side of the ship. Mariam clung to her son's shoulders reluctantly, fearing that the creaking side of the boat might contract and smash his delicate fingers. Good hands were essential in the family's jewelry business. Nothing must damage his hands. The family understood painfully well the cost of a smashed hand. Mariam relaxed her grip.

Mariam's extraordinary inner strength made the small gentle woman seem much larger than she was. Although Jewish custom dictated to the contrary, she was really the tacit authority in the family. Mariam wore her forty years well, with only a few streaks of gray in her coal-black hair, yet wisdom was etched in her face. She must keep her composure for the sake of the others.

Suddenly the boat lunged forward, and Mariam

was slung across the bow. She slid to the bottom where the collecting sea water immediately turned her outer robe into a wet sop. For a moment she looked back at the stern. Philip was still holding her father, Jarius, as one does a small child.

At sixty-seven, the titular patriarch of the Ben Aaron family had been a poor candidate to sail across the vast sea to Rome. He had shown absolutely no sign of apprehension when they boarded at Caesarea, and all had gone well for the first day. But Jews were a land-bound people. Sailing was reserved for fishermen like Shimon Kefa* and his small fleet that crossed the Gennesaret† where sight of land was never lost. The terrors of the sea soon played their cruel tricks on mind and stomach. Jarius had turned green well before the sailors mentioned that pirates were sighted. During the half day that the renegades trailed the Roman merchant ship, Jarius quoted and sang psalms as if oblivious to the ominous threat looming on the horizon. But he had sung too loudly and sat too erect on the stern of the ship. His quaking voice betrayed him.

Mariam couldn't stand to look at her father's misery any longer. "Please!" she cried aloud.

"He's secure," Philip yelled when his eyes met Mariam's. "Grab something or you'll be knocked against the bottom. The storm is increasing!"

"I'm all right!" Mariam knew she must sound secure. Her son or husband might feel they must come to her immediate rescue. Any precipitous action on her part could only jeopardize them further. "I can hold to the window," she called back confidently.

Mariam grabbed for the porthole in the hull. An-

* Simon Peter
† Galilee

other deluge of sea water crashed into her face, filling her mouth and nose with the bitter brine. Instantly she felt the icy water run down her chest, sending jolting shivers through her body. In all her years in Judea, Mariam hadn't experienced anything like the violence of the storm that was tearing their boat apart.

The craft was a small commercial vessel about nineteen rods* long with the interior divided into sections. The front chambers were filled with clay vessels of oil and wine. The rear compartment belonged to the Ben Aarons with only thin wooden walls keeping the cargo from shifting and crushing them. The family had no idea other valuables were on board, but the presence of Roman soldiers implied that gold might be stashed away in the ship.

"Can you see the raiders?" Stephanos tried to call over the increasing storm. "Are they still out there?"

Once more Mariam pulled herself up against the side of the boat. The boat heaved and tilted in her direction. As if boosted by an unseen hand, Mariam was immediately pushed up into place. Lightning cracked against the darkening purple sky and thunder crashed into her ears. She squinted, fearing the sea water. Slowly the boat righted, and the sea slid down its side. Not more than three hundred cubits away, the brigand's boat was bearing down on the smaller Roman cargo vessel.

The long, flat battleship had many oars sticking out of the hull, probably rowed by slaves chained to their places within the attack vessel. The immense ship looked twice as long as their boat. Because they did not depend on the wind as did the sail-driven boat,

* about eighty feet

the attackers could easily slice the commercial boat in half as soon as the storm subsided.

The *Pax Romana* virtually guaranteed the safety of the shipping lanes from Ysrael to Greece and on to Rome. Yet when ships strayed too far south, Phoenician pirates often plundered and looted. Even so, no one would have thought the renegades would not encroach on a standard route. Maybe some small nation wanted to shake free of Roman rule and had chosen the sea rather than land as the place of revolt. Mariam had no idea who the sailors were, but obviously the men standing on the approaching boat's bow were ready for battle. The pirates beat their swords against the railing ready for boarding. Only the turbulence and the heavy rain kept them from hurling giant balls of fire into the sails of the cargo vessel.

"Pray!" Mariam called out to Philip. "We are going to be attacked. Pray! There are far more of them than of us."

Mariam knew her father would be quickly killed. Stephanos would make a valuable slave, and Philip would be of considerable worth. She shuddered when she reflected that even at her age she would bring a price in the slave markets—after they discovered if there was any worth left in her.

"O Adonai," Philip groaned, "be merciful!"

At that moment Jarius vomited and went limp. At first he looked dead; then he began to sputter and gasp. The bow of the boat pitched forward in a great surge. The sea water that was rising in the bottom exploded against the stern and drenched both men. Jarius was suddenly washed clean, though soaked to the bone.

Mariam heard the Roman soldiers running overhead on the deck. The small detachment of soldiers would be no match for the horde pulling alongside. Although she understood Latin, Mariam could not catch what they were saying, but no interpreter was needed to decipher the panic in their voices.

A great cracking was followed by the sound of sails tearing. The planking over their heads shook as an enormous pole smashed into the decking. Many of the boards splintered, and other planks seemed about to snap.

"It's the rigging," Stephanos screamed. "The storm has snapped the mast. We don't have a sail up anymore. I know it! There's no way to guide the ship. We're doomed!"

Sea water began running down through the broken boards overhead. At the rate that water was rising on the bottom, the boat would sink, just from the leaks. Even though Mariam couldn't see other cracks, she wondered if the hull might be breaking up. Should that happen, the boat would disintegrate, and they would disappear into the sea.

Death did not frighten Mariam. She had already been there once and come back. Since that miraculous day when the Rabbi Yeshua had said *"Talitha cumi,"* Mariam had seen death—and life—through transformed eyes. His resurrection offered the final evidence that death's threat was vastly overrated. The Master had called her forth from the grave and, she believed, had called them out of Yerushalayim on this mission to Rome. Then why were they perishing at sea? If her faith was rightly placed, surely she would not be knee deep in freezing water. If God was in control, why were they sinking?

Maybe Ha Elyon* had not sent them. Mariam felt

* The Most High God

overwhelmingly bewildered as she did when she remembered the night that the young men had brought the body of the first Stephanos back to her father's house. The stone pounding that had beaten the life from him had also scattered any simple explanations she had for how the Almighty and the world operated. Some pieces in the puzzle never fit. Once again confusion displaced faith.

General Honorius, their old friend, had promised them safe passage. His personal aide was sent to be their companion. The young soldier was his surety against harm. And where was the aide now? Undoubtedly, Lucius was preparing for the battle to the death on the top side. No. In this world nothing was guaranteed.

The spray of sea water exploded through the window again, plastering Mariam's hair to the side of her head. Her eyes stung and the salt tasted bitter. Her fingers were numb and her feet burned. When Mariam glanced from the side of her eyes, she saw that Stephanos' eyes were clenched shut. He was wet, shivering, and terrified. His lips murmured some undiscernible prayer for survival.

Her father looked as if he had slipped into a coma. Perhaps sheer terror had shut his mind off. All the better if Jarius was to die at the hands of some wild savage who would shortly drop through the overhead door. Philip still held Jarius about the waist, trying to keep both of them upright and out of the rising water on the floor.

How did they ever get here? Mariam tried to remember the events, the decisions that had caused her to leave two of their children behind and venture into a pagan world that was beyond their comprehension. Mariam wanted to pray but couldn't. Anger clutched at her throat and distorted her best thoughts. Mariam knew she should be in deep supplication seeking devout hope. Yet she felt confused and distracted. Her extraordinary experiences and the holy interventions were washed out of her mind. They might even drown in the lake that was forming at her feet!

Bracing herself against the side once more, Mariam also closed her eyes, trying to remember. As death pressed in, she must recollect clearly why they had taken this journey. Having escaped certain death before, Mariam desperately knew she had to understand why she had agreed to their impending destruction in this boat-shaped tomb. Why had they left the secure soil of Ysrael? What had pulled her away from her children, whom she loved more than life itself? Mariam had to recall why they had been so sure that God had called them forth on the sea in disaster's wake. Memory was her only defense against despair.

Once more the faces of Leah and little Zeda floated before her eyes. She saw the entire family seated around the supper table. But the boat's sudden dip jerked her head forward, obliterating the tender images.

''Remember,'' she said aloud. ''Remember . . .''

II

YERUSHALAYIM A.D. 50

Mariam moved quickly around the supper table, making sure each of her three children had taken adequate portions of the lentils. Though the hour was getting late, Philip and her father, Jarius, continued their intense discussions, oblivious to the rest of the table. She placed the pot back in the small fireplace in the corner.

"Are you ready now for us to bring the dates and pomegranates?" the servant girl asked Mariam.

"I suppose," Mariam said in an uncharacteristically loud voice. "No one seems to be interested in the rest of their supper tonight—or what's happening with us."

Philip blinked twice and looked at his small wife in surprise. Jarius turned toward her with questioning eyes. Mariam continued in her usual quiet tone as if nothing had happened. "No, perhaps *the children* and *I* will take a few more moments to finish the lentils."

Supper was usually a warm family time. Little Leah and Zeda always reported their childhood adventures, and their grandfather Jarius lectured them on the proper behavior expected from good Jewish children. Philip always smiled at these righteous little

11

admonitions as everyone took Jarius's lectures with polite half-hearted seriousness. Stephanos continually remained aloof as if the two-year age span between ten-year-old Leah and his four-year edge on Zeda constituted maturity.

The family dining room was large by Yerushalayim* standards but as plain and simple with its undecorated stucco walls as were the rest of the houses. The Torah's prohibition against graven images stifled creativity. Halfway up the wall by the fireplace was a little niche. Years earlier Mariam had placed a brightly colored vase that once belonged to her mother into the indentation, and it had not been moved since. Of late, she had begun hanging long strings of garlic bulbs woven together by the door. A large old water jug had become a pot to hold long-stemmed dried flowers. Situated at the opposite end from the fireplace, the purple and yellow dried plants gave the room its only distinctive touch of color.

"Please clear the empty bowls," she instructed the servant. "I think we are finished with the bread. At least those of us who have paid attention to supper are." Mariam cast another reprimanding look in her husband's direction.

Though small, Mariam was anything but fragile. Since that awesome day when she made her journey back from Sheol,† Mariam had been a picture of vibrant health. Thirteen years of marriage and three children had not added many wrinkles to her delicate features. Her smoothly contoured face still retained the gentle flowing line of her adolescent years. At thirty, Mariam looked in the prime of her life. Her

* Jerusalem
† The place of the dead

snapping black eyes and coal black hair had lost none of their shine.

Since her mother's untimely death during her childhood, Mariam had been the mistress of her father's household. Mariam directed the household the way a captain guides his ship. When the children came, little changed. There was no question that Jarius Ben Aaron remained the patriarch of his family with his son-in-law ready to receive the venerated position someday. Neither was there any question about who really ran the house.

"Children—" She cleared her throat. "Perhaps there is something you would like to say in this adult world of talk."

Philip and Jarius smiled sheepishly at the rest of the family. "Yes," Philip asked, "how was your day?"

"I would like to know what is happening at the great Yerushalayim Council," young Stephanos asked. Although he was only twelve, Stephanos had his mother's remarkably spiritual perceptiveness and ability to assess the meaning of things. He, too, was able to see more than his years had taught him. "I keep hearing about this man called Paul and his friend Bar Nabba.* Some call him Shaul. Why the difference?"

Philip's eyes caught Mariam's. For a moment they stared at each other before she looked away. Jarius bit his lip.

"Every time I bring up this Shaul, you get quiet," Stephanos pushed impatiently. "The People of the Covenant talk about him all the time, but we seem to

* Barnabus

have trouble even mentioning his name. I don't understand.''

"My friend Marta* says that our family doesn't like him," ten-year-old Leah chimed in. "What did he do to us?"

Leah was small like Mariam, but Philip always said that she looked like his mother. Although no Ben Aaron had ever met Philip's family, they treasured his stories of growing up in Athens. Often he spoke of his mother, Lydia, whose complexion was much fairer than Mariam's. Her hair was also lighter and of a finer texture. Leah was her heir.

"I thought we were supposed to like everybody." Leah questioned her parents.

"Do I have to eat any more lentils?" eight-year-old Zeda complained.

"Yes," Mariam said firmly.

Zeda twisted his mouth in disgust and drummed on the table with his fingers. Talk was not Zeda's idea of passing time. Named for his Uncle Zeda who had died many years before, he had the nimble fingers that the Ben Aaron brothers needed in their business, making the finest gold pieces in Yerushalayim. Uncle Zeda's fingers had been crushed when he was a child, which forced him to be the family business manager. The rest of the brothers were the artisans.

"Well?" Stephanos pushed. "Why don't we like this Paul or Shaul or whoever?"

"The story is difficult," Philip continued, looking at his wife thoughtfully. "And it is important that we love everyone. However, sometimes—" Philip fumbled for the right words. "Sometimes . . . there . . . are people with whom we have problems."

* Martha

"What problems did we have with this man?" Leah persisted.

"He didn't like lentils either?" Zeda asked.

"We should be forthright," Jarius interjected. "They should know the full story."

"Do you remember the first Stephanos?" Philip asked his son. "The man for whom you are named."

"Of course! I am very proud to be named after the first martyr for our faith. He was a brave man."

"And our best friend," Philip added. "He was very important to your mother and me."

Mariam explained, "Over twenty-eight years ago, your father and Stephanos sailed here from Greece. They were best friends and had come to Yerushalayim on a pilgrimage to make sacrifices and observe Pesach. They did not know that the Messiah had come."

"But when we heard his story," Philip continued, "we knew we had to follow the truth—regardless. Stephanos immediately became a great spokesman for our new faith."

Stephanos stirred the lentils on his plate with his finger. "Sure, sure. We all know that Stephanos was your best friend. Tell us the good part of the story."

"There is no *good* part." Mariam sounded irritated. "Your father is telling you of a very serious matter. Stop playing with your food."

"The day Stephanos was killed, a group of men from the Sanhedrin took him out to be stoned." Philip paused. "Shaul was the ringleader of the group that killed our friend."

"No kidding!" Stephanos' mouth dropped.

"Really!" Leah sputtered. "Then he must *really* be a bad man!"

"No, no." Jarius shook his head. "We don't call

people bad. We offer them the opportunity to find the good that is within them.''

"Then why don't we talk to this Shaul?" Leah asked.

"Because he killed Stephanos, stupid," the older brother lectured his sister.

"But Yeshua* forgave the men who killed him," Leah countered. "That's not stupid."

"Oh, children," Mariam rubbed her forehead, "you do have a way of posing the impossible questions."

"Your mother and I will be discussing the matter," Philip answered sternly. "Yes, we must make sure there are no barriers between us and this man. You are not to speak of this matter with your friends. We must not discredit Paul in any way."

When Mariam had married Philip at fifteen years of age, he had become part of the household of her father. Philip had simply moved into her room. The place of her childhood memories was the cradle that nurtured her first hours with her new husband. Her world had been small, stable, and dry. Mariam had known only security and protection.

The terrible persecutions that had befallen the People of the Covenant had not driven the Ben Aaron family from their home into the streets. They had been spared the displacement that had scattered many of the believers.

In the years that followed, Philip settled into the family. Consequently, Philip's surname never really stuck, and for all practical purposes, he became a Ben Aaron. The family remained wealthy jewelry mer-

* Jesus

chants as Philip filled her Uncle Simeon's role in the business.

"The most important leaders of our movement have come to Yerushalayim for this conference," Jarius explained to his grandchildren. "Shaul is a significant leader now, and he is doing the right thing. We do not want to harm him in any way."

"The matter is among us," Mariam instructed the children. "We will keep it that way."

"Can we leave now?" Zeda asked impatiently.

"You haven't eaten your fruit," Mariam objected.

"We will get some from the kitchen." Zeda stood quickly to seize the opportunity to leave. As he darted from the room, his brother and sister quickly followed.

"The child is right." Jarius stroked his gray beard. "We must reconcile with this man. I'm sure he has no idea that after a decade and a half such ill will remains."

"Shaul knows that our family has always pushed for a mission to the Gentile world. He needs *our* support." Philip got up from the table and walked to the window to look out into the night. "He spoke to me today and said that we must talk. Strange, isn't it? He wants to talk with me."

"Ironic indeed!" Jarius agreed. "The point of this Yerushalayim conference is reconciliation. Here we are trying to bring the two halves of the world together while we and Shaul are split apart. Curious indeed that we are confronted with the only true *enemy* our family ever had."

"They brought Stephanos' body in there—" Mariam pointed toward the large gathering room just beyond the dining room. The single candelabrum in the corner cast haunting shadows across the large dim room. "I can still see Philip and the others carrying Stephanos wrapped in a sheet. I will never be able to erase that memory."

"And yet the Lord Himself has put His hand on Shaul," Jarius lectured. "Can we do less?"

"I know," Mariam said softly. "I know."

"Shaul believes I can silence the opposition of the local brethren," Philip continued, still looking out the window. "He wants me to speak forcefully tomorrow. He believes that the Yerushalayimites are too narrow in their views because they have not seen the larger world as I have."

"He has a strong point." Jarius shook his finger at Philip. "You and Stephanos came here from the Jewish colony in Athens. You were the first person to go to the Samaritans. Many of our people have never been beyond the surrounding countryside."

"Yes," Mariam added, "most of our local leaders believe we should wait for the Gentiles to come to us. They still expect the exaltation of Mount Zion to come with the second return of the Messiah. They believe we will hasten His return by bringing in all the Jews first."

"Exactly." Jarius agreed. "They believe going out among the Gentiles is a waste of time. But you know how to refute them."

"I really don't want to talk to Shaul," Philip admitted. "But I know I am wrong. It is our problem—not his."

"Having to lay down the last vestige of my resentment is like a little death that I don't want to face," Mariam agreed.

"No small price," her father agreed. "But not too great to pay for preserving our integrity, our faith."

"Why?" echoed from the corner of the room.

The family turned to discover that young Stephanos had slipped back in unnoticed and had been listening to the entire conversation.

"Why?" he asked again. "We always seem to pay such a great price. Why?"

Mariam walked to her son and pulled him close to her. "Someday you will understand." She stepped back and looked at his boyish face. He was standing on the threshold of the upheavals of adolescence; before long, erratic whiskers would turn the smooth terrain of his face into a field of stubble. In a few months he would be thirteen, and the time for Bar Mitzvah would be at hand—the world of childhood would be gone forever.

"I was just about your age when it all began," Mariam smiled compassionately. "No, my son, the road is never easy, but we cannot take the way of compromise. We must never deceive ourselves into believing that there is another way. No matter the price, the way is worth it."

Mariam hugged her son and shuffled him through the door back down the hall toward his bedroom. As Jarius and Philip continued their discussion of the events of the day, Mariam walked into the dim gathering room and sat down in the shadows. She allowed the dusk to settle over the distractions of her household. Stephanos must learn never to shrink back in the face of any threat to his integrity and their faith. Somehow he must learn not to fear such danger. Mariam knew, with the strange inner knowing that only she could understand, that someday her son would be called on for a great task and he must not retreat before that moment. Her son had touched a long-displaced memory, and Mariam knew that she must remember that experience in her past. With her eyelids half closed, she began to see in her mind the all too familiar garden tomb where the inner confrontation had occurred.

Once again the terrain came into view. Spring had dotted the hills of Judea with the purple, yellow, and red wildflowers of the valley. The almond trees were exploding with white blossoms. Mariam had gone to the grave of her betrothed, Stephanos. For months after his death, Mariam had come to the garden tomb, both mourning and wrestling with the seeming ineptitude of the Almighty in failing to rescue her beloved.

Returning to the garden tomb was natural. Resurrection was pivotal in Mariam's world. Life truly began when the Rabbi in Gennesaret* raised her from a deathbed. Her near-death experience brought strange gifts and capacities that Mariam did not fully comprehend. An inner eye saw what others never suspected. Often Mariam heard the secret whisperings of the world of the soul. In the beginning she struggled to know whether these experiences happened in her spirit or in the space before her face. Always a sensitive child, Mariam's return from death imparted a consciousness of extraordinary proportions. Of course, the Great Resurrection here in the tomb of Yosef of Ramatayim† changed everyone's world! Then Stephanos' death seemed to reverse and destroy the very hope that the other events had given Mariam. He still rested in this very garden in anticipation of the final resurrection. It had taken months for her to recover perspective. Mariam always needed time

* Galilee
† Joseph of Arimathea

in this place to get her bearings—particularly on the eve of her wedding.

"Hail, O favored one, the Lord is with you!"

Mariam had jumped. Believers often visited the site, but no one had been in the garden when she arrived. Mariam turned and stared at a large man standing only ten cubits behind her. Not having heard one sound of his approach unnerved Mariam even more. She was not sure whether the man was physically present or walked in her spirit.

The stranger was large, with long hair but no beard. His white robe seemed to glisten in the afternoon sun. Moreover, the man's face had a timeless quality that conveyed no hint of age. Young and old were strangely seamlessly blended without distinction.

"What—" she blurted out, "What—do you want?" Mariam had clutched her cloak tightly around her neck.

"Do not be afraid." When the man lifted his hand, the palm was strangely creased and shriveled as if it had been soaked in water for hours. "Mariam, you have found favor with Ha Elyon."*

"Who are you?" Mariam's knuckles had turned white.

"Behold!" the man answered, ignoring her inquiry. "You will conceive in your womb and bear a son."

"I am not married," she had stammered.

"But the hour is at hand." The man slowly lowered his hand. His countenance was awesome and his presence commanding. His black hair was pulled

_____
* The Most High God

straight back in a most uncharacteristic manner for the local Yerushalayimites. The sun sparkled in his coal black eyes, making them appear to burn with fierce intensity like the eyes of an angel of light. "Shortly after the marriage, you will conceive a man-child."

"W—w—hy are you here?" Mariam had inched backward.

"You have been chosen for a special task. A great honor has come to you." The messenger had taken several steps forward. As he closed the distance between them, he moved directly in front of her. He did not need to speak to radiate an invisible intensity, which created an ominous sense of power. "Rejoice!"

Mariam could only stare. The words were strangely familiar. Somewhere, someplace before, Mariam remembered the words. Immediately she searched her memory. His phrases belonged to another time and place. Were they from Torah?

"The son that you are about to bear will have a great potential. You have been selected to rear one who shall have a special place among the People of the Covenant. You must listen carefully to my instruction."

Mariam had nodded mechanically as her mind raced backward searching to remember where she had heard the man's words. She had heard them before. Yes, she wrote them herself—in the scroll about Yeshua.

"Your son will be great and a child of the Most High. You must protect him carefully. Teach him about the terror that stalks by night. Warn him of the attacker who waits in the dark alley. The boy must learn the meaning of wise retreat."

"Retreat?" Mariam had swallowed hard. "I don't

understand.'' The messenger pointed his finger at Mariam's face. ''Hide him in the shadow of the Temple, and never let him leave the Holy City.''

''I don't understand.'' Mariam had wrung her hands. ''I'm sorry, but I don't grasp what you are saying.''

''Fear death!'' the figure shrieked. ''Even *your* escape from darkness was momentary. Teach your son to guard his life well. His potential can disappear from the earth as quickly as the flowers of spring fade.''

Mariam rubbed her eyes. ''I'm confused—''

''Remember my warning,'' the messenger barked. ''Let my words overshadow you. Guide him into this truth. Teach him the meaning of fear!''

Overshadow me? Miryam, the mother of Yeshua, used that exact pronouncement when she told Mariam the story of the birth of the Messiah. Yes, Miryam had used these very expressions. Mariam and Mattiyahu* had written these words in their Gospel.

''You must raise this boy to know the error of the impulsive. Of all the believers, you especially understand the tragedy of the one who might have avoided burial in this place.''

''Avoided—'' Mariam had grimaced.

The messenger had scowled. ''Darkness swallows its victims. I know the abode of the dead. Have you forgotten?'' he smirked. ''Was it not a lonely, empty place?''

''Why would an angel of God know *that* place?'' Mariam's question had slipped from her mouth almost an afterthought, leaving her in total bewilderment.

---

* Matthew

"Warn him!" the foreboding figure demanded. "Teach him prudence!"

"You are *not* a messenger of light," Mariam said hesitantly. An overpowering dread settled like an evil fog, and her heart began to pound uncontrollably.

"Stand *not* against the tide that flows through this world," the pitch of his voice raised. "Receive the hour of your visitation." As the man spoke, his face lost its neutral quality and aged. Wrinkles lined his mouth and cheeks. "Do you question the Most Holy?" the figure shook his fist.

"N—o—o—o," Mariam choked and sputtered, "but I do question you." She brought her arm up, partially shielding her face.

The messenger's eyes had widened in intimidating intensity. The black pupils deepened until they became fathomless, like a pit without a bottom. "Do not refuse me," he pointed both fingers at her. "You will pay a great price if you do. Decide now! The fate of the unborn child is in the balance," he snarled.

Mariam took several steps backward. "I have heard of you. You are evil!" She spread her fingers in front of her face. "You came to Yeshua on the mountain, and He resisted you. Rudach Ha Kodesh!"* Mariam suddenly screamed to the skies. "Be my defender. I am not sufficient. Yeshua Ha Mashiach,† be my strength!"

When Mariam had looked back, the figure was gone. To her astonishment there was no trace of his ever having been there. Mariam shook her head hard as if trying to determine whether she was awake or

* Holy Spirit
† Jesus, the Messiah

asleep, coherent or incoherent. Was the conversation a hallucination? A delusion?

Mariam started to run backward, but she stopped. "Retreat! I will not be afraid!" she said defiantly. *A son?* Mariam pondered the words, *a child of the Most High. Even now the Evil One pursues my child that is not yet conceived.*

Even as Mariam sat in her own living room, she felt the cold clammy terror of that afternoon thirteen years before. She blinked several times to ease the memory.

Philip called from the dining room. "Are you still awake? You are so quiet."

"What?" Mariam jumped. "Oh my! I was just lost in my thoughts—remembering." She blinked several times.

"This matter with Shaul upsets you, doesn't it?" her father asked.

"The time has come," Mariam slowly stood up. "We must completely reconcile with this man and put the past behind us. If we do not, we give evil a gateway into our lives."

"I agree," Philip said simply.

"No price is too great to ensure that evil has no toe-hold here." Mariam walked out of the shadows.

"Tomorrow," Philip agreed, "we must face this man."

"Tomorrow," Mariam agreed and squeezed her husband's hand.

There had been a time when Mariam was sure that no one could ever replace her first love. When Stephanos swept into her life, he had been like a Greek god in his statuesque athletic handsomeness. In those days Philip was only his incidental comrade, along for the adventure. Mariam had not given him a second thought. But during those long months of mourning, Philip cared for her with a pure concern that was the essence of love. When he finally asked for her hand, Jarius had wisely not forced a new betrothal. Time had been allowed for Mariam to know this thoroughly good man. The marriage day came, and Mariam went joyfully with no regrets. In the years that followed, Philip's love and devotion were validated daily.

"Together," Mariam kissed Philip. "We can do anything together."

III

For the fifth of Nisan,* the midday temperature was unusually warm. Doors and windows were wide open to allow as much ventilation as possible to flow through the inn that now was called simply the *Upper Room*. The big rack of candles that hung in the center of the room had been pulled to the top of the high ceiling and all of the furniture removed. Even the sacred table was pushed back to the wall out of the way.

The large open room was packed with men who both stood and sat shoulder to shoulder. The entire leadership of the Yerushalayim Church was scattered among the assembly. Even delegates from far-off Samaria and Antioch were present. The apostles sat together in an inner circle around the center of the room. An open space had been cleared in the very center for the speakers to present their positions.

Philip and Jarius sat just behind Yochanan,** and the three leaders exchanged comments when the debate became heated. Philip watched Shimon Kefa's†

* March to April
** John
† Simon Peter

27

face carefully as Shaul and Bar Nabba* answered questions from the assembly. Shimon's bold features and strong square jaw spelled determination and persistence; sparks could quickly fly from his black eyes. But whatever the leader of the apostles was thinking today, he gave no hint.

"We must not put a yoke on the Gentiles!" Bar Nabba shook his fist at the group. His Greek-styled haircut distinguished him from most of the men. "Even we, who were trained from our earliest memory to be observant, have often failed to keep the kosher rules completely. Even the best of our forefathers could not keep all the traditions perfectly." His brown tunic fell back on his shoulder as he swung his fist in the air. "We cannot expect the goyim to do better! You make a mockery of the grace of God!"

Shaul gently pushed his companion's hand down. "Has not Shimon Kefa argued the same?" Shaul said more softly. He was short and slight; premature baldness matched his Spartan appearance. Although not physically attractive, he was magnetic. "We bear witness that the mighty signs and wonders of God have been poured out equally on Gentile and Jew. Who can deny that Ha Elyon† has made no distinction?"

"But there are fundamental issues of simple decency," an old man in the rear called out. His long, flowing tallith partially covered his gray head. "We cannot ignore the Noahkite covenant that has always been binding on the goyim. Idols cannot be tolerated. Humane treatment of animals must be observed. We must always oppose the infamous immorality of the pagans."

---

* Barnabus
† The Most High God

"Hear, O Israel!" an elderly man next to him bellowed.

"Yes! Yes!" echoed across the length of the room.

Shaul held his hand in the air and silently waited until the uproar subsided. "Of course, basic morality is always taught. There are many in the world beyond your boundaries who are good and sensitive people. They would never in any way diminish the high standards of our Jewish way of life."

"Moreover," Bar Nabba added, "we have the teaching of Yeshua." He held up a scroll tied at the center with a leather thong. "Is not His teaching on worship and uprightness clear? Did you not compile His teaching here in this very room? The goyim hunger for direction. There is no problem here."

"I believe the issues can be settled." Shimon Kefa abruptly stood up. "If we agree not to require circumcision but replace our ancient ritual with baptism. Food laws can be waived for Gentiles if they will keep the moral teaching of Yeshua. I believe our congregations can accept these changes. Can we not agree on these adjustments as binding on all of us?" Shimon Kefa looked slowly and carefully around the inner circle. His preeminence among the apostles prevented any unruly response from the crowd. He continued smiling kindly, but his countenance was firm.

The old men in the rear appeared to be grumbling under their breath. Many in the crowd frowned.

"We are close to a final decision," Shimon Kefa announced. "I would suggest that we take the rest of the day to ponder our thoughts privately. We must pray and then vote what we believe to be the will of Adonai.* We must be bold and of good courage. Most of

* The Lord

all, we must be faithful. Let us pray before we adjourn until tomorrow at the end of the first hour of the day."

Talliths were pulled over every head. Some men piously covered their eyes as the entire assembly prayed. A babble of holy sounds filled the Upper Room as many prayed aloud. Finally Shimon Kefa prayed loudly above the gentle rumble of intercession, *"Baruch ata Adonai Elohaynu, melech ha—olam,"* As he blessed God, the others became quiet. When his prayer ended, a resounding "Amen" filled the room.

The crowd quickly dispersed as some went through the front doors while others departed down the stairway to the floor below.

"I believe the issue is settled," Shimon Kefa shook Shaul's hand. "When we return tomorrow I expect the Lord to speak clearly in our midst. Peace." The chief of the apostles shook Shaul's hand again and then moved on toward the front door.

"We shall pray so," Shaul called after him.

"Well done." Philip stepped into the center near Shaul. Jarius stood close behind him. "You suggested that we talk today. Perhaps we might go to our jewelry shop, which is not far from here."

"Excellent." Shaul extended his hand. "I've been anticipating our conversation. "I am ready to leave now."

As Jarius, Philip, and Shaul made their way down the narrow winding street that led out of the neighborhood, Shaul enthusiastically recapped the morning's debate. Children were playing in the street quite secure in the shadow of the great building, which had become the major gathering center for the People of the Covenant. Shaul's excitement grew as he explained his expectation of imminent victory.

"You must be cautious now." Philip pulled at Shaul's sleeve, pointing to the major thoroughfare at the end of the neighborhood. "Our streets have become dangerous. There is so much violence these days that one must never walk blindly into an unprotected area."

"Yes." Jarius timidly peered around the corner. "Sicarii may mistake us for someone they are pursuing."

"Sicarii?" Shaul dauntlessly pushed ahead. "Who are they?"

"A new group of political assassins formed out of the Zealots," Jarius instructed. "Anyone with *any* suspected sympathies toward Rome is their target."

"Ah!" Shaul nodded his head. "*Sica* is Latin for a curved dagger. I understand."

"Many years ago my eldest brother was killed in such a senseless attack of the Zealots. Since then matters have become much worse. After King Agrippa died everything deteriorated."

"I hear talk about a disastrous upheaval in the city." Shaul stepped ahead of Philip into the broad street.

"Fools!" Jarius struck his fist into his palm. "Stupid fools. The Romans provoked the whole debacle."

Suddenly two men bolted in front of the trio. Running as hard as they could, the two dissolved into the market at the other end of the area. Soldiers abruptly entered the open space, looking for the men. People in the square mingled together, seemingly oblivious to the disruption.

"Provocations have become as routine as shopping." Philip shook his head. "During Sukkot* a Ro-

* Feast of Tabernacles

man soldier contemptuously bared his backside to the crowd. The crowd exploded in rage. Stones were thrown at the soldiers and the Procurator Ventidius Cumanus sent in reinforcements. Chaos followed.''

Jarius stepped carefully around two beggars who were huddled together against the wall. Each man extended a dirty palm upward. Shaul reached for his leather pouch at his side. Immediately two other filthy wretches rushed out of the crowd with their hands extended. As if by signal, three rag-tattered children ran toward them.

''Stop it!'' One of the beggars swung his makeshift crutch at the children.

The beggar at his side cursed and spit on the ground. ''We saw them first!''

One of the children kicked him.

Immediately the three men rushed on to avoid the escalating hassle. The beggars continued shoving, shouting, and cursing each other.

''They multiply like sparrows as the times get worse.'' Jarius complained. ''Who can tell the needy from the thieves? Riots have made them more aggressive. But we still try to help the poor in every way possible. We feed them at the Upper Room.''

''There was more than one riot?'' Shaul picked up the pace.

''Oh, yes,'' Philip continued. ''Another soldier found a scroll of the Torah. He tore it up and threw the pieces in a fire. The whole countryside was enraged. People stormed the Roman headquarters at Caesarea, demanding punishment. I suppose Cumanus had learned the lesson we taught Antiochus Epiphaneus. He saw a rebellion coming, so he ordered the man's head cut off. Only then did the fracas subside.''

''Everywhere I look I find revolt.'' Shaul shook his

head. "Our holy land is on the verge of total disintegration. The burden of Rome has become intolerable."

"Repent!" rang through the air. "Repent now before the day of the Lord falls!" Someone was shouting from a corner at the far end of a side street.

"Is that one of our people?" Shaul stopped to look down the street at the crowd gathering around the man.

"No, no." Jarius shielded his eyes from the sun as he peered down the narrow street. "Messianic fever is just infectious. Visionaries and prophets pop up on every street corner."

"The disease has become epidemic," Philip added. "Every day a new savior appears. Rational hope is gone. People have lost sight of intelligent alternatives to the chaos that has settled over us. We live under a blanket of confusion. Madness begets madness until only the extremists seem rational. The more bizarre the vision, the more credible it becomes."

"I understand there are many self-proclaimed messiahs." Shaul stood for a moment, trying to hear what the distant preacher was shouting.

"Pathetic." Jarius shook his head. "Shameless in their pretensions. These wild men come down from Galilee and grow up out of the wilderness."

"We are in the last days." Shaul abruptly turned back to his companions and stopped. "The end of our age is at hand. Final judgments of God are being rendered."

"You believe that Yeshua is about to return?" Philip asked.

"We are living in the fullness of time!" Shaul's eyes became intense. He began pointing his finger at them in staccato rhythm. "I believe the Rudach Ha Kodesh* has shown me that certain conditions must be met that have not yet fully occurred. But the end of this world is in sight." Shaul gently tapped on Philip's chest. "We must not let anything hinder our teaching that the kingdom of God is at hand. The whole world must know."

"It is difficult now to get our own people to listen to us," Jarius began walking again. "There are thousands of believers living in Yerushalayim, but the lines have been drawn between us and the rest of the Jewish population."

"This is exactly why we must go to the goyim," Shaul said, becoming even more animated as they walked toward the cross section. "I know that Toma argues that once all of the Jews believe, the messianic age will arrive and the Gentiles will just naturally come to us. But I know that they have confused the divine time table. We *must* go to the Gentiles."

Jarius pointed to the left. The great inner wall of the city loomed before them. "Our shop is just ahead at the end of the street of the jewelry merchants."

"The Holy One of Israel is doing something new." Shaul seemed to be lost in his own sermon. "From out of the ashes, a new institution will appear. A new covenant has been made through our Messiah. The goyim are being engrafted onto the olive tree that has been old Israel. We are the ambassadors of the new order."

"My daughter is waiting to meet you," Jarius interrupted.

"Even now," Shaul continued, oblivious to what had been said, "some of the apostles do not fully realize the universal implications of our faith. Our Mes-

* Holy Spirit

siah is cosmic!'' He raised his arms in the air, unaware that the merchants who lined the street were staring.

"Here we are.'' Jarius held back the canvas awning that was the entryway into their building. "Please enter.'' His invitation also hinted for an end to Shaul's soliloquy.

The coverings on the windows were still in place, keeping the room in shadows. Seated in a dim corner was a slight figure of a woman.

Large hanging strips of bright-colored cloth decorated the wall. The empty display tables awaited the latest creations of the Ben Aaron family. Philip quickly began taking down the window shades. As light filled the room, Mariam stood.

"My pride and joy—'' Jarius hugged his daughter. "I hope we have not kept you waiting long.''

"May I present my wife?'' Philip set the coverings on one of the counters. "Please meet the man that the world has come to know as Paul, Shaul of Tarsus.''

"I am deeply honored.'' Shaul bowed at the waist and deferred with a slight nod of his head. "Only today I discovered that you were the one who helped Mattiyahu* write the great scroll. *The Gospel According to the Hebrews* is the most important tool we have for teaching the goyim. I know you wrote it for the Jews, but its value for the Greek world is inestimable.''

Mariam stiffly extended her hand.

"Obviously I have missed the best treasure to be found in this holy city,'' Shaul clasped her hand warmly as he talked.

"We have some important matters to discuss.'' Ja-

* Matthew

rius set a large clay wine jug on the little table at the rear of the room.

"Yes," Shaul continued enthusiastically, "we must make sure that our rebuttal is fully prepared for the final meeting lest anything go wrong. I am glad Mariam is with us. Women have a unique place in this new order that is emerging."

"Actually," Philip spoke firmly, "we have another matter to discuss. Something more personal."

"Of course, of course." Shaul sat down. "How can I be of service?"

"Perhaps I should tell you something about this place," Jarius began. "Originally there were three brothers. Zeda, the eldest, was killed by the Zealots."

"Yes," Shaul answered soberly, "you mentioned him earlier."

"Our second brother became a well-known rabbi at an unusually early age. He was even granted a seat on the Great Sanhedrin. You met him many years ago."

"Oh," Shaul mused, "I don't recall anyone named Ben Aaron—" He stopped.

"His name was Simeon," Jarius said bluntly. "Simeon Ben Aaron."

Shaul blinked several times before settling back in his chair. "Oh," he muttered. "Simeon."

"You remember," Mariam observed.

"How could I forget?" Shaul stared at Jarius. "You are brothers?"

"We have not seen or heard from Simeon for many years." Jarius explained. "He lost his honor and place with the Sanhedrin. He disappeared."

"I never met him," Philip added.

"He was discredited because of me." Shaul leaned into the table. "When I became a believer, he was no longer trusted. He brought me here—to Yerusha-layim.''

''Oh, yes, we know.'' Mariam said flatly.

''Shortly after my conversion in Dammesek* I saw him.'' Shaul shook his head in amazement. ''He ran from me. I've really not thought much of him since.''

''All ties were severed.'' Jarius looked down. ''We lost contact.''

''But,'' Shaul answered compassionately, ''I remember Simeon as an honorable man. He tried to protect your family at all costs. He was strongly opposed to violence.''

''We have trouble remembering Simeon in that way,'' Mariam looked away.

''Most certainly,'' Shaul protested, ''even though Simeon rejected our Messiah, he was an honorable man.''

''Something else happened during that time,'' Philip spoke slowly but deliberately. ''Simeon was involved and so were you.''

Shaul's forehead wrinkled in a knot as he searched back and forth, looking into their faces. ''I was young, impulsive,'' he admitted. ''I made many mistakes. I— I—,'' his voice trailed away. ''I hurt many people.''

''Perhaps,'' Philip tried to sound casual, ''you remember a young Hellenized Jew named Stephanos?''

Shaul's neck turned dark red and his face flushed. ''Of course.'' He hung his head. ''The young man was brilliant. I believed him to be my archenemy. I could never forget him.''

''Do you remember how he died?'' Mariam asked.

* Damascus

"Please," Shaul's voice was barely audible. "Please, tell me what you want to know." His eyes became watery and he swallowed hard. "I can never forget how he died."

"I was betrothed to Stephanos." Mariam's hand held the table tightly. The muscles in her thin neck were taut and drawn. "We were to have been married. He was also Philip's best friend."

Shaul looked down at the table for a long time. His mouth bent in a broken line. "I am sorry," he choked. "I am so sorry. No, I didn't know any of this. You must find it difficult not to hate me." He put his hand over his mouth. "I am so sorry. I am so very sorry." Shaul covered his eyes. Awkward silence hung over the room like a funeral pall.

"Simeon had absolutely nothing to do with his death." Shaul kept his eyes covered. "The charge is to be laid to my account, God forgive me. But Simeon did nothing. He forbade injury to anyone. He knew nothing of the plot against the Greek. Simeon did everything he could to protect you as well. Can you please forgive me?"

"Simeon knew nothing?" Mariam strained forward. "Nothing?"

"I swear it."

"That's exactly what he tried to tell us," Jarius exclaimed.

"All these years—" Philip dropped his arms. "We thought Simeon was responsible."

Once again the long silence became all-absorbing. Suddenly Mariam stood and walked around the table. She reached down, putting her arm around Shaul's shoulders. "The time is long overdue for us to put all this aside. We did not invite you here to humiliate you. We wanted to reconcile and heal the past."

"Yes." Jarius extended his hand. "But we had to know your heart."

Shaul reached for Mariam's hand. "No one is more evil than they who think that God has chosen them to be the agents of His vengeance. The most violent deeds always come from us who self-righteously seek to impose His judgment. I was so very wrong." Shaul kept shaking his head.

"And we did not forgive as Yeshua instructed us," Philip added. "None of us around this table is without error. No one is righteous."

Shaul looked at Mariam, then at Philip and Jarius. "Thank you. . . thank you."

"I must hear the words again." Mariam bit her lip. "Simeon knew nothing of Stephanos' death?"

"Absolutely nothing."

"In my condemnation of you, I committed the same sin against my uncle." Mariam hung her head. "We all have our amends to make."

"I do not expect to ever see my brother again," Jarius sighed. "But we have learned many lessons today from which we shall profit in the future. Thank you, brother Shaul, for helping to set us free from the past."

"Perhaps, you have also liberated me today," Shaul answered.

"I feel that we should ask the risen Messiah to bless our conversation." Philip reached out to join hands around the table. "We must ask Him to seal this meeting with His love."

"And I must pray for my uncle," Mariam held tight to both her father's and Shaul's hands. "Wherever he may be . . ."

IV

While dawn still lingered over the city, Philip and Jarius moved quickly about their one-room jewelry shop. They had begun working well before the first hour in order to complete at least two special orders. Time spent in the special Yerushalayim conference had cost the Ben Aaron business dearly. Now that the issues were settled, lost income had to be recouped.

"Yesterday's decisions will remove all confusion about our mission to the world," Philip said to his father-in-law while filling the display tables.

"Shaul was certainly vindicated," Jarius replied.

"I believe we have selected the right men to go back with him and Bar Nabba to Antioch." Philip hovered over the necklace he was adjusting. "Tonight's service of commissioning is to be a new beginning."

The first bright light of day streamed through the small windows, falling on the colored banners hanging from the wall. Once the cloth strips had been brilliant reds and greens. Years of morning and afternoon sunlight left only dull, faded ribbons of decoration. With the exception of the wall hanging, little in the shop had changed through the years. The display tables and work benches were in exactly the same places as always. Seasons came and went, but even most of the chains and bracelets stayed the same. Jarius preferred the predictability.

"We're running low on Elilat stone." Jarius rubbed the necklace with a soft cloth. "I have not seen much good amalekite lately. We must make inquiries."

"Way ahead of you," Philip laughed. "Did you think that all you have taught me for these many years has gone to waste?"

"No, no," Jarius used his patriarchal condescending voice. "Just making note of our need."

"I woke Stephanos when I arose this morning and sent him into the city to make inquiries. It's time he learns about the buying end of our business. He already has enough skill to make gold pieces."

"Our family's talent lives on in his fingers." Jarius beamed. "He may yet be the best of us. Certainly his Uncle Simeon's ability to make gold necklaces was never excelled."

"Come now," Philip chided his father-in-law, "you remain the master artisan of Yerushalayim. People even come from other countries just to purchase one of your *dedahebas*."* Philip looked admiringly at his father-in-law. The years had turned his hair white and curved his back. Yet when Jarius stood tall, the countless hours of bending over a table no longer took their toll, and he looked as erect as ever. Still, the family tragedies and Jarius' serious disposition had left their mark in the creases on his face.

"The Holy One of Israel has blessed us. Jarius held the necklace at arm's length, carefully inspecting his work. "Praise be to Adonai."

---

* Elegant woman's headdress

Philip tied the canvas door back so that shoppers would know business had begun. After arranging the jewelry in a final artistic pattern, he returned to his own bench. Business was likely to be light until midday. Each man should have time to finish a few pieces that might yet go on display.

As the morning passed, a gentle breeze blew through the shop, clearing out the mustiness of the old oil lamps and the acrid smell of the lye and fuller's soap used to bleach and clean metal. The dry air carried a touch of almond blossoms and the other hints of spring that filled Yerushalayim when the wind swept down from the hills around the city and brought the scent of the fields across the houses. Both men felt the invigorating zest of spring.

"Surprise!" boomed a voice from the entryway.

"Stephanos!" his grandfather jumped. "You walk like a cat."

"We businessmen must move quickly." The young boy broke into the room. "We have to be on our toes to get the best buys of the morning. Right, father?"

"I didn't expect you back until the afternoon." Philip eyed his son suspiciously. "You couldn't have talked with all the merchants in such a short time."

"You *doubt* the skill of your son?" Stephanos chided.

"I would suggest that you'd better have a good reason for returning so soon." Philip stood up and put his mallet down.

"Of course!" Stephanos sat down at the little table in the back. "I have already discovered something new and unusual."

"Oh?" Jarius set his work aside and stood up. "Let's hear what the new master of the trade routes has to say."

Philip sat down beside his son. "It had better be good."

"I found a new merchant who brings exquisite jewels from afar." Stephanos beamed. "No one knows about him. I alone have found this source of supply."

"You?" Jarius wrinkled his forehead. "Why you?"

"Because I am clever. I am a Ben Aaron. That's why."

"Yes, yes," Jarius rolled his eyes. "You must learn that such a ploy is an old trick of merchants. They want you to think you are special so you won't be as critical in your dealings with them. Many people know about this man I'm sure."

"No . . ." Stephanos shook his head. "I don't think so. I was in the area near the Pool of Siloe* and stopped at the tents of the Phoenician traders. You remember Ishmael? You know the Arab who sold us emeralds when you made the huge *dedaheba* for the Roman general?"

"How can we ever forget him?" Philip threw up his hands. "He is a pest—like the hungry dogs of the street."

"He called out to me, 'Young Ben Aaron come here.' At once this other man stepped from out of the shadows and began to ask about me. After Ishmael introduced me, this strange man invited me to drink hot tea with them. He told me he had found the best gems Yerushalayim has ever seen. He knew of our family and said we were exactly the type of merchants who could profit from the exceptional quality of his stones."

Philip looked knowingly at his father-in-law. Both

* Pool of Shiloam

men smiled kindly at the enthusiasm of their young buyer.

"You think I am a fool," Stephanos groaned and looked away.

"No, no, my son." Philip patted him affectionately on the back. "I am sure you have assessed the situation correctly." A hint of solicitude diluted Philip's assurance.

"*No, you don't,*" Stephanos fumed. "But think about this!" He reached into the belt around his waist and produced a leather pouch. "The man told me to bring this stone back to you as a proof of his wares."

"He trusted you with a gem?" Philip's eyes narrowed.

Stephanos turned the pouch upside down, and a large smooth piece of lapis lazuli slid to the table. A dark blue stone with flecks of gold sparkled in the light. The highly polished surface almost seemed to glow.

"Good heavens!" Jarius stared at the gemstone. "Such a cut is worth at least thirty denarii.* You have been walking around the city with such valuable merchandise!"

"I know, I know. Stephanos smirked. "I'm not dumb. Have I not brought you a prize?"

"The man trusted you with this stone?" Philip shook his head. "I can't believe what I see."

"Perhaps, next time you will give me the respect I am due." Stephanos sat back in his chair and smiled.

"We must get this back at once." Philip grabbed the stone. "This man could tell the Romans that you stole it from him. They might even come for us, charging that we are dealing in stolen jewelry."

---

* Equals one month's wages

"Now wait a minute!" Stephanos protested.

"Yes." Jarius stroked his chin and looked gravely at his grandson. "I am sure you have been set up for some diabolic plan. No one would give a boy such an expensive stone to carry through the city."

"Who was this man?" Philip took hold of his son's robe. "Did you get his name?"

"Yes—yes," Stephanos stammered. His eyes darted back and forth between his father and grandfather. "I thought I—"

"Later!" Philip cut him off. "What was the man's name?"

Stephanos looked blank for a moment. "Yochanan," he said slowly. "His name was Yochanan Ben Zakkai."

"I have never heard of him." Jarius shook his head. "Never in all my years have I heard of this jewelry merchant."

"Perhaps this time Ishmael has set a little trap for us." Philip grabbed Stephanos' arm. "We must find this Ben Zakkai at once."

Jarius pushed his grandson toward the door. "Get back to him before a trap can be sprung. Jarius pushed the canvas flaps aside to let Stephanos out. "Hurry!" he called after them.

Philip pulled his son along as he raced through the back streets of the city, steadily descending toward the Pool of Siloe. He kept firing questions at Stephanos, barely giving him time to answer one before he asked the next one. Philip cut between houses and vendors' stalls as he pushed on toward the wall that separated the new part of the city from the old Jebusite village of David.

"Think carefully," Philip demanded. "What did he look like?"

"His hair was nearly white." Stephanos struggled to keep up with his father, "But he really didn't look a lot different from anyone else in the city except that he was blind in one eye. He had a black patch over his left eye."

"Anything else unusual about him?"

"No," Stephanos puffed. "He was Jewish just like us. In fact, he looked a lot like grandfather, must be close to the same age."

"Blind in one eye? I don't remember such a man."

Stephanos kicked at a rock and scratched his head. Ahead he could see the stairs that led down to the pool area where the merchants gathered. "A chain!" Stephanos suddenly exclaimed. "Around his neck was an unusually large gold chain. No one in Yerushalayim wears such chains. The old man must be very wealthy."

"What was on the chain? Think. Was there a jewel, a symbol?"

"Yes, there was a *Morgen David** in the center. The design work was exceptional."

"Watch your step—the steep part of the path is just ahead," Philip warned. "The descent down to the pool is abrupt." Philip reached for the stone wall to keep from walking too quickly.

"The Phoenician tents are always near the back." Philip pointed to the row of jewel merchants, who had inhabited the landing halfway down to the pool. The path broadened, forming a natural rest area before the trail cut back and descended to the bottom. For centuries merchants had set up tents in the open flat expanse. The daily flow of visitors to the Pool of Siloe always brought buyers by Ishmael's open door-

---

* Star of David

way. Conveniently seated on a stool, the crafty Arab only needed to call out his list of bargains to attract customers. Other merchants lined the well-worn path, but most only offered trinkets and cheap junk. Everyone knew that the Arab dealt in truly valuable precious gems and metals. "Now where is this Yochanan Ben Zakkai?" Philip demanded.

"I will show you, Father." Stephanos moved in front as if giving directions might redeem him. "Ishmael's tent is just ahead, and the man was with him."

The tent was red and green. The large pavilion backed up to a high retaining wall. Anyone who took the winding path down to the pool could not miss this particular location. Either going up or coming down, people paused to catch their breath there, but—there were no signs of activity. The front flap on the multicolored canvas tent was down.

"Ishmael!" Philip cupped his hand to his mouth. "Ishmael, are you there?"

"You have called forth a humble son of the desert," a voice answered. "Is it not the time to rest before the afternoon sun overtakes us?"

"We must talk with you *now*," Philip answered impatiently.

The side of the tent turned back, and a small, swarthy man wrapped in the baggy robes of the desert stepped out. A *keffiyeh** covered his head and much of his face. Life in the burning sands had blackened his skin. His coal black eyes seemed without pupils.

"It is I—Philip, of the Ben Aaron family. We must talk."

* Arab headdress

"Ah, my brother." The Arab made a sweeping bow. "Welcome to my humble tent. I see you have brought your purchasing agent with you."

"Where is the man who was here this morning—the white haired man? The man with one eye?"

"Man?" the Arab rubbed his chin. "There have been so many. Which man?"

"Don't trifle with me," Philip snapped. "I speak of the man who gave my son this piece of lapis."

"H—m—m . . ." The Arab pulled at his ear. "Yes," he said slowly, "I remember your boy bargaining with such a man. But you must know that hundreds of people come here. Are we not the finest gem merchants in the city?"

"The man had a large chain around his neck," Stephanos pushed. "Surely you remember him."

"Well . . ." Ishmael swayed his head back and forth. "Now that you mention the chain, the face comes back to mind. Perhaps you would like to do business with this man? Have you ever seen a better gem than the one sent with you?" A sly grin crossed his face.

"What game are we playing?" Philip looked hard at the Arab. "Of course, you know this man. Perhaps there is some scheme afoot?"

"We have done business for years." The Arab stretched out his arms as if measuring a vast expanse. "How can we not trust one another? Do not be afraid to say that you would like to trade with this merchant. I will not be offended. He brings great treasures from afar."

Philip dropped Stephanos' leather pouch in the Arab's hand. "Sending a boy into the city with such a valuable stone is more than suspicious. I don't know what's afoot here but we don't want any part of it. Give the man the gem when he returns.''

''But I may not see him again for days.''

''Good!'' Philip backed away. ''Then you are responsible for his merchandise.'' Philip pulled his son's robe as he started back up the winding stairs. ''If we want to do business, we'll find him.''

''I'm sorry,'' Stephanos apologetically called back.

''Just learn a lesson today,'' Philip continued as he pulled his son up the path leading out of the area. ''Never let anyone give you gems or gold unless the transaction is sealed. We cannot trust the intentions of *anyone.*''

''Yes, father.'' Stephanos hung his head. ''I will remember.''

The Arab stood in the doorway of his tent watching the pair disappear. Another shadow fell alongside his own. From the back of the tent a man emerged to watch Philip and his son leave. The tall, thin, white-haired man wore a heavy golden chain around his neck with a magnificent *Morgen David* in the center. A black patch covered his left eye.

V

Philip kissed his wife on the forehead. "We will eat with the brethren. The meeting may go quite long tonight."

"Stephanos is staying here?" Mariam asked.

Philip frowned. "I think so."

"Now, son," Jarius pleaded as he threw his outer cloak over his shoulder, "I think you were *too* hard on the boy today. After all he was trying to do his best." Jarius tried to sound indifferent as if he could conceal his bias toward his favorite grandchild.

"I think not," Philip said stiffly. "Stephanos can be frighteningly naive."

"But his heart is always very good," Jarius pleaded.

"Wondrously good." Mariam was pensive. "Yes, our son is without guile. And that is both his strength and weakness. He comes as a lamb into a world of wolves. His eyes are not trained to perceive cunning and deception. He does not see evil."

"Jarius," Philip said, looking at his father-in-law, "the first time I met any of your family I was amazed. I had come from a Greek world where men cheat, lie, and steal as easily as they buy fruit in the market.

50

Such a world is foreign to all of you. In your own way you are as guileless as is my son. The years have done their work on you, but your heart is still wrapped in kindness. Stephanos has inherited a double portion of your tribe's gift. We do not want to crush his spirit, but we must open his eyes to what lurks in the minds of wicked men."

"Yes, yes," Jarius reluctantly agreed, "but we must encourage his independence too."

"Certainly, *Abba.*" Mariam shook her head. "But Stephanos has almost no capacity to recognize evil. Unless he learns to read the cunning in the eyes of men, one day he will be prey for the scavengers that roam the back streets. I fear because he naturally trusts everyone to have the same pure motives. At some critical moment he will walk into a trap that could take his life."

"I don't want my son to be disillusioned," Philip spoke to Jarius. "But I don't want him to be a fool either. He must learn to be aware without being cynical."

"I suppose," said Jarius, sounding disgusted. "I just don't like it."

"The Holy One of Israel has a unique plan for our son's life," Mariam insisted. "We must help him learn to be prudent. I know that is what Philip wants for him. Perhaps, today was just one of those lessons he must learn along the way."

"Of course," Philip smiled. "Actually the stone was quite a prize. Stephanos has a good eye. He'll learn."

Jarius pushed his son-in-law toward the open door. "We must hurry. Tonight is a big night."

Philip waved over his shoulder as they hurried out into the darkness.

Once the evening meal was finished and the initial

fellowship completed, Yaakov,* the brother of Yeshua and the bishop of the Yerushalayim Church, began the Agape Feast. The apostles sat at the far end of the Upper Room around the sacred table while the company of believers huddled together throughout the room. The center tables had been cleared of the remaining food.

The assembly sang familiar Jewish hymns before they drifted into the new songs of the People of the Covenant. "Having the form of God," they chanted. "Taking the form of a servant," the haunting melody drifted out the open windows. "Not counting equality a thing to be grasped, emptying Himself," the lyrics floated down to the many believers who sat on the street around the walls of the inn listening and praying. "He humbled Himself," one group sang. "He humbled Himself," the side of the room answered back. "Obedient," the words of the chorus were sung together. "Obedient, obedient." As the other verses continued, a holy hush settled over the entire building and the street below. Everyone seemed to sense the historical importance of the evening.

Songs became prayers. Some men sat on the floor with their faces in their hands while others knelt holding their arms toward heaven. Jarius and Philip sat in the traditional Jewish posture with their heads covered and their palms extended upward.

When the prayers subsided, Yaakov picked up a large silver cup. Holding the chalice over their heads, he proclaimed, "On the night that He was betrayed our Messiah took the bread." He held a large disc of flat bread above his head and tore it in half. He handed half the loaf to the apostles on each side of

---

* James, called the brother of Jesus, is also referred to as His first cousin.

him. Each man took a piece before passing the bread on to the next person. Yaakov held the sacred vessel above his head. "The cup is the new covenant in His blood. As often as we do this, we proclaim the Lord's death until He comes." After he took a sip, he passed the cup on to the next apostle. Slowly the bread and wine went from person to person across the vast room.

After each person had received the cup, Shimon Kefa moved to the center of the table and called for Bar Sabbas* and Sila to come before the apostles. "We have called you out as envoys to the goyim in Antioch, Syria, and Cilicia. Take our greetings to them. Proclaim the gospel." Each of the men nodded his head solemnly.

"We have come to a holy moment," Shimon Kefa explained to the entire room. "Never before has the house of Ysrael sent missionaries into the Gentile world. If our blood brothers hated us in the past, how much more shall they now despise us? And yet how can we not recognize what *Abba* God has done? Brother Shaul has challenged us to accept the complete calling that Yeshua gave us when he ascended. We are now ready to go into all the world."

A murmur of affirmation sounded around the room.

Shimon Kefa continued giving instructions and counsel to the two men sitting before him. The youthfulness and sincere intention of Bar Sabbas and Sila were obvious on each man's face. Philip and Jarius stood in the back and watched the apostles gather around the two men. Shaul and Bar Nabba stepped forward also to lay their hands on each one. As the

* Barsabbas, Son of Shabbat

young men were commissioned, prayers were made for their safety and health.

Shaul began to pray more loudly. His voice boomed over the other prayers arising from the congregation. "Listen my people!" Shaul's head was thrown back and his eyes were closed tightly, but his arms were lifted upward and his chest extended as if he were offering himself as a sacrifice. "I, the Lord, will bless you and prosper my church because of this day," he prophesied. "I will open the windows of heaven and unlock all sealed doors that nothing may hinder the message. From this hour onward the fullness of my new covenant will be made known. What has begun as a star in the night will fill the sky like a blazing sun until the empire itself is swallowed by the light."

Silence seized the room as everyone turned his attention to the little man who prayed as if he were the very mouthpiece of God. The Yerushalayimites who traditionally prayed or sang the psalms were awed by the exploding prayer that gushed out of Shaul like the Jordan tumbling down from Mount Hermon.

"Even Shimon Kefa gawked at him. "Rome itself shall bow at your feet." Shaul paused only to catch a large gulp of air. "What has begun here in the lowliest of places shall be exalted on the top of the seven hills. The day shall come when your *ekklesia** will exceed the glory of the realm."

Silence became breathlessness as reverence mingled with consternation. Philip and Jarius stared. The atmosphere of the room became super charged with divine energy.

"From your midst will I choose my ambassadors who shall confront even the mighty Caesar when the

* Church

exalted are brought low," Shaul continued as if speaking out of a trance. "Yea, from this room will come my envoys of grace. The house of Ben Aaron shall be my voice. In that day they will be my messengers of the truth making known the covenant to the evil city. Fear not, for I shall be with you as you are called out and sent forth." Shaul's voice trailed away. Slowly he lowered his hands and head.

The awestruck group turned their attention from Shaul to Philip and Jarius. Both men looked blank and uncomprehending. Obviously few in the room knew what to do with Shaul's strange ecstatic message. None dared to probe the implications of what had filled their ears. Finally Yaakov* broke the silence by inviting the assembly to come forward and bless Bar Sabbas and Sila. Jarius and Philip stood in place watching the men push past them.

"What did he say?" Philip finally asked his father-in-law.

"My ears heard, but my mind did not understand," the older man replied, shaking his head. "I've never heard anything quite like this. It is as if Eliyahu** and Yesha'yahu† have returned. Someone must clarify Shaul's words to us."

"I can," a man spoke behind them.

Philip and Jarius turned to find a tall thin man standing behind them. His unusually fair complexion and extremely round eyes clearly set him apart from the Yerushalayimites.

"I am Mark of Cyrene. Paul invited me to come with him from Antioch. Is his prophecy not of the same order as Agabus gave when he foretold in our

* James
** Elijah
† Isaiah

city that there would be a great famine during the reign of Claudius? Believers in the Greek *ekklesia* are accustomed to receiving such direct guidance."

"Perhaps," Jarius said slowly, "we are a bit more traditional here."

"You will learn from us." Though he was respectful, a hint of condescension seeped into Mark's explanation. "On many other occasions, the Holy Spirit has spoken a similar message. The Christianios will some day conquer Rome itself."

"Conquer Rome?" Philip blinked.

"Someone here named Ben Aaron is being called out to go there," Mark explained factually. "Possibly you might know this person?"

"Oh yes," Jarius fumbled, "but who are 'Christianios'?"

"Greeks in Antioch have given our movement this name," Mark sounded superior. "My, but you people are isolated. Rather than saying Yeshua Ha Mashiach, Greeks call the savior Jesus the Christ. Since we all owe our lives to Him, the pagans refer to us as Christianios—as Christians, the slaves of Christ."

"I see." Jarius stroked his beard.

"Whoever this Ben Aaron is, he must learn such things. The new ways are the customs of the real world." Mark sounded very knowing. "We are truly living in a new day. Please excuse me, I must speak to Barnabbas. The man hurried on past two apostles to shake hands enthusiastically with the man Jarius called Bar Nabba.

Philip and Jarius did not move or speak as the self-appointed authority from Cyrene walked away. They watched in consternation while the packed room emptied. Men hurried out the door as well as down the inner staircase, but Jarius and his son-in-law waited until Yochanan approached them.

"What can I say?" the handsome apostle asked them.

"What did we hear and see tonight?" Jarius asked him.

"I'm not sure. Who knows what to make of this Shaul and the Gentiles he brings with him?" Yochanan threw his hands up. "He brings new ideas, ways, people that are so different. It is hard to know what to do, to think. And yet the hand of Adonai is clearly upon his life."

"Did you understand what he said?"

"Somewhat . . ." Yochanan spoke slowly. "I'm not sure I grasp all of it." Yochanan looked intensely at Philip. "But I understand the implications for your family. His words for you were heavy indeed."

"Indeed," Philip exhaled.

"We shall see." The apostle put his hand on Philip's shoulder. "We shall see." Yochanan turned away.

The candles in the large rack hanging from the center of the room had nearly burned down, and their smoke blackened the ceiling. Some of the *gaba'im** were setting the room back in order. The father and his son-in-law knew it was time to leave.

"Friends!" someone called out.

Jarius and Philip had almost reached the door when they realized Shaul was calling to them. Shaul darted around the few remaining people as he continued waving and hurrying toward them.

"Tonight is more than a special time," Shaul said quickly. His dark eyes burned with intensity. "The

* Deacons

Rudach Ha Kodesh has moved once more as if *Sha-vu'ot** itself had returned. The eye of the Almighty is on your family.''

''We have not heard anyone speak as you did tonight.'' Philip rubbed his hands together. ''I'm sure we have much to learn.''

''The call has been extended to you,'' Shaul's words were clipped and staccato. ''Doors are opening everywhere, and we must be ready to move at a moment's notice. You have been called.''

''What do you mean?'' Jarius asked hesitantly.

''Sometimes images flood into my mind.'' Shaul looked back and forth between the two men. ''At other times, only words come. The Holy One fills me with understanding that exceeds my capacity to know. Perhaps this process seems strange to you.''

''Yes. What really happened tonight?'' Philip pressed Shaul.

''Someday we will work together in Rome. I saw five of you standing in the midst of the glory of Rome. As I looked, I saw the house of God rising on the horizon and increasing until the whole city was overshadowed by its glory.''

''Five of us?'' Philip puzzled.

''I do not know when but the day will come, *Ha Elyon*† has ordained it.''

''Our life has always been in Yerushalayim,'' Jarius explained. ''I am an old man. I am sure my value would be quite limited.''

Philip began to wring his hands.

''What the Lord reveals is never wrong,'' Shaul said.

* Pentecost
† The Most High God

"There are five in my family," Philip answered.

"Then I won't have to go," Jarius jokingly shrugged.

"Either way, if you go or not," Philip said slowly, "someone is missing from that scene."

"Do not try to second guess Adonai," Shaul insisted. "Accept His handwriting, but do not try to read between the lines. His mercy always prevails. Surely this call is not a complete surprise?"

"Many years ago my wife was given a similar prophecy by Miryam, the mother of Yeshua. I have not thought of the matter for years."

"Prepare yourself." Shaul put his hands on the shoulders of both men. "He is planning a great adventure for us. You will be in my prayers and thoughts until we meet again."

"Perhaps you would come to our home for a little refreshment?" Jarius pointed toward the door.

"Thank you," Shaul answered, embracing Jarius, "but we must leave early in the morning." He turned to hug Philip in the same way. "We depart for Antioch with the dawn. May God bless and keep you. *Mizpah*."*

As quickly as he had come, Shaul was gone. The two men watched Shaul blend into a circle of apostles and immediately take charge of the conversation. Jarius and his son-in-law turned and followed the last of the group out the door.

Crisp, invigorating air rushed into their faces. Philip and Jarius stood on the landing for a moment looking over the city. Just ahead they could see the rise that was Mount Tziyon.† On the other side, the skyline

* A covenant of departure invoking God's blessing
† Mt. Zion

was broken by the irregular shapes of the flat-roofed houses of the city. Candles and oil lamps still filled the windows of hundreds of homes.

"I cannot imagine living anywhere else," Philip mused as they descended the stairs. "As was true of your fathers, so I expect it to be of my children. I don't know what to do with what we have heard tonight."

Jarius shook his head. "At least we have reconciled with this man. If nothing else, these days have made things right between us."

Philip paused at the bottom of the steps, "If we are to leave here, we would all have to go. No one could be left behind."

Jarius laughed. "There must always be a Ben Aaron left in Yerushalayim. I am the logical candidate."

"Never!" Philip said fiercely. "You are the leader of our clan."

"Hard to believe." Jarius picked his way carefully down the dark cobblestone street. "In the beginning, there were three of us. Three brothers from the tribe of Levi. None of us dreamed of anything more than living out our days together in the shade of the great city wall. Now they are both gone. I am the only one who is left. Passing strange, indeed, the ways of God."

Jarius and Philip walked down the narrow street without noticing that a man was watching them from the shadows. Standing underneath the steps, the man had been able both to see who came down from the Upper Room and to eavesdrop on their conversations.

When Jarius and his son-in-law disappeared around the corner, the man stepped out into the street. The bright moonlight reflected from the large gold chain around his neck.

VI

YERUSHALAYIM A.D. 52

Even though the month of Elul* had passed, summer heat still lingered over Judea. The usual aridity of the dry months made the sixth hour somewhat more bearable, but nothing diminished the repugnant smells of the food vendors' stalls. Mariam and Stephanos crossed the marketplace, exchanging few pleasantries. Other shoppers transacted their business with the same sober intent. Mariam walked near the buildings, keeping Stephanos to the outside as an extra precaution against the unexpected. Agitation and irritation were the order of the day. Where there had always been one Roman soldier, now there were two. Soldiers were surly and shoppers curt; merchants seemed abrupt and easily annoyed.

"More and more people leave for the wilderness every day," Stephanos said, staying close to his mother's side. "Some join the Essenes or the Pious Ones. Others just disappear."

"You can also smell the fear." Mariam pulled her

* August to September

veil across the bottom half of her face. "People know that disaster can explode at any moment."

"Would this not be a good time for the Messiah to return?"

"Yes, my son, but I don't expect His return soon." Mariam picked up the pace as they left the plaza and turned off the great boulevard down the narrow street that led to the family business. "Much is yet to be fulfilled before the Great Day can arrive."

"Did not Yeshua predict that Yerushalayim would fall?" Stephanos shifted the purchased vegetables from one arm to the other.

"The account is in our Gospel. You have read the scroll."

"Is this why the woman from Joppa wants to talk to you today, Mother? She is afraid?"

"No, my son. Our visitor from Joppa received her life back as I did. One's world is changed after such an experience. She searches for understanding."

"So many people come to talk to our family." Stephanos held his mother back when they reached the corner. "Surely our influence is well known to our enemies."

"Indeed! But long ago we decided to live by faith— not fear." Mariam stepped ahead of her son into the narrow street. "Because we were eyewitnesses to all that Yeshua did and taught, we must be bold. Ha Elyon* will protect us."

Suddenly three men darted out of an alleyway only half a furlong in front of them. As the men dashed across the street, sunlight flashed on the blade of a dagger. Stephanos immediately pushed his mother

---

* The Most High God

against the wall, spreading his arms in front of her. Their purchases scattered into the street. Within seconds a detachment of soldiers burst into the street. A soldier hurled his spear at the trio just as they turned into the adjacent alley and disappeared.

"After the swine!" The lead soldier charged ahead. Immediately the rest of the soldiers raced after him. Once more the street was empty.

"Don't move," Stephanos warned his mother, "I must make sure the way is safe before you go further." He quickly ran to the alleyway and looked back and forth.

Mariam crouched down against the wall. A cold chill settled over her. She could feel impending disaster. Although she saw nothing unusual, the oppressive dread increased. Inexplicably her attention was drawn to the roof line above the street. Mariam thought she could see a man standing with his hands on his hips, surveying the scene below him. He smirked as if what he saw greatly pleased him. Mariam blinked several times trying to discern whether she saw or envisioned the specter hovering above her.

Large, with long, flowing hair, the man did not have a beard. His white robe almost glistened in the sun. His black hair was pulled back in an uncharacteristic manner for Yerushalayimites. He looked awesome and commanding. His coal black eyes were fixed with fierce intensity upon her son. As Mariam stared, she realized she had seen him before. He had annnounced her son's birth.

"No!" she barely exhaled. "No! I know you!"

As if he had heard, the man turned his head slightly toward her. Though wrinkled, his face still seemed timeless. His deeply furrowed cheeks and mouth contradicted the aura of immortality that hovered around him. The ferocity of his look made Mariam shudder.

"*Rudach Ha Kodesh!*" she cried, "Help me."

Slowly the man raised his hand as if he alone could command the winds without interference. Wicked laughter filled the air without a sound falling into the street.

Mariam pulled her veil across her eyes. When she looked up again, he was gone, and Stephanos was running back to her.

"Don't be afraid, Mother. The men are gone."

Mariam did not move as she stared at the roof once more.

"I said, they are gone." Stephanos gently shook her. "Mother, the danger has passed."

Mariam did not move.

"There is nothing to fear now. Please—Mother. Don't look like that. I will protect us."

Mariam turned slowly toward her son. "No," she mumbled. "Only God can protect us."

Stephanos helped his mother to her feet. He quickly gathered up the vegetables lying all over the street. Locking his arm in hers, he hurriedly pulled her past the intersection. "Really mother, it wasn't *that* bad."

Mariam said nothing as they hurried down the familiar thoroughfare that ended at the inner wall of the city. She only nodded at their friends and competitors in the other jewelry stores. When they reached the jewelry shop, Stephanos held back the canvas door, allowing her to enter first.

"Mariam," Philip called from the back, "friends are here. They bring news from Shaul."

"Father—" Stephanos started to speak. Mariam jerked hard on his sleeve.

"Say nothing," Mariam cut him off. "Put the vegetables in the back. I will explain later."

"Yaakov has come with a letter from Shaul, and
your visitor Tabitha is here." Philip motioned for his
wife and son to join them in the rear.

A very small, black-haired woman sat meekly at
the table. Yaakov, the bishop of Yerushalayim, leaned
over a scroll, which was unrolled in front of the two
men. Mariam quickly embraced each person before
finding her place at the little table.

"I was telling your husband," the white-haired patriarch of the Yerushalayim church began, "that it appears that Antioch is becoming the center of our
missionary work. Shaul has certainly been a busy
man."

Philip frowned. "Shaul and Bar Nabba have had
some sort of disagreement. Apparently Shaul took Si-
las on another journey to the north and left Bar
Nabba behind."

"I came immediately." Yaakov began, rolling up
the scroll, "because Shaul sent you a personal greeting. He still believes the Holy One has a special mission for your family among the goyim."

Mariam smiled for the first time. "Oh, really!"

"The man pushes too hard." Philip shook his head.
"But I will certainly give him credit for tenacity.
We've not even seen him for two years."

"He forgets nothing," Stephanos added.

"I must talk with my friend who has come from
Joppa," Mariam abruptly changed the conversation.
"How do you fare?"

The small woman with big black eyes smiled but
only nodded.

"We remember your story well, Tabitha." Yaakov
patted her hand. "Do not be shy. Even Shimon Kefa

was overwhelmed when he prayed and you were raised from the dead by the power of our Messiah." Yaakov turned to Philip. "Tabitha's father is also named Stephanos. He is a well-known dispenser of medicines in Joppa. Of course, his expertise makes her story all the more remarkable. And your mother, Elizaveth? She is well?" the apostle asked Tabitha.

"Yes," the young woman answered quietly. "Quite well."

"Since your return from Sheol," Mariam asked, moving toward her, "you have had unusual experiences? You see things that others cannot perceive? You know what others cannot comprehend? Sometimes you cannot trust your own eyes?"

Tabitha nodded defensively.

"Yes, I understand. The way is not easy. You have gifts that are given only to those who have gone to Sheol and returned. Do not fear. Once you have seen the world of death, you are attuned to the One who uses death as his weapon. The Evil One will try to frighten you because you can see behind his mask. I will help you understand your abilities."

"You have come to a unique teacher," Philip assured Tabitha. "Mariam understands these matters as no one else."

"Perhaps we should leave them alone." Yaakov tied the scroll together. "I must return to some other matters anyway. A blessing upon the house of Ben Aaron!" Yaakov stood up.

Mariam began talking intently with Tabitha, and Philip walked Yaakov to the door. Stephanos hovered around the two women until his father called him to the front. Knowingly Philip suggested that Stephanos rearrange the pieces of jewelry on the display tables at the front of the store.

"I want to listen," Stephanos protested. "I never tire of her story."

"Tend to business," Philip barked.

"How can I learn if—" Stephanos caught the stern look from his father and stopped. Without another word, he began picking up the jewelry on the counter.

"We'll not disturb you," Philip called back to Mariam.

Mariam patted Tabitha on the hand. "Let's begin. Perhaps you understand the pain of others even before they speak?" Mariam probed.

"Y—e—s—s," Tabitha said carefully. "But what frightens me most is that Evil has become so real. No one has heard of such a thing."

Mariam looked at her visitor intensely for a moment. "There is another world on the other side of what can be seen. We've been there. We know it."

"Sometimes I am terrified. I can sense when Evil stalks the streets."

"We can see what the eye doesn't register." Mariam spoke in soft, low tones, but her voice was urgent. "The Evil One knows and will try to frighten us. You must take courage at such moments."

A man suddenly bolted through the canvas door. His abrupt entrance ended all conversation. Stephanos instinctively covered the counter with his hands. "Peace to the house of Ben Aaron," he called out in a thick accent.

"Welcome to the finest offerings in Yerushalayim," Stephanos answered defensively. "You have come to the house of the master craftsmen—" He stopped. "Ishmael!"

Philip dropped his small mallet. "Ishmael? The Arab gem trader?" He stood up.

"We have not seen you in— in— two years. Since I was in your tent . . ." Stephanos stammered.

"Peace to your house," the dark, swarthy man bent low in a sweeping gesture of honor. "Two years has been much too long."

"What brings you to us?" Philip asked cautiously.

"Great respect," the Arab grinned, showing toothless gums. "Perhaps, you will remember the wonderful stones that suddenly appeared in the city two years ago? Your young son greatly impressed the remarkable trader who brought them from afar."

"We remember well." Philip walked to his son and put his arm around his shoulder.

"The trader has come again," Ishmael rubbed his hands together as if he had just discovered a great gift. "This time he brings even greater gems. Soon the whole city will be questing after this clever man. Your competitors will even pay for the directions to where he can be found. *But*—" He lifted his hands in the air as he shouted. "Your house alone has found favor with the stranger. He has sent me to fetch you for a private showing."

"Why us?" Philip asked skeptically.

"Many years ago he was befriended by the house of Ben Aaron. He wishes to return the favor."

"What favor?" Philip crossed his arms.

"Ah!" The Arab waved his hand in the air, "But this is a man of great solemnity. He did not share his secret with a desert dog such as I."

"Tell me his name." Philip was unaccustomedly blunt.

"Yochanan Ben Zakkai," the Arab said softly.

"—the same name, Father," Stephanos interjected.

Philip looked hard at his son immediately silencing

him. "Why doesn't this Ben Zakkai just come here? We will be glad to talk directly with him."

"O—o—oh," the Arab crooned, rolling his eyes, "he wishes to honor your young son, with whom he was much impressed when they last met. He asks for you and this fine young man to come to our tent."

"Jarius is our buyer." Philip shook his head. "We do nothing without—"

"No!" The Arab cut him off. "My client will deal only with the two of you. He felt you might be somewhat reluctant to come alone, so he sent this gift ahead." Ishmael reached inside the large sash that held his dirty robe together. He pulled out a leather pouch and opened it over the counter, letting a bundle fall out. Carefully, he unwrapped the piece of cloth until an exceptionally brilliant large ruby red gem lay before them. "Is it not flawless?"

"Father! I've never seen such a stone!"

Philip picked up the great sparkling jewel. "Remarkable!"

"Yochanan Ben Zakkai remembers that his last meeting with your son created some misunderstanding and possible difficulty for the young man. Therefore he sends this stone as his personal gift to your son."

"Gift?" Stephanos sputtered.

"Ben Zakkai is not some unworthy son of the Sahara." The Arab clapped his hands. "He is one of your own. His word is as good as your Torah. I cannot return to him with the gem. I must leave it as a gift to your son. Is it not customary for fellow businessmen to exchange gifts of appreciation?"

Philip kept turning the gem in his hand. "I can't believe my eyes. The color is perfect red."

"Perhaps you are ready to come with me now?" Ishmael grinned slyly.

"What can I say?" Philip held the piece to the light.

"You will not be sorry." The Arab continued rubbing his hands together. "Shall we depart?"

"My wife will know where we are," Philip warned.

"Of course, of course."

"Mariam," Philip called to the back of the room, "Stephanos and I are going to the tent of Ishmael near the Pool of Siloe. Understand?"

Mariam returned his serious look and then waved them on as she continued talking to Tabitha.

"We should not be gone long. Send help if we tarry."

"Walking in your presence down the streets honors me greatly." The Arab bounded for the door. "Prosperity has come to your house today."

Ishmael chattered as the trio quickly walked down the street, but Philip and Stephanos said almost nothing. Although two years had passed since Stephanos had trampled down the steep path that led to the gem trader's pavilion, he immediately recognized Ishmael's familiar faded red and green tent.

"Our father Avraham is honored today," Ishmael stopped at the entrance and waited for father and son to enter before him. "Please be seated while I summon our friend." Ishmael pointed to the padded floor of the tent. He quickly disappeared through the back entrance.

The floor was covered with heavy Persian carpets that overlapped each other and extended to the very edge of the large tent. In one corner a large copper brazier still simmered and smoked from cooking at midday. Several lamps hung from the ceiling. Along the back sides of the tent, heavy trunks were chained together. A short table was situated at one end. Wine and cups were set out ready for use. An unusually large Greek urn covered the center of the table.

When a large flap to the back swung open, Ishmael stepped in. "My honored guest and trader of renown, Yochanan Ben Zakkai!"

A tall thin man in his early fifties entered quickly. His hair and beard were nearly white. Ben Zakkai's countless miles of travel across the deserts had tanned his skin into a leathery wrinkled brown. The black eye patch over his left eye did not completely cover the scar that ran down his cheek. His silk robe was of a pattern and regal quality seldom seen on Yerushalayim streets. Around his neck was a heavy gold chain with an elegant Morgen David hanging in the center.

"*Baruch ata,*" Ben Zakkai offered his hand to Philip. He turned to Stephanos, suddenly embracing the boy and hugging him for an unusually long time. "Peace to you, young Ben Aaron," he beamed as he held both the boy's shoulders.

"Never in all of my years," Ishmael began, "have I known a trader such as this man. He forgets nothing. Remembers the price of gems from years past! Knows the value of everything! Ah, who can deal with such a one?"

"Thank you, old friend." Ben Zakkai deferred to the Arab. "Your kindness to me will never be forgotten. Tell me about yourself, boy!" He abruptly turned to Stephanos, "I have not seen you for two years."

"Well," Stephanos struggled for the right words, "I— I— have—"

"You have an unusual interest in my son," Philip interrupted.

"No, no," Ben Zakkai assured Philip, shaking his head, "it is only that I recognize talent when I see it. The moment I saw this lad I knew that all the talents and gifts of the Ben Aaron family had finally come to rest in him. Unlimited skill!" He rolled his eye at Stephanos in mock wonder.

"Ishmael says you once knew our family," Philip pushed.

"Indeed!" Ben Zakkai's words were almost a sigh.

"Long ago?" Stephanos asked.

"Too long," the older man mused. "Almost in another lifetime. But that is yesterday. We have come to do business today. Tell me, young man. Did you like the ruby?"

"Oh, yes. Thank you very much. Never have we seen such a stone. What is it? Where did you find it?"

"I purchased it myself," Ben Zakkai spoke to Stephanos as if he were the only person in the room. "It is spinel. No one knows for sure where they come from, but the land is beyond Scythia and Armenia on the other side of the Mare Caspium in the country of very high mountains. They unknowingly call them rubies or balos rubies, but this is a red spinel with the brilliance of a diamond. It can even detect people with evil supernatural power. A clairvoyant's arms will convulse when touched by the stone."

"Really?" Stephanos' eyes danced.

"I knew I must carefully save such a rarity for the right moment. Perhaps a king would seek a gift for one of his many wives. Possibly the gem might ransom me from attacks at sea. I might trade it for a slave. Or I might use it as a gift to begin a new business with a skilled and learned trader. Immediately I knew you were the man!'' Ben Zakkai patted Stephanos on the sleeve as one does a special comrade.

''Excuse me,'' Philip interrupted. ''Stephanos is but a lad. He—''

''His mother could have been betrothed at his age! Has he not been Bar Mitzvahed?''

''His mother?'' Philip questioned.

''Now here is a lesson.'' Ben Zakkai shook his finger at Stephanos. ''You must carefully preserve such a stone. Save it just for the right moment. The value of such an investment can only grow with the years. A good trader measures time very carefully. We turn our waiting into money or opportunity,'' he confided.

''Excuse me,'' Philip started again. ''You mentioned my wife. Ishmael said you had once been befriended by the Ben Aaron family. When was this?''

''Oh, many times. Too long ago to mention.''

''But I must know,'' Philip said firmly.

Yochanan Ben Zakkai sighed deeply and looked away. ''Perhaps the story is not quite accurate. There was an unfortunate misunderstanding some many years ago with your father-in-law. I am sure that he is too much of a gentleman to have mentioned the matter to you. I would hope to rectify an old disagreement. Reestablishing our business relationship might help settle the matter.''

''You owe us something?'' Philip folded his arms across his chest. ''Money?''

''Something of that order . . .'' Ben Zakkai suddenly clapped his hands twice. Immediately two men entered through the back entrance, carrying trays covered with gems and stones. ''Feast your eyes on my offerings.''

Stephanos dropped to his knees as the trays were placed in front of them on the soft Persian rugs. Philip looked in silent astonishment.

"Notice the lapis." Ben Zakkai pointed to one tray. "I never liked the stone much myself, and I know it is relatively unusual in Yerushalayim. Now I offer you the opportunity to become the exclusive merchants for a new treasure. You always worked only with Eli-lat stone."

"How do you know this?" Philip puzzled.

"A good trader knows everything," Ben Zakkai spoke directly to Stephanos. "This tray alone will bring an endless flow of customers to your store. The word will quickly spread across the city. Look at the other tray." He picked up a brilliant emerald. "Would this not make a prince envious? Think about this one as a centerpiece in one of Jarius' magnificent *dedahebas.*"

"We could not possibly purchase such expensive treasures," Philip protested. "Maybe one or two but only Jarius makes such decisions."

"Of course!" Ben Zakkai suddenly swept the entire tray into a velvet bag. "I am going to send them home with you for his inspection." He quickly emptied the other tray into a similar bag. "There will be no problem with arranging terms."

"But— But—" Philip pushed the bags away.

"Of course my men will accompany you back to the shop to ensure your safety. Once Jarius is satisfied with the quality, we will deal on any terms that you set."

"No one trades like this," Philip stammered.

"No one seeks the opportunity I do." The white-haired man again spoke only to Stephanos. "Now, Ishmael, entertain my friend with the special new drink that I brought from the vineyards of Greece. I must speak further with my new business partner, Stephanos Ben Aaron."

"But—" Philip helplessly reached out.

"You will see," the Arab winked, "that Yochanan has found the nectar of the gods—as the Greeks say." He poured a cup of amber liquid from the Greek urn on the table. "Taste this."

The Arab began an endless dissertation on wines and the superiority of the unique aged brew of the Greeks. Ben Zakkai inched closer to Stephanos, asking him endless questions about his likes and dislikes. Stephanos was completely enchanted by the one-eyed stranger. The young boy talked freely and completely about his dreams and hopes. Ben Zakkai drank in each fact as if sampling vintage secrets.

The thick amber wine was exquisite beyond anything Philip had ever tasted. An almost unquenchable thirst demanded more than he customarily drank. The warmth in his stomach soon drowned out his skepticism of the one-eyed stranger. A new pleasantness filled his mind and he began to think only of the incredibly good fortune that had befallen them.

"We would not want your wife to worry," Ishmael finally whispered in his ear. "I think we should return."

"So soon?" Stephanos protested.

"No more misunderstandings," Ben Zakkai reminded him. "You must go back, for the afternoon is drawing to a close."

"Will you come to our house?" Stephanos asked Ben Zakkai.

"Only if I am invited."

''Then I shall personally make sure that it is done!'' Stephanos beamed.

''You will hear from us,'' Philip added thickly.

''I trust so.'' Ben Zakkai bowed low. ''I pray so,'' he said more softly.

VII

Jarius listened intently as Philip and Stephanos re-
counted every detail of their afternoon encounter
with the Arab and Yochanan Ben Zakkai. Jarius kept
running his hands over the jewels and stones spread
out before him on their dining room table. Mariam
held Stephanos' large spinel ruby before the candle.

"The man gave you this piece?" she asked her son
a second time.

Stephanos solemnly nodded his head. "He wants
to do business with us."

"I smell a rat in all of this." Jarius bit his lip. "But
for the life of me, I can't see how we are being set up."

"Aren't the stones genuine?" Philip asked.

"Absolutely!" Jarius gently rubbed the top of the
large emerald. "We must be cautious in transporting
this collection. People have been murdered for far
less."

"Could that be it?" Stephanos snapped his fingers.
"Could we be an assassin's target? Everyone knows
that our family are leaders of the People of the Covenant."

Philip and Jarius looked at each other.

"No," Stephanos answered himself. "I know that

78

Ben Zakkai truly likes *me*. When we talk I feel that he cares."

"Evil walks across our rooftops," Mariam said sharply to her son. "Do not be naive. Devious people are masters of deception. Convenience creates their smiles. Be warned. The fraudulent wear genuineness like an expendable cloak."

"Ishmael is probably such a man," Philip pondered aloud, "but I tend to agree that Ben Zakkai is different."

"We must meet this man," Jarius concluded. "Out of the multitude of our counsel we will know the truth. I do not believe that he can fool all of us."

"Great!" Stephanos clapped his hands. "I told him that we would invite him for dinner. Now, we can—"

"You did what?" Mariam looked startled.

"No, no . . ." Jarius shook his finger at his daughter. "A relaxed evening would give us ample time to measure the man. I think we should immediately make arrangements for tomorrow night. We need to have a sense of direction as quickly as possible."

"I'll take the message." Stephanos stepped forward.

"You certainly are the right connection," Philip agreed. "First thing in the morning we will send you to the Arab's tent. By tomorrow night we may know this man's intentions."

"What do your intuitions tell you, Mariam?" Jarius asked his daughter. "The Spirit speaks to you as to no one else."

"I don't know." Mariam shook her head. "Usually I have a clear sense of direction, but everything seems murky. I don't know," she muttered. "Something strange is at work here, and yet I do not feel fearful. Perhaps I will be more clear in the morning."

Servants scurried about the family dining room, lighting the last candles and two remaining oil lamps. Jarius had instructed that there be no shadows on this evening. A fire roared in the corner fireplace. Bowls and cups were already in place on the table. A flat clay bowl of flowers was in the center. Fresh flowers had been placed in Mariam's mother's vase in the niche by the fireplace. Even the long-stemmed dried flowers in the old water jug were replaced. The Ben Aaron family sat looking at one another, awaiting the arrival of their strange guest.

"I will question him about the source of these gem stones." Jarius looked from person to person. "We will soon see if he truly knows the trade routes. Perhaps Philip can push him on the terms that he wishes to offer us. This ploy will allow me to be a mediator if an argument should develop. Mariam must carefully observe."

"No one can listen like you do, Mother. What about me?" Stephanos asked. "What shall I do?"

"Watch." Philip's answer was quick and short. "Just observe. You may learn an unexpected lesson."

"If I smell too much intrigue," Jarius warned, "I will thank him for coming and end the conversation. We will simply retreat and send this one-eyed trader and his merchandise on their way."

Mariam folded her hands in front of her on the table. "I only sense that what happens tonight will be of great importance for our future."

Ten furlongs away Yochanan Ben Zakkai quickly turned from the cross street into the narrow lane that ran in front of the Ben Aaron household. Even though the night was pitch black, his steps were sure and decisive. Because his left eye was covered by the black patch, he walked to the right side of the street to better gauge depth and proximity.

The few remaining merchants in the marketplace and the soldiers stationed on the corners had turned when he passed. In these days of austerity, few people dressed in slick and shiny silk unless they were men of position and power. No one could see his face, which was covered by the hood on his outer cloak. Only his thick white beard hinted at the identity the covering concealed.

Ben Zakkai had not asked for directions but walked straight up the hill to the large two-story stucco house that towered imposingly over the surrounding neighborhood. The faded brown color and the black night only made the oil lamps in the windows seem to burn more intensely. Halfway up the hill, the merchant slowed his steady pace as if to measure his every step carefully.

The traveler came to a complete halt before the Ben Aarons' massive wooden door. For a long time, Yochanan Ben Zakkai looked at the long slender *mezuzah* on the doorjamb. At first he only touched the sides; then he rubbed the little container, invoking the blessing on the tightly wrapped scroll inside. He set his feet firmly before the door frame and finally rapped on the door.

The family servant did not need Ben Zakkai's introduction. He immediately ushered the stranger down the long hallway. The servant held back the curtain to allow his guest to enter the gathering room first. Immediately the Ben Aaron family stood and walked across their dining room into the dim, long living room. The servant stood beside the stranger, keeping his lamp close to the visitor's face.

"Yochanan Ben Zakkai," he announced stiffly.

"*Shalom.*" Jarius extended his hand as he crossed the dim living room.

"We're glad you are here," Stephanos fell in beside his grandfather. "Thank you for accepting my invitation."

Ben Zakkai folded his hands and bowed deeply. As he slowly straightened up, his hood fell back over his shoulders. The lamplight made the black eye patch, framed by white hair, like a black hole in his face. "*Shalom aleichem,*" he answered cautiously.

Jarius blinked several times and then stared silently.

"We are greatly honored," Stephanos blurted.

"Good heavens!" Mariam's hand came to her mouth. She reached out to her husband for support. "It can't be!"

The stranger clutched his hands together until his knuckles turned white. His head turned slightly so that his good eye had full survey of the people in front of him.

Philip looked back and forth. "Who is it?" He whispered to his wife.

Jarius' hand rose mechanically from his side. He reached toward the man's face, very slowly stopping just inches away. He could only shake his head.

Mariam stepped directly in front of the man. She put her hand to her heart as her chest rose and fell rapidly. "Uncle?" her voice was barely a whisper. "Uncle Simeon? Is it you?"

The guest nodded his head up and down very slowly.

"Uncle!" Stephanos sputtered.

"My brother—" Jarius choked, "—my brother." Wrapping his arms around Simeon's neck, he suddenly hugged him so tightly that he nearly twisted the cloak off Simeon's shoulders.

Mariam leaped forward, embracing both men at once. As she clung to the two men, her sobbing became so intense that she could not speak.

"What's happening here?" Philip took the lamp from the servant and held it high in the air. "I— I— I— don't understand."

Speechless the guest slumped over his niece and brother. The trio swayed back and forth while Philip and his son stared uncomprehendingly.

"Ben Zakkai?" Jarius sniffed and stood back. "Where in the world did you get that name?" Suddenly Jarius broke into uncontrollable laughter. "My brother—Yochanan Ben Zakkai—is the mystery man of the jewelry world!"

Simeon coughed in little spurts of laughter until he was chuckling and crying at the same time. Mariam clung to Simeon, too overcome to speak.

"You are Uncle Simeon?" Stephanos asked in wonder.

"Yes," Simeon smiled weakly. "I am your great-uncle."

Mariam felt his brown leathery cheek gently. She touched the wicked scar that ran up under the dark patch. Wiping the tears from underneath his other eye, she moaned, "We have all been wounded, God forgive us."

Simeon wrapped both arms around Mariam, swaying back and forth once more as he clutched her in desperation. Uncle and niece wept together.

"I have never met you." Philip extended his hand.

"Well, I mean— I've never met you as a Ben Aaron." He clumsily lowered his hand. "I'm glad to know you as . . . as . . ." His words faded. ". . . one of us."

"One of us?" Jarius exploded. "Indeed! My brother has returned!" He shouted in the servant's face. "Pour the wine! Prepare the feast! God has restored the House of Ben Aaron! Praised be His name!"

"Please," Mariam said weakly, "let us sit around the table. I don't think that I can stand much longer."

Jarius quickly offered his brother the place carefully prepared near the candles and oil lamps. All of the Ben Aaron family scurried to their places. An amazed servant backed out of the dining room and began calling to the rest of the servants.

"When I was last here . . ." Simeon paused uncomfortably, then continued, "there were no children, no husband; only the two of you. Over seventeen years have passed since we sat at this table together."

"Much has happened in those two decades," Jarius sighed. "We have lived many lifetimes."

"I remember painfully well the last time I touched the mezuzah," Simeon continued. "And I remember the day we attached it. Is the same message there?"

"The psalm is still there:

> Behold how good and how pleasant it is
> For brethren to dwell together in unity!

Just as the day *we* placed it."

"I feared returning." Simeon's eye darted back and forth from face to face. "Perhaps after tonight, you will not—"

"No," Mariam stopped her uncle. "We were wrong. No matter what happened then, we acted badly. We did not practice the forgiveness we preach."

Simeon bit his lip. "There was much misunderstanding."

"We know," Jarius comforted his brother. "Rabbi Shaul explained many details that we did not know at the time."

"Shaul?" Simeon recoiled. "Shaul of Tarsus?"

"He is our friend now," Jarius continued. "We hear from him often. Shaul told us that you did not intend harm and tried to protect us when the persecution arose. But all that is behind us now."

"Wherever I go, I find Shaul has preceded me." Simeon shook his head. "I cannot escape the man or his reputation. And to think *I* introduced him to the Great Sanhedrin."

"Shaul is taking our faith to the goyim. His mission is to spread the message of Yeshua across the world."

"Apparently so." Simeon looked away. "Even the goyim are infected—" he stopped abruptly. "I must be honest," he began again. "My mind has not changed. Even though the whole world seems to be chasing after your messiah, I am the same Jew I always was."

"And you are still my brother." Jarius patted his hand. "This time we must find our way better than we did before."

Simeon stared at the table. He arched his eyebrows. "I hope so," he sighed. "I hope so."

"Uncle?" Mariam asked gingerly. "Your eye? What happened?"

"Jewelry business is a bit more dangerous in the desert than it is in Yerushalayim," Simeon smiled once more. "I found a desert rat who wanted to relieve me of the burden of my prize purchases. I caught him going through my tent in the middle of the night."

"He attacked you?" Mariam asked in horror.

"After I hit him with a pole," Simeon laughed. "If it were not for my servant I suppose he would have killed me. I have always lacked the instincts of a true warrior."

"Oh—" Stephanos leaned closer. "Do you ever take the eye patch off?"

"Son!" Philip chastised him.

Simeon laughed loudly, "Now I will tell my new partner my greatest secret. Someday I will show you." He leaned toward his nephew. "Now I have the perfect place to hide my greatest gems. I have a safe in my face that no thief in the night can rob."

"Fantastic!" Stephanos' eyes danced. "And you will show me?"

"At the right time!"

"Stephanos!" Mariam pinched him. "Please."

Three servants began bringing food into the room. As the man and the two women placed the bowls on the table, each paused to stare at the one-eyed man. They backed out of the room, not taking their eyes from Simeon for a second.

"No one must know who I am," Simeon quickly warned the family. "You must instruct your servants to seal their lips. I must remain Yochanan Ben Zakkai to the world."

"But you are one of us again," Jarius protested.

"I have made many strange connections and allegiances in faraway places. These alliances demand that Ben Zakkai live on. Don't forget that I left this city in disgrace. It is better for all of us that the Great Sanhedrin believe that Simeon Ben Aaron is dead. Believe me. I know more of these matters than you do."

"But you must come back to our family business," Stephanos blurted out. "How can I be your partner if you don't return?"

"Perhaps I can serve you best from afar. No one in the entire city knows the secrets of the trade routes as I do. I can make us rich quickly with just a few of the tricks of the trade that I have learned over the years.

"Simeon," Jarius pleaded, "no one could make the wonderful chains that you do. Even after all these years, people still inquire about the craftsmanship that was the hallmark of your work."

"My fingers have grown stiff with age." Simeon flexed his fingers very slowly. "I'm afraid they will not serve the intentions of my mind as they once did. God has graciously replaced my skill with economic opportunity."

"But something can be worked out," Jarius insisted.

"We have two other children." Mariam pointed to the back of the house. "I want you to meet them. They're in bed, but I will awaken them."

"I have often watched Leah and little Zeda play," Simeon smiled kindly. "Leave them sleep tonight. The truth is that I have observed all of you from a distance for many years. Whenever I returned, I hid and watched."

"Oh, Uncle!" Tears filled Mariam's eyes. "If we had only known. I am so sorry."

"I have become quite good at observing quietly," Simeon chuckled. "Now you *must* allow me to protect you."

"Protect us?" Philip puzzled. "Something is wrong?"

"Everything is wrong," Simeon snarled. "The whole world is filled with craziness and evil. Believe me when I tell you that the times will become much worse. Walking the streets of Rome, I have seen the shape of the future."

"You have been to Rome?" Jarius' mouth stayed open. "I am amazed."

"I must be honest." Simeon's voice fell. "I like this new faith of yours no better than when we last spoke. But I do not know what to do with it. Belief in your messiah is even sweeping through that filthy city."

"Wonderful!" Philip clapped his hands together.

"I accept it as a sign of how bizarre the world has become," Simeon said cynically. "Rumors fly around Rome that the imperial family members systematically poison and kill each other. Executions and assassinations are routine. Cruelty and deceit are the order of the day. Women, men, children are sold like animals."

"Would not our Messiah make Rome a better place?" Mariam asked her uncle.

"I care nothing for Rome," Simeon said disgustedly. "Yerushalayim I love and cherish. I know the day is coming when the Romans will no longer tolerate our rebellion. They will turn us into slaves for their marketplace. I have seen what they have done in places like Pontus and Cappadocia. I know the results of their invasion of Britannia and the far corners of the world. They break cities in little pieces and plow the fields under with salt. Children are herded onto slave boats bound for Rome. Someday the Romans will descend on this city like a swarm of locusts."

"Yeshua prophesied this would happen," Mariam said sadly. "I have written His words in a scroll. Perhaps—"

"I am a practical man." Simeon cut her off. "Believe me when I tell you that the day will come when my wealth will be of more value to you than the messiah you profess."

"We will have ample time to discuss such matters." Jarius nervously raised his hands in the air. "All of these details can be worked out in due time. Tonight we must celebrate and rejoice. Let us begin by blessing the name of our God. Let us thank Him for your return to this table. Once more we can join hands and pray together as a family."

Jarius reached for his brother's hand and held his other palm open for Mariam. Jarius squeezed his brother's hand tightly as Stephanos immediately grasped Simeon's other hand. Philip completed the circle, holding his son's and wife's hands. Jarius closed his eyes and looked heavenward. Mariam and Philip dropped their heads forward and closed their eyes. Only Simeon continued to look at each face around the table.

"*Baruch ata adonai,*" Jarius prayed, "*elohaynu melech haolam.*" As Jarius blessed the Lord and thanked God for the return of his brother, Simeon looked from person to person with tears running down his right cheek. He kept shaking his head in disbelief.

VIII

In the seven years that followed Simeon's return, the house of Ben Aaron prospered greatly. None suspected that the mysterious Yochanan Ben Zakkai was one of the family. Stephanos was his spokesman as well as the family broker in precious stones. Simeon came and went, traveling during the cooler months and avoiding the deserts in the summer. Sometimes Ishmael, his Arab friend, traveled with him while on occasion Stephanos worked the trade routes with his uncle.

Simeon remained troubled that the faith of the People of the Covenant continued to spread with explosive success. Wherever he went, synagogues were in turmoil and marketplaces rife with religious discussion. While everyone argued about Rabbi Yeshua, by common unspoken agreement the family Ben Aaron avoided discussing the beliefs that had torn them apart two decades earlier. Yet the tensions remained.

When Simeon traveled with Stephanos, their differences became unavoidable. Each morning as the sun rose, Stephanos slipped from beneath his blankets to bow with his face on the ground. Stephanos' prayers always began the same way. Simeon could not avoid hearing.

"Our Father in heaven! May Your Name be kept holy. May Your kingdom come." Stephanos' voice was quiet but intense. "Your will be done on earth as in heaven." Finally he concluded, "in the name of Yeshua Ha Mashiach."*

By the time Stephanos ended his prayer, Simeon stomped out of the tent. The sun was rising and quickly dispelling the bitter cold of the desert night. Simeon pretended to be checking the camels to cover his explosive exit from the tent. "Keep your mouth shut," he grumbled under his breath.

"You all right?" Stephanos called from the door of the tent.

"Sure."

"I will prepare breakfast," Stephanos called back cheerfully.

"At least they've stayed kosher," Simeon said to himself. Simeon stood up as straight as he could and threw his head back. "Well, he keeps all the festivals," he concluded and then marched back inside the tent.

The faith of Jarius' family was very much like that of Simeon. Sukkot** and Pesach† were always observed. Shavu'ot had become even more important to them. Jarius, Philip, and Stephanos prayed with the *tefillin*‡ strapped on their arms and heads. No one could level the slightest criticism of how Philip's children observed the Sabbath. Mariam devoutly kept

---

* Jesus, the Messiah
** Feast of Tabernacles
† Passover
‡ Leather straps holding boxes containing written prayers that are bound to the body during worship

every ordinance the Law of Moses required of women. The family still regularly worshiped at the Temple. Simeon might have blended into their worship with ease if it were not for their constant references to Yeshua.

In recent months, Simeon had returned to the rabbinic debates that were always rumbling within the Temple precincts. Introducing himself as Ben Zakkai, he found that he could still easily hold his own in the heated discussions over Torah and the traditions. Occasionally one of the combatants would admiringly encourage him to take his point of view before the Great Sanhedrin. Although he always smiled in satisfaction, Simeon quickly retreated after such a suggestion and then disappeared for months.

Simeon watched from a distance when Leah was married. Philip and Mariam proudly presented their only daughter in a ceremony that differed only slightly from what generally occurred in the synagogues. Since most of the guests were believers, Simeon did not mingle or talk much with those who attended the celebration. He remained Ben Zakkai, the mysterious business partner. The radiant couple affirmed their faith in Yeshua and pledged their future family to him as well as their hope for His imminent return. Simeon looked away.

Although Simeon was never very comfortable around his niece, he liked his younger nephew immensely. Even though Zeda was twenty years old and betrothed, the marriage contract had never been fulfilled. Everyone talked of a wedding in the near future, but Zeda repeatedly slid away from the final steps that would seal the pact. He was far more interested in developing his ability to work gold. Simeon instructed, and Zeda quickly acquired the skill of making fine necklaces. His nimble fingers easily wove fine strands of gold wire together as well as created the tiny links that make the royal necklaces, which had always sustained the reputation of the house of Ben Aaron. Simeon's only complaint was that Zeda might well be the most devout believer of the three children.

So much alike, Simeon and his family were worlds apart. They reached but never quite touched.

Like the rest of Yerushalayim, Simeon's hopes had soared when the news swept across the land that the Praetorian Guards had assassinated the mad Emperor Caligula. A better day seemed possible when he was replaced by the more kindly Claudius. But Claudius died five years ago, and the new rumor in the streets was that his wife, Agrippina, poisoned him. Because Rome was incurably and fatally infected with every vile manifestation of lust, madness, and gluttony that the world had ever known, both emperors and citizens were capable of anything. Simeon knew the truth and trembled before the implications.

Tebeth* has been unusually mild. There had not been a hint of the snow flurries that occasionally dusted the jewelry shop during the cold months. Simeon and Stephanos made a fall trip to Damascus where "Yochanan Ben Zakkai" had special connections. After securing a large supply of lapis, they returned on the King's Highway, trading along the way. Uncle and nephew worked several days preparing their offerings for the new display tables that had been erected near the windows where sunlight was constant throughout the day. Even though the afternoon was warm, a small fire still burned in the corner

---

* December to January

fireplace. Zeda worked intently at Simeon's old bench while Jarius and Philip talked.

"Yaakov said he would arrive near the end of the sixth hour," Philip reminded Jarius. "I hope there is no problem."

Jarius rolled his eyes. "There is always a problem, But if something serious had occurred, I'm sure we would have already had a hint. Being a *zekenim** and a *tzedakah*** gives us access to the eyes and ears of the city. We shall soon see."

Everyone froze in place when the canvas door to the shop opened and a young Roman soldier stepped in. He wore the full uniform of the legions with a metal breastplate and the plumed helmet of an officer; an expensive red cloak hung from his shoulders. The sword and sheath were decorated with metal scrolls and designs. The man was obviously a considerable cut above the common troops who patrolled the streets, harassing the merchants.

Stephanos immediately stepped forward. "And can we be of service to the noble servant of Caesar? Perhaps an exquisite ring for a lovely lady?" He pointed toward the jewelry table. "The finest in gold necklaces are also to be found here."

The soldier looked slowly and carefully around the room, studying each face. "I seek a man, not a purchase." His voice was cold and professional. "I am here on business for Rome."

Each member of the Ben Aaron family stiffened. Simeon pulled his robe more closely around his face, and Zeda held his mallet more tightly but did not turn around.

* Elder
** Deacon

"There is some problem?" Philip stood up and stepped forward. "Someone is unhappy with some item we have sold them in the past?"

"I am looking for an older man." The soldier ignored Philip. "The man would be the age of the two of you." The soldier pointed at Jarius and Simeon.

"What is your concern?" Philip held his ground.

"Is one of you named Ben Aaron?" The soldier spoke as if Philip were not present. "Jarius Ben Aaron?"

"Why?" Jarius stepped beside Philip. He gave no hint of fear or intimidation.

"You are the man?" The soldier carefully measured the white-headed man in front of him.

"Why?" Jarius did not flinch.

"Soldiers usually ask the questions." The soldier's words were firm but not threatening.

No one answered or moved.

"Well," the soldier continued, tossing his head, "I know this is the shop of Jarius Ben Aaron, and I'm sure that one of you is the man." He removed his helmet and set it on the jewelry counter on top of several pieces. "As a matter of fact, I have a special letter for this Jarius. I have been instructed to place the scroll in no one's hand but his. I can go no further until I know which of you is the man."

"Who is the letter from?" Jarius' expression did not change.

"The communiqué is from none other than the illustrious head of the Praetorian guard, General Gaius Honorius Piso."

"Honorius!" Jarius clapped his hands. "My old friend! I've not heard from him in years. General?" He paused. "You said General Piso?"

"Indeed." The soldier bowed his head in respect.

"The general is one of the celebrated heros of Rome."

"I had no idea," Jarius exclaimed in wonder. "No one could deserve it more."

"I take it then, that you are Jarius Ben Aaron," the soldier persisted.

"Of course, of course." Jarius removed the helmet from the display table and set it to one side. "Let me see the letter at once. I am delighted."

"The seal has not been broken." The soldier reached into his belt and pulled out a small scroll wound on two wooden dowels. "I have been instructed that the matter is of the utmost confidence and to be shared with no one but Jarius." He held the scroll firmly in his hand.

"They are my family," Jarius protested. "We have no secrets here."

"My life is on the line," the soldier said solemnly. "I will exact the full toll if I am misled."

Jarius stuck out his hand. "Let us not tarry. I am eager to hear from my old friend."

"I have been instructed to ask one final question. What is it that General Piso always wears around his neck?"

"His neck?" Philip grimaced. "How should we know?"

"Oh . . ." Jarius sighed. "He still wears the chain and golden cross I made for him just before he left."

"You are the one!" the soldier's reservations instantly disappeared. "I am honored to meet the friend of my general." The soldier swung his fist into his breastplate, giving the Roman salute. "Please forgive the interrogation, but it was necessary that I not be misled. I am Lucius Capena, special aide to the general."

"Lucius! Come and drink with us." Jarius pointed

toward the table in the back. "You are most welcome. Come meet our friend." Jarius waved for the family to gather around. Only Philip followed his lead. "Come on," Jarius beckoned to his brother and grandson. "Gather around and see what our friend has to say."

"Perhaps, I should explain," Lucius hesitated, "I am not yet a believer in your faith. I honor the general and know what happened to him here but I am still learning. I sought this assignment in order to more fully investigate."

"Excellent," Jarius beamed. "We will help you in every way we can." Jarius broke the seal and un-rolled the scroll. "*Dominus illuminatio,*" he read aloud. "The Lord remains his light!" he exclaimed. "Lucius, please read since my Latin is a bit defective."

The young soldier sat down and began:

> Beloved brother in the Lord, grace and peace be unto you. I have not ceased to pray for you since I saw you last. You and your precious daughter have remained in my memory as guiding lights. I have attempted to be faithful to all you taught me and still read the Torah every morning and night.
>
> The Holy One has greatly prospered me and my house granting to us a place of honor in this great city. As was foretold so long ago, the time has come for you to visit us here. The hour of destiny is at hand. The season of reckoning has come.
>
> My trusted aide, Lucius Capena, will make all the arrangements and care for your every need. You will live in my house as one of the family and I will cover all of your expenses. Mariam must come and teach from the scroll that she wrote. Even in this far away place we have heard of the *Gospel According to the Hebrews*.

    Do not linger but come at once. Surely our call is
    the will of the Divine.

                        Your friend and brother,
                        General of the Praetorian
                        Honorius

"I have been instructed," the aide continued, "to arrange for a ship to take you across the Mare Internum. Your entire family is included. As soon as you are ready, I am prepared to act."

Stunned silence settled over the room. Several moments passed before Philip spoke. "Was this trip not prophesied long ago? We should not be surprised."

"Rome!" Simeon sneered. "You have no idea of what you say. I have stood on those dirty streets and watched whores ply their trade. There is no abomination that is not practiced there."

Jarius slid into a chair and leaned on the table. "I am an old man now. Perhaps I would never return from such a trip. I don't know. I just don't know."

"There are many believers in Rome," Lucius interjected as he began rolling up the scroll. "Every day new inquiries come about your faith. Teachers are desperately needed. I would gladly sit at your feet as we travel."

"Mariam has always known that she was to stand on the streets of Rome and bear witness to what we have seen and heard." Philip put his hand on his father-in-law's shoulder. "The only question is whether you are to go with us."

"I am to go!" Stephanos insisted. "You will need me."

"We must pray." Jarius shook his head slowly. "I just am not sure. We must have confirmation."

Simeon slipped back into the farthest corner. He slumped against the wall and then slid down to the floor.

"Time is of the essence," Lucius urged. "Rome is filled with intrigue and instability. We must act with dispatch. No one knows what each new day will bring."

The canvas door abruptly swung once more, and two men entered. "Shalom."

"Yaakov!" Philip answered. "Come here. We have remarkable news. Nicholas, we weren't expecting you."

Both men stopped when they saw the Roman soldier standing beside the table.

"Do not be apprehensive," Jarius said in Hebrew. Then he returned to Greek: "Please meet Lucius, aide to General Honorius."

"Honorius?" Yaakov puzzled. "Our old comrade?"

"The very same! Sit down and read his letter." Jarius once more unrolled the scroll on the table. "Honorius has become a very important man."

Jarius continued talking as the two read over his shoulder. "Remember? He stood at the foot of the cross. In fact, Mariam wrote of him in the gospel scroll. He recognized the truth about Yeshua even on that terrible Friday."

Yaakov picked up the scroll, holding it close to his eyes, reading each line again carefully.

Jarius explained to Lucius, "Yaakov is the bishop of the People of the Covenant in Yerushalayim. He can teach you many things about our Messiah."

"He wants you to come to Rome!" Yaakov looked up from the scroll and blinked his eyes several times. "I'm astonished."

"I am confused," Jarius nodded. "At my age—"

"No, no," Yaakov stopped him. "The whole matter is God's timing. I am amazed. Only He could have arranged the details so perfectly."

"I don't understand." Jarius wrinkled his forehead.

"We have also received a letter—from Shaul," Nicholas explained. "Of course we pay little attention to new reports of his imprisonments because he is constantly being thrown into jail. But this time the matter is far more significant.

"Herod Agrippa himself has sent Shaul to Rome to appeal his case before the highest tribunal." Yaakov gestured frantically. "He was sent from Adramyttium with an officer from the emperor's regiment. Now Shaul is a prisoner in Rome itself."

"Shaul has sent word for many of us to come and help him," Nicholas looked around the room. "He particularly asks for the Ben Aarons. Can it be an accident that these requests have come at the same moment? I think not."

"Rome!" Stephanos shook both fists in the air. "Praise be to Ha Elyon!"

"You do not know what you say." Simeon spoke bitterly from the darkest corner of the room. "When has Rome been other than the city of death?"

Lucius stiffened and looked annoyed.

"Perhaps we should show our newfound brother, Lucius, something of our city." Yaakov stepped forward. "Obviously the family will need time to discuss this matter privately."

Nicholas eyed Simeon with disdain.

"We are honored you are here." Jarius moved to cover any affront the soldier night have felt. "I think Yaakov can show you sights that even many of our citizens have not seen. Let us meet tomorrow and discuss the matter further."

Lucius agreed and left with Nicholas and Yaakov. The family had barely returned to their heated discussion when Mariam appeared in the doorway. She quickly read the scroll from Honorius while the debate continued.

"Don't go," Simeon begged her. "We have become a family again. What will become of the business and your children if you leave?"

"I've expected this door to open for a long time." Marian squeezed his hand. "No more than a year; two years at the most. Then we will return. Surely Leah will soon have children. They must have a grandmother."

"You and Zeda can run the business," Stephanos quickly insisted. "Since I am not betrothed, there is no reason for me not to go. But Zeda will soon have family responsibilities. Only the trading in precious jewels will suffer in our absence. The two of you will be a team."

"My fingers are no longer nimble and agile," Simeon protested. "Production would be limited and the quality poor."

"No, no," Jarius laughed. "Skill is in your mind. Practice will bring everything back. It will be good for you to stay put for a while."

"Madness!" Simeon ground his teeth. "Madness! You will all die in Rome. Don't you understand? I know how easily these dogs of prey kill. The Romans didn't object to putting your messiah to death. Are you any better?"

"We believe that His death served the highest purposes of Adonai," Mariam explained to her uncle for what seemed like the hundredth time. "Even the cruelty of Rome serves the purposes of God."

"These matters are best left undiscussed." Simeon looked up to heaven and held his hands in the air. "But I have lived on the sea routes and I know that danger lurks everywhere."

But no one heard him. Even a week later, his warnings were ignored. Simeon finally agreed to oversee the family business. He would remain Yochanan Ben Zakkai, who advised Zeda, the family proprietor. Overnight the youngest son and the vanquished brother had become the surviving remnants of the Ben Aaron jewelry business. Simeon insisted that Zeda would not be married until Mariam and Philip returned. He would be father to both Zeda and Leah in their absence.

"A year," Mariam had insisted. "Only a year. If we are not back by then, you should proceed with the wedding. Yaakov and the *zekenim* will help you make the arrangements. But life must go on."

"The future remains in the hands of our God," Philip said firmly. "Yeshua may yet return before we do. Regardless of what happens, you are to be brave and to act with integrity. Never fear our displeasure."

Zeda recoiled before the idea of becoming the titular head of the Ben Aaron family in Yerushalayim. Only after a long discussion with his father and mother did he acquiesce to the inevitable. He had always liked being the baby of the family and gladly allowed Stephanos to have preeminence.

"Remember the song that we sing?" Mariam asked her youngest son. " 'He emptied himself taking the form of a servant.' " She hummed the simple melody. " 'Becoming obedient unto death, even death on a cross.' Let the words guide you," she encouraged Zeda. "Then you will find your way."

In the end, the hymn had encouraged Mariam. What Simeon could not believe spoke deeply in her own heart. Even the prophecy over a decade earlier by Miryam, the mother of Yeshua, did not ease her pain in leaving her children behind. Night after night she remembered each admonition and inspiring word that led to their departure, but the reluctance that tugged at her deepest sensitivities never left. Only a passionate decision of faith sent Mariam packing.

Yeshua said, *"Talitha cumi,"* and her life began again. Once more she had to stand up if life was to go forth. That knowledge—and that knowledge alone—brought peace to Mariam when she finally set her face toward Rome.

IX

MARE INTERNUM A.D. 60

ariam's scattered reminiscences were interrupted once more when a wave violently
rocked the boat and bounced her against the hull.
Jarred back to the present reality, Mariam tried one
more time to look out the small porthole in the side of
the ship. The sounds of the approaching pirate ship
were drowned out by the storm, but Mariam could
see the attackers just off the bow of the boat. Unex-
pectedly a large island now loomed on the horizon.
Mariam saw rock outcroppings near the shore. Another violent upheaval of the boat slung her back to
the water-covered bottom of the boat. She pulled
Stephanos close and hung on as if he were a wooden
harbor piling. Once more doubts poured in like the
sea water, drenching her in apprehension.

"There's land ahead!" she shouted to anyone who
could hear.

"Can't be!" Philip yelled back.

"The storm's knocked us far off course," Stephanos
answered, clutching his mother tightly.

"Pray!" Philip called back. "I don't think the boat
can hold together much longer."

"Evil!" Stephanos sputtered, spitting out salt water. "The Evil One himself pursues us."

"Yes." Mariam was barely able to answer. "Yes, I have no question that we are under spiritual attack."

Instantly Mariam remembered the wrinkled, knurled, craggy face that was indelibly etched in her memory—just as he had looked the first time in the garden when he tried to confuse her about the destiny of her son, just as he appeared the day he stood on the roof during the street attack. Sometimes he looked younger; sometimes he looked older. His eyes might momentarily seem benevolent, but the deception could not be sustained. Leer and lust always surfaced in the lines around the all-seeing eyes.

Just before the ship cast off, Mariam saw him standing in the crowd on the dock. He seemed only to be one of the crowd waving goodbye to the voyagers. A cloak partly concealed his face. As the well-wishers waved, Mariam noticed that one man stood above with his hands at his side. The boat drifted happily out into the Great Sea; he glared. Mariam leaned over the railing to look more closely, and their eyes locked. Instantly an invisible force clutched at her throat.

The valleys in the contour of his face remained frozen while his eyes burned. His grotesque, bulbous nose reddened. No word or gesture was needed to convey his diabolic intent more completely. With slow, mechanical precision his cold, calculating stare shifted from Mariam to Stephanos. While her son joyously waved to the crowd, the man's glare surveyed Stephanos like that of an undertaker measuring for a coffin.

Mariam grabbed Stephanos' hand, pulling it down.

"What's the matter?" he said to his mother. She looked fearfully into his innocent eyes. "Wave at the people. They wish us well."

But when Mariam pointed to the crowd, the man had disappeared.

"Wave," Stephanos said again.

At that moment Mariam knew that her son was especially marked for the conflict in Rome. As the scene slipped away, the ship seemed to be rocking less violently, though it still felt out of control. Mariam was sure that Stephanos was right about the rigging having been torn away. Probably the pirate ship was circling while they floundered like a wounded seagull.

Philip braced himself against the side by setting his feet on a beam that ran the length of the bottom of the boat. Straddling Jarius, he held the older man tightly around the waist. The family patriarch had still not regained consciousness. His arms dangled limply at his sides. At least Mariam could see that he was breathing heavily. Jarius looked so much like his brother at that moment that tears came to Mariam's eyes.

The ship was definitely rocking more gently than it had for the last hour. Mariam's grip around Stephanos' chest was gradually loosening, but her stomach still cramped and she had to keep her jaw tightly clenched.

"The storm seems to be lessening," Mariam said in Stephanos' ear.

"That's not good," he answered. "The attackers can board the boat if the winds die down. They'll make quick work of us."

"Then the final battle is surely about to begin," Mariam looked overhead at the heavy timber planking that supported the deck.

"Listen to me," Stephanos whispered in his

mother's ear. "I have hidden the great ruby-red spinel jewel that Uncle Simeon gave me. No one could find the place. It's one of the tricks that he taught me." Stephanos clutched his mother's hand tightly. "If the boat is overrun, I will use it to buy your safety. The stone is worth a fortune. I know it would secure your release."

"No, no!" Mariam bit her lip. "Don't even think such things."

"The stone has been carefully sewn inside the leather in the sole of the extra sandals in my pack." Stephanos looked down at his mother. His eyes had a new strength and resolve that his mother had never seen before. Each word came quickly, with new decisiveness. "Uncle Simeon gave me a knife. When the door opens, I will kill the first man who comes through. Perhaps I can stop only one man, but it will give you time to get the pack if need be. If I fall, you will have the stone."

"Son—" Mariam tugged at his hand. "We cannot kill. Yeshua taught us to welcome our attackers with kindness. We must depend on Him and not our own strength. We could not possibly bargain with murderers."

"I will protect you." Stephanos' voice became much louder and broke. "I am not afraid."

Mariam squeezed his hand. "Our Messiah has not taken us on this journey to abandon us to these seafaring thieves. We must not lean on our own understanding but trust Him." Mariam used Stephanos' hand to pull herself up. "I am proud of your bravery, but what we must do now is pray."

"Stephanos," Philip called, "help me rest your grandfather against the hull."

The ship jerked and rocked up and down as father

and grandson moved Jarius to a more comfortable position. Overhead they heard men starting to run back and forth. Someone began shouting, but they could not make out the words.

The family joined hands and knelt together in the cold water that covered the bottom of the boat. Mariam shivered as she held her son's and husband's warm hands. The pungent, acrid smell of sea water and rotting wood filled their noses while they prayed aloud. Periodically they listened for the sound of the attack.

Finally Stephanos crawled back up the side to look. "Good heavens!" he exclaimed. "We're heading for the rocks!"

Philip and Mariam quickly found portholes. From the three different angles the family could piece together what was happening. Not only was their rigging down, but a similar disaster had befallen the pirate ship. The wind and current had carried both vessels into the shoreline, but the larger ship, which sat more deeply in the ocean, seemed to be helplessly caught in the undertow.

"They're going backward!" Stephanos cried out.

"Look at the oarsmen," Philip answered. "They're in complete confusion!"

As the boat was sucked backward toward the rocks, the oars that jutted out of the boat whirled in chaotic disorder. Like the feet of a centipede in convulsion, the tottering oars evidenced panic in the hull.

"The sailors on the deck are stampeding," Mariam called back.

Suddenly the back end of the ship went straight up in the air, slinging many of the pirates out into the roiling ocean. When the ship came down, the hull cracked in the middle. Even from their distance the Ben Aarons could hear the terrible splintering sound.

"Their ship's breaking up!" Stephanos pounded on the hull. "Look at them! They're sinking!"

A huge wave lifted up the front half of the boat, tearing it completely away from the stern. When the wave dropped the bow, the family could see that the stern was hung up on rocks. The bow sank immediately, leaving only the scattered remains of the stern protruding out of the ocean. When the waves recessed, the hull of the ship looked like the skeleton of a dead whale impaled on the barnacle-encrusted boulders.

"I can't believe it." Stephanos turned and slid down the side of the boat. "Gone—the whole lot of them! Gone in an instant."

"Only the hand of God has spared us." Philip stood steadily on the gangway for the first time.

"We seem to be drifting parallel to land," Mariam said as she finally turned from the window. "We're passing the rocks. I really don't feel very well." She sat down again holding her stomach.

Stephanos was the first to realize that the overhead hatch was being opened when he heard a heavy timber being dragged to one side. Sunlight poured in when the large cover was lifted away.

"Are you all right?" Lucius' familiar voice called out.

"Lucius? That's you?" Stephanos inched toward the hole.

"Is anyone hurt?" Lucius asked.

"Grandfather's in bad shape, but the rest of us are not injured—just badly shaken."

"Excellent," the Roman soldier lowered himself down into the hold of the ship. "One of the worst storms I've ever seen. Nearly tore us to pieces."

"They're gone," Mariam said in astonishment. "Gone."

"Absolutely amazing!" Lucius wiped the sea water from his eyes. "It was almost like a great hand sliced them into two pieces. The whole crew disappeared in the waves. Simply amazing."

"*Baruch ata Elohaynu.*" Jarius weakly lifted his hands in the air. "We have been spared."

"Father!" Mariam reached for his hand. "You're better."

"Jews weren't made for the ocean," Jarius coughed. "I swear that if I survive this trip, I'll never get in a boat again."

For the first time in what seemed like an eternity, the family laughed.

"Come now," Lucius chided Jarius. "You've done very well. We had to tie some of our men to the railing lest they panic and fall in. Your God seems to have brewed up the storm to defeat our enemies for us."

"Were there many of them?" Stephanos asked.

"We would have been greatly outnumbered," Lucius said gravely. "The battle would have been grim."

"Our little skirmish is only a prelude." Mariam stood up. "The great battle is before us. Something monumental is waiting for us in Rome."

PART TWO

X

ROME A.D. 62

Gaius Honorius Piso, you are our only hope," the senator with the purple-striped toga over his shoulder begged. "You must act."

Jarius and Mariam had never called the general by his first name. In fact, Honorius preferred everyone, except his wife, to use his last name. The nomen implied he was worthy of honor, and so most people knew him only as Honorius. Piso was the cognomen, the extra surname that his grandfather had added three decades earlier. The old warrior liked its literal meaning, "I grind down." The significance of "Piso" was not lost on the battlefield. However, professional acquaintances and military associates generally addressed him as Gaius Honorius Piso.

"If you delay, Nero will make sure that Sextus Afranius Burrus consolidates his control of the Praetorian Guard." The senator shook his finger. "You must not let that happen."

The general looked out over the large courtyard as if he were deep in thought. The maneuver gave him a few more moments to ponder the implications of what Marsi Crossus Laenas was saying.

Although the Forum of Caesar was seldom packed,

113

senators and Roman notables crowded about the porticoes, talking loudly and making sweeping gestures. This unusual place had been chosen for their informal meeting. General Honorius and his aide, Lucius, stayed at the far end, near the temple dedicated to Venus Genetrix. Standing on the steps of the octastyle Corinthian building, they could easily observe events in the open-air area.

Julius Caesar had spent over a million sesterces to buy up the property on which he had built this new curia from where Rome was supposed to be ruled. Now, over a hundred years later, the representatives of the people of Rome could do little more than talk and complain. Fear ruled the people as the despotic descendants of Augustus Caesar governed in a manner that would have made even the imperial-minded Julius blush.

''I appreciate your confidence, Marsi Crossus Laenas.'' Honorius was distant and aloof. ''You are a trusted friend.''

''So am I.'' Felix Carbo stood next to Laenas.

But there were no trusted friends in the crowd. With the exception of his aide, Lucius Capena, it would be every man for himself when the final showdown came. Gaius Honorius Piso knew well that they were in such an impossible dilemma precisely because the elite of Rome did only that which served their personal interests best. Treachery was the order of the day, not friendship.

Lucius kept looking behind them, inside the temple at the extraordinary works of art that lined the walls. On one side was a picture of the mythical Medea and on the other a portrait of Cleopatra. Toward the front were large statues of Caesar and Cleopatra. Overhead was the splendorous lacunar ceiling. Such a sight easily diverted attention.

Honorius was trapped in a constantly changing circle of senators. Yet the theme was constant. Each one wanted someone else to do something about the emperor's behavior. Finally the general took a deep breath, only to catch a tinge of the foul odor that was omnipresent in the streets of Rome after a flood. The amalgam of rotting food, feces, and general filth crept into even the hallowed halls of the city.

"I'm afraid I have another urgent meeting," Honorius lied. "Your advice has been most helpful," he mumbled, "but we must be on our way now. Thank you, gentlemen." He beckoned to Lucius and pointed toward the far exit of the Forum.

Honorius and his trusted aide and friend quickly crossed the Forum and headed toward the marble steps to the street. The tall columns that bordered the open-air plaza cast long shadows as the late afternoon sunlight faded.

Honorius had listened to the angry grumblings without making any comment. Such open criticism of the emperor had not been heard in many years. The nobles of the Great City were drunk with despair. Cynicism and malice were blending together into an intoxicating brew that anesthetized normal precautions.

Lucius knew the cries for vengeance were meant for the ears of the general. While no one had the courage to do more than talk, the spineless nobility hoped that the old and respected leader of the Praetorian Guard might do what they would only dare to think. Lucius feared that Honorius could be implicated in some wild plot simply by being present during such loose talk. He felt relieved when Honorius nodded to leave.

"I want to talk with Jarius and Peter," Honorius said under his breath when they passed two senators. "There's much on my mind tonight." He picked up the pace when they passed the men. "Trouble is about to break loose again. I need their advice."

"Caution, my friend." Lucius was unusually forward. "You have survived many times what would have been the downfall of a lesser man. I fear for you if you venture forth again."

"I'm an old man," the general grumbled. "I want to live in peace. I hate this intrigue, but I can't avoid what's happened either." As they walked down the street, Honorius pointed in the direction of the Circus Maximus that towered above the rest of the buildings. "That way," he muttered.

"Chaos has been unleashed." Lucius pulled about him the long flowing crimson robe that hung from his shoulders. "Educated men are thinking like rabid dogs. The rabble in the streets could quickly become uncontrollable. We must not underestimate the danger that lurks around every corner of Rome."

"Yes." Honorius lifted his plumed helmet onto his head and tied the strap under his chin. "Vigilance must be constant." The visor on the front of the helmet cast a deep shadow, almost making his black eyes disappear. Only his proud nose and strong chin jutted out. Once the strap was secure, his hand automatically felt for the handle of his sword. Honorius let his fingers slide down the ornate metal sheath, which housed the weapon that had protected him for two decades. "I'm ready," he said.

"They're baiting you," Lucius finally blurted out.

"They want you to stand up so they can cower behind you."

"Evil people come in all shapes and sizes." Honorius picked up the pace. "But the worst kind go to war with their tongues. Such cowards hide behind anonymous accusations using words to fight for them. They start fires, but they lack the fortitude to put them out."

"The nobility is our nemesis," Lucius said boldly. "Greasy little men sit in back rooms manipulating brave men like you to cover for them. When the matter is settled and the outcome clear, they come crawling out to line up with the winners."

"Caution Lucius. Don't let anyone hear you say such things." Honorius slapped his aide on the back. "Your kind is rare in this city of duplicity. I couldn't do without you. Come. We must walk faster. The evening will catch up with us." Once more both men became silent as each pondered their plight.

Rome had always been decadent. Filth and obscene opulence roomed together. Slaves from conquered nations had built the marble palaces that lined the streets the two men walked. Wealth stolen from the storehouses of vanished national treasuries paid for the splendor. Yet the flow of wealth into the city could do nothing to stem the tide of evil and hate that came with the trophies. Greed and an insatiable appetite for power drove the Roman legions on their endless worldwide forays of conquest. Each success only added another layer to the veneer of hate. In turn, the once-noble ideals of the republic and the senate had crumbled under the fear of losing control to the rabble in the streets. Slave rebellions fed their desire for stability at any price. When the reins of power were handed to the Caesars, only the semblances of justice were left. Now the whims of the royal family were the only absolute authority.

But Honorius knew how to use the system for his purposes as well. The same laws ensured that Paul be given his proper due as a citizen of Rome. Although he was a Jew by birth, his legal privilege made it possible for Honorius to arrange for him to teach while a "paid guest" of the Roman state. Honorius made sure that every right accorded special victims of the judiciary were his. Paul's transfer to Rome had fulfilled one of the petitions that the general had long prayed.

When Honorius had returned to Rome from Israel nearly thirty years earlier, he found it nearly impossible to explain fully and comprehensively the awesome discoveries he had witnessed in Jerusalem. At first his wife, Julia, feared that his time in the Judean province had deranged him. But in time she came to share his faith. Their home had slowly become a center of inquiry as word about the new religion filtered across Rome. Even though Honorius felt completely inadequate for the task, he had eventually become a leader in the new movement, spreading the story of Yeshua whom the Romans now called the Christus.

As more believers from the Greek churches migrated to Rome, the name of Jesus became common. Once these leaders from the Jerusalem church were assembled in Rome, their movement spread like wildfire. Certainly Jarius and his family had fanned the flames. The believers were a bright light in the dreary Roman world of intrigue that had swallowed all Honorius' hopes for a better day. Now that Nero had once again demonstrated the royal family's unlimited capacity for conspiracy, matters would only deteriorate further.

"Do many people know what Nero has done?" Lucius leaned close to Honorius as they quickly walked toward the center of Rome.

"Too many," the general growled. "The story will be gossiped all over Rome within hours. Nasty business," he mumbled.

The sinking afternoon sun had thinned the crowds out so the two soldiers could walk relatively unobserved down the back streets. Years before an imperial edict of Julius Caesar had forbidden any wagons on the streets of the city at night. Drivers hurried their horses to get their carts out of sight before sundown. Nothing interrupted their brisk pace.

At the great Circus Maximus the general and Lucius turned abruptly to the left and made their way up the winding cobblestone street that led to Honorius' home.

Rome was a strange mixture of dazzling unexpected colors and dull drabness. Terra cotta buildings intermingled with marble palaces. Tall buildings lined congested streets where people lived in constant fear of fire. Surrounded by the seven great hills from which Rome had sprung, temples, monuments, and streets were filled with tall, narrow cypresses and spreading pine trees. The mansions of the Palatine lined the Via Triumphalis, which ran to the great Circus Maximus. Streets spread every which way. There was little rhyme or reason to the strange hodgepodge clustering of buildings, set at divergent angles. There was a slipshod, random quality to the great city that considered itself to be the very center of the universe. Order in Roman society came from its class structure, not the city blocks.

Gaius Honorius Piso was a recipient of the opportunities that the highest rung in the social ladder offered. Birth offered the natives of Rome one of two options. Ordinary citizens were plebeians. In the beginning plebes could not be senators, priests, or magistrates. But the plebeian class had chiseled away at the privileges of the nobility, creating various ways of buying and earning their way into the ranks of the elite. Because Honorius was born a patrician, he had automatically inherited the opportunities of aristocracy. Even before there were kings, the patricians had held positions of distinction in Roman society.

Honorius' mother was a granddaughter of General Pompey, who had first captured Jerusalem nearly one hundred years earlier. Through her family, Gaius Honorius Piso had inherited the house of Pompey. On his side the Piso name embodied the bloodline of the ancient Manlius clan. Such aristocratic origins had made Honorius a natural candidate when the opening came for a new leader of the Praetorian guard. The senate would never entrust the generalship to some commoner or even a knight who had qualified for office because of his wealth. A true soldier of the highest order was the only possibility. Honorius' time in Jerusalem was not particularly distinguished, but it linked him publicly with the previous service of Pompey. He was the right man at the right place at the right time.

The old estate of Pompey suited the office of the head of the Praetorian. Indeed! The house of Piso was glorious to see. The marble facade was a soft elegant ivory color with streaks of red running through the slabs. Large support columns across the front gave the house a fortresslike look appropriate for a military man. Two huge torches on each side of the large bronze door had now been lit.

In front of the door a young soldier stood at attention. The emperor himself provided this special attaché to maintain constant vigil over the house of this trusted guardian of the state. Everyone recognized this gesture as one of Nero's not-so-subtle ploys to keep constant surveillance on the man who had engineered the coup that toppled Nero's brother Caligula twenty years earlier. Honorius was not a man to be taken lightly. In turn Honorius had done the unexpected. Rather than treat the young soldiers as spies, Honorius brought the detachment into his household, treating them as brothers. The strange generosity of the general made the emperor all the more suspicious of him. Because each soldier quickly became devoted to Honorius, Nero had to change his assignment constantly. Many of the soldiers became believers in the new god that Honorius followed, which infuriated Nero all the more.

"Salute!" the guard brought his fist sharply against his breastplate as the general and his aide approached.

"Peace to you," Honorius answered with his usual unusual greeting. Immediately the soldier opened the large bronze door.

Once the door was shut behind them, Honorius instructed Lucius on gathering his Jewish guests in the assembly room where large banquets were often held. "Dispatch the servants on assignments outside the house," he whispered. "No one is to have the slightest opportunity to eavesdrop on the evening's conversations."

Jarius was the first to arrive. For a long time he sat looking at the walls of the inner banquet hall. In sharp contrast to the plain living room with low ceiling in his home in Jerusalem, the walls here were remarkably high and lofty. Bright panels of red and yellow leaped out at him. Each wall was divided into many sections with exquisite designs everywhere. Paintings created optical illusions, making the walls look as if they were filled with compartments and indentations. Even though Jarius' home was large by Jerusalem standards, the whole house would still almost fit into this one room alone. He stared at the frescoes that bordered the ceiling. Although he had seen them many times, the scenes still fascinated him.

Directly in front of Jarius was an ornate niche in the wall. The *laraium* was the household shrine for the *lares*. Every Roman household had such a shrine that held the household guardian gods. The *lares familias* granted protection to a particular home. *Lares permarini* granted safety to voyagers while *lares praesities* defended senators. Long ago Honorius had removed all vestiges of this Roman practice from his household.

Shimon Kefa entered quietly and sat opposite him in a large ornate wooden chair with a hand-tooled leather seat slung across the bottom. Years spent in the open air of the Sea of Galilee had taken their toll on his skin. Shimon's dark, leathery face was deeply creased and wrinkled. His stark white beard made a striking contrast to his dark complexion. Although he had adjusted to being called Peter by most Romans, he didn't particularly like the loss of his Jewish name. He sat silent, patiently keeping his thoughts to himself.

Stephanos came in a side door. He immediately kissed his grandfather on both cheeks and sat down beside him. Even wearing the Roman toga reserved only for citizens of Rome and cropping his hair short could not conceal his Semitic ancestry. Maturity had pushed the family nose and chin forward, making it virtually impossible to take Stephanos for a native Roman. "Obviously great thoughts are being formed here tonight," he said to Shimon Kefa.

The apostle smiled but made no reply.

"Something's afoot," he continued his monologue. "Lucius sent the servants scurrying. Got any hints?"

Neither man answered.

"I smell trouble."

"All I hear is noise," his grandfather answered wryly. "Sooner or later you're going to be in trouble for wearing that toga."

"Now, Grandfather," Stephanos rolled his eyes, "you're getting a little crotchety."

"*Shalom!*" Mariam and Philip called out, "A little something to make your stomachs happy," Mariam carried a plate of fruit, olives, and fresh-baked rolls. Philip followed her, holding a pitcher of wine and a tray filled with goblets. "I understand we have important business to discuss tonight. We had food left after we made sure that Shaul had good kosher food sent to him at his quarters tonight."

Shimon Kefa stood respectfully and helped Philip set the pitcher and tray on a small table. "Peace to you," the apostle smiled. "I've missed seeing you the last several days. So much is happening it's impossible to keep up with all the doors opening to us. I'm glad we could gather tonight."

"Something is wrong." Philip frowned. "I saw the servants leaving early."

"Yes," Jarius agreed, "but I don't know what has happened."

Shimon Kefa nodded his head. "When I saw such

signs in K'far Nachum,* I knew it would be dangerous to sail on the Gennesaret.

"I fear that we are faced with a treacherous voyage.
I have been praying for the One who stilled the storm
to walk with us."

"I don't want any more tempestuous boat rides!"
Jarius shook his head vigorously. "Once was
enough!"

Mariam laughed at her father. "You will never
make a sailor, Father."

Jarius shivered and shook his head again.

"*Pax!*" The greeting boomed across the room.
Honorius entered through the large ceremonial doors
at the far end with Julia on his arm. Lucius followed
them.

Petite like Mariam, Julia had gray hair combed up
and braided around her head as was fitting for an elegant lady of Roman society. Her long, flowing gown
was gathered at the waist with a small golden belt.
Though simple in line, her silk dress was elegant.

"Thank you for coming," Honorius began, shaking
hands. "Your counsel is coveted." Lucius stood behind the couple.

The group drew their chairs together in the center
of the room, as far from the walls as possible. Philip
poured water into the wine in the goblets. "What's
going on?" he asked the general.

"Nero has murdered his wife," Honorius said
bluntly. "With the exception of Claudius, every emperor has been polluted with the foul poison of Lydia.
Now we have another monstrous murder to contend
with!"

"Murdered his wife?" Jarius gasped. "Octavia?"

* Capernaum

"Tomorrow her death will be explained away and official mourning will be proclaimed, but everyone already knows the truth," Honorius gritted his teeth. "Nero is as crazy as was Caligula."

"Lydia?" Stephanos quietly asked Lucius. "Who was she?"

"The wife of Caesar Augustus," Julia answered. "Killed her own children and grandchildren to make sure Tiberius became emperor."

"Certainly Octavia wasn't any better than Nero." Honorius picked up a full goblet. "But the act can't be overlooked. She was still a human being and justice is due her. Caligula's downfall began when he killed his sister."

"Caligula lived with his sister as his wife," Lucius snarled. "Then one night he gutted her in their bed-chamber. Absolutely mad!"

"I heard the old hints in the forum today." Honorius took a long swallow. "Oh, no one would say the words out loud, but the thought was in their eyes. Senators looked at me, hard and straight. They knew that I got their message. The time is approaching when someone must do something about Nero."

"Allegiances are already being made," Lucius said, wringing his hands. "Silent agreements are being struck. More and more people are afraid of what Nero might do next."

"I fear for the future." Honorius set the cup down. "Tonight I need your counsel and prayers. In the past I would have thought only about what was best for the future of Rome. Now I have a more important consideration. I must ponder carefully what serves the purposes of the kingdom of God." Honorius looked intensely at Peter. "I know Rome, but you understand eternal matters. What should I do?"

For a few moments the big fisherman stroked his beard and closed his eyes. Then he spoke slowly and deliberately. ''We must not be surprised at the fiery ordeals exploding around us. We are part of a much larger conflict than simply the wicked indiscretions of a corrupt man. The kingdoms of this world are locked in a final conflict with the kingdom of God.''

''I don't understand,'' Lucius frowned. ''What sort of struggle do you mean?''

''The Evil One is on the prowl.'' Peter shook his head hard. ''He knows his time is short. We must recognize each catastrophe as an extension of his intentions.''

''Yes,'' Jarius said gravely, ''Rome is the major focus of worldly power as Yerushalayim is the spiritual capital. Nowhere else on earth is the battle for righteousness as intense as it is in these two key cities.''

''So what should I do?'' Honorius shook his hands in the air.

''Whatever you do,'' Peter cautioned, ''you must not succumb to the temptation to fight the enemy with the enemy's weapons. Your deeds must be motivated by love.''

''But how can we fight evil with love?'' Honorius shrugged his shoulders.

''The answer is not always clear,'' Jarius pursed his lips. ''Remember that you and I both stood at the foot of the cross, Honorius. We can never forget how He returned good for evil. The key to these issues lies in returning forgiveness for vengeance. If we act with malice, even our attempts to bring justice will open a Pandora's box of wickedness. Mercy and forgiveness are the only implements of war worthy of our calling.''

Honorius rubbed his forehead and massaged his

temples. "I am confused. I'm just not sure which way to turn."

"My friend," Shimon answered. "Often the way is not clear and we must find the best among bad choices. But even in such an hour, we must guard the heart. The ultimate battlefield lies there. Evil must be resisted"

Mariam added. "Nothing about the pursuit of righteousness guarantees that a sword will not pierce our souls—even when we are squarely in the middle of God's perfect purposes."

"What will become of us?" Julia wrung her hands. "I don't want anything to happen to my husband or to your family. I just want to live a peaceful life."

Jarius patted her hand. "How well I understand," he smiled. "But our Lord gave us clear direction. If your husband follows what the Holy One directs him to do, he will have the best insurance he can have against uncertainty."

"Pray for me." Honorius lifted his head. "Pray for me to know the truth. I truly want divine guidance."

"We shall," Shimon assured him. "We will pray about this time of testing and ask that all of us be delivered from the Evil One."

XI

In two days the month of mourning will be past," the young servant told Stephanos. "Then we can officially be merry once more. Life goes on."

"Titus, you surprise me." Stephanos leaned back from the dining table and looked up at the frescoes of grapes and vines that bordered the ceiling. Underneath, a gold strip ran around the top of each wall. Panels and blocks of bright colors on the walls made the entire room look rich and luxurious. At the far end was a mural of Rome painted to appear as a view from an open window. "Here we are in the exquisite dining room of the house of General Gaius Honorius Piso, a guardian of imperial Rome. You don't sound properly sad."

"We have come to know each other well in these last two years." The tall, slender young man collected the empty dishes on a tray. "At the very least we both have Greek names and come from conquered peoples. Why the pretense? We both know the truth. Who cares about dead Octavia or who killed her?" Titus smirked.

"I don't understand you," Stephanos raised his

eyebrows in mock consternation. "Is not the death of the emperor's wife a cause for grief for even the unaccepting guest of Rome?"

"Guests!" Titus snorted. "The only difference between us is the nature of our captivity. We are all slaves of one variety or the other."

"You speak your mind freely tonight, my friend."

"You are afraid to speak yours?" The slave shrugged. "After all, you have your god to give you special protection. I am nothing but chattel for the marketplace. Do I have greater courage than you?"

"You know that our family never speaks of politics." Stephanos shrugged. "Who knows what ears might be attached to these very walls?"

"Then I am more courageous than you!" Titus taunted.

"Or possibly more foolish," Stephanos quipped. "At any rate, I never listen to the gossip of the streets. Loose talk and gossiping are against our beliefs."

"What a strange religion you have." Titus put the last cup on his tray. "You don't believe in the lares, in any protective spirits. Yet you believe in a god without a face or form. You talk of his son as one looking like us yet you drink his blood—or so you say. How can you dare to say I am foolish?" The servant began carrying the tray toward the cooking area.

"I will joke with you about almost anything," Stephanos called after him, "except our religion. Levity is never an option."

"H-u-m-ph!" Titus called over his shoulder. "I'll be back. I have something really worthwhile to tell you."

Stephanos slumped back in his chair, crossed his

arms over his chest, and watched the door shut behind the young man.

Perhaps he had made a mistake in becoming so familiar with the slave. But then Honorius treated everyone more like family than like property or employees. Because Titus was only a year younger, he naturally was a potential friend. In fact, the general had virtually assigned Titus to Stephanos as a valet and guide to Rome. Honorius had warned him that the slaves went up and down the street trading gossip as if it were a commodity. While Stephanos didn't like Titus' constant pumping for opinions and information, the young servant made a good companion.

Stephanos and Titus looked a great deal alike with their black hair, olive skin, and the same lean build, Romans sometimes even took them for brothers. Because Honorius dressed Titus well, the slave was able to move through the city like a freed man. Occasionally Stephanos almost felt a genuine kinship, but at such moments Titus seemed to withdraw as if some invisible wedge kept an enforced distance.

Perhaps slavery is the problem, Stephanos thought. *Possibly Titus' resentments won't allow any free person to get beyond a certain point. Titus never speaks of where he came from or of his dreams. A piece is missing and Titus offers no clues. He talks easily and boldly but never personally. No one ever truly knows Titus,* Stephanos concluded.

"Do I get another lecture about your religion?" Titus bounded back into the room. "More on the mysteries of these early-morning gatherings where you practice cannibalism?"

Stephanos did not smile but studied Titus carefully. He was a ruggedly handsome twenty-five-year-old man. His arms were strong, his muscles taut and defined. Like a Greek god's, his profile was clean-cut and finely chiseled. His black eyes danced as they always did when he was willing to violate any propriety in making his little jokes. He meant nothing offensive with his bad humor.

"We don't cast our pearls before swine," Stephanos answered sternly.

"A Jew speaks of pork?" Titus sat down across the table. "At dawn you eat the flesh of your leader and at night you speak of pork? You are *very* strange."

"You are tempting the fates in which even you believe." Stephanos' reply was abrupt.

"Indeed!" Titus took a handful of grapes from the decorative bowl on the polished wooden table. "If Nero can dispatch his wife with a snap of the finger, why should I live with less abandon?"

"You tread heavily on the leniency and generosity of your owner," Stephanos warned. "Someday you may step too far over the line."

"No offense!" Titus poked Stephanos in the ribs. "I jest with you tonight because I have special news for you. Tonight is a time for merriment. I have a special message for you."

"What?" Stephanos looked askance.

"How can I share the news of a young noblewoman's infatuation with a grouch?" Titus indifferently stood up and began lighting oil lamps around the room.

"Young woman?" Stephanos blinked. "What do you mean?"

"Oh, you wouldn't be interested." Titus smiled as he reached up to light a hanging lamp against the wall. "Almost bedtime."

"Who are you talking about?"

"What would the affections of a beautiful woman of wealth be to such a serious scholar of other-worldly matters?" Suddenly Titus laughed. "Come on, Stephanos. Smile! You are a very lucky man."

"You toy with me?"

"Quite to the contrary!" Titus grinned broadly. "I have been entrusted with a secret for your ears only. What am I offered for this priceless information?"

"Come on. I know your tricks, Titus. I'm not biting."

"Such a pity. And the lady is so lovely."

"Lady?"

"Ah, there is a little life left in you." Titus jabbed him again. "Yes, you are most fortunate. One of the most beautiful women of Rome has been smitten with you."

"Who?"

"Guess."

"I'm going to bed . . ." Stephanos acted as if he were about to leave.

"Priscilla!" Titus blurted out.

"Who?"

"Priscilla Rutilia Laenas," Titus beamed.

"Priscilla Laenas?" Stephanos puzzled. "I don't remember meeting such a person at any of our gatherings."

"You didn't." The slave's smug smile returned. "Priscilla is a friend of the general's family. Her father is a very significant senator—rich too. The family cognomen means a priestly mantle. You should like that twist. Many times she has visited here when you weren't aware. You are a lucky man. You have caught her eye."

Stephanos suddenly laughed aloud. "What an entertainer you are, Titus! Are you now the household provider of pleasant diversions on a regular basis? Am I the only one who is so honored? Are there others?" Stephanos laughed again.

"I don't understand you," Titus frowned. "Any other man in Rome would have leaped to his feet before such an opportunity."

"Well, Titus, I will give you credit for trying." Stephanos finally walked away. "But the hour is late and I have much to do tomorrow."

"Listen to me—" Titus reached for the sleeve on his robe. "I don't think you understand. One of the most eligible young women in Rome thinks you're very attractive. Her family has power, wealth, influence. People kill for such opportunity."

"No, you don't understand, Titus. Jews are a separate people. We don't marry outside of our race, our religion. No matter what some woman brings, I am not interested in her offerings. If it were not for the intentions of the Holy One, we would not be here in Rome at all."

"Religion again?" Titus threw his hands in the air. "Everything you do circulates around your religion!"

"Yes, it does." Stephanos leaned very close to the slave. He smiled, but his tone was very firm. *"Everything."* Stephanos turned toward the door.

Titus watched him for a moment. He scratched his head, and his eyes darted back and forth. Just as Stephanos reached the door, Titus cried out. "You didn't give me a chance to tell you the most important thing. Yes—the most significant fact. She is interested in exploring your beliefs," he blurted out.

Stephanos stopped and turned slowly. "You're making that up."

"No, no . . ." the slave stammered. "You didn't give me time to explain fully. She wants to meet with you to discuss your ideas."

"You know that we share our faith with anyone." Stephanos shrugged. "This woman is no different. Let her come to one of our meetings." He disappeared through the door.

"O—o—o—oh," Titus heaved. "I nearly blew that one." He turned toward the lamps he had been lighting, extinguishing them one by one. *Priscilla wants private lessons,* he thought to himself. *I must remember to tell her that she must be interested in his beliefs. She'll have to start where he is. Oh, well, I'm sure she's clever enough to understand what to do next. These Jews! Who can understand them!*

Titus extinguished the last lamp and stood alone in the dark dining room. Through the open door, he could see the hall lit by the moonlight. For a few moments he looked around the room, which was shaped so much like the houses of Greece. In the dark he could almost imagine that he was back in Corinth where he was born but could never return. Because he had caused a man's death, the Romans threw him into slavery. He bit his lip to fight back the overwhelming loneliness that such moments always released. Only then could he dare to let himself feel the deep hate that he harbored for every Roman, every slaveholder, every free man.

Oh, yes, he thought, *I am well fed and, by the standards of Greece, treated like royalty, but it could change in a moment. Should the general die or his political fortunes change, I would instantly be reduced to the level of the rabble in the street or be sold off. By Zeus, I loathe them all!*

He closed the big door behind him and looked

down the long hallway toward the high window where the bright moonlight was streaming in. He turned down the hall toward his quarters. Titus heard voices coming from the *tablinum*, the general's office, but the door was closed, so he did not stop lest he appear to be eavesdropping.

"Someday," he said softly, "—someday."

The lamps in the *tablinum* had burned down, and the light was dim. Long shadows fell against the walls. Honorius sat with his arms across his chest as Peter spoke to Mariam and a young man seated next to her. To his left was a tall, slender, aristocratic-looking man.

"I have asked Linus Decius to join us," Honorius explained. "He has become one of our significant leaders and has access to many resources that will be very important to us. He is also a deacon."

Linus smiled kindly. His eyes sparkled with intelligence and awareness. "My family was originally from Umbria, to the north," he explained. "We have large farm holdings. My father decided that I should come to Rome to promote our interest. They wanted me to get involved in politics here." As he spoke, Linus made large gestures with his long arms. Because he was exceptionally tall, Linus had a commanding appearance. He was extraordinarily handsome. His strong, square jaw and distinguished nose made him someone who would be noticed. Linus looked like a natural leader. "Currently I am a *tribuni aeraii* working with the state treasury."

"Linus is in a good place to be our eyes and ears,"

Honorius added. "He also can help us distribute the history of Jesus that you are going to write."

"You really believe that this project is important?" Mariam asked. "I worry that my time might be better spent working with the people who come to talk with me."

"No question about it," Linus encouraged her. "You already know what we are desperately hungry to learn. We can multiply your influence through your writing."

Peter nodded solemnly. "I have come to believe they are right, Mariam. Even if the Lord returns quickly, we must tell our story to everyone we can. John Mark has been my traveling companion long enough that he has heard me tell many of the most significant stories about the ministry of our Lord. He will know what I feel must be included in the writing."

"You want me to help him as I did Mattiyahu* when we wrote the book for our people?" Mariam asked.

"Yes." Peter nodded his head emphatically. "You helped Mattiyahu sort out and include what was most important. This time we must be more brief and just tell about the years of ministry."

"I believe," Honorius interrupted him, "that we must also translate the first book from Hebrew into Greek. People are clamoring to know the story of Jesus. Writing is the fastest way to get the message out."

"Many, many people are in despair," Linus added, shaking his fist. "Romans are morally confused people. With all of our affluence and power, we live in

* Matthew

fear of treachery and betrayal. Many of our people are heartsick. When we can tell them the story of Jesus, we will immediately speak to the longing that is everywhere. We have an opportune moment for our cause."

"I agree." The big fisherman stroked his white beard. "We must proceed on all fronts. At the same time, we must prepare a story that is particularly for the Gentile world. Genealogies and messianic connections with the ancient writings will distract them from the heart of the message. I believe Mariam can help us tell the story more concisely."

"When do we begin?" John Mark asked.

"Immediately!" Peter shook his fist. "We all know the climate of evil that hovers over this city. But in these past few days I feel an even greater urgency. As I prayed, God gave me a vision of a great disaster sweeping across the city. I must confess to you that I believe our time here is short. We must work in haste."

"What are you saying?" Honorius leaned forward against his desk.

"I don't know." Peter shook his head. "Often one does not understand a vision fully until after it has been fulfilled. But I do believe that Adonai has shown me that a fiery ordeal is coming. We must use every minute we have to get ready for what is ahead."

Honorius breathed deeply and sighed. "I, too, fear for the days that are before us. Nevertheless, as a general I know how to prepare for battle. You will have everything that you need ready and at your disposal, Peter."

Mariam added thoughtfully. "Once Miryam, the mother of Yeshua, told me that my words would go across the world and be heard by a people yet unborn. Perhaps she was speaking of this hour." Mariam stood and put her hand on the shoulder of John Mark. "At dawn we begin. So let us end this day by praying."

The little woman from Yerushalayim, a fisherman from K'far Nachum, a general of the Praetorian Guard, and a young man whose mother owned an inn called the Upper Room knelt on the cold marble floor and joined hands with an official of the Roman treasury. Together they prayed in Greek.

Across the city, not far from the Caelian Hill, another meeting was ending. Oil lamps were hung from the low ceiling. Men and women crowded around the teacher to hear each word. Paul's room was so packed with people that little space was left, even for shadows. Although he was an official prisoner, Paul's quarters were relatively spacious. Honorius had made sure he had the best the law allowed. His suite of rooms in the *insulae* wasn't any different than one any other Roman citizen could obtain.

Most *insulae* were very tall, with many stories. Rome was filled with these apartment buildings. Literally meaning an island, the *insulae* were beehives of human activity surrounded by alleys and streets. Paul lived in the center of everyday life in this city of apartments. Even though a guard was always in the vicinity, Paul's guests appeared to be the true captives of the moment.

"The hour is very late. . . ." Paul leaned forward in his chair. "Let me summarize what I have been saying. We must be subject to our rulers. Even when they are corrupt, their exalted positions serve as a defense against the Evil One." Paul turned to Jarius, seated next to him. "If we don't break the law, we have no need to fear those in power over us. We give tribute to whom tribute is due."

"We remain moral people," Jarius added. "We put on Yeshua, Jesus Christ, and walk in His ways regardless of what the rest of the world does. Let us ask our brother Paul to bless us as we depart."

Jarius covered his eyes and bowed his head. Some of the Romans looked down while others continued glancing about the room. "Now to Him who has the power to establish you," Paul prayed with his hand aloft, "may He keep you safe and secure. The grace of our Lord Jesus Christ be with you all. Amen."

The men and women seated on the floor stood. Some of the gathering hugged each other while others only shook hands. Paul was thanked profusely for his thoughts, and the group quickly dispersed. As the last inquirer left, the guard poured wine into Paul's amphora cup. "I must retire," the man yawned. "I will be here in the morning."

"Bless you, Julius," Paul called after the guard. "Sleep well."

"I want you to know two of the young men who have become very important to our movement in recent days." Jarius beckoned for the two young men to come forward. "Paul, meet Clement and Urbane."

Both men quickly bowed in deepest respect.

"Ah, Clement," Paul acknowledged, "yes, I have heard of you but not your friend. I am pleased to know you."

"Clement is a companion of Epaphroditus, and they work together in helping the poor."

"Indeed!" Paul beamed. "For years Epaphroditus has been more than a brother. He has been invaluable to our work."

"You can trust these two," Jarius told Paul. "Whatever they say will be reliable. You will be seeing much more of them in the days ahead."

"Wonderful!" Paul shook Clement and Urbane's hands enthusiastically. "I will look forward to your visits."

"We are greatly honored to know you." Clement solemnly folded his hands in front of him and bowed again.

"Please call on us for any need," Urbane added.

Both men quickly departed, leaving Paul and Jarius alone.

"You spoke wisely tonight," Jarius said quietly. "No one could accuse us of being part of the dissension that is running rampant in the streets. People are very angry. But I suspect there were spies among the group."

"Indeed!" Paul stood and stretched. "These are evil times. I understand that Seneca has resigned from the government in protest."

"Honorius confirmed the report this evening. Apparently Nero is already planning to marry Poppaea Sabina. She is as immoral and arrogant as the last one. The senators are rumored to be in confusion and disarray."

"Now they are saying that Nero actually killed his mother three years ago." Paul drank from the cup. "Even these young believers whisper such reports. Honorius has said the same himself."

Paul blew out several of the lamps, leaving lit only a little clay lamp on a table near the door. For a moment he looked around the room at the plain, un-adorned stone walls. There were a table, two chairs, and, in one corner, a small camp bed. The room was at least adequate by Roman standards but had none of the frescoes the wealthy enjoyed. ''I suppose most Roman citizens feel that my quarters are quite aus-tere,'' Paul chuckled. ''Wouldn't be meager in Yerushalayim, would it?''

''Adonai has provided well for all of us,'' Jarius smiled. ''Who would have believed twenty-five years ago that we would end up in the center of the Roman Empire spreading our faith? Who would have be-lieved that we would be friends?''

''We have always been at the center of the world.'' Paul sat down. ''Wherever the purposes of Adonai are manifest, there is the axis of all things. So it has always been and remains. And thus has He bound us together.''

Jarius stroked his beard thoughtfully. ''You are very important, my friend. Your teaching remains a light for all of us.''

''Our struggle is not with a mad emperor.'' Paul peered into the night. ''We contend with principali-ties and the powers of darkness. We must help these Roman citizens learn how to stand against spiritual wickedness in high places. Make no mistakes! None of us is adequate for this warfare. Only the arm of God can enable us to stand.''

''What do you see ahead, Paul?''

Paul folded his arms across his chest. ''The worst has yet to come. I expect an explosion of evil to break loose in the days that are before us. Perhaps none of us will survive.''

''I see.'' Jarius' forehead furled. ''Yes, I expect

much the same. I can almost smell the smoke in the air.''

''I was praying in the middle of the night.'' Paul looked into a dark corner. ''An extraordinary vision fell upon me, and I saw a great battle unleashed. At first I was terrified by the sight, but then a great peace came over me. A glorious cross rose up from among the dead on the battlefield as if it had been created out of their flesh. An unquenchable light shone from the center. An incredible sight!''

''Mariam has similar premonitions,'' Jarius finally answered. ''She says little these days, but I sense that her soul is filled with more than she dares speak.''

''Our ancient enemy remains relentless,'' Paul added. ''He knows his time is short. I do not fear the conflict, for the victory of our Messiah is also at hand.''

''Yes!'' Jarius stood and walked toward the door. ''But in the meantime we must be prudent and vigilant.''

''Are you sorry you came to Rome?'' Paul suddenly turned to the old man.

''I want to see my grandchildren and great-grandchildren grow up. Yes, I want to be buried in the tomb of my ancestors,'' Jarius' eyes were moist. ''I fear that will not be so. But I also believe that the final great Resurrection is at hand.'' He stopped for a few moments and sighed. ''What Jew doesn't want to live out his life peacefully with his fig tree and vine bearing plentiful fruit? Such are the gifts that old age should bring. And yet I am part of a greater good. Ours is an adventure that even Moshe* and David would have longed to see.''

---

* Moses

"Bless you, Jarius Ben Aaron." Paul put his hand on his friend's shoulder. "You are a righteous man."

"Bless you, Shaul of Tarsus." Jarius dropped a leather pouch on the table by the door. "A few sesterces for the morrow. Peace to your house." Paul closed the door behind Jarius as the old man slipped out into the bright, moonlit night.

XII

Priscilla Rutilia Laenas sat in the peristyle garden of her home, looking pensively into the small reflecting pool. Her mother, Livinia, picked at the narcissus and violet flowers in the clay basins standing at the side of the granite-lined pool. Average by the standards of the nobility, the house of Marsi Crossus Laenas was magnificent by any other measure. Like all true Romans, the family prided themselves on maintaining the appearances of the elite.

And elite they were. Tucked within the folds of their ancestral memory was the claim to descent from Ancus Maricus, the Fourth King of Rome. Livinia was from the patrician Servilius family that had been prominent in politics during the Republic. Because they were nobility, Livinia constantly drilled Priscilla on her particular responsibilities in Roman life. The scrolls of the ancient stories of Cornelia, the Mother of the Gracchi, had been placed before Priscilla as soon as she could read. Cornelia's perfect example of honor, industry, integrity, and perseverance was Livinia's constant point of reference for her daughter. Any possible infraction of the Roman behavior code

144

was met with an example from the life of the Mother of the Gracchi.

"You do remember that your father has the paterfamilias right to marry you to whomever *we* choose," Livinia said sharply.

"Have I ever suggested anything to the contrary?" Priscilla sounded distant and aloof.

"We have carefully tried to instill in you the virtues of our class." The mother tightly clenched the flowers in her fist. "Why must you be so exasperating?"

Priscilla stiffened. If Livinia invoked the name of Cornelia, Mother of the Gracchi, one more time Priscilla would scream. Not that she didn't fully adhere to the ideals of tenacious loyalty to family and state; still the Cornelia-shaped mold had been imposed on Priscilla one too many times by her mother's heavy hand. Several years earlier something had snapped inside Priscilla and torn a huge hole in the picture of Roman noble life that her mother and father had spent over a decade hanging on her. When Priscilla looked into the place her mutiny had evoked, she saw only boring emptiness. Marriage to some patrician counterpart—whether he be named Caesar, Sulpicus, Claudius, or Sergius—no longer interested her. Priscilla was in love with life, not position.

"Perhaps no man will find me enticing." Priscilla tossed her head indifferently. "After all, my dowry isn't all that inviting."

"You know better on both accounts!" Livinia snapped.

Priscilla did know better. Men had been taking her measure since she turned thirteen. At seventeen she now had a full ample figure. Her high breasts and narrow waist flowed out into long shapely legs. The looseness of her gown only seemed to tease the eye, hinting further at her promise. Her milky skin was flawless. Sparkling black hair framed her noble face, which made a flawless setting for her large almost purple eyes. The richness of her countenance was well matched by investments her father had made in her name through the years. The family could easily choose any suitor who best fit their purposes.

For a moment Priscilla looked down at her well manicured hands. She sat on a gilded, encrusted couch with a silk-covered seat. Her fingers were long and quite delicate. Priscilla smiled sweetly. "It would be a tragedy if a proper suitor was found prematurely and I was not yet emotionally disposed to proceed. I might ruin everything inadvertently. I would think my compliance would save all of us possible embarrassment." The smile lingered long after the words faded.

Livinia straightened. Her face hardened as she stared menacingly at her recalcitrant daughter. "Maybe we should take you to the Temple of Vesta and place you in the college of the vestal virgins. You're a mite old, but you could still serve in the temple for fifteen years. Or we might ship you off to my cousin, Aurelia, who lives beyond the Isarcus River. Let's see how you find the farm boys. . . . Then again, we might lock you in your room and let you mellow a bit with age. It has been done before." Livinia bore down, "Don't trifle with me, daughter. These are serious matters."

Priscilla only continued to smile.

She had not been a particularly rebellious child, but Priscilla had romped through the streets of Rome from the time she was eight. Slave attendants had been hard pressed to keep up with her endless antics, trying to lose them. As a teenager she had climbed the Palatine Hill a hundred times, exploring every possible avenue through the heart of Rome. Priscilla even delighted in wandering the Subura back streets where the riff-raff of Rome lived. Pushing propriety to its limits was an art with her. She had poked her nose into the temples of the mystery cults, watching rituals that would have scandalized her father and mother to the core. Every boundary was a new test for this child of spring.

"You think you can wind your father around your little finger," Livinia exploded. "but this time you won't! By the gods, I'll not stand for it." Livinia threw the flowers she was holding on the ground and stomped through the colonnades.

Marsi Crossus Laenas was an unrelenting business-man as well as a senator, but his daughter always found the chink in his emotional armor. Priscilla's warm way with her father drove many a wedge be-tween Marsi and his wife. Priscilla could afford to smile.

A fantasy had danced through her mind more than once. Occasionally, under special circumstances, a Roman woman might choose her husband. Although it was the exception, the possibility was there. At the right time—when Priscilla was alone with her father—she would present the option. As her mother disappeared into the house, Priscilla continued to smile. When the slave from the house of Honorius ar-rived that afternoon, he was quickly and warmly re-ceived by Priscilla. As Titus apprised Priscilla of his conversation with Stephanos, he avoided mentioning the Jewish custom of separation of the races, and he did not say anything about the young Jew's indiffer-ence to her. Instead, Titus launched into a lengthy discussion of the Ben Aaron family's preoccupation with the new religion that they taught. Interest in their cult was clearly the best avenue for Priscilla to pursue. She thanked the slave, pressed several sesterces into his hand, and sent him on his way.

"So my handsome Jew teaches religion at night," Priscilla mused as she strolled back into the peristyle garden where she had begun her day. "Tomorrow night he will have a new student." Sitting down on the edge of the marble ledge around the atrium pool, she looked at the fish, which lazily wound their way across the bottom among the green water plants. *Like fish in a pond, the world seems to be filled with gods,* she thought. *What's another one or two? Maybe this enchanting man will even tell me something interesting. Whether or not, he will be well worth the time.*

Priscilla purposefully arrived late. She wished to slip into the gathering after everyone was settled.

Huge torches flickered in the night air on each side of the bronze doors of the house of Honorius. Priscilla did not even have time to knock. As if on cue, Titus, the slave, greeted her at the entrance. He led her quickly through the peristyle garden and through the colonnades that separated the front of the house from the back section. When they emerged from the hallway into the immense atrium, Priscilla was astounded. The room was packed!

"I have a place for you near the wall," Titus whispered. He pointed to his left. "I believe the seat is where you wished to be."

Immediately a servant stood up and pointed at his chair. Priscilla quickly edged her way along the wall. A few were scattered around the room, but most of the assembly were seated on the floor so that anyone sitting in a chair could see clearly across the whole atrium. Seated in a strategic place, she would view the composition of the assembly as well as take proper and careful measure of the young Jew who fascinated her.

"We do not present speculations or arguments," the large man in a foreign robe was telling the group. "I personally walked with Him. Even though I had a prosperous fishing business, I left everything behind to listen to His teaching." The man's hair was completely white, but his skin was very dark. He was clearly Semitic. "We have come to tell you about Him."

Priscilla looked carefully at the large group. What a strange mixture of rich and poor! There were even a few tunics with the purple stripe of senatorial nobility. She was amazed that white-haired Senators Livius Pyrrhus and Felix Carbo were standing by the back wall. Priscilla wondered what her father would think if he knew his old friends were at such a meeting. "We believe the Holy One is now making Himself known through our Messiah. He offers a new beginning to everyone who comes to Him." The speaker's voice was booming and powerful. His self-assurance was magnetic.

Priscilla noticed a number of soldiers seated near the front. Poor people sat or stood next to men wearing purple-striped togas over their shoulders. *How unusual*, she thought. *If there is any place in the world where class distinctions are sacred, it is Rome. Yet this hodge podge looks like the marketplace on a busy day.*

"Tonight I've asked my companion, Stephanos, to speak briefly and then we will pray for you." The big man sat down as the young man stood.

''*Shalom*,'' the young Jew grinned with embarrassed innocence. ''*Pax*. Thank you for coming.'' He cleared his throat nervously. ''Shimon has asked me to speak on one of the teachings of our Lord.''

Stephanos' black, wavy hair and sparkling eyes had caught her attention the first time she saw him. He was handsome in a very masculine way, and yet his manner was so different from her swaggering Roman pursuers who so often exuded nothing but pure arrogance. As he talked, she immediately recognized a gentleness seldom seen in her social circles. Stephanos was really far more fascinating than she had even imagined he might be.

''Jesus taught us that the poor in spirit, the humble are blessed,'' Stephanos said in measured tones. ''I know that must sound absurd to the people of Rome who have always lived by the might of the sword.'' He paused and took a deep breath. ''But do you find joy in your lives?'' Suddenly Stephanos spoke with a new, decisive authority. ''Has conquering other people given you peace of mind? Does the pride of power give you contentment when you lie down at night? Does striking fear in others make your hearts happy? I think not,'' he concluded emphatically.

Priscilla blinked. She had expected a discourse on some new animal-shaped god or maybe a description of a new exotic ritual to give one strange powers. This man was challenging the common assumptions of her class! And he was right. Peace of mind was as rare as the ground powder of a rhinoceros horn—and prized even more.

''The humility of which I speak,'' Stephanos continued, ''is the brokenness that we experience when we are crushed by life. The loss of a parent, a friend, a love, the losses that shrivel our self-confidence, leaving us hurt and demeaned. At such moments we feel abandoned by life itself. You Romans speak of the fates turning against you. But I tell you that at such times our Messiah stands close at hand and is ready to offer you new strength and promise. Is this not hope?"

She stared incongruously. Priscilla expected to be titillated but not confronted. Not only was his message unexpected, this young man's whole demeanor was disconcerting. Nothing was hidden or pretentious. He spoke with a certainty not rooted in his own self-importance. *Never* had the patrician maiden seen such qualities.

As Stephanos continued to talk, Priscilla realized that she had no point of reference for what she was hearing. While she had lived a chaste life, the common assumptions of Roman life did not include strict sexual morality or any ethic of kindness. It had never occurred to her that the hovering atmosphere of depression and acrimony that hung over Rome might arise from the behavior of its people. Betrayal and infidelity were the norm. Although she had never faced her own apprehensions, Priscilla suddenly realized that marriage had little attraction for her because it offered no emotional security. And now this Jew was offering her a new starting point. The ashes of loss and dissipation would be heaped up as the mortar out of which to build a new way of life. Priscilla wasn't being offered a new religion as much as a new existence.

"Now we want to pray for you," Stephanos continued. "We find that as we intercede, the Holy Spirit often falls. At such times, our risen Messiah walks among us. His holy presence touches people as surely as my hand is extended to you, and that is how new life begins. Simply open your hearts and ask Him to help you. In the silence of your thoughts, offer Him your pain. Your need will be the place of contact."

The big man and Stephanos stood side by side with their arms lifted. Priscilla saw several other people rise to stand with them. Two seemed to be husband and wife. To their left was a white-haired man. Priscilla gasped! General Gaius Honorius Piso was standing with his arms uplifted. She couldn't believe it. Not only had he made his house available, he was one of these believers!

"I am going to ask several of the believers to assist," Stephanos explained. "Epaphroditus, Linus, Clement, please come forward."

Priscilla watched as a white-haired man began to walk from the back, but her attention was immediately drawn to the unusually tall and handsome man who stood up in the center. He wore the toga of a tribune. Such a man always caught her eye. She watched as the three men joined Stephanos at the front.

"Each of us will be glad to pray with you individually," Stephanos continued. "Often we lay our hands on people as we do so. Just raise your hand and we will come to you. Urbane, perhaps you could assist. Simply stand where you are."

Another young man only a short distance away stood up. Priscilla was impressed by the genteel demeanor of each of these leaders.

"Now, let us silently invite the Holy Spirit to come." Stephanos closed his eyes and held his hands up in a typical Jewish way.

The room became extremely quiet for several minutes; then sounds of weeping broke the stillness. An unseen force swept across the room like an invisible summer storm. What couldn't be seen was felt.

Stephanos, the big man, and several other leaders did little more than stand praying silently as if they were calling down the winds of heaven on the assembly. Shimon began to explain that the unseen Messiah was walking among them offering gifts of forgiveness and healing. He talked briefly and then began to walk through the group, stopping to touch people. The others followed suit. Even General Piso placed his hands on people's heads. While Priscilla could hear people crying, nothing accounted for the intense emotion that filled the room. Neither could she understand the acute inner sensation that gripped her own heart. The whole atrium was pulsating with vibrant life that took her breath away. Although Priscilla was confounded, she was not disturbed. Quite to the contrary, an extraordinary sense of peace surrounded her.

Eventually Shimon called the meeting to a conclusion. He explained something of the cult's practices and invited the listeners to come for further instruction. Then he raised his hand and blessed the assembly, and the meeting was over.

Most of the people began leaving, but some gathered around the leaders at the front. A white-haired old man and a husband and wife were busily answering questions. Many of the younger people talked to Stephanos, while the men with purple-striped togas questioned the general. Priscilla watched from a distance, trying to sort out what she had witnessed. Only after most of the inquiries had thinned out did she approach Stephanos.

''I am Priscilla,'' she said.

Stephanos nodded politely and started to turn away.

''Priscilla Rutilia Laenas,'' she said slowly. He

blinked and looked again. "You've been in this house before. You have visited on other occasions. Titus knows you."

"Yes." Priscilla smiled cautiously. "I know the family of the general."

"Yes," Stephanos mused, "I see."

"Please," Priscilla said earnestly, "I came tonight out of curiosity. I have heard of your gatherings and simply wanted to see what strange things might go on. I meant nothing malicious, but I certainly wasn't prepared for this evening." There was nothing flirtatious in her manner. She looked Stephanos in the eyes with deep sincerity. "I'm not sure what I have seen here, but I want to know more about this Messiah of whom you speak. May I talk with you further?"

The young Jew looked away for a moment and then looked back. He tilted his head slightly as if bringing her face into focus. "No one is ever turned away," he said slowly, and for the first time he smiled at her.

"I have always believed in the gods of Rome." Priscilla was straightforward. "My family has attended thc ritual in the temple of Jupiter Optimus Maximus, the great god of Rome. I believe in the lares. We have our household gods." She shrugged. "But what happened here tonight is so different. I just don't know what to say."

"Yes." Stephanos smiled kindly. "Our way is different. You will find a greater reality than you have ever known before."

And there it was! The flicker of recognition in his eyes that Priscilla had learned to watch for. He did notice what an attractive woman she was. She had caught his eye, and Stephanos had taken her measure. But something had changed in her interests in the course of the evening. The man was no less of interest to her. In fact, she had found him to be infinitely more than she dreamed was possible. But Priscilla knew she had touched something undefinably more important than anything she had ever known in her life. The young Jew was a part of a puzzle that must be fit together very carefully. He could not be treated as a seasonal diversion. Any interest he showed must be treated with a respect far greater than she had ever given. What had begun as an adventure had changed into a quest.

"I do not offer you one more selection among the pantheon of gods," he smiled. His shield that had been raised in the beginning was gone. An attraction was evident. "We speak of the One True God."

"I wish to know more," Again Priscilla was straightforward.

"I will be glad to offer you my help. Please feel free to come again."

"Thank you." Priscilla bowed her head in deference. "I will make an appointment." She returned his smile.

Priscilla quickly exited through the long hallway that opened out into the peristyle garden at the front of the house. Titus stood by the door, letting people out.

"Well done." Titus bowed as Priscilla passed.

She neither answered nor acknowledged what the slave implied. He looked puzzled, but before the Greek could speak, Priscilla was gone.

XIII

The Greek slave finished combing her mistress's jet-black hair before standing back to make sure the linen gown was properly adjusted. "As always you look most alluring."

"Thank you, Dorcus," Priscilla whirled around. "I'm going to meet Stephanos at the Forum Boarium on the edge of the meat market, at the foot of the huge statue. I can't wait." She started down the hall.

"You've seen much of this man in the last month. Much. Please be cautious." Dorcus frowned. "I don't want you to get into trouble."

"Come now," Priscilla chided her. "I'm a big girl these days."

"I know, I know," the slave muttered as she walked behind her. "Just the same, I've been chasing behind you since you were a baby and I—"

"Priscilla!" Her father's voice called from the *triclinium*, the dining room. "Please come in here."

When Priscilla entered the room, she saw her mother reclining on her couch across from her father, Marsi Crossus Laenas, who sat upright, staring at the floor.

"We wish a word with you." Marsi pointed to a

156

third couch on the far end of the dining table. The stern white-haired senator crossed his arms across his chest. Livinia sat up.

"I must be on my way," Priscilla smiled. "I don't have much time."

"Not today," Livinia answered sternly. "We have much to say."

"What?" Priscilla looked at her father. "I have someone to meet."

Marsi Crossus Laenas shook his head. "Sit down child. Other things must wait. We have serious matters to discuss."

"But—" Priscilla protested.

Marsi pointed at the couch with uncharacteristic firmness.

Priscilla reluctantly settled onto the couch. "Well?" she said impatiently. "Let's do this as quickly as we can." Priscilla stared insolently at the wall. The fresco depicted a mythical hunting scene with Hercules carrying a dead stag on his shoulders. The surrounding panels of bright red had always made the picture seem garish to her.

"Where were you going?" her mother demanded.

"Why? You've never asked such—"

"Where?" Livinia barked.

"I was going to meet a friend," Priscilla said slowly. "A teacher. Am I now the object of the hunt?"

"The Jew who lives in the house of Gaius Honorius Piso?" her mother pushed.

"Well, yes." Priscilla tried to sound factual. "I often discuss religion with—"

"Exactly!" Livinia cut her off. "We are quite aware that during the last three months you have done nothing but secretly meet with that man, supposedly to learn about the weird sect that he and his friends promote. As best I can tell, you have done nothing but pursue this Semitic pest.''

''What's going on here?'' Priscilla stood up. ''I demand to know what this interrogation is about.''

''Sit down,'' Marsi said gravely. ''There are issues afoot that I am sure you don't understand, child. The time has come for us to face this problem.''

''What problem?'' Priscilla shook her hand in the air. ''I have done nothing wrong! This 'Semitic pest,' as you call him, is a man of personal morality beyond anything I've ever heard of in Rome. Oh, if I had been around some of your precious friends, like Aulus Baebius, I would have been sexually ravished for at least eleven of the past twelve weeks. All I have done is listen. After all Judaism is a respected religion in our city.''

''These are not our concerns.'' Marsi again pointed to the couch and waited until Priscilla sat down again. ''First of all, these people are not teaching Judaism. They have brought something new to Rome.''

''And you've changed,'' Livinia interrupted. ''In the last weeks, you've become quiet, moody—distant. I think they are bewitching you. You don't—''

''P—le—ea—se!'' Marsi stared hard at his wife. ''I was trying to talk. Let me continue.'' Marsi turned back to his daughter. ''Religion as such isn't the issue. You know we have always observed the official religious customs of Rome. Frankly I have been taken of late with the lectures of Caius Musonius Rufus. If anything I embrace the Stoicism that he teaches. No, I don't care what gods and goddesses you pursue. We have a more serious issue.''

Priscilla folded her hands in her lap. She bit her lip and looked down. Turning so that she would not have to face her mother, she asked, "What is the problem, Father?"

"Twofold." Marsi shook two fingers at her. "First, the rumors are circulating widely that this new sect meets early in the morning to drink blood and eat flesh. Cannibalism is suspected. In fact, some are saying that they steal babies and eat them."

"Come now!" Priscilla threw up her hands. "Would I be a part of something so repugnant? Really!"

"You might not know until it was too late," Livinia asserted, and then she looked down to avoid her husband's eyes.

Marsi cleared his throat. "My point is that these people already have a bad name in some quarters. You don't even need to be close to such gossip."

"And the servants have told me—" Livinia started to shake her finger, but this time her husband caught her eye. She stopped in midsentence.

"These rumors fly because of the second problem," he continued. "The emperor has great fear and contempt for Gaius Honorius Piso. Anything vaguely associated with him is being discredited. Nero is spreading these stories. Honorius' new and strange religious inclinations are an excellent place to attack. The house of Piso is under constant surveillance. Everyone who enters and leaves is observed. We must distance ourselves from all of these people."

"I don't understand." Priscilla lowered her defenses for the first time. "Please say more, Father."

"Nero is a madman!" Marsi Crossus Laenas' face turned crimson, and the veins on the side of his temple bulged. "We are all captives before the tyranny of a mad dog. No one can predict what this insane fool will do next. Matters are more serious than either of you can grasp." His eyes shot back and forth between his wife and daughter as he stood up and began to pace back and forth in front of the tables. "Honorius might have been of help to the senate. Everyone knows he's strong enough—and smart enough to know how—to rid us of this vermin that sits on the imperial tomb. But he won't move! Now all of the power of the praetorians is slipping into the hands of Sextus Afranius Burrus."

"Why?" Livinia reached out for her husband. "Why won't he use the Praetorian Guard as he did with Caligula?"

"It's his foolish religion!" Marsi snorted in uncharacteristic anger. "He talks of love and morality these days. Now he has waited so long that I think he's lost his grip on power. I don't think he *could* do anything if he changed his mind. Can you imagine it? A Roman general has to contemplate the morality of killing? I can't believe my ears."

"Then why should Nero fear him?" Priscilla wondered.

"Because fear stalks the twisted tunnels of that warped little mind." Marsi ground his fist into his palm. "When Nero thought Honorius had the strength to depose him, the emperor kept a safe, respectable distance. Now Nero sees the general in a potentially vulnerable position. If he could kill Honorius, Nero would appear to be invincible. At least in his own eyes, he would think so. Of course, others would find it more difficult to plan a coup if Honorius fell. Don't you see the situation? Priscilla, we must stand wide of the house of Piso, lest we be hit by the bricks when it falls. And fall it *will*."

"I can't understand where she is," Stephanos complained to Titus. "Priscilla should have been here long ago."

"She's never late." Titus kept looking into the crowd that milled around them.

Stephanos looked up at the huge sculpture behind him. "I know we agreed to meet here beneath the Hercules Triumphalis statue. I wonder if something has happened." Stephanos stepped up on the base of the statue and looked over the heads of the people.

As Stephanos surveyed the street, he saw two huge men standing at the edge of the meat market staring at them. At first he discounted them, but when he looked again, he realized that they were spying. He glanced back a third time, recognizing that the men were definitely studying him.

"Titus," he said softly, "turn slowly and look over your shoulder. We are being watched."

"I don't know who those apes are," Stephanos continued as the slave looked, "but they are mean. I'm sure they are going to do something."

"Gladiators." Titus turned back. "People hire them to do their dirty work. They're a deadly lot."

As Stephanos watched from the corner of his eye, the two men began to edge their way toward the statue. One was a black man who towered above the ground. The other was a blond-haired German of equal size. Apparently they weren't aware that Stephanos had observed them.

"Here they come," Stephanos warned the slave. "They're closing in on us."

"I'm sure they are after me," Titus froze in place. "Because I belong to the general, they have probably been sent to kill me in order to send him a message from the emperor. You must run away fast, my friend."

"Of course not," Stephanos snapped. "At least the two of us are better than one. Never would—"

"I'm going to run." Titus pointed to the left with his thumb. "You go to the right and find Honorius. It's our only hope."

"No," Stephanos said emphatically as he watched the two men narrowing the distance between them.

"Run hard lest they lose me and turn back for you," Titus warned. Before Stephanos could answer Titus shot straight toward the Temple of Ceres, the headquarters of the Plebeian Order. Clearly Stephanos could not follow him with such a head start. Impulsively Stephanos jumped to the back of the statue and darted up the opposite street as fast as he could run. When he reached the corner, he looked over his shoulder for the first time. To his horror, he saw both men chasing him. He was clearly outrunning the gorillas but not by enough to escape them. Instantly Stephanos darted up the broad street.

Why? he thought as he ran. *Why me?* Then he realized that attacking the personal property of the general might be too much of an affront. A foreign Jew would be quite expendable, a much better way to send Honorius a warning. *Just kill a friend, his guest.* By separating, Titus had played into their hands. For the first time, Stephanos realized that the two men always intended to kill *him.*

A second glance over his shoulder and Stephanos saw that he was still outdistancing them, but his heart was pounding with a fury. Because they were trained athletes, the gladiators would soon wear him down. All they had to do was keep up the pursuit. Suddenly Stephanos saw the great temple that was at the end of the street.

The Temple of Artemis, sometimes called Diana of the Ephesians, was large and typical. Many steps led up to the marble base of the building, which supported many columns that held up the ceiling. Inside, many small rooms would be adjacent to the large center hall where the statue of the goddess was worshiped. The anterooms were used for sacred temple prostitution. If Stephanos could get inside the building, he might be able to find a place to hide or another way out that would lose his pursuers. Ducking his head, Stephanos bounded up the seemingly endless flight of stairs. Nearly falling to his knees at the top, he stumbled into the main hall.

Stephanos paused momentarily to catch his breath and clutched at his chest. To his amazement, he saw a two-story statue of the goddess at the far end of the enormous room. Stephanos had often heard of the infamous statue of the fertility goddess Artemis but as a good Jew had avoided all possible contact with the cult and its strange symbol of a bare-chested woman with many breasts. He stared in disbelief as the smoke rising from the incense braziers curled up around the marble base of the huge statue. Stephanos blinked several times before bolting toward the small cubical rooms on the right side. He slipped through the door into a small hall. Trying not to look too conspicuous, he moved quickly toward the light at the end of the passage.

When he burst into the adjacent room, a woman who had been seated on a bed stood up. The thin veil barely covering her nakedness concealed nothing.

"Help me," Stephanos panted.

"I would be delighted." She smiled seductively. "I will help you with your offering to the goddess."

"No, no—" His heart was beating so fast, he could barely speak. "I'm in trouble—"

"Of course," the woman smiled sympathetically. "This must be your first time."

All Stephanos could do was shake his head and push past her. When he looked out the door of her room, he was back in the great hall. At that moment the two gladiators rushed into the assembly room, knocking a man sprawling on the floor. Immediately one of the priests ran toward the pair shouting and waving his arms in the air. The black man with the enormous arms caught the priest by the neck, lifted him off of the ground, and hurled the hapless man into the nearest column. The priest's head snapped back, cracking into the marble. For a moment he seemed suspended in air; then he slowly crumbled to the ground in a lifeless heap.

Stephanos stepped back into the room and grabbed his head. "Have no fear." The woman's voice was low and husky. "Just relax. . . ." She put her hand on his arm.

"Thank you," Stephanos muttered incoherently, and then he ran back through the side door from which he had come. By this time the sounds of struggle rang through the temple.

A man and a woman were lying together in this room with another young woman, who was staring indifferently at the ceiling. As Stephanos bounded past them, he grabbed the man's toga and slung it over his shoulder. Running down the passageway, he wrapped the toga over his easily recognized foreign robe. Cautiously he peeked out. By this time, four of the priests were embroiled in a battle with the gladiators. One glance made it clear that the warriors were enjoying themselves immensely as they knocked the priests around like pieces of firewood. One of the great braziers crashed to the floor, spilling live coals everywhere. From somewhere a priest charged with a long metal pole. He smashed the blond German across the shoulders, knocking him to the floor. In that moment Stephanos saw his opportunity. Clutching the toga about his neck, he leaped toward the main entrance.

Stumbling out into the light, he lost his footing and went tumbling down the marble staircase. Instinctively, he grabbed his head, but nothing protected the rest of his body from the sharp edges of the unforgiving marble. At the bottom, he rolled onto the street. His knees and elbows were bloody. Pain shot up and down his back and legs. The toga was left far up in the middle of the stairs. Blood was running from his nose.

The pain must be ignored. Staggering to his feet, Stephanos could at first only hobble. Sheer willpower made his legs pump once more. He half ran, half stumbled down the street. At the corner he looked back. Apparently the battle inside the temple was still going strong. As best he could, Stephanos hobbled toward the marketplace and the route back home.

As soon as the guard at the front door saw Stephanos hurriedly limping down the street, he ran out to help him. Together they entered the house and found their way into the *triclinium* where the household of Honorius was gathered. The rest of the slaves and servants crowded along the back of the dining room.

"Son!" Mariam leaped up. "We were terrified. Oh heavens, look at you! They've beaten you!"

"No, no." Stephanos slumped down in the nearest chair. "They didn't get me. I was just hurt in the chase."

Immediately a servant brought an oil lamp on a tall stand. He lit the oil and pushed the light close to Stephanos.

"Let me look." Jarius immediately began to examine Stephanos' arms and hands.

"Titus told us his version of the story." Honorius turned Stephanos' head slightly to look at the blood crusted under his nose and across his chin. "What did happen?"

"I eluded them by running into the Temple of Artemis." Stephanos looked down, realizing that his legs were trembling uncontrollably. "When I got away, the two thugs were fighting with the priests. I just slipped out."

"Praise God!" Philip hugged his son's shoulders. "Adonai has intervened."

"It makes no sense." Honorius patted Stephanos' shoulder. "No sense." Honorius stared at the brightly colored panels around the room.

"I was sure," Titus said sheepishly, "that they wanted me."

"You should *never* have left him," Honorius said menacingly. *"Never!"*

"I— I— I thought they were after your property," Titus hung his head.

"Stupid thinking!" Honorius turned his back and began to pace. "You must have been followed from our house."

"No," Stephanos said slowly, "there was no one in

sight when we left. In fact, I turned at the corner and looked back. Those two men would have been obvious."

"You weren't followed?" Honorius cocked his head sideways and looked intensely at Stephanos. "You must have been."

"No, no," Stephanos said slowly, "I remember carefully looking over the crowd from the base of the great statue of Hercules Triumphalis just as they arrived. In fact," Stephanos puzzled, "they knew exactly where we would be. Those men came knowing that we would be at *that* place."

"Someone told them you would be there?" Honorius was intense. "Who would have known?"

"No one." Stephanos looked hard at Titus to silence any comment that he might make about Priscilla. "Possibly the guard at the door overheard some comment about where we were going."

"There is something very wrong in all of this," Honorius snarled. "Of course, Nero is behind this business, but betrayal is in the air. Someone is a spy."

"Maybe another servant inadvertently told someone outside the house of our trip." Titus glanced around the room at his fellow servants but they looked back with deep hostility.

"You shouldn't have left him," Honorius barked again before turning to the others. "Do any of you remember hearing where they were going or telling anyone else of the trip?"

The domestics vigorously shook their heads.

Julia spoke to her attendants. "We must be very careful. You could be attacked without warning. From now on, when you leave the house, go in pairs."

"My own guards must be posted both on the outside and inside of all doors," Honorius ordered. "Until we sort this out, we must assume nothing. There is more afoot here than meets the eye."

Titus stepped into the group of servants and tried to edge his way to the back. Honorius looked hard at him.

"All right. Everyone back to work," Honorius barked, sounding irritated. Immediately the household dispersed. Titus quickly disappeared.

"I just don't know how to read any of this." Honorius spoke mostly to Julia. "A piece in the puzzle is missing."

"Stephanos isn't hurt badly," Philip sighed. "Everything else can be accepted."

"No." Honorius began pacing again. "I am as bothered by what I don't understand as I am by what has happened. Everything smells about this nasty business."

Jarius helped Stephanos stand. "We will attend to his wounds. I suspect he'll hurt more tomorrow than today. Let's go to the kitchen and get some damp cloths and olive oil." Philip took his son's other arm and went with them.

Honorius and Julia left Mariam sitting by herself. After a few minutes Mariam rose and went to the little room at the back of the house, which Honorius had set aside for John Mark and her to write. The room opened onto the atrium, allowing her a nice view of the plants and the little pond. In the center of the writing room was a simple, long table on which she and John Mark had spread their scrolls and parchment.

Mariam felt ill. The sight of her son's face covered

with blood, his arms and hands bleeding, had affected her more profoundly than she had revealed. Her stomach churned, and her forehead felt moist. The scrolls on the table became more of a blur than objects. At that moment, an icy-cold sensation sent chills down her spine. Something deep within her soul churned as her inner knowing stirred. Without moving, Mariam looked toward the open doorway. Instantly she stopped breathing.

He was standing there, framed by the flowers and the water in the pool. Mariam had last seen the specter on the shores of Caesarea-by-the-Sea when their boat departed for Rome. He was much larger now, his face more knurled and wrinkled, his nose more bulbous and red. His bloodshot eyes were almost pink.

Mariam swallowed hard and closed her eyes for a moment. Breathing as effortlessly as she could, Mariam looked again. To her surprise, she realized that this strange creature was not looking at her. He was carefully assessing the manuscripts on the tables as if he could read even the ones that were rolled up. It was as if she were not in the room at all. Slowly she reached for her *Gospel According to the Hebrews*. As soon as her fingers touched the wooden spindles, she grabbed the entire scroll.

At once he looked at her. Only his eyes turned; his expression remained frozen. But when their eyes met, an awesome magnetism locked onto Mariam's mind. Behind those diabolic eyes was a world that terrified her. He said nothing but slowly bared his sharp-pointed teeth.

"They will yet be mine," he said.

His words took Mariam's breath away. When she looked again, he was gone.

Mariam sank down on the table. Her knuckles turned white as she gripped the wooden planks. Her knees wobbled and she breathed rapidly.

XIV

During the weeks that followed the attack in the marketplace, Titus stuck to Stephanos like the cement castings on the city buildings. The household clearly held the unspoken opinion that cowardice—not self-sacrifice—had caused him to abandon his Jewish charge. Fellow servants and slaves made no comment, but their continuing silence spoke volumes.

Titus scurried about doing everything possible to appear unusually dutiful. No conversation was held without his appearing with a plate of sweetmeats or figs. When Stephanos left the house, Titus trotted along at his side, paying rapt attention.

Within a week, Stephanos' wounds healed. He resumed his teaching activities, meeting with as many inquirers as possible. He met privately with Linus, Clement, and Urbane to give them special instruction in the Way. Their discussions often lasted until well past midnight. However, all contact with Priscilla Rutilia Laenas had come to an end. His questions about her health were turned away. His only information came from slave gossip. She seemed to have disappeared from the streets of Rome like a goddess returning to her place among the Pantheon.

Mariam and John Mark worked continuously on their story of the Messiah. Each day they talked, argued, and worked to reduce Mariam's *Gospel According to the Hebrews* to a more compact story, giving only the essential details of Yeshua's work and teachings. They worked in a new form that had begun to appear around Rome. Rather than using a scroll, they wrote on flat sheets, which would be bound together in what was called a codex.

Periodically, Shimon Kefa sat with them to talk about his memories. But Peter's visit did not slow their work as much as Mariam's insistence on praying three hours each morning before beginning. At first John Mark chafed under the restraint. As time went by, he made his own spiritual discoveries, which changed his view of what was important. Each evening Mariam labored to condense further what they had written during the day.

Rome's political life rumbled on, punctuated with whispered tales of the wild excesses in the imperial palace. The latest episodes concerned the bizarre obsessions of Poppaea Sabina. Rumor had it that Nero's new wife was obsessed with bathing in the milk of an ass, which was supposed to offer wondrous regenerative properties to preserve youth and beauty. Everywhere Poppaea Sabina went, a herd of donkeys preceded her to supply her evening bath. These tidbits of gossip provided snickers, which were a relief from the terrible reports that usually drifted down from the southeastern side of the Palatine Hill where the emperor ruled. Donkeys were everywhere.

Periodically Stephanos returned to the stall in the Porticus Margaritaria where the Ben Aarons made a pretense of doing jewelry business. The large open-air shopping plaza was the best gold market in the city. It was famous for its pearls, and the aristocracy of Rome made their purchases in the Porticus. Stephanos' gold work kept his fingers nimble and made sure he didn't lose his touch. Most importantly, the business made a good neutral point of contact, where debate and conversations could linger on until the sun had set. While the pressure of a full, busy life kept Stephanos more than occupied, it did not keep him from often wondering what had become of the wondrous Roman beauty with sparkling black hair and nearly purple eyes.

But Priscilla Rutilia Laenas had not disappeared; neither had she forgotten Stephanos. When both her mother and father were summoned to the imperial palace for some social function, she knew the time had come to make her move. Without telling anyone, Priscilla slipped out a side door. She quickly walked three blocks to the plaza where she could blend into the crowded market, making it hard for anyone to follow her. Priscilla took a circuitous route down side streets until she came at last to the familiar hill that harbored the estate of General Gaius Honorius Piso.

For several minutes Priscilla looked up and down the cobblestone street in front of the general's house until she was satisfied that no one was watching the door. When the last pedestrians on the street disappeared, she darted across to the door and asked the guard for entry. The soldier disappeared into the house and came back with Titus.

"The house of Piso is honored." The slave swung the door wide open.

Priscilla walked in, nodding pleasantly but distantly.

"I am surprised to see you," Titus followed her into the peristyle garden directly in front of the door.

"Stephanos is in?"

"Well— a— yes, I think so." Titus seemed generally perplexed.

"I wish to speak to him *alone*."

"Of course." The slave hurried away.

Quickly the Greek returned with Stephanos following him. "Stephanos Ben Aaron of Jerusalem," he announced and stepped aside.

Stephanos cast a long annoyed glance out of the corner of his eye as he stepped past Titus, "We've not seen Priscilla Rutilia Laenas in a long time." Stephanos bowed from the waist in the Roman formal fashion. "I trust your health is well."

"Thank you." She returned the formal gesture. "Quite well. I wish to speak in private. Is that possible?"

"There is a problem?" Stephanos showed no emotion.

"A question needs clarification," Priscilla persisted. "I'm sure you can quickly give me an answer."

"I see." Stephanos was distant. "Possibly we could spend a few moments in the general's *tablinum*. He will not be using his study today. Please follow me."

"I know the way well," Priscilla answered with a touch of sarcasm.

As Stephanos shut the doors he looked out at Titus with a hard stare that signaled the servant to disappear.

"Yes?" Stephanos pointed to a gilt bowl-shaped chair along the wall. Behind the chair the wall was honeycombed with compartments filled with scrolls and manuscripts. Several other chairs were against the other walls. Beneath a high open window was a large heavy wooden table that Honorius used as his desk. A block for holding pen and ink was next to a hinged writing tablet. A stylus for cutting on the wax was next to the tablet. As on all the walls in the house, blocks of bright-colored fresco were everywhere.

"Oh, Stephanos, are you all right?" Priscilla reached out. "Are you physically well? I heard that you were terribly injured."

"What?" Stephanos stiffened and tilted his head slightly as if to hear her better. "I don't understand?"

"I've been so terribly concerned."

"Just a moment." Stephanos held up his hand. "I've not seen or heard from you in months. Three months to be exact. In fact, the last contact we had was to agree to meet beneath the statue of Hercules Triumphalis—and you did not come. Oh, yes. I made sure nothing had happened to you. Our rendezvous turned into an attack on me. But all I received was a message via a servant that your household wished no further contact with the Christianios. Very strange. Now you show up here today asking about my health? What's going on?"

Priscilla sank into the chair. "I'm sorry, so very sorry. Yes, yes, I know about the attack. I wanted to contact you, but I didn't know how."

"Oh, come on," Stephanos folded his arms across his chest and stood in front of her. "You forgot which street we live on?"

"Please listen to me carefully," Priscilla implored. "I was warned not to come here. I was forbidden. Did you know that everyone who comes here is put on a list that goes to Nero?"

"The guards at the door are our friends. We know about the surveillance the emperor maintains. Everyone does," Stephanos answered indifferently.

"I know what I am talking about," Priscilla bore down. "There are other spies, and you don't know who they are. The emperor has already started a campaign to destroy the house of Piso. Your attackers were only one part of a terrible plot."

"How do you know such things?"

"I didn't come to the market that day because my parents forbade me to do so. They had servants watching me. I don't know how, but my father knew that something serious was in the air and that General Honorius was very vulnerable—more so than any of you grasp. Your religion is the device by which Nero will discredit the general."

"Our religion? Come, now. You jest with me."

"Absolutely not. I don't know the details, but I think I see where all this intrigue is going. Eventually the emperor will find sufficient reason to come for you and your family. I am here to warn you about the spies. You have no idea how devious the people of Rome can be."

Stephanos sat down opposite her and looked carefully at the beautiful woman across from him. During the weeks they had met to discuss his faith, he worried because of his attraction to her. At night he found himself lying awake thinking of her. She was beautiful, intelligent, intriguing, and certainly seemed sincere. Her wit and humor delighted him. No, she hadn't fully embraced his faith, but her interest had been far more than curiosity. At the same time, he remembered his parents' warnings about his incessant naivete. His mother hadn't liked the time spent alone with Priscilla, regardless of the motives. She *did* know where the gladiators could find him. Maybe he was a fool. Maybe he was being taken in.

"We know the people of our household well,"

Stephanos answered defensively. "How is it that you know more than we do?"

"In all of Rome, I've never found the honesty that I see in you. If I tell you more, can I trust that what we say will remain between us?"

Would I regret such an agreement? he thought. *Could I be walking into a trap? The earnest plea in her eyes says no.* He answered, "I will keep your confidence."

"Two weeks ago, the emperor called my father into his chambers and questioned him at some length about what goes on in your meetings."

"Nero?" Stephanos choked. "The emperor?"

"I don't know all that was said, but my father was quite shaken when he returned home. He said the time was short. He didn't tell me how, but he implied that the emperor has a special way of tracking everyone that comes and goes in this place. I am here at risk to myself—you must trust no one."

"How can I not tell my family?" Stephanos threw up his hands.

"Warn them—but you must not disclose your source."

"Why are you telling me this?" Stephanos looked straight in her eyes. "Coming here is a violation of your father's orders. Why should you jeopardize yourself?"

"In the beginning, you, this religion, the first meeting was only a new adventure, a diversion. But after the first night, I knew that I had found something more. I wanted to know what you were about. I watched you, I listened to you. I had never seen anyone like you. Before my eyes you grew in stature." Priscilla breathed deeply. "I care . . . about what happens to you."

Stephanos looked away slowly, carefully considering each word. "You are indirectly defying the emperor. You could be in great danger."

"Probably so."

"Then why? Why should you?"

"I care about you." Priscilla reached for him. Stephanos didn't move.

Priscilla smiled and then blushed. She dropped her hand. "I want to keep on being a part of your life. You are more important to me than my father and mother think. I want to stand with you in what is ahead."

"You don't understand what you are saying," Stephanos protested.

"Oh, but I do." Priscilla stood up. "Yes, I am a woman of Rome, trained to be completely obedient to her family—and her husband. But I also know how to act with courage and integrity." She boldly took his hand in hers. "If you must walk through danger, then I want to be at your side."

Her eyes offered even more than she said. The old feelings that had stirred Stephanos in the past surged forward. He gently touched her cheek and then drew back. "But our worlds are separated by an uncrossable chasm. No. We can't possibly cross the mountains of customs and traditions that separate Romans and Jews."

"You say your Messiah moved mountains. You speak of a Master who moved the boulder away from His tomb and offered new life. Can He or can He not take us through this place?" Her sudden audacity made all duplicity impossible. She demanded an answer that challenged any easy response that Stephanos had to offer.

"Well, yes. But this? I don't know. I'm not sure."

"I am ready to find out." Priscilla squeezed his hand tightly.

During the next month, Priscilla Rutilia Laenas came each day. Sometimes she came in the morning and other days in the afternoon, but she was careful not to establish a predictable pattern for her visits. Titus was the only one who knew about Priscilla's coming by the back entrance.

A large garden separated the general's house from the villa on one side and another large house on the other. His property backed up to a hill that was a permanent barrier to anyone's ever building behind him. Years earlier a high wall had been built along the base of the hill. The servants' quarters formed another barrier because their two-story building ran perpendicular from the wall toward the back of the general's house. The garden that meandered around the sides and back of the property was bordered by another stucco wall that kept casual intruders out. However, the back wall had a gate on the far end, opposite the servants' housing. Priscilla simply came over the top of the hill, walked the length of the wall, and found the gate Titus unlocked every morning. She entered the house through the gate the servants used.

Although Stephanos and Priscilla always talked with the door to the *tablinum* closed, there was simply too much activity for her clandestine visits to go completely unnoticed. Several times as Stephanos closed the door, he looked up to discover that his mother was watching. On another occasion, Priscilla passed Philip as she entered through the servant's doors at the rear of the house. But nothing was said.

After several weeks, Priscilla asked, ''Have you

talked with your family? Have you told them about the danger, the spies?"

Stephanos held her hand between his as they stood in the center of the study. "I have waited—" He stopped. "I guess—" His voice faded. "I just don't want anything to intrude between us. We already must move heaven and earth to avoid your parents." He glanced at the door that was their only guarantee of privacy. "I fear that my family may be even more unreasonable if they know our relationship has changed. My mother and father will not like any hint that . . . that my feelings for you have grown."

Priscilla looked lovingly into his black eyes and smiled. "No, I think you really don't believe me yet. You haven't decided that the danger is real."

"That's not true," Stephanos protested.

"On some level it is." Priscilla put her finger on his chin. "You are hoping to tread water, waiting for me to tell you the storm has blown over."

"They will pressure me about where I got the information."

"You must not tell them I am the source." Priscilla shook her head. "There is more at work here than even I know. Secrecy is our only security."

"I know, I know," Stephanos suddenly put his arms around her, holding Priscilla close. "I will tell them tomorrow. I just don't want anything to happen to us."

"I love you," Priscilla said softly.

That night Stephanos asked the general to meet with his family the next morning. John Mark sent word to Peter, asking him to join them. As the sun set, the young Jew prayed for wisdom and guidance. Stephanos knew that his report could have very unpredictable repercussions.

On one hand, he did believe Priscilla. It had taken several weeks to come to a firm conclusion. He wasn't about to expose himself to the charge of being naive again. No, this time he had thought carefully about the matter. Yet, he worried that his feelings were an uncertain factor. Stephanos desperately wanted to believe that he was seeing everything correctly, but he couldn't even let himself think that Priscilla might be deceiving, tricking him. Stephanos had to believe that their love for each other was genuine. Nevertheless his sense of certainty was eroded by some undiscernible component in the mystery. After all, how did Priscilla really know? Where were these spies? Who? Everyone in the general's house was like family. Something didn't add up, and it made Stephanos very uneasy.

The next morning Peter came early. "Ah, Shimon," Titus greeted him at the door. "The family is meeting in the general's study."

"Thank you," the big apostle smiled. "I must speak with Jarius first." Titus immediately spread the word of Peter's arrival.

Stephanos waited nervously in the study for everyone to gather. His mother and father came first. They greeted him affectionately and sat down. Mariam sat in the gilded chair Priscilla always used. Shimon came next, explaining that Jarius did not feel well and would stay in his room. Finally, Honorius marched in and sat behind his desk. He greeted everyone politely and then looked sternly at Stephanos as if expecting a military briefing. Without looking down, the general pushed the ink block aside and pushed the hinged writing tablets away. He leaned forward like a battle commander ready to signal the charge.

"Please hear me out before you respond." Stephanos walked back and forth. "I have pledged my confidence to not tell anyone the source of my information, but I must warn you about what I have discovered. Nero has found a new way to spy on us. He is preparing to attack the general by using our religion as an excuse. I don't know how Nero is planning to do so, but I know that he is spinning a deadly web."

"My boy . . ." Honorius sounded condescending. "Spying has been my business for as long as I have run the Praetorian Guard. Do you think I don't know what that vile little toad is up to?"

"With all due respect, sir, something unique is happening. Old friends are betraying you. We are being set up by an ingenious, diabolical plan that I don't fully understand."

"Our religion?" Philip questioned his son. "How could our teachings be subversive?"

"They are saying that Honorius has lost his ability to rule with force," Stephanos answered. "His enemies believe that he no longer has the nerve to kill. Therefore he is weak and vulnerable. If Honorius falls, the emperor's position will be invincible."

Honorius' eyes narrowed and his skeptical smile faded. "Where did you hear such a thing?"

"Please, I can't tell."

"Such is not street talk." Honorius rubbed his chin. "Nor is this slave gossip."

"I mean what I say." Stephanos stood firm. "We are all in the middle of a carefully conceived plot.

Honorius, do your old friends confide in you even as they did two months ago, one month ago?"

The general stared at Stephanos a long time before responding. "Your informant knows a great deal." The general leaned back and folded his arms. "I'm afraid I must take what you say seriously."

"I do not know where the eyes are hidden, but we are being watched."

"Who else knew you were going to the market the day you were attacked?" Honorius responded.

"No one—" Stephanos shook his head. "—except the other person that we were to meet there."

"Who?" the general shot back.

"Priscilla." Stephanos shrugged. "You know her family. She is the daughter of your friend, Marsi Crossus Laenas. Priscilla Rutilia Laenas."

"Isn't this the young woman I have been seeing talking with you the last several weeks?" Mariam's question was obviously rhetorical. She was quite aware of the answer.

"Of course," he answered defensively.

"She enters by the back way," Philip observed sternly. "Strange indeed."

"Please—" Stephanos gestured nervously with his hands. "Only Titus knows that she comes. Her family has forbidden her to study the Way. We must not jeopardize her."

"Marsi avoids me everywhere," Honorius' voice was detached as if assessing attack points on a battlefield. "A week ago I started toward him when I happened onto him in the Forum of Augustus. He turned in the opposite direction and quickly disappeared. At the time it seemed to be a deliberate action. Now I know it was."

"And his daughter sees you regularly?" Philip looked askance at his son. "Strange coincidence indeed!"

"No, no," Stephanos protested, "I know her intent is sincere. She would not bring harm to any of us."

"You know?" Philip raised his eyebrows. "I believe we have had reason in the past to worry about your tendency to be deceived."

"She would make an excellent ploy." Honorius began to drum on his desk. "Possibly she is innocent. But she knew where you would be when the gladiators attacked."

"I think you must tell us everything," Philip insisted. "You may trust this woman, but you may also be completely deceived. We must be the ones to decide what is the truth."

"No." Shimon Kefa spoke for the first time. "We must not make Stephanos break his vow. We must respect his pledge."

"Yes," the general said slowly thinking out loud. "The young woman might yet prove to be helpful. We could plant information with her that would deceive our enemies. She might prove an effective tool for *us*." He stood and walked from behind his desk. "Stephanos, I am sorry to say that she is more likely to be a spy than any in our household. You must not trust her. Listen, but be cautious. Marsi Crossus Laenas is not above using his daughter for his own ends."

"I know her too well." Stephanos' voice cracked and rose in pitch. He sounded strained and annoyed. "She is as much at risk as we are." He kept pacing back and forth.

Philip looked knowingly at his wife but said nothing.

Peter smiled kindly at Stephanos. "You are a man without guile. I trust your heart. Do not worry. The Holy One of Israel will guide you in these matters. You did the right thing by telling us what you could."

"Thank you." Stephanos looked disappointed. "I am trying to do what I think I should, but I must say that I trust Priscilla." He stood with his feet apart and his arms across his chest.

"No one else knew you were going to the market?" Honorius probed one more time."

"No one."

"Let us ponder carefully what we have heard," Honorius concluded. "Continue to see the daughter of Laenas, but don't play the fool. Perhaps we will have a message for you to send with her later. Thank you, Stephanos. Let us all walk carefully."

The general left the room, taking Philip and Peter in tow. Honorius began talking again after the three stepped outside the room.

"Your interest in this young woman is far more than evangelistic," Mariam said to her son. "Rome has thousands of Jews, and many of our own women seek to know the Messiah. None of them qualify for private instruction."

Stephanos said nothing but turned nervously toward Honorius' desk.

"I see the truth in your eyes, but what I see also tells me that something is happening in your heart. You have crossed a line with this Priscilla." Mariam tugged at his tunic. "Have you forgotten that you are first and last a Jew?"

"I am completely aware of who I am." Stephanos turned and crossed his arms once again. "I am not a fool."

"Most certainly not." Mariam softened. "But you

may not be aware of how important you are in the plan of God. The Evil One would do any and everything possible to destroy you. Would not a Roman woman be a most effective snare?'' Mariam looked straight into her son's eyes.

''She is not evil, nor a spy. She could be a very important person in the spread of the Way in Rome.''

''Yes,'' Mariam said evenly, ''such a noble woman could be a great asset—or a great disaster. You are standing on treacherous ground, Son. I think you must talk with your father.''

''Mother,'' Stephanos pleaded, ''please listen to the Spirit. Yes, I could be wrong, but I believe you will hear a confirmation. I can't talk with my father. I heard his thoughts today. I saw it in his eyes. He's always distrusted my judgment.''

''He only wants to protect you, Stephanos. You must talk to someone who will help you maintain perspective.

''If it will comfort you, I will promise to speak with one of our leaders. Perhaps Paul would guide me. But you must not turn against me. I need you to trust me. If Priscilla is a spy, then I will need your forgiveness and help. But if I am right, you must assist me in protecting her. You have a gift of discernment. Please lean on that gift and not on your prejudice.''

Mariam folded her hands and shook her head. ''I am troubled. That is the best I can say now. I am troubled. But if you will talk with Paul, I will try to be open. In the meantime, be cautious, my son. I tell you again that you do not realize how important you are. Promise me you will be prudent.''

''I will do my best.'' Stephanos hugged his mother and hurried out of the *tablinum*.

XV

Stephanos realized he might be unduly sensitive, but he felt his parents were constantly watching him. Because he no longer felt comfortable meeting Priscilla in the house, he began seeing her near the back gate at the bottom of the hill. Shrubs and trees concealed their rendezvous. He casually let his mother know that he had talked with Paul twice, and she seemed somewhat relieved. Still he felt it best to let the family mention her name.

"Tell Priscilla that we pray daily for the emperor," the general taunted one evening over supper. "It's true!" Honorius snorted. "Let her pass that word along. Surely such a thought will confound our enemies."

Stephanos told Priscilla the next day, not because he wanted to put her to the test but because the practice was true. However, Stephanos didn't insist that she tell anyone. He simply agreed that she should know.

After his third conversation with the apostle from Tarsus, Stephanos knew that it was time for Priscilla to meet Paul. They agreed to meet together at the temple of Caesar on Via Sacra across from the Arch of

Augustus. By coming from two different directions, they would be harder to follow. Titus insisted on coming along but after Stephanos' stern refusal, the subject dropped. "You look wonderful," Stephanos beamed.

"Only for you," Priscilla beamed back. Her underdress of expensive cerise wool shone through the thin drape that hung from her shoulder. When she walked, the light blue drape floated around her. The sky color accented the purple in her eyes. Priscilla's black hair had been pulled back in a tight bun, which was unusual for her. She looked older and more mature.

"Walking down the street with you makes me look like a prince."

"And a prince you are," Priscilla laughed. "My prince."

Stephanos laughed somewhat nervously as if he didn't know what to say.

Flirting and teasing were not easy for him. Romance was a foreign idea for Stephanos. Young Jewish men and women always kept considerable physical and emotional distance. Parents simply arranged future marriages, and the seasons took their course. Only with the ensuing years did a couple develop deep emotional attachment. Time, not proximity, produced romance.

But the old ways were being scrambled. In Judea, only after betrothal was social contact allowed, and then chaperons were always present. The dance of courtship was foreign but strangely alluring to him.

Coquetry and even aggressive suggestions were common in Priscilla's world. In fact, her mother had begun Priscilla's schooling in the ways of men early on. Priscilla knew her intentions well before

Stephanos was even aware of her. Their daily conversations had only increased her resolve.

As Stephanos shared his faith and answered her questions, the old lines faded. Priscilla sat close and her touch lingered. The walls fell quickly. He found himself holding her hand. After she left he tried to retain the feel of her touch, and he thought about her all of the time. Stephanos was clumsily trying to find his way into this strange new world of Roman customs—and passion.

They passed the temple of the Dioscuri as well as the shrine and fountain of Juturna. The couple turned up the Vicus Tuscus to complete their journey to the *insula* where Paul was under house arrest. No one noticed or looked twice at the Roman woman of aristocracy being openly affectionate with a foreigner. The happy couple enjoyed the anonymous nature of the crowded city.

Stephanos and Priscilla finally found the narrow street that descended from the top of the Caelian Hill. Turning left at Via Salaria, two blocks down they saw the large *insulae* where Paul lived. The five-story tenement building was immense and imposing. On the ground floor were little shops and offices with stairs in the center of the building going up to living rooms. Fortunately Paul's quarters were only on the second floor. Some people stuck up in the attic had to climb long flights of stairs.

Boys and girls chased each other in and out of the staircase. The warmth of the afternoon sun made the street pavement cozy for children's play. Stephanos and Priscilla wound their way past the toddlers and the older children, playing hide and seek games at the bottom landing of the stairs. The children, like Paul, were fortunate to live in such well-kept housing. Because Rome was mainly a city of extremes, the wealthy and the poor, little space was left for the small middle class.

"Look who's here!" a voice boomed from the top of the stairs.

Stephanos looked up. "Epaphroditus! Good to see you. What are you doing here?"

"I was going to ask you the same thing," the elderly man answered, coming down the steps, "but why would any of us be here but to see the great man?"

"Indeed." Stephanos stopped on the landing and offered his hand. "Please meet my friend, Priscilla."

"I've seen you at the meetings in the home of General Honorius," she smiled.

"My pleasure." The white-haired Greek bowed. "I've been asking Paul questions about the letter he sent us several years ago, the one he wrote from Corinth. I swear the man is a spiritual genius."

"We shall test his mind further today." Stephanos started on up the steps. "Peace to you."

"Peace to you," Epaphroditus called back as he carefully picked his way down the steep stairs.

"Tell me about him." Priscilla hurried to keep up with Stephanos' long strides.

"Epaphroditus has been somewhat of a patron of Paul for a long time. Originally he immigrated from Philippi. When Paul came to Rome, Epaphroditus met him on the Appian Way with gifts and food to welcome him. Some ten years ago Paul wrote him a special letter of instruction that has become almost like the Torah to the people of Rome."

"I see." Priscilla stopped at the top to catch her breath. "And you've told this Paul about us?" Priscilla probed. "All about us? You told him that I am willing to pay any price to forge a new way of life with you? I'm sure he doesn't approve."

"He is a very understanding man, Priscilla. He has seen so many customs change that he has learned to be very open-minded. He is more concerned with what you believe than with the old customs."

"There is so much that I don't know." Priscilla bit her lip. "I'm afraid that I'll make you look bad."

"Don't be silly. We're nearly there. His place is at the end of the corridor. I've been here many times." Stephanos led her down the dimly lit hall.

Julius, Paul's special Praetorian Guard, let them in. Paul was sitting at a wooden desk in the corner with a scroll before him. A stylus and inkwell were beside his hand. In contrast to the general's house, the walls were plain and unadorned. The room was simple with a bed in one corner and a small table and chairs in the other. The plainness felt much more like Judea than Rome.

"You came in the nick of time." Paul waved his two guests in. "You caught me starting a letter. Epaphroditus was just here."

"Yes." Stephanos stood politely but nervously before Paul. "We passed him on the stairs."

"So this is the young woman of whom you spoke," Paul smiled. His unusually high forehead merged into his nearly bald head. The remaining hair was very white and thin. Though he certainly was not a handsome man, kindness emerged from his wrinkled face when he smiled.

"I am honored to meet the great teacher." Priscilla extended her hand. "Thank you for seeing us."

Paul looked thoughtfully at the young woman standing in front of him and then spoke to Stephanos. "My connection with the Ben Aaron family begins with your namesake. It all started with the first Stephanos. Now you are his replacement in this world filled with Gentiles. I trust you will prove as steadfast as he."

Stephanos blushed and shifted his weight uncomfortably from one foot to the other.

"And you are from the family of Marsi Crossus Laenas." Paul once again looked at the woman in front of him as if charm and beauty were quite secondary to his unarticulated criteria. "Surely your family have the pick of Rome at their disposal. I am well aware that they might even lock you up if they knew you had any serious ideas of cavorting about with a foreigner—much less a Jew. Why should you have even the slightest interest in my special young friend?"

Priscilla breathed deeply, taken back by such immediate and direct confrontation. "I feel—"

"You must realize that our religion is our life," Paul suddenly continued. "We are a people of destiny. None of us can compromise this calling without placing our very personhood in jeopardy. This is why Jews have always been a separate people. Even more, Adonai has placed His hand uniquely on the family Ben Aaron."

Priscilla stood quietly until he stopped, and an awkward silence fell between them. "Do you wish me to continue? To answer now?"

Paul smiled. Her self-assurance and spunk clearly pleased him. "Of course,"

"I am trying to understand everything I can about the People of the Covenant. I want to be one of you, and I am a candidate for baptism. Stephanos told me about your instruction to him that we must not be unequally yoked. I am more than willing to pull my share."

"We are very different from the people in your city." Paul was straightforward. "Our faith cannot be added to your life as if you were putting a new statue of a lare on a pedestal on the wall. Our way is exclusive, narrow, and very morally demanding. We believe in only one God."

"Yes," Priscilla said hesitantly, looking at Stephanos for reassurance. "Each of these issues has been stressed to me. I was raised to believe that different gods dispensed various benefits. One protected the state while another saved us during childbirth. The gods saved us from fate and the course set by the stars. I learned about Apollo, Jupiter, Athena, and Zeus, and now I have discovered a new way."

"These are not easy ideas to give up." Paul spoke sympathetically. "You have a divinity to cover every need."

"Indeed!" Priscilla answered. "We have ancestral gods as well as territorial protectors. We are really a thoroughly religious people. In my house we received instruction on the Olympians as well as Pan, Hecate, Dionysus, and many others."

"Why would you change your mind?" The old man settled back in his chair. "We only bring you trouble."

"Several years ago a Greek teacher presented the ideas of Xenophanes in a class on philosophy. He taught that there had to be one god who was the greatest in the Pantheon. But this god would be different from the many stories that we hear about the endless disgraceful things that the gods do. The more I thought about that idea, the more troubled I became.

I realized that the people that I knew were more moral than most of the gods we believed in.''

"Very interesting,'' Paul mused. "You do have a theological turn of mind.''

"I heard many other things,'' Priscilla continued. "Among them were the teachings of your Moses and his belief in the one creator god. Perhaps these ideas helped set the stage for what I experienced when I came to the first meeting at the house of General Honorius. I must tell you that nothing really prepared me for what I experienced in those gatherings. I saw a reality of spiritual power and certainty that I didn't dream existed. You were not just sharing ideas but an actual encounter. My mind was changed by what I saw.''

"H—m—m—m!'' Paul waved her on. "Tell me more about what you found there.''

"It is hard to put in words.'' Priscilla looked at Stephanos once more for encouragement. "I have always burned incense to the gods and made the prescribed sacrifices, but when the deed was done nothing was any different. I just went home, and life went on its way. Your meetings were nothing like that. I saw power and new strength released in the lives of people. I knew I had found a way that was real, tangible, that made a difference.''

"Well, my boy,'' Paul stood up and addressed Stephanos, "you are proving to be a good guide for this young woman, but it sounds as if the Holy Spirit is doing all the work. A good sign,'' he laughed, "a very good sign. I think we should have a little refreshment. Julius, would you pour us something to drink, please?''

Immediately the soldier began pouring a honey drink in cups for each of them.

"Perhaps," Priscilla persisted, "I can best tell you what happened by speaking of love."

"Love?" the apostle raised his eyebrows.

"My time with Stephanos and the other Christianios has redefined what love means. Passion and fierce loyalty have always been a part of the Roman world, and we greatly honor courage. Yet the love that I learned about in the story of your Master and His cross amazed me. I have seen this love in Stephanos and experienced it in your gatherings. I have been changed by this wonderful love."

"And so you have become special friends with our Stephanos hoping to learn more of this love?" Paul tried to conceal a grin.

"I know about the courage that Roman men exhibit in war," she pressed. "As I watched your people, I saw a greater courage, the courage to love without reservation or limit. Yes, I want always to live this way."

"But you and Stephanos are from two different worlds," Paul protested. "Even in Rome, your class stands apart from the rest of the citizens. How can a patrician cross the Tiber, much less the Mare Internum* into our world?"

"Well, am I not from a separate people also?" Priscilla's reply was polite but firm. "Even as you, we have always seen ourselves as set apart for a great destiny. Rome rules the world because my class has so purposed it. I was raised on the stories of Cornelia, Mother of the Gracchi. Each account was designed to remind me of who we are. No, Stephanos and I are not different—only our contexts are dissimilar."

Stephanos laughed. "Spoken like a Greek orator!

* Mediterranean Sea

Her mind is worthy of her wonderful face.'' He took another drink from the cup Julius had given him and beamed.

''You teach a Christ who has broken all boundaries between life and death.'' Priscilla continued. ''Why cannot the barriers between our worlds also be removed by Him?''

''Indeed!'' Paul sat back down in his chair. ''Have *I* not taught that in Christ there is no east and west, slave and free, Jew and Gentile? I, of all people, would be the first to agree that all of the old social boundaries have been rendered obsolete in Him. But I am not sure that you understand what we are about.'' He got up from his chair and began to pace about the bare room. He walked from the desk to the bed and back. ''Jews have always been exiles. Believers are even more in exile. We know that time is short. The end of the age has already begun.'' Paul talked even more rapidly as he moved back and forth. Julius, his guard, listened intently. ''The Lord may return at any moment. Even now, Antichrist sits on the throne of Rome, and a great tribulation is about to begin. All of us are going to be swept along before the tides of history. Eternity is in the balance. Do you understand me, child?''

''Perhaps not completely . . .'' Priscilla hesitated, ''but I think I know the implications.''

''No,'' Paul said, shaking his head, ''none of us really understands the significance of what is ahead. But I know that the Ben Aaron family will play a key role in what is to follow.'' The old man stopped and looked deeply into Stephanos' eyes. ''In the days that are just ahead, you will be tested beyond your wildest imagination. This love your friend has seen will be pushed to the limit. When it is over, you will be a principal leader in the church of Rome. In the twinkling of an eye, the blade will fall. You must gird up your loins. I tell you that you must be Stephanos— standing before the Sanhedrin unafraid, unmovable."

"I am prepared to be with him," Priscilla said softly. "I will stand *by* him. I am not afraid to be renounced by my family and my class. This day I choose life, not position. I will listen to the voice of your God, not the calling of the ancient gods of Rome."

Paul turned toward Priscilla. She was young, beautiful, idealistic. "Yes," he said slowly, "I believe that you will. I believe Adonai can use your Roman stubbornness and persistence to His glory. But child, it may well cost you everything you have."

"I stand before a treasure that exceeds any I have ever seen. Can I be a fool to invest what little I have to acquire that which is beyond price?"

Paul reached for Priscilla and took both her hands in his. "Our Lord told us, 'He who loses his life for my sake will find it.' Possibly that is the path He has ordained for you, my child. I don't know, but I have not regretted one step I have taken on this road. Beatings and shipwrecks have never hampered the great adventure that has given me a splendid life. It shall be no less for you."

"Then you will give us your blessing?" Priscilla beamed.

"You cannot have Stephanos by himself. If you embrace him, you must accept his calling and his people. If you are ready to take on that mantle, then you have my blessing."

"Thank you." Stephanos put his arm around Priscilla's shoulders. "Thank you, thank you."

"Be careful," the apostle warned. "I am not sure what is happening, but my travel about the city has been restricted of late. We stand near the edge. Now go on your way. Go home and face the consternation of your parents, Stephanos."

"Ah, yes," the young Jew laughed. "We have *our* class barriers to hurdle as well." Taking Priscilla's hand, he started to leave.

Paul called to them one last time as they opened the door. "Your namesake believed that our gospel was for the Gentile world. He wanted the old divisions broken. I think he would be pleased to know that the one who carries his name is crossing the final bridge between our worlds. Go in God's peace, Stephanos and Priscilla."

At the same moment that the young couple left Paul's *insula* on the Caelian Hill, across the city Lucius Capena was entering his commanding general's house. As always the guard at the door smartly brought his fist against his leather breastplate and snapped to attention. Lucius saluted but did not break his stride. He immediately crossed the peristyle garden and went down the hall that led to the study room in the back of the house. Mariam was there working on her manuscript. Jarius stepped out of his room into the hall just as Lucius passed.

"*Shalom*, Lucius. I trust all is well with you."

"I have something for you." The aide reached in his waistband and held up a scroll.

"A letter!" Jarius clapped his hands.

Lucius laid the small scroll in Jarius' hand. "The last boat that arrived at Puteoli brought mail from Judea. This little epistle was included in the general's communiqués. I hope I bring you good news. Apparently the boat has been at sea for at least three months. No telling how long since it was sent."

"Thank you very much," Jarius said as he shook the soldier's hand.

The old man clutched the cloth-wrapped scroll and hurried to the back of the house. "Mariam!" he called out. "Come quickly. We have word from home!"

He burst into the back room where his daughter was bent over a table with a stylus in her hand. "Look!" He held out the roll. "A letter has come from Yerushalayim."

Mariam dropped the pen and pushed the parchment in front of her out of the way. "Right here, Father." She patted the table in front of her. "Put the letter here."

Jarius quickly untied the leather thong and unrolled the cover. Inside was another binding that held the two spindles together. Once the leather was untied, he could roll out the little scroll. Mariam looked over his shoulder as Jarius' trembling finger began to trace the letters. Since the lines were solid letters with no spaces between the words, he had to study each line carefully and slowly, pushing the words apart with his eyes.

"Chislev* 15," he read the date. "Five months have passed!" he exclaimed.

"*Baruch Adonai ha-mevorakh l'olam va'ed,*" he read reverently. "*Adonai yimlokh l'olam va'ed.*"

"Bless the Lord," Mariam responded.

"You are missed more than I can express." Mariam

---

* November to December

began to read aloud over her father's shoulder. "Leah and Zeda lament your absence no less with the passing days. What irony that I return home and you leave!" Mariam clutched her father's hand. "The letter is from Uncle Simeon. Wonderful."

"You promised only to be gone a short time, but now three years have passed and time lengthens," Jarius continued. "We fear that we will never again see your faces. Even as I write, your children are at my elbow. You will be pleased to know that in the late spring, you will be grandparents. Jarius will indeed become the great patriarch!"

"I won't be there!" Mariam threw up her hands. "And it will be a year before we know whether Leah had a boy or a girl. Oh my! Let me read, *Abba*."†

"You must come to some conclusion about Zeda's betrothal. There is some pressure to get on with the marriage. Zeda will be compliant with your wishes but is hoping we can move forward. If we had some idea of your return, we would know how to proceed."

Mariam straightened up. "So many important matters to be settled and we are very far away. Who knows when we will be back? Philip and I must talk immediately."

Jarius leaned over the scroll and began again. "I am sorry to be the bearer of bad tidings. Your friend, Yaakov, the bishop of Yerushalayim, the cousin of Yeshua your Messiah, has been put to death." Jarius stiffened. "Oh, not our dear brother! Yaakov—" His hands came up to his face and he slumped forward, "Oh, Yaakov," he moaned.

"How, *Abba?*" Mariam reached for the scroll.

† Papa

"How could such a thing happen?" She read while Jarius stared vacantly into space.

> The previous procurator Festus died. Before he could be replaced by Albinus, Ananus, the high priest, struck against his perceived enemies. Using Sadducean law, Ananus took control and opened court proceedings against some Pharisees and Yaakov because he was the leader of your sect. We sent a delegation of Pharisees to meet the new procurator as he was on his way to Yerushalayim. We were of no avail. Yaakov was executed before Ananus could be stopped. Now the high priest works hand-in-hand with Albinus and everyone loses. The new procurator is making a fortune by releasing Festus' political prisoners if relatives pay high enough ransom. Once again justice is mocked and insult is added to injury. You have my profound regrets.

"Can it be that our dear friend is gone?" Jarius' old eyes filled with tears. "I just can't believe it—from the family of Messiah! We must tell Shimon as quickly as possible—and Paul too."

Mariam swallowed hard. "Such a terrible blow. Such a tragedy. But, Father, we must finish the letter first."

Each read silently.

> The city is filled with chaos, murder, and turmoil. Sicarii attack, and soldiers strike back. The whole countryside is boiling and revolt is advocated openly. Yet our only unifying force is hatred for the Romans. Our people are irreconcilably broken into many factions. The country folk can't be united into an army. The political divisions turn the city people

against themselves. Only the crazy messiahs who keep cropping up like the spring weeds really think we can overthrow our oppressors.

I fear that should another rebellion begin, our conquerors will spare nothing in subduing the people. They would attempt to make us an example to the world this time. There is no limit to what they will do. Therefore, it is difficult to know whether to encourage you to ever return. However, should a war begin, do not try to reach us here. Yerushalayim would certainly become the main center of hostilities.

The name of Yochanan Ben Zakkai has become known in the Great Sanhedrin. I have been given a seat there. Of course, I am not associated with the Ben Aaron house, except in business matters. A one-eyed, white-haired old man has effectively distanced himself from his past. My only joy these days is being the constant thorn in the foot of the Sadducees. But I stop short of real political battle with the likes of Ananus.

Consternation and trepidation reign supreme in this holy city. Could there be a more ideal time for the Messiah to come? Or as you believe, to come again? Arrogance displaces justice as despair swallows hope. In the face of such perversity, your children stand tall, steadfast, and unshakable. They do you proud. The house of Ben Aaron will stand when other walls crumble.

Ve-ne' emar ve-haya Adonai le-melekh 'al kol ha'artz, bayom ha-hu y'yeh Adonai ehad u-she-mo chad.

Your brother and uncle

Jarius' tears dropped down on the vellum. ''I will never see Yaakov—or Simeon—again. My spirit knows the truth. The faces of Simeon, Leah, Zeda will be only final memories. I will not know my great-grandchild.''

''Father, don't say such a thing. Don't draw conclusions. We have much to—''

''No, no!'' Jarius rose very slowly. ''Look into your own spirit, child. You see the truth there even better than I. Yes, look and you will know.'' With trembling hands, he rolled the scroll up and handed it to his daughter. He kissed her on both cheeks, staining her face with his tears. Then he walked out of the room without saying another word.

XVI

Stephanos tossed restlessly in his bed for a long time before he finally awoke. His mouth was dry, and his throat hurt. Up in the darkness, the walls of his sleeping cubicle seemed like sheets of opaque black slate. The only hint of light came from a lamp far down the hallway. He knew that it had to be the middle of the night. Always a sound sleeper, Stephanos suspected he had been dreaming. And yet something ominous pounded on his senses. After several uncomfortable moments, he forced himself to sit up in bed.

Once Stephanos inhaled deeply, any notion of dreaming evaporated. His nose burned and his eyes stung. The cubicle was filled with smoke! Instantly he leaped out of bed and stumbled toward the hallway. Immediately he discovered that the oil lamp had long since burned out. Light was coming from flames that were leaping up above the hill behind the general's house. The sky behind the open areas of the atrium was a glowing crimson. Rome was burning!

"Fire!" Stephanos cried at the top of his voice. "Help! Everyone up! The world's on fire!" He shouted from cubicle to cubicle.

As soon as he heard shuffling behind the doors, he darted out to the slaves' quarters. Just as he reached the back door, the servants began pouring out.

"Titus!" he shouted. "Help me get the people out of the house. Titus? Where is he?" Stephanos grabbed a servant, but the older man shrugged and bolted for the garden.

"Titus!" Stephanos screamed again. "Just when I *really* need him!" Stephanos looked over his shoulder at the sky. From one end of the horizon to the other, fire and smoke filled the night. There was no time to lose. He darted back into the house.

"Mother! Father! Get up!"

Two servants ran past Stephanos. After calling one more time, he started to run across the atrium. At that moment Honorius came down the opposite hallway with Julia following him. Mariam and Philip burst out of their rooms. Stephanos leaped over the end of the *impluvium* pool in the center and ran toward them.

"Rome is on fire," he sputtered as smoke filled his nose.

"I must get to the soldiers," Honorius strapped on his sword, talking in rapid staccato tones. "People will panic. The city will riot. Looters will plunder."

"What's happened?" Philip rubbed his smarting eyes.

"I don't know," Stephanos covered his nose. "I was the first to wake up."

"Don't worry about our house," Honorius spoke to his wife. "The hill out back and the gardens are a natural buffer. Most of the house is marble and granite anyway. Don't worry about me. I've got to reach the poor sections where everything is wooden. The shacks around the bottom of the Caelian will go up like kindling. I'm sure that's where a fire would naturally begin."

"What shall we do?" Mariam asked.

"For the moment wait here until I assess the situation." Honorius held up his arms, and a servant rushed forward to place the leather breastplate on his chest. The man quickly fastened the straps across the general's back. "I'm sure many of the believers will be driven from their homes. I will find out as quickly as I can."

"I must get a tunic on." Stephanos looked down at the loincloth around his waist, realizing for the first time that he was not even wearing sandals.

"Hurry, son," Mariam encouraged. "Who knows what we will need to do."

Stephanos ran into his room. He grabbed a tunic and threw it over his head. As he reached for his sandal, the thought struck him: *Paul lives near the poor section at the bottom of the Caelian Hill! We must get to him. I must tell Honorius. I must catch him before he disappears.*

Nearly slipping on the slick marble floor, Stephanos ran out of his room for the front entry door. The large bronze doors were strangely ajar. *Perhaps, the guard left with Honorius,* he thought.

An inner premonition caused Stephanos to peer outside cautiously before he threw the door open. To his surprise he saw that the general was at the bottom of the steps surrounded by a group of soldiers. But something was strangely wrong. One of the men was pointing Honorius' own sword at the general's chest. Another soldier held a spear at the general's throat.

Stephanos slipped down on one knee and cracked the door open a bit more. As Stephanos watched, one of the soldiers began tying a cord around Honorius' wrist.

"They are arresting him!" Stephanos gasped. "Good Lord, the house is under attack!"

Instantly, Stephanos inched backward and then raced toward the back of the house. "Mother! Father! Honorius is being arrested!" he screamed at the top of his voice. "Titus! Titus! Where are you?" Stephanos spun around, looking in every direction.

Suddenly Mariam stepped out. "What are you saying?" She ran toward her son. "Soldiers? Arrest?"

"Mother, the street is filled with guards. They have taken Honorius captive. They will soon be in here!"

"Quick!" Mariam grabbed his hand. "Follow me." She pulled him toward the workroom off the atrium. "You must take the writing and run."

"I can't leave you!"

"We will follow you!" Mariam shouted as she ran into the office. "We will be right behind you, but you must not stop until you are over the back hill."

Mariam grabbed the codex on the table. Several half-completed sheets were still lying on the flat table. When she grabbed the manuscript, the bottom sheet caught on the table and tore part of the page away. She shoved the pages into a leather pouch.

"The end is ripped off!" he cried.

Mariam pressed the codex in his hand. "We will write it again." She pointed to the window. "Jump out. Don't chance anything. Run, my son. We will meet you on the back side of the hill. Run! The writing must survive. It is more important than we are. Don't stop!"

Stephanos leaped through the large window opening. To his surprise he landed in a big bushy shrub several feet beneath the window. He rolled onto the ground, tearing his tunic. Even though the smoke made him choke, he scrambled to his feet. Clutching the leather bag tightly, he ran for the back wall. Staying close to the fence, Stephanos ran in and out through the trees and bushes until he found the gate, which had been left unlocked for Priscilla. Quickly he raced up the hill. Twice he stumbled when his foot caught a protruding vine. Halfway up he looked back for the first time.

Soldiers were coming around each side of the house. With torches held high in the air, they charged the back entrance. Other men ran into the servants' quarters while a few began walking carefully through the garden. The soldiers multiplied as he watched. Every escape route was sealed! No one could leave now.

Despair settled like the smoke. Stephanos sank to his knees. His chest heaved as he fought back tears and coughing. His friends and family were clearly the victims of a well planned and orchestrated attack. Terror clutched at Stephanos' throat. There was absolutely nothing he could do. His mother's last words rang in his ears. "The writing must survive."

The only thing left to be done was to protect the codex and wait to see what followed. Only then did he realize that a soldier with a torch and another man were walking straight across the garden toward the back gate. Once they discovered it was unlocked, they would be up the hill. Unless he ran quickly, the soldiers would have him as well.

Reluctantly, Stephanos struggled to his feet and stumbled up the top of the hill. Once he cleared the edge, he ran straight down into the street beneath him. Throngs of people were shoving and pushing their way through the smoke-filled night. He charged into the crowd and instantly disappeared into the terrified mob.

At first he trotted down the cobblestone street, swept along with the horde. Animals ran wild; dogs barked incessantly. Children screamed and people panicked. When someone fell, the crowd surged over them without hesitation. Cinder and ash filled the air. Wherever Stephanos looked, flames leaped over the buildings. As best he could tell, the fire was burning mainly to the west and south, but the winding, erratic streets made it impossible for him to have any sense of direction at night. Stephanos knew that until he found some familiar landmark, he was hopelessly lost.

Despondent, he edged his way out of the street and slumped down on a high ledge in front of a house. He watched a mother and child pass. When the child fell, his mother jerked him forward without stopping. The little boy screamed, but she didn't even look down. Abruptly, five soldiers on horseback bolted through the crowd. People parted before the riders but merged back into a continuous flow when they galloped past. Finally an older man slipped out of the traffic.

"What's happening?" Stephanos called to him as he passed.

"The whole bottom area is burning," the man barked hoarsely. "No one can stop it. The winds are sweeping the flames in every direction."

"How did it start?"

"I don't know." The man spat the words out. "Some say it was deliberately started. Too big. Too fast to be an accident."

"Who?"

The man shrugged and threw up his hands. He turned and started down the street.

Stephanos pulled his knees up to his chest and buried his face in his tunic. He clutched tightly the writing that his mother had elevated above her own life. He felt confused and frightened. There was nowhere to turn. The jagged edge of the manuscript rubbed across his cheek, and he flinched.

The codex? he thought. *Who would understand the value of the document? Who would think that the story of Yeshua was of supreme worth? Who? Who . . . but Epaphroditus! Yes, he would gladly provide security and shelter.*

Immediately Stephanos stood up on the ledge. For the first time, he could see that dawn was breaking. The fire hadn't subsided, but at least he could tell east from west. Standing on his tiptoes, Stephanos searched for something familiar. Slowly, against the backdrop of dawn, he began to see the outline of the Campidoglio, the natural fortress that overlooked the Tiber River. The Temple of Jupiter Optimus Maximus was there. Everyone knew that the hill allowed the Romans to control the river and the link to the sea. The Arx stronghold at the northern summit was the ancient protection for Rome. Now he knew which direction to take to find his friend Epaphroditus.

On the right bank of the Tiber River the villa of Epaphroditus was behind the suburb gardens of Alcilua Glabrius and the Anicius family. Originally planned to demonstrate a continuous flow of unity between nature and architecture, the rich, lush public park was even surrounded by a portico to provide shelter when people walked in the rain. Villas were generally outside the city, but Epaphroditus' residence had a country appearance with the abundance of trees and greenery that surrounded the house. Not far away across the river were the slopes of the Caelian Hill.

Inside the villa, Linus and Clement paced as Epaphroditus drummed on the table with his fingers. Looking out the window, the two younger men watched dawn's light begin to fall on the Tiber. Large pieces of cinder drifted down into the river and park below them.

"What do you make of it?" Clement asked his companion. "You're a tribune *aerarii*. You're around the treasury where you hear all the political talk. You know what makes the city run. How could such a disaster happen?"

"This is no accident," Linus said dogmatically. "A fire couldn't spread this quickly. Something evil is afoot. We will long remember this nineteenth of July."

Epaphroditus looked at the two young men. "I'm an immigrant, but I never cease to be amazed at the treachery that weaves itself through this city. More intrigue occurs in Rome in a day than happened in Athens in a century. No one seems to know what is happening until all the bodies have been counted.

"I am glad we sent Urbane over to the other side. I am very concerned that Paul's *insulae* might have been caught in the crosswinds. I wonder if the soldiers are letting people through yet."

"It's almost as if they were holding the people in," Clement interjected, "rather than sealing them out. I just don't understand."

The river's always been our friend." Epaphroditus stood up. "The flames couldn't reach us even if the winds picked up again. But Paul is another matter. At least he had a guard to protect him. I'm sure Julius knew what to do."

"Are you sure Peter got out of the city?" Clement asked the older man.

"Yes, yes," Epaphroditus assured him. "He had a premonition that something was in the air. My servant was instructed to accompany him until he was well down the Appian Way. I'm sure he is near the harbor by now."

Linus kept looking down on the river. "The sun will fill the sky shortly. Then it will be easier to move about the city. But I don't think the flames have subsided."

"You have become key leaders in our movement," Epaphroditus said forcefully. "In the past you have given guidance that vastly exceeded the wisdom of your years. Now we will need both of you more than ever. You are invaluable and indispensable. The believers will depend on your insight."

A sharp knock interrupted him. Epaphroditus unlocked the chain and carefully opened the door.

"Stephanos! What a shock! Come in. Come in."

Linus immediately hurried to the door. "What are you doing here? You have word about Paul?"

Almost unable to speak, his chest heaving in and out, Stephanos slumped into Epaphroditus' chair at the table. Between gulps of air, he unfolded the story of the night's occurrences. After explaining its value, he laid the codex on the table.

"I don't know what's become of my mother, my father, my grandfather, any of them." His head was so low that his face nearly touched the table. His lips trembled. "I don't know what to do next."

"We must either find some way to get into the general's house or find out where they have taken them." Epaphroditus wrung his hands.

"We will need inside information to get a lead on what's happened to Honorius," Linus said rapidly. "Surely Nero is behind this business. We must be doubly cautious. No one's word can be taken at face value."

"People are on the verge of total panic," Clement added. "The city will be alive with rumors and chaos. It will not be easy to sort things out."

Once again someone pounded on the door. Stephanos leaped from the chair, frantically looking around the room for a place to hide. Without a word, Linus pointed to a sleeping cubicle. Stephanos jumped into the small room while Epaphroditus walked slowly to the door.

"Who is it?" Epaphroditus asked cautiously.

"Urbane," the voice answered. "I'm back."

"Quick. Let him in." Clement rushed to help unlock the door.

Epaphroditus nervously pulled at the chain. When Urbane darted in, Stephanos immediately came out of the cubicle. Both men looked at each other in surprise.

"Stephanos!" Urbane gulped in large mouthfuls of air.

"Soldiers captured General Piso's house, and only Stephanos escaped," Epaphroditus explained to Urbane as he locked the door behind him. Beckoning to all the men to assemble around him, Epaphroditus quickly sat down at the small table in the center of the room. "Urbane was sent to make sure nothing happened to Paul," the white-haired man said to Stephanos. "Well, what did you discover?"

"He's gone!" the young man exploded. "I had to push hard to ferret the story out, but finally I found a woman in the *insulae* who listened to Paul's teaching. The fire did not reach the apartments, but soldiers came late last night before the inferno even started. They took Paul away under guard—no one knows where. He's just vanished!''

''The plot thickens!'' Linus crossed his arms and stood with his legs set apart. ''Before all the destruction began, Paul was taken. In the midst of the chaos when soldiers are needed the most, a large detachment is sent to arrest the very man who should be leading them. And the fire begins at the same time. Gentlemen!'' Linus pounded the table. ''A master plan lies behind all of this, and I tell you it comes straight from the imperial palace. We must act quickly to find out everything we can.''

Stephanos held up his hand for silence. ''I think I know what to do,'' he said very slowly, ''but only the five of us must know. Can I trust each of you to hold your tongues?''

''Of course, of course,'' echoed around the room.

Stephanos tapped his chin nervously as he looked from man to man. Stephanos thought of his infernal tendency to be too trusting. Yet he had no choice. This little group of believers were all that he had left in the vast corrupt city of Rome. ''I must speak of the woman I have come to love,'' he blurted out. ''Her name is Priscilla Rutilia Laenas.''

''The woman who was with you when you came to see Paul?'' Epaphroditus asked.

''The same. She is the daughter of Marsi Crossus Laenas.''

''Laenas the senator?'' Urbane puzzled.

''Yes,'' Stephanos said hesitantly.

"Laenas has access to the emperor." Linus shook his head. "That's really playing with fire."

"Her parents do not know she has become one of us," Stephanos explained nervously. "Nor do they know about my relationship with her. I must protect her."

"But can you really trust her?" Epaphroditus threw up his hands. "She's a patrician. After all, blood holds more together in Rome than love. If she gets caught, she'll not turn against her family."

"All I can tell you is that I love and trust her." Stephanos sounded defensive. "I know she can find out what we need to know."

"And she could lead us straight into a trap." Linus shrugged.

"I am not a fool," Stephanos snapped. "After all, my family is on the line. I have the most to lose."

"Of course." Epaphroditus patted him on the shoulder. "We are all nervous. There's been no sleep tonight. We, too, are frightened. No one means anything personal. How would you go about contacting her?"

"If I just had my servant, Titus . . ." Stephanos shook his head. "But he was captured in the raid. We need someone who can call at her house without being suspect."

"Who better than a *tribuni aerarii?*" Clement pointed to Linus. "It would be natural for a tribune of the treasury to come to a senator's house. Civil servants do so all the time. If Marsi Crossus is home, you could be prepared with some question about how tax money is to be used for this disaster. If he's out, you ask for his daughter."

"I don't know . . ." Linus hesitated. "Since I am not

identified as a follower of the Messiah publicly, I have
been useful in the past. If I become known—"

"What more important reason could there be to
risk identification?" Clement interrupted him. "We
must find out what is going on."

"Yes, yes." Linus scratched his head. "It makes
sense. Probably the sooner I get there, the better."

"I will go with you," Stephanos insisted. "If you
are able to see Priscilla, she will want to talk with me.
She might even be able to come out. I can tell you the
details as we go." Stephanos stood up from the table.
"But this writing must be secure. A great price may
yet be paid to insure its survival."

"I will keep it with my copy of the letter Paul wrote
to the believers in Rome," Epaphroditus picked up
the flat codex. "We will also have several scribes
make copies to guarantee nothing happens to our one
copy."

"Excellent!" Stephanos shook his host's hand. "I
knew you were the man to depend on. I am ready to
leave as soon as Linus is."

"First, my son, we must eat a little something."
Epaphroditus put his arm around the young Jew.
"You will need all the strength you can muster. This
day will be very long. Let us eat a little bread. I will
prepare some pease-porridge with bacon. My servant
made preparations before going home last night. I'm
sure he will not come this morning! We must eat—
and pray—before you venture back into the storm
raging out there in the streets."

At the same moment Priscilla and her family gathered around a breakfast of figs, fruits, hard-boiled

eggs, and a few sweetmeats. Priscilla only stared at the food while her mother picked at an eggshell. Her father both ranted and beat on the table.

"Madness!" Marsi Crossus Laenas said for the tenth time. "We are surrounded by total madness. You must not go outside today, Priscilla. Nor probably for a month. Who knows what the rabble in the street will do? They even marched on the palace gates last night. People have lost children, property, homes! Irrationality is the order of the day."

"Where did it start?" Livinia asked her husband.

"The whole disaster began in the Subura near the Esquiline Mount. All the foreign mongrels live in that jungle of *insulae*. Lots of Jews down in there. Sure, the whole place needed to be cleaned up—but not *this* way!"

"What are you suggesting, Father?"

"Nothing, Priscilla!" Marsi snapped. "Nothing. Just stay out of the streets."

"Does anyone know how it started?" Livinia munched on the egg.

"Oh, the divine Nero did," Marsi spit out the words in disgust. "Yesterday afternoon, he called several of us in and told us that the 'other' gods had warned him that a disaster was at hand." Marsi Crossus Laenas threw back his head and laughed in contempt. "None other than Mars came to warn Nero to protect himself."

"Are you saying he was hinting that the fire was coming?" Priscilla strained forward.

"Just a week ago, Nero had senators look at his new model for a rebuilt Rome," Marsi continued. "He casually pointed out that the Subura area near the Viminal Hill must be razed to the ground if the city is to be rebuilt properly."

"What do you ever mean, husband?" Livinia frowned. "Who did start the fire?"

"Didn't I mention their names? Marsi leaned nearly across the table and spoke cynically. "The Christianios! This new sect that follows some dead Jew is responsible."

"What?" Priscilla's hand flew to her mouth.

"I told you to stay away from General Piso's house." Marsi shook his finger at his daughter. "I told you Nero would get him. Well, get him indeed! By midmorning all of Rome will be hearing that the general and these crazy cannibals burned the city. Piso will be the temple sacrifice for this crime!"

"They couldn't have!" Priscilla shook her tightly clenched fists.

"Of course they didn't!" her father yelled back at her. "*Nero* started the fire. Even the simplest moron in the senate will eventually recognize the truth, but it won't make any difference. We have a nice easy culprit to blame, which allows all of us to look the other way."

"But you can't!" Priscilla pointed back at her father. "You have to stop this monster before—"

Marsi reached across the table and grabbed his daughter's hand. He held it so tightly that pain shot up her arm. "Nero controls the world right now!" Marsi spoke in slow, measured syllables. "He has no opposition in his control of the military. Those who speak out will end up in the same cell with Piso and the others in the Mamertime Prison. There will be no heroes, daughter—only dead fools. *Keep your mouth shut*. Stay in this house and I may live to have grandchildren."

The senator dropped her hand and stood up. He

looked hard and mean in a way that neither wife nor daughter had ever seen before. Marsi Laenas turned and marched out of the room. "Madness," he muttered. "We are surrounded by total madness."

XVII

The hot noon sun beat down on Linus. July heat and the fire made sweat roll down his forehead while he knocked on the front door of Senator Laenas' house. The air smelled of smoke, and flames could still be seen in the distance. Stephanos stood across the street behind a tall, spindly cypress tree, trying to blend into the foliage. Pushing and shoving people, carrying bundles on their backs and pulling animals along, filled the streets. When the door opened, a small man in a white tunic barely stuck his head out.

"A *tribuni aeraii* to speak with the senator," Linus spoke loudly and with professional demeanor and distance. "Is the senator in?"

The servant looked sternly at Linus. His toga *praetexta* was carefully draped over his right shoulder with the multitudinous folds resting on Linus' left arm. The necessary purple stripe ran across his shoulder and across the edge near his left wrist. With one quick glance at his feet, the servant saw red leather callous sandals worn only by a patrician.

"Well?" Linus tapped his feet impatiently.

"The senator is out." The man shouted over the deafening street noise.

"Then I have been instructed to speak with his daughter."

"Priscilla?" The servant frowned.

"Priscilla Rutilia Laenas," Linus snapped back.

"Ah, yes." The servant pursed his lips, "please come in. I will call her."

Linus shut the door behind him and stood in the entryway until the servant returned with Priscilla. Her eyes signaled recognition. Linus immediately bowed at the waist.

"*Pax*," he said politely. "*Shalom*."

Priscilla smiled and looked at him carefully.

"I wish to share some information with you," Linus said hesitantly as he looked intently at the servant.

"Thank you, Silvanus." Priscilla dismissed the servant with a wave of her hand. "I can handle the matter."

The servant nodded and left.

"What word do you bring?" Priscilla quickly asked in a low, intense voice.

"We must talk where we cannot be heard."

"It is difficult anywhere—this entry is, perhaps, the best place."

"Stephanos is across the street," Linus murmured.

"Oh, thank God!" Priscilla gripped Linus' wrist. "Is he all right?"

Linus leaned next to Priscilla's ear, rapidly whispering the details of the capture of the Ben Aaron family and Stephanos' narrow escape.

"I must go to him." Priscilla rubbed her temple. Her eyes darted back and forth. "I must take some sort of wrap with me, but yes, I must go to him." She turned toward the hall.

"Regardless of the cost . . ." Her words trailed after her, "I must go to him."

When Priscilla returned, a light linen drape was slung over her shoulder. She took Linus' arm without even breaking stride and opened the front door with her other hand. "Where is he?" She led Linus down the stairs.

"Easy . . . slowly . . ." Linus looked up and down the street. "He is close at hand, but let us be cautious."

"In this tumult?" Priscilla pointed toward the mass of people surging past. "No one even has time to pay attention to themselves. Where is he?"

Linus took her arm firmly and pushed out into the crowd. Once they were across the street, he pointed behind the cypress.

"Stephanos!" Priscilla reached for his hand. "You've not been hurt?"

"Only harassed." Stephanos squeezed her hand. "Everyone else has been captured. Probably in prison, but I have no idea where to turn. Soldiers have also taken Paul."

"You were right to come here." Priscilla put both of her hands over his. "But we must act quickly. I have been forbidden to be on the streets, and I fear the results if my father finds that I have been out. I think I know where we should look."

"Where?" Stephanos and Linus said simultaneously.

"Walk down the street alongside me," Priscilla started out. "We need to get away from here. There is something else you must know."

The two men fell in beside Priscilla, edging their way past people and quickly walking out of the area in front of her house. Only when they turned the corner could they talk in a normal voice.

"Nero is deliberately spreading the rumor that the Christianios started the fire," she began.

"What?" Stephanos stopped.

"The believers will be hunted people," she continued. "The general will be charged with being a ringleader. You must realize that this is a life-and-death matter."

Linus smashed his fist into his palm. "That's why they came for Paul! They're rounding everyone up."

"Yes," Priscilla confirmed, "and the Mamertine Prison is the place to begin our search. I heard my father mention it. I can get away with making inquiries, but we must hurry. The Forum isn't that far from here."

Everyone in Rome knew the Forum was in the small valley between the Palatine and Quirinal Hills. The Julian Basilica and the Forum of Caesar with the temple of Venus were the most common landmarks in Rome. The square in the center was the very fulcrum of all political, religious, and commercial life. Great processions and triumphal marches always came through this nerve center of the city. Triumphal arches and temples with honorary columns filled the area. On the east side of the highest hill was the cold miserable Mamertine Prison. Paradoxically, to be locked in this dungeon was to be planted in the very heart of Rome past and present.

The trio quickly found the Via Nova street that ran alongside the house of the vestals. They turned at the temple of the Dioscuri and took the Via Sacra past the

Lacus Curtius to Clivo Capitolino street, winding its way up the hill to the jail. Everywhere they turned, masses of people were surging through the streets.

The ascent up the hill was steep and lined with bushes as they left all the temples, statues, and marble buildings behind. Near the top they could see the entrance to the prison. Five guards in plain leather breastplates stood with spears in their hands. Each man wore a helmet and carried a sword. The heavy door was built into the side of the hill; once it was locked there was no means of escape ever. The guards stood talking to each other.

"Ask for Julius," Linus instructed Priscilla as they walked. "If he is still with Paul, he will be our best source of information. Stephanos and I ought to wait at some distance—particularly Stephanos. If Julius is no longer assigned to Paul, you might try to get direct access to Paul himself. God be with you."

The two men stopped at the last bend in the path, and Priscilla went on alone. Linus stayed close enough to the turn to be able to watch Priscilla while Stephanos waited in the shadows of the retaining wall. When she reached the entrance, she spoke to one of the men briefly. Linus watched as the guard disappeared inside. In a few moments the metal door opened, and Priscilla was ushered into the prison.

"She's in!" Linus exclaimed. "At least she's in!"

"I just hope we haven't let her walk into a trap." Stephanos wrung his hands. "I don't like any of this."

Linus watched while Stephanos alternately leaned on the stone wall next to the walk and paced. Time dragged.

"She's been there way too long," Stephanos fretted. "We should not have let her go alone."

"She's coming out!" Linus brightened. "Yes, she's

walking away alone. That's it, Priscilla! Slow and easy. Here she comes!''

"You're all right?'' Stephanos pulled Priscilla into the shadows as soon as she turned the corner.

"Watch and make sure no one is following me.'' Priscilla nodded her head affirmatively as she kept walking. "Yes, Julius was inside with Paul. Paul is held in irons, but he is all right. I think I have the information we need.''

"Where are they?'' Stephanos pushed.

"Only Paul is inside.'' Priscilla spoke rapidly. "The general and the men of his house are in the cells of the Lautumiae on the back side of the Arx of the Capitol. It's just down the way on the lower side of the Forum. We're very close. But neither he nor Julius knows anything about where they took the women. Apparently the emperor is more concerned with the general and Paul now.''

"I know the jail.'' Linus talked rapidly as they hurried back down the path. "They don't use that place often. Basically it's a big room with broken-down cells around the sides. Usually the dungeon is guarded by *lictors*, not soldiers.''

"*Lictors?*'' Stephanos asked.

"Something like me, like tribunes. They're civil servants who generally serve as escorts for senators and important people. If you see guards wearing plain white togas, you'll know they are *lictors*. I think we could bribe our way into the place if they are on duty.''

"Wouldn't soldiers be there?'' Priscilla breathed heavily, trying to keep up with the men.

"Not necessarily. Soldiers are needed all over the city right now, and Nero might also fear that the general would have some sway with anyone in the military. He just might turn to the employees of Rome to do his bidding. That would be perfect. Soldiers wouldn't be easy to bribe, but the civilians would be a snap."

The flames above the city had diminished considerably by the time they crossed back through the Forum. People were still running through the streets, and there was no sense of order. The two men and Priscilla easily went unnoticed in the continuing chaos.

Once they cleared the Forum proper and passed the capitol, they found the narrow path down the back side, which became a steep hill sliding down to the flat plain below. As they had descended the slope from the Mamertine Prison, so they virtually ran down the backside of the Arx. Trees and shrubs covered the hillside and provided a natural cover when they reached the bottom. Immediately they saw the Lautumiae just in front of them.

"*Lictors!*" Linus pointed to the gateway into the prison. "Three of them. White togas! Perfect. I have an idea. Just follow me and say nothing. Priscilla, stay in the shadows until we return."

"What are we doing?" Stephanos dropped slightly behind his friend.

"Just act like you're my servant," Linus said under his breath as he walked even faster. "Priscilla, stay right here until we return."

"We have come about the food arrangements," Linus addressed a short, fat man who was sitting on a boulder outside the metal door. The other two looked puzzled.

"Who are you?" the squatty, balding man asked indifferently.

"A *tribuni aeraii*," Linus avoided using his name. "We are concerned with the expenses."

"I don't know anything." The tall man shrugged. "They hauled me up here when the whole city went up in smoke. I don't even know who is ultimately in charge except we've got some important people in there. Everything else is some kind of big secret."

"I need to inquire about the head count and their needs. Please let me and my servant in."

"I don't have any orders to do so." The fat man puckered his fleshy cheeks. "I don't want any trouble." He looked at the other two men, who shrugged indifferently.

"Listen," Linus' words dripped with irritation. "If I have to walk all the way back to the imperial palace in the riot that's going on in the streets to get an order, I guarantee you will have real trouble!"

"All right! All right—" The man stood up. "But it's going to be your responsibility not mine."

"Why do you think I'm here?" Linus barked.

The other two men dropped the heavy timber that secured the outer door. "Dark in there," the fat one muttered, "pitch black, stinks. I wouldn't advise staying long. Don't know how many of what are rooting around in the mud and darkness."

"Possibly so." Linus beckoned Stephanos on. "But it will take time for our eyes to adjust to the dark. I'll need my servant to go ahead of me."

"As you wish." The man nodded disdainfully.

Once Linus and Stephanos stepped inside, they stopped. The prison was far darker then they would have thought. A damp, muddy stench replaced the stale smell of smoke. As their sandals slipped into the ooze beneath the straw-covered floor, they could only see shapes moving around the large open area.

"Look!" came from one of the corners. "It looks like my son!"

Stephanos peered in the direction of the voice. "Father? Philip of the Ben Aaron family, is that you?" he called.

"Son!" The form moved out of the darkness. "We are here!"

"*Abba!*" Stephanos reached out, trying to find his way without slipping. "Are you here? Where are you?"

"In the corner," Philip answered as he came forward. "They caught you! How terrible."

Father and son found each other at the same moment. Tottering to keep their balance in the slippery wet mud, they embraced. Honorius emerged from the darkness to hug Stephanos.

"They didn't get me. I escaped! I'm in here because they think I'm Linus' servant."

"Linus? The tribune? The deacon?" Honorius groped in the darkness.

"Yes." Linus edged his way toward them. "Is anyone else here from your household?"

"No," the general answered. "You can speak freely."

"Good." Linus found them. "I must not be identified if I can help it."

"Where is Mother?" Stephanos probed immediately.

"All the women were taken to a large blue house on Vicus Patricii just before it goes up the Viminal Hill. Just outside the Subura Major. The soldiers left them there when they brought us here last night."

"I don't know the place well," Honorius interrupted. "It's a terra-cotta two-story with a new coat of blue paint belonging to a prominent *lictor.* A private home. There's a tavern across the street. Two columns in front." Accustomed to the dark, the general walked straight toward them.

"Why there?" Linus probed.

"Julia's high nobility," Honorius answered. "You know how shy and retiring she is. Never says anything. Too bashful to come to our meetings. I think they're not sure if she is one of us. The emperor is playing his hand cautiously. He wants me, but he's probably not sure yet whether he's after my aristocratic wife. Your family is substantial."

"I'm sure they fare better than we." Philip added.

Stephanos realized his father was just in front of him, reaching out. Taking his father's hand, Stephanos asked, "How were we betrayed?"

"Who knew that you went to the market the day that you were attacked?" Honorius answered.

"Just Titus and . . ." he stammered, "and Priscilla." Stephanos could now see the general's shape to his left. "But I know Priscilla didn't betray us. She is waiting outside and without her—"

"Who knew?" the general asked again.

"Just Titus and . . ." Stephanos stopped.

"Who knew?" Honorius said once more.

"No! No!" Stephanos gasped. "Not Titus!"

"He was standing outside among the soldiers when I left the house last night." Honorius' voice cracked. "He unlocked the doors for them. He even led them to the back gate. After all I did for him! Nero's special guards at the door were better friends to me. For months he has been sending information to the emperor. Lists of names. Everything. I'm sure they knew every time Priscilla came to the house. The back entryway—everything."

"I can't believe it," Stephanos' voice trailed away. He was glad he could not see Honorius' eyes.

"A man can defend against his sworn enemies . . ." The general sounded as if he spoke to himself. "But when a friend or one of your family seeks your throat in the night, even God's hands are tied. You are defenseless. No strategy can save you from such treachery."

"What can we do?" Linus begged. "Tell me anything. We will see that it is done."

"You cannot save us." Honorius' voice fell. "As soon as the city is settled again, they will surround the Lautumiae with a small army. The word will spread that I am here and my friends will want to help, but Nero will make sure there is no escape. The best you can do is try to get the women out immediately. Make no mistake. No one can help us."

"But the citizens won't believe you set the city on fire," Stephanos protested. "The senators know better."

"The cowards won't buck the emperor this time." Honorius disagreed. "There's too much at stake now for anyone to admit Nero burned the city. Later the facts will creep out, but we'll be gone before they face the truth. We're an easy target to pacify the masses who lost everything in the fire."

"No!" Stephanos shouted. "I won't accept the—"

"Yes!" The general cut him off. "You must not come back here again. They know you escaped, and Titus will fear that you will find him. You must shave your beard and do everything to look like a Roman or a Greek. Don't return. It's your only hope."

"I can't," Stephanos anguished.

"You must," Philip rebuked him. "You have come to Rome for this hour, my son. God has always had a great plan at work in all of this. Your escape was not an accident. You may be the only voice that is left to speak. You must hide until you know what you are to do next. Do not be anxious for us."

"I do not fear death," a tired voice said behind him.

"Grandfather!" Stephanos had not seen Jarius because the older man had difficulty standing.

Jarius hugged his grandson and kissed him on both cheeks. "We ran a good race. God has not abandoned us. We do not have to be afraid. Now you must stand up as the man you are. You must be a Ben Aaron. When you walk out the door of this prison, you must do honor to both of your names. Carry our title well and keep the spirit of Stephanos, our first martyr."

"I can't leave you," Stephanos sobbed as he clutched his grandfather. "I must protect you."

"You serve us best by helping our women," Honorius reassured him. "But time is short; you must not stay here lest the soldiers return."

"Father!" Stephanos reached for his father. "You have always been my rock."

"I love you more than my life, my son. I cannot tell you how proud I am of you. You are a credit to your family and your God. I thank God that He allowed me to be your father."

"No, no!" Stephanos hung on his father's neck. "I can't leave you."

"Honorius is right." Jarius patted his grandson on the back softly. "You must leave for your own sake. Let me bless you, and then you must go."

Jarius and Philip placed their hands on his head. In the darkness Jarius prayed, "*Heenay anokhee meit,*

*v'hayah eloim imakhem, v'heisheev etkhem el eretz avo-
teikheam.''*

And then Philip answered, ''The God before whom
my fathers Avraham and Yitzchak* walked, the God
who has led me all my life long to this day, the Messiah who has redeemed me from all evil, bless you,
my son. And in you let my name be perpetuated, and
the name of my fathers, Avraham and Yitzchak,''
Philip choked. ''And my father Jarius.''

Grandfather and father removed their hands and
kissed Stephanos on both cheeks.

''I can't leave you,'' Stephanos anguished. ''This
cannot be.'' Linus kept tugging at his arm. ''I'm sorry
but the general's right. We must hurry.''

''It is only the beginning.'' Jarius gave his grandson
a final kiss. ''We will not flinch. The Roman Empire
will see how invincible our faith is. You must help
them see the truth.''

''Do everything you can to seek the release of Julia
and your mother. Your best efforts will comfort us
sufficiently,'' Honorius called after him. ''God be
with you.''

''*Shalom,*'' Philip's voice faded.

Stephanos could not speak. He stumbled toward
the light coming through cracks under the heavy
door. Hot tears ran down his face. He felt dizzy and
unable to swallow. When the fat man opened the
door, Stephanos staggered into the blinding sunlight
with his hand over his face.

''Told you it was a pig sty,'' the guard chided him.
''Always offends my nose too.''

Linus thanked the guard politely. ''Soldiers coming
soon?'' he asked casually.

---

* Isaac

"Should have been here already. Special detachment coming, they say. Wish they'd get here. I'm hungry."

By the time Linus left the fat man and the other two, Stephanos and Priscilla were well on their way. Nothing needed to be said. Everyone clearly understood the implications of the guard's offhand comments.

Stephanos plodded along in a daze while Linus told Priscilla everything they had heard. Instead of returning to the Forum area, they took a side street, leading toward the Tiber River. Finally Stephanos could go no farther. He slumped down next to an arch in front of a red terra-cotta house. He brooded on the sidewalk, sobbing with his face buried in his hands. Priscilla cradled his head in her arms. For a long time no one said anything.

"I always wanted to be completely independent of my father," Stephanos breathed heavily. "I chafed under his restraint, his advice. Now I would give anything in the world to hear just a word, one word of direction."

"We are not finished." Priscilla slipped her arm around his shoulders. "Now we must think about getting your mother and Julia released. We won't have much time."

"Titus!" Stephanos shook his head back and forth. "He betrayed all of us. I completely trusted him."

"Rome is bought and sold every day," Priscilla rubbed his neck. "Money is the grease on which the machinery of this city operates. I'm sure Titus went for a low price. Perhaps his freedom and a bag of gold."

"*Lictors* may also be guarding the women. We can't wait." Linus suddenly stood up. "We can bribe them.

We must act very quickly. A few hours could be all the time we have. We must find a way to bribe them if a *lictor* is still on duty. We can't waste any time.''

''I will return home.'' Priscilla stood up. ''I need to cover my absence if my father returns. I will search for enough sesterces, gold, or anything to help buy them out.''

''We will do the same,'' Linus continued. ''Within two hours we will meet on Vicus Patricii street at the base of the Viminal Hill. Find the tavern across from a blue house. The house must have two columns in front. We will trust God to provide enough by then.''

When Stephanos got to his feet, Priscilla kissed him tenderly on the mouth. ''I trust that God will protect and provide for us.'' She smiled. ''I will stand by you no matter what happens. What you have lost today, I will try to provide again in the best way I can.'' She ran her fingers through his hair and kissed him again. Then she ran toward her house.

''I have some gold hidden in my flat,'' Linus said rapidly, ''but I must run very fast to get there and be back in two hours. I had best go alone. In the meantime, you must shave. Find a Greek headband. You'll make a better Greek than Roman.''

''Yes,'' Stephanos said slowly, ''I have no choice. The beard must go. I know what I must do. I know *exactly* what I must do. I have one treasure left, and it should be enough to tip the scales. Two hours. I will be there.''

XVIII

By the time Priscilla passed the garish green and yellow Temple of Cres, the office of the Plebeian Order, Linus was running up the Via Triumphalis away from the Circus Maximus. The broad boulevard used for the victory parades after great conquests now looked more like the scene of a mob revolt. Drivers of broken-down carts piled high with furniture edged pedestrians out of the way. People screamed and cursed at each other. Linus quickly wound his way through the traffic jam, ignoring the insults.

The sky was still red, but the flames were not as evident above the houses. However, rancid smelling smoke was just as heavy as it had been at the beginning of the day. Linus had to travel fast as his house was the farthest away. Stephanos more quickly found his way to the Palatine by avoiding the swamp area below the Carinae and the Fagutal and running without stopping.

Long before Priscilla reached her house, she decided to enter by the back way lest her arrival be obvious. She quickly entered by the loggia at the rear and hurried toward her sleeping cubicle. Her father's *tablinum* was not far away. Something of real value could be easily found in one of the cubicles or his office. Once she was inside her room, Priscilla began gathering up the money she had stashed away at different times. Unfortunately she could only muster a small bag of sesterces and a handful of denarii.

A noise far down the hall interrupted her search. Several people were walking down the walkway. Startled, she shoved the money back into a pile of clothes and covered it with a cloak. Priscilla patted her hair, hoping she didn't look too disheveled.

"Daughter!" Livinia called, "Please come here quickly."

"Yes, Mother." Priscilla casually shut the door behind her. To her astonishment she saw two soldiers standing beside her mother. Each man was in full battle regalia with a red tunic draped from his shoulders. Hanging on the right side of a heavy leather belt was a sword in a metal scabbard while at the left hand was a dagger in a similar scabbard. Their metal breastplates were molded and shaped to portray the extraordinary muscular definition of a superb athlete. Each man's helmet was buckled under the chin. Because the soldiers had not even removed their helmets, the long red dyed horsehair plume stuck up like an attacking porcupine. No one had ever brought a spear into the house of Marsi Crossus Laenas, yet one soldier carried a lance as if he might use it any moment. Their eyes were set like flint.

Livinia's face was taut, and her eyes were filled with terror. "They have orders to take you to the emperor," Livinia was barely able to say the words. "You are to be questioned immediately."

"Why?" Priscilla protested.

"I don't know," Livinia turned to the men. "Why?"

"We only have orders," the first man answered indifferently. His face was set as if he could kill without feeling the slightest emotion.

"Immediately," the man with the spear snapped. His bushy eyebrows were so thick that they seemed to ingest his black, cold eyes. "Now!" He thumped his spear against the floor.

"Where is Father?" Priscilla looked desperately around the house.

"He is already at the imperial palace." Livinia's hands shook. "He went there early this morning and never returned. Oh, my child!" Livinia grabbed Priscilla and hugged her. "I hope this time you haven't gone too far."

"When will I be back?" Priscilla asked nervously.

"I don't know," her mother sobbed. "The soldiers will tell me nothing."

"Let me wash up." Priscilla eyed the back door.

"No!" the soldier with the spear barked. "Don't trifle with us." He looked hard at Priscilla. "Our orders are to return with all haste. Come as you are."

"But, but—" Priscilla tried to protest.

"Do just as they tell you," her mother pleaded. "We don't want any more trouble."

"Thank you, madam." The soldier stepped back for Priscilla to walk between the two of them. "We leave at once."

Before Priscilla could speak again, one of the men took her arm firmly and marched her between them toward the front door.

Stephanos was sure the general's house would be guarded, but he reasoned that soldiers would not expect anyone to return over the hill. Instead of using the back gate, however, he climbed the wall near the opposite end adjacent to the servants' quarters. For a few moments Stephanos lay flat on the top of the wall, watching to see if any soldiers were stationed in the garden or at the back entrance. The smoke burned his eyes and filled his nose with the rancid smell of old charcoal. Soot was everywhere, making his arms and legs feel gritty and dirty. When he looked at the house, he could see that the cinder and ashes in the air had left a gray stain that dulled the normal luster of the general's home, but there was no movement.

Satisfied that the area was empty, he dropped to the ground and hurried toward the servants' quarters just a few spans from the house. He found that the dormitory was completely empty. The two-story building had a large open area in the center with sleeping cubicles around the side. At one end was a cooking area with tables and chairs for the servants. Utensils, clothes, knocked-over lamps were scattered around the room as silent witnesses to a desperate fracas. Everything was just as it was left after the soldiers arrested everyone.

Stephanos immediately went to Titus' personal cubicle near the back. Rummaging through his possessions, Stephanos found one of the leather headbands Titus always wore. He discovered a solid brown Greek *chlamys*, tunic, and a sash. Wadding up his bundle, he walked into the common area where a bowl of water was still sitting on a table. The feel of water on his face was wondrously refreshing. He dampened his face and left his beard wet, hoping to minimize the pain of shaving. In his entire life, he had never cut his beard, and he knew that it was going to hurt. When he looked back down in the basin, Stephanos was surprised to see that the water had turned black. Stephanos could only guess at how much soot and ash was still in his hair.

Stephanos picked up the sharp razor the servants used to shave Honorius. As he began to cut away the beard, the pulling and nicking of his face hurt as much as he had feared. Periodically Stephanos stopped as his eyes watered and his nose ran. The whiskers slowly fell away, leaving his face smarting and burning.

As soon as the beard was gone, Stephanos pulled his long hair to one side and hacked away at it. In short order he had turned his Judean looks into something like the latest Greek style. Once he donned the dark-brown tunic, he tied the band around his forehead. He looked around the room one last time. The smell of cooking grease and stale food filled his nose. He adjusted the tunic and tried to hurry. When the sash was secure, he quickly and stealthily approached the general's house.

Stephanos waited a long time after he slipped into the back atrium before he ventured on into the house. Finally, however, the hollow, empty sound of the large room assured him that he was alone. He stood still for several moments straining to hear the familiar voices of his mother, father, and grandfather. Stephanos even hoped the walls would echo some long-forgotten conversation with Honorius, but there was only silence. What had been the reassurance of security became painful loneliness. Quickly he slipped into his own cubicle. Stephanos knew exactly what he wanted.

Immediately he found the sack where his special possessions were stored. Using the razor, Stephanos quickly cut away the leather concealment to get the one thing that could help him most. Without putting anything back, he slipped out of the cubicle, walking as softly as possible toward the general's office. At that moment he saw a soldier's shadow fall across the back entrance.

Stephanos instantly dived onto the slick marble floor and rolled toward the ledge that surrounded the *impluvium* pool in the center of the atrium. Suddenly someone knocked on the front door. When there was no response, the person rapped more forcibly. Inching his way upward, Stephanos looked around the pool just as the shadow disappeared. He strained forward, listening as intently as he could. Footsteps faded out as if the solider was running back around the side of the house toward the front door.

Stephanos reasoned that a guard probably made rounds from the front door to the back. Someone's appearance at the front door had sent him back. When Stephanos slipped over the wall, the soldier must have been standing at the front door. Stephanos knew he needed to leave quickly but carefully. He looked down at his hand—at the one thing he thought could make the difference in securing his mother's release. Now the question was whether he, Priscilla, and Linus could get to the blue house on Vicus Patricii in time.

Linus turned left when he came to the end of the Via Triumphalis. Breaking out of the jammed street, he stopped to think. After a few moments he abruptly turned in the opposite direction and started running down the gently sloping streets that halted at the Tiber River. He looked up at the Temple Jupiter Stator as he trotted past the marble edifice. The shrine to the god who protected soldiers in retreat seemed strangely appropriate at that moment. People were running in every direction like frightened animals. He laughed, realizing how the old religion seemed like nothing but foolish superstition now. Instead of going toward his house, he headed for the gardens that bordered the Tiber River. He hoped there would be less smoke along the river. While he was standing by the Via Triumphalis, it had occurred to him that more money would be hidden at Epaphroditus' villa, and it was much closer. While Linus had far greater resources, he didn't keep much cash around. Because Epaphroditus was not a citizen of Rome, his reserves were hidden at home. Linus knew where he should go. No one paid any attention as he ran down the side street. Everyone was far too occupied with the problems created by the great fire.

Linus cut through the portion of the gardens of the Anicius family and shortened his path considerably. Epaphroditus' house was set on the edge of the hill overlooking the river. The river gardens stretched out beneath the Villa. Although the exterior was plain, the property was extremely expensive. Surrounded by large cypresses and shrubs, the house looked as if it was set out in the midst of the Umbrian plain.

When he found the flight of stairs up to the Villa, Linus bounded up several steps at a time. He beat on the door mercilessly. Epaphroditus opened it quickly, and Linus nearly tumbled in on the floor. Only then did Linus realize that he was so out of breath he could hardly speak.

"You're being chased?" Epaphroditus asked urgently.

Linus shook his head vigorously.

"You've heard about Peter?" Clement asked as he joined them at the door.

Once again Linus shook his head as he bent over to catch his breath.

"Listen!" Clement spoke rapidly. "Peter has disappeared. He was nearly to the harbor when he turned around and came back to Rome. Apparently he had just left my servant when something happened that changed his mind. He turned around, caught up with the servant, and came back. When they reached a place where they could see the city was on fire, he sent my servant back to me and disappeared into the city. His only explanation was that he would not make the same mistake twice. No one knows where he is.

"I know nothing," Linus was finally able to say. "But I need money. I need money to help Mariam Ben Aaron and Honorius' wife escape."

"Escape? I don't understand." Epaphroditus beckoned for Linus to sit down at the table in the center of the room. The large central area had cubicles on the sides and chairs along the wall. The center table was used both for eating and conversations. "A little wine, Linus. Compose yourself and tell us what is happening."

For the first time Linus was aware that his body was wringing wet. He did need more than a little composure. Blood pounded in his temples, and he felt drained. While he slowly sipped the wine, Linus told both men the details of what had transpired since daybreak. While Linus talked, Epaphroditus began producing little sacks of money from various corners of the room.

"Will it be enough?" Epaphroditus asked as he pushed his accumulations to the center of the table.

"I don't know." Linus shook his head. "All we can do is try. We must act quickly and hope *lictors* are standing guard. Where could Peter have gone?"

"We fear that he came back to Honorius' house. If so, they will have grabbed him," Clement explained. "Of course, in all the confusion in the streets, he might be anywhere. He might be safe."

"We pray so!" Epaphroditus produced a leather satchel for the money. "Mustn't look like you're a walking bank," he warned. "You must appear simply to be a tribune. People have been killed for a fraction of what's in here."

"I will tread carefully. What will you do about Peter's disappearance?"

"The word has gone out," Clement answered. "We will have people across the city on the alert. Our people will soon know about Paul's arrest and what happened to the Piso household."

"Our troubles have just begun." Epaphroditus bit his lips. "They will hunt us down like dogs in the street. Peter often spoke of the fiery ordeal that was to befall us. His words are being literally fulfilled."

"I must hurry!" Linus stood up. "Pray for me, brothers. The next few hours will be crucial."

Stephanos was the first to find Vicus Patricii street at the base of Viminal Hill. The damage made it obvious that he was approaching an area where the fire had either begun or just swept though. There were no carts or crowds on the street, and the smoke was thicker than anywhere else he had been. The Subura Major section looked like a total disaster. Stephanos could see that a few houses down the street were still smoldering. Looking through the spaces between buildings, he saw nothing in the far side of the Subura area but charred smoking ruins. He found it hard to breathe.

Stephanos slowly and carefully walked near the buildings, looking for the landmarks that would identify where his mother was imprisoned. The unburned houses seemed empty as if the occupants had fled the fire and not returned. Even some of the doors were still open. Stephanos pulled his robe over his nose and tried to protect himself from as much of the smoke as possible. Most of the time he walked with his head down. When he came to the edge of the curb, he looked up. To his delight, he saw a tavern just across the street.

Stephanos immediately walked to the entry way and looked around. There it was! Just up the street was a large terra-cotta house with columns. The entire facade was blue. No guards of any kind were posted at the door. Nothing else marked the place as any different from any other house on the street. Obviously a very good residence for a place so close to the lower-class Subura Major section, the house also appeared to be abandoned.

Stephanos looked into the dim tavern. It was nearly empty. He stepped inside. Several men were seated at small wooden tables around the room, talking and drinking.

"You live in the area?" Stephanos asked one of the men nearest the door.

The man shook his head and looked away.

"What do you need?" A large disheveled man called from the back. He appeared to be cleaning up the mess left by a fight at one of the rear tables. "This is *my* place."

"Must have been terrifying last night." Stephanos tried to sound casual.

"Thought the whole place would go" he snarled. "If the wind hadn't shifted, sure would have."

"I'm trying to find a friend." Stephanos spoke casually. "Of course, the fire has made everything difficult."

"Tell me about it!" the owner answered caustically.

"Know who owns the blue terra-cotta house over there?" Stephanos pointed up the street.

The tavern owner eyed him suspiciously. "A *lictor*," he answered cautiously. "The president of one of the colleges of *lictors*. Why?"

"Wonderful!" Stephanos exclaimed. "I mean— a, er— this is exactly the place I'm trying to find. Good. Very good."

The owner went back to picking up broken clay cups and filling wine jugs as if to distance himself from this strange Greek-looking fellow with the shaggy hair. Stephanos turned back to the door watching for Linus or Priscilla to show up. He did not have to wait long before Linus stepped out of the smoke.

"Over here," Stephanos called out.

"Holy Jupiter!" Linus exclaimed when he recognized Stephanos standing in the doorway. "I didn't know who you were."

"Do I make a good Greek?"

"Well, yes, but with a bad haircut."

"I wasn't trying to be fashionable." Stephanos pulled him outside.

"You aren't," Linus laughed. "We'll have to trim

you up. You look like a Greek who just escaped from the auction block. But at least they won't take you for a Jew. What have you found out?''

''The house is owned by a *lictor*,'' Stephanos pointed across the street, ''Couldn't believe my ears. There's a good chance we will be dealing with *lictors*.''

''Excellent,'' Linus answered. ''Let's get out of here. Taverns in this area are good places to get mugged.''

Both men walked up the street until they were directly across from the blue house. ''Where's Priscilla?'' Linus ask impatiently.

''Priscilla should be here.'' Stephanos looked nervously up and down the street.

''I would have thought she might be the first one. I don't like it.'' Linus covered his smarting eyes. ''We can't wait long. Let's figure out how much money we have between us.''

''I don't think we can even come close to getting everyone out.'' Stephanos lamented.

''Don't worry about releasing the servants,'' Linus counseled. ''They won't do much with them anyway. We've just got to have enough to spring Julia and your mother. Everything hinges on how greedy—or how desperate—the guard is.''

Stephanos kept looking up and down the street as they discussed their approach to the house, but Priscilla was nowhere in sight. ''Do you think something has happened to her?''

''Anything is possible,'' Linus answered. ''Maybe she couldn't get back out of her house. I'm sure she's all right, but I know that we can't wait much longer. I desperately had hoped she would add to our bribe. We need to wait as long as we can.''

At that moment a man in a white toga stepped out

of the front door. He looked up and down the street as if to appraise the situation before departing.

"We can't wait." Linus yanked Stephanos' arm. "We must act now." Without another word the tribune started across the street with his Greek-looking servant following him.

XIX

Priscilla stood between the two guards, waiting nervously in front of the ornate bronze doors that opened into the courtroom of the emperor. Both men kept eyeing her, and their constant surveillance added to her apprehension. She tried to find a distraction. Everywhere she looked, Priscilla saw the opulent symbols of Roman wealth and power. Frescoes around the ceiling were edged in gold. Green jade marble, the finest in the world, lined the walls, and the tall columns were of the finest polished Nanite. Terrazzo mosaics filled the hall floors with wonderful designs of brilliant colors. Statues and busts of former emperors and generals sat on each side of the door as well as around the hallway. Priscilla's eyes kept returning to the gold-bordered niche in the wall just to the left of the door. Inside the little shrine in the wall were the lares, the offerings to the spirits that protected the palace. Even the exalted Caesars made sure that, regardless of their evil deeds, the gods were appeased.

By now, she thought, *Linus and Stephanos must be waiting for me. They will wonder why I have been delayed. Oh, I hope they don't wait too long.* "Dear God of the Jews," she prayed softly under her breath, ''please keep Stephanos safe.''

Slowly, the doors opened before Priscilla, and a *lictor* in a plain white toga stood ready to escort her and the soldiers into the imperial chambers. Everywhere she looked senators and soldiers stood around the room. Immediately Priscilla saw her father standing not far from Caesar's throne. Marsi Crossus Laenas looked worried and frightened. The men around him were sober and stone-faced. She saw many familiar faces but no friends.

Priscilla walked forward, looking frantically around the crowd. A man moved quickly from behind a column as if trying to blend into one of the clusters of men. On the back of his head was a little conical beanie denoting that he was a freed man, a freed slave. His quick movement caught Priscilla's eye. Although he disappeared behind a group of men, she clearly saw his face. The freed man was Titus.

''Hail Caesar!'' the two soldiers snapped to attention in front of the emperor's platform and struck their breastplates with their fists.

Priscilla bowed solemnly.

The emperor sat hunched forward on his gilded throne. His white toga was edged with a gold stripe, and he wore a golden laurel wreath in his hair. Nero's silk tunic was bordered with maroon clusters of hand-embroidered grapes. The emperor was a fat-faced, pudgy man, grossly overweight. His smooth, puffy checks and swollen eyelids had witnessed too many a banquet where he had both gorged and purged himself only to gorge again. Nero looked edgy and tense. He kept turning in his chair, more like a caged animal than the imperial ruler of the most powerful nation on earth.

"Come here, child." Nero beckoned with a fat finger.

Priscilla took two steps forward, looking down to avoid eye contact.

"Do not be afraid," the emperor smiled cynically. "People are always overwhelmed in my presence. Do not condemn yourself for being unable to look directly on my glorious countenance. Today I have condescended to meet you with my splendor concealed. You may look upon me."

Slowly Priscilla looked up, trying to conceal her contempt. She bit her lip when she remembered Honorius calling him a toad. Nero did look like a bloated frog.

"A hideous deed has been done," Nero lectured her. "The new sect that follows one Christus has attempted to burn Rome to the ground. We must act quickly to protect ourselves from these vermin who run between our houses with their tails on fire." He spoke to the crowd as if to convince them that he was truly in control. "Apparently these Christianios seek to destroy even me, your beloved emperor."

Priscilla tightly clutched her hands together. She took several quick, deep breaths to still her pounding heart. Rather than listen to the emperor, Priscilla tried to concentrate on what she would say.

"Now . . ." Nero settled back in his chair. He rested his elbows on the chair arms, touching his fingertips together. "We are informed that you have even attended the public meetings of this group and that you have received private instruction. Perhaps you and your family grow tried of the protection your benevolent emperor offers you?"

Priscilla felt every eye fastening on her. She dared not look at her father because she knew that terror would be etched in every wrinkle in his tired face. Her mind raced, trying to organize her defense.

"Speak up child. Time is limited," Nero whined. "Just tell us the truth."

"If it please your majesty," Priscilla began haltingly, "I must begin by telling you that I have been raised as a true daughter of Rome. From my earliest memories my parents taught me to guard and protect the traditions of our city and people. I would never undermine any aspect of our great society. As soon as I was taught to read, my mother put before me the stories of Cornelia, the Mother of the Gracchi. As surely as I was raised on milk, I was nurtured on these accounts of Roman strength and patience. Integrity and endurance for the sake of Rome were always stressed in our household."

"I am pleased to hear so," Nero retorted. "But why have you abandoned such a solid foundation?"

"I have not," Priscilla answered softly but forcefully. "Let me be clear that my personal explorations of this new religion have nothing to do with my family. I have inquired after new ideas as I would of any new thought that the Greeks might bring us. Is not the study of philosophy honored by all?"

A slight smile broke across the senators' faces. Priscilla immediately felt a surge of self-confidence. "Moreover," she pushed on, "you must know that my father has always put the well-being of the emperor ahead of our family. In fact, if it were necessary, we would be sacrificed for the good of Caesar."

For the first time, Priscilla looked at her father's eyes. Relief had displaced fear. Almost imperceptibly, Marsi Crossus Laenas nodded his head up and down. Priscilla chilled, knowing that what she had just said was frighteningly accurate. She paused for a moment as something not quite definable happened in her mind. The realization of how expendable everyone was to her father pulled her across an invisible line, taking her beyond his sphere of influence. Any lingering indecision about completely embracing Stephanos' faith was gone. Priscilla had no time for reflection, but the shift brought increased courage with the new awareness.

"Such loyalty pleases our ears," Nero commented. "Your daughter speaks well for you, Senator Laenas. But child, the city burns around us!"

Priscilla straightened her back. "Noble Caesar, such rumors about this fire are not worthy of you. You have heard slave talk."

Nero dropped his hands and sat up. "What?" he choked. "What are you suggesting?"

"Slaves and servants spread such tales," Priscilla stood her ground. "I am quite aware of their gossip about the meetings at General Piso's house. In fact . . ." Priscilla turned slowly toward the senators. ". . . the general had one servant who bragged that he supplied information directly to you, your majesty. Some Greek named Titus talked far and wide that the wilder the story, the more money he received. So he made up every crazy tale he could think of."

"Where did you get this?" Nero sputtered.

Priscilla saw that the senator's smile broadened. Her father was clearly delighted with the nerve she had struck. "My slaves report such matters to me," Priscilla answered. "After all, a woman of Rome must keep abreast of such matters if she is to protect her emperor."

"You don't know what you are saying." Nero shook his hand at her.

"Please forgive me," Priscilla answered respectfully, "but I simply report the common knowledge of the streets. Only General Piso's magnanimity kept him from selling the little fool. In fact," Priscilla paused to make sure she had everyone's full attention, "the Greek boasted that if the story he brought was important enough, you might give him his freedom."

"Stop it!" Nero pounded the chair's arm. "We are not here to talk of a slave but of these Christianios. They started the fire!"

Priscilla wanted to look around for Titus. She would give anything to catch a glimpse of his face at this moment, but she feared giving herself away so she looked down at the floor.

"Don't you know this sect started the fire?" Nero shouted at Priscilla.

"If so," Priscilla replied, looking straight into the face of the ruler of Rome, "then they contradict everything that they taught me. Yes, I have listened to their ideas and they advocate love and truth. Never have I ever known such purity of purpose or benevolence of intention."

Nero's angry eyes blinked and shifted quickly from hers. Fear was hidden behind his bluster. For reasons Priscilla couldn't grasp, her straightforward response confused the emperor. She wasn't saying what he wanted to hear, and her answers kept him off balance. He was no longer in control of the hearing.

"The kingdom of which they speak," Priscilla continued, "is spiritual. They have no political designs."

"They undermine the state!" Nero charged. He stuck his lip out like a pouting child. "They wish me harm."

"I must say," Priscilla answered to the gallery around her, "that every day General Piso prayed to this Christus for peace for the state." Priscilla turned back to Nero, "And he prayed for your well-being."

"No more!" Nero stood up. "They have bewitched you. You have been deceived. Take her home! Marsi Crossus Laenas, straighten out your daughter's mind."

Laenas stepped forward to stand beside Priscilla.

"No more of this!" Nero waved them away. "We must get on with rounding up the leaders of this sect. Go home now."

The senator bowed, and the two soldiers who had been standing to the side immediately escorted father and daughter to the door. Priscilla tried to see if she could locate Titus, but he seemed to have disappeared. She and her father walked quickly out of the courtroom, and the bronze door banged behind them.

"Brilliant defense!" Marsi hugged his daughter. "You couldn't have given a better account of yourself. Your performance was worthy of your ancient ancestor King Ancus Maricus."

"Thank God it's over," Priscilla shuddered. "I was terrified."

"Now he will leave us alone," Marsi hugged Priscilla again. "Where did you find out that slave story? He was Nero's big secret. I would give one hundred denarii to see the emperor's face again. I thought his eyes would pop out."

"What I said was true," Priscilla said soberly. "The general and these believers wouldn't hurt anyone. They are innocent of any sedition."

"Of course," Marsi agreed. "But they make good scapegoats. At least we won't have to worry anymore. Your mother can thank you for keeping us out of the emperor's clutches."

"But what will happen to Piso and his friends?"

"I don't know." Her father shrugged. "They will probably be executed. My guess is that they will be sent to the wild beasts. But that's unimportant. They are expendable."

"The general was *your* friend."

Instantly her father put his hand over Priscilla's mouth and started walking her out of the palace. "Don't ever say that again anywhere," he warned. "Piso was a fool. Now he's gone. His fanatic friends mean nothing to Rome or to us. Just keep away from all of them, and we will be all right."

"You would let innocent people die?" Priscilla pulled away.

"Innocent people die every day," the senator snapped, "and no one cares. Nothing matters but saving ourselves."

"No!" Priscilla shook her fist in his face. "I won't live by such a standard any longer. If you and your senator friends can stand back and let that evil madman destroy good people, then you are the betrayers of Rome and every good thing it ever stood for. You are as cowardly as Nero is diabolical."

"Don't you dare talk to me like that!" her father yanked Priscilla forward by her arm. "Don't let a little success make you heady. If you hadn't disobeyed me in the first place, we wouldn't even be here today." The senator pulled Priscilla so close that their noses nearly touched. He looked down into her face with intense rage. "Now hear me well. Piso and the rest will be fed to the lions or the dogs or whatever else the emperor chooses to unleash on them. And probably such a performance will be for the ultimate good of Rome. The populace cannot be allowed to entertain the idea that the emperor thought he could rebuild the city by first destroying it. You will go home and not come out of that house until I tell you.''

''I won't!'' Priscilla shook her head defiantly.

''You will!'' Laenas shook her arm so violently that Priscilla nearly fell to the floor. ''I'll not allow you to jeopardize me, your mother, all we have acquired. I'll lock you in your room forever or turn you out on the streets with only the clothes on your back. Now you get back to the house and stay in your cubicle until I return. Understand?''

Priscilla jerked away and ran down the marble corridors leaving her father standing by himself. Her tears made it difficult to see where she was going. Once she stumbled out of the palace, she ran down the Palatine Hill as fast as she could. Night was falling, and the black smoke hanging in the air made the hour seem later. However, when she reached the crossroads in the street, she did not go toward her house. Priscilla went in the opposite direction.

The small heavy *lictor* looked at Linus suspiciously. He kept his right hand inside his white toga as if a knife were hidden beneath the folds. ''You say you are a tribune?'' he asked skeptically. The sun was setting, and the smoke made it doubly difficult to see beyond the end of the block.

''How else would I know who you are holding as prisoners?'' Linus smiled and answered indifferently. ''I have friends in the very highest places.''

''You don't know who is inside,'' the *lictor* defied him. He kept looking up and down the empty street.

''Piso's wife.'' Linus leaned toward the *lictor*. ''His

household. You are a bold man to have kidnapped such personages.''

The *lictor's* mouth dropped. ''Who told you?''

''When the general is freed,'' Linus smiled arrogantly, ''and he will be released shortly, I'm sure he will be looking for the man who did harm to his wife.''

''I've done her no harm.'' The *lictor's* face turned dark red. ''She's been quite well cared for, all things considered. No one in there has missed a meal. I swear it.''

''For your sake, I hope so.'' Linus kept smiling. ''But surely you are aware that what doesn't happen publicly can occur in a dark alley. A *lictor* is an easy target.''

''I am only doing as I was told,'' the man protested. ''They said I was acting on orders from the emperor.''

''You have that in writing?'' Linus queried.

''No . . . No,'' the lictor fumbled, ''but the instruction came by a senator.''

''If I were you,'' Linus said, his eyes narrowing and his voice becoming intense, ''I would be making plans to get out of Rome for a while. You are caught in a cross-fire, and the arrows are likely to end up in your neck.''

''What do you want?'' The small fat man pulled his toga more closely around his shoulder. ''What's the point of all this?''

''We're here to help you get out of the bind.'' Linus smiled. ''We can take you out of the middle.''

''How?''

''Release the women to us.''

''You're joking,'' the *lictor* sneered.

''We are associates of General Piso,'' Linus began to

talk quickly. "We have been dispatched by Praetorium Guards who are concerned about what happened last night. You let us have the women, and we'll tell everyone that they simply escaped. You're off the hook with everybody and the powers that be can *fight it out* for themselves."

"Do you think I'm a fool?" the *lictor* retorted. "I don't even know who you are."

"Exactly," Linus shot back. "Our anonymity is also a safeguard." Linus moved closer so he could see the man's face clearly.

"I'm not about to do something dangerous on the basis of no more than your word."

Linus saw the man's shifty eyes clearly. He was confused and somewhat bewildered. The *lictor's* indecision was the opportunity Linus sought. "You are a shrewd man—intelligent," Linus cooed. "I wouldn't expect you to act without some sign of assurance. The fact that we have money to give will certify the wisdom of a quick decision."

"What are you offering?" the *lictor* demanded.

Linus pulled the leather satchel from beneath his toga. "I have a bag full of sesterces." Linus shook the bag vigorously.

"Talk in terms of denarii or save your breath," the fat man snapped.

"I have fifty denarii for you," Linus smiled broadly.

"Don't toy with me. Twice that wouldn't entice me."

"Two hundred denarii," Linus said soberly.

"I thought you were somebody," the *lictor* sneered. "You are a fraud."

"Two hundred and fifty." Linus turned to Stephanos with pleading eyes. "We will go no higher."

"Then don't waste my time. I'll not play this game for such a paltry sum."

"Perhaps," Stephanos answered, "I can seal the bargain." He reached inside his robe and brought out a leather pouch. "Seldom has anyone in Rome seen such a priceless gem." He poured into his hand the large red ruby that his uncle had given him years earlier. "Don't touch it," he cautioned the *lictor*. "The stone is a king's ransom. When it passes into your hands, the bargain is sealed. Look carefully at the opportunity of a lifetime."

The *lictor* peered into Stephanos' palm. The beauty and the brilliance of the stone hypnotized the greedy little man. "Done," he finally concluded.

"All right!" Linus talked as he poked on the man's chest. "Get the women out here. As soon as we have them, the money and the stone are yours."

"Give me the stone now," the *lictor* insisted.

"No!" Linus shook his head. "Get them out here and you've got it all. Those are our terms."

Stephanos held the gem up slowly, letting the light from a distant torch retract from the surface. "Make it quick," he demanded.

Without a word, the *lictor* bounded back into his house with his toga flying beneath him. Stephanos and Linus walked back and forth in front of the house for what seemed like an eternity. Then the door opened and Julia and Mariam walked out.

"You only get these two," the *lictor* snarled. "The slaves will cost you more."

"Keep 'em!" Stephanos pressed the gem into the man's fat hand. "We are finished."

"But— but—" The *lictor* clutched the ruby in one hand and reached out with the other.

"You'll let them all go right now if you know

what's good for you." Linus pushed the satchel into the *lictor's* hand. "And I'd take a quick vacation at the seaside if I were you."

"Wait . . ." the *lictor* shook his head.

"Let them all loose!" Linus yelled back. Stephanos had already started down the street with his arm around his mother and his hand on Julia's arm. Linus didn't look back as he trotted to catch up with them. They disappeared into the twilight.

The only good thing about Paul's dingy cell in the Mamertine Prison was that the openings to the outside were so restricted that none of the soot and little of the smoke from the great fire filtered in during the day. Paul had been able to hear the confusion in the streets, and his conversations with the guards had kept him abreast of the details. Early in the day Julius had been dispatched to the imperial compound, and another guard replaced him. Paul could tell additional guards were posted outside.

Through the months Julius had become Paul's constant companion and friend. He struggled to understand Paul's new religion and did not reject it. but he found the idea of one God not completely comprehensible. Whatever he lacked in insight, Julius made up for in devotion to his charge. When Julius returned, Paul knew he would have a better source of information than would be available to the vast majority of Rome.

Julius walked in with the manner of a disinterested soldier. He waited silently until the attending guard left. "Nero is sending soldiers all over the city to capture the believers. They arrested General Piso and the

Ben Aaron family,'' he explained in quick clipped words. ''Looks very bleak.''

Paul listened without comment. He nodded apprehensively as the briefing continued but kept his composure. When Julius finished, Paul thanked him and then retired to a distant corner to pray.

When his replacement came on duty, Julius returned to his indifferent pose and left without saying goodbye. Paul looked at him leave but said nothing that might betray their relationship.

Late in the afternoon Peter was brought in, shackled with chains around his legs. The two old comrades embraced but said little until two hours later when the guard changed. Before he left, the replacement for Julius set a torch near the entry, then secured the door behind him. The fire did little to remove the pervasive damp, musty smell of the leaky prison.

''How did they catch you!'' Paul asked as soon as the soldier's footsteps died out. They sat side by side leaning against the cold stone wall.

''I came back to Honorius' house this afternoon.'' Peter shifted the manacles around his wrist. ''I had no idea what was happening. Of course, I feared what the fire had done. A soldier came around the side of the house and grabbed me. Even then I did not fully comprehend the situation.''

''Why did you come back?''

''Very amazing,'' Peter answered slowly. The flickering torch on the wall threw deep shadows across his face. Peter's eyes disappeared beneath his white eyebrows. His face looked ancient and very tired. ''I was on the Appian Way going toward the harbor. I had just sat down to rest when I heard a voice say, *''Quo Vadis?''* I looked around and saw no one but I swear I heard the question plain as I hear you. I suppose the ring of the Latin caught my ear, but I couldn't see anyone and I couldn't understand why a stranger would ask about my journey. I kept looking for the caller but saw no one. Only then did I have a haunting premonition. I had been so sure that the Only One of Israel had called me to leave that my mind was closed to any other possibility. Then I remembered the story of the boy Samuel being called in the night. So I began to pray, "Speak, Lord, for Your servant hears."

"And?" Paul edged nearer his friend. "And what happened?"

"Within my soul, I felt that Yeshua was speaking directly to me, saying that once more the master was about to be crucified in Rome. He asked me if this time I would join Him." Peter spoke pensively, "I did not do well the first time. I have longed to redeem myself, and I felt that I was being given a second chance. Even though I didn't understand, I knew that I must return quickly. I had no idea that the city was on fire."

"Extraordinary!" Paul exclaimed. "Another piece to the puzzle. Priscilla Laenas was here this morning while Stephanos Bar Aaron hid outside. I learned that Nero is blaming the believers for setting the city on fire. Julius confirmed the stories."

"Us?" Peter recoiled.

"Our worst premonitions have come to pass. What you envisioned earlier is literally upon us. A cross is being erected high above this evil city. Perhaps the final battle is at hand. Certainly the Antichrist sits on the throne and we are in the midst of a great tribulation."

"Is this what you make of it?" Peter probed.

"You've always been the thinker, the scholar among us. What do you conclude?"

"Perhaps, we have come to another *akeda*, the binding of Yitzchak,"* Paul pondered. "The Holy One of Israel will test us as He did Abraham at Hedid. I believe we may well be stripped naked. If so, our hearts will be fully revealed."

"*Akeda?* I tremble before such an idea." Peter lowered his head. "So it was on Mount Moriah—and at Golgotha. The Holy One momentarily averts His face and seems to turn His back. Nature cowers and the sky turns black."

"But Yeshua taught us that a table is prepared for the meek there," Paul comforted him. "Even if His face is turned, He hears from on high. The God of Israel promises that all the ends of the world will remember these times and turn to Him because of these very difficult hours."

Peter smiled faintly but wrung his hands. "Ever since our fathers were chosen by Ha Elyon,** we have been a hunted people. Evil has pursed us like the hounds of Gey-Hinnom."†

"We are the rope in a tug of war between the purposes of God and Evil," Paul concluded, "perhaps a dubious honor."

"A hard place to live for sure. When Athaliah nearly killed her own grandson Joash, it was so. And it was no less so when Herod tried to destroy the little ones at the Messiah's birth. Life was purchased by the cost of death."

"And now our time comes," Paul said wearily. We must pay the price. Even thinking such a thing scram-

* Isaac
** The Most High God
† Jerusalem's garbage dump

bles my thoughts. Just considering the idea twists all sense of reality. I tremble before the horror that might be ahead of us.''

''I do not know whether I dread the torture or the uncertainty the more. I think maybe the agony of physical pain is easier then the dread of the soul. Unless the Holy One upholds us, fear can consume our best intentions.''

''I know.'' Paul raised his hands. ''I have stood at this place before. I have felt the rod and the lash: forty blows minus one, shipwrecks, beatings, chains. But even as the leather thongs were tearing my flesh apart, the covering of the Lord was there. Oh yes, sometimes I thought the excruciating pain could not be borne. At those very moments of despair, the hand of God sustained me with such reality that I cannot describe what a wonderful thing happened in my mind and spirit. He was there.''

''I believe,'' Peter said slowly, ''and I place my trust in His provision. But I have also failed. I have little confidence in myself. I bluster and bellow, but at the most critical time in my life, I turned coat and ran like a frightened puppy.''

''And you came back today.'' Paul grinned broadly. ''Is that the act of a coward? Ah, Peter! We are all fragile and often break at what seems to be the paramount moment when intelligence and fortitude are most needed. Here is the secret that I learned lying on my face on stone jail floors.'' Paul put his arm around his friend and spoke in his ear. ''Our weakness serves Him best. He asks for no more than our availability. You have always been that supreme variety of man and apostle.''

''I do not intend to hear any more roosters crowing

at the dawn. I will stand unmovable and yield no ground this time."

"History turns on such moments," Paul assured him. "We stand at the crossroads of time and eternity. Take heart, my good brother. It is an enviable position that we have found—an honor granted only to aliens and exiles."

XX

After nearly thirty hours, flames still blazed across Rome. Late into the night a glow hovered over many areas of the city. The smoky foglike covering lay over the gardens along the river and around Epaphroditus' villa where the refugees who had made their escape were spending the night.

Julia and Mariam stayed in their host's cubicle. Stephanos, Linus, and Epaphroditus slept on pallets on the floors throughout the house. They awoke as out of a deep, troubled dream. For some time no one spoke as each tried to recover from the events of the day before. Clement and Anacletus arrived early and heard the details of the rescue as well as the prognosis for the future.

Epaphroditus set out the food he had on hand. Bowls of onions, walnuts, sticks of celery, and some salted fish provided sustenance. Mariam and Julia sat at the table while the rest sat around the room. Most of the group simply ate large chunks of bread. During most of the meal little was said.

"Paul is so completely sequestered that no one can reach him," Epaphroditus lamented. "Peter seems to have completely disappeared. Honorius, Philip, and

266

Jarius are locked up and surrounded by soldiers. In one day, we have completely lost all our leadership. We have been cut loose and set adrift.''

''What can we do?'' Clement looked at the floor. ''We can't stay here. Epaphroditus is too well known. By the end of the day, soldiers will have paid us a visit.''

''Maybe not,'' Epaphroditus answered, ''but you're right. We can't chance a raid.'' He added, ''But someone must pick up the pieces and lead us. This is not a time for indecision.'' He pushed the loaf of bread away.

''God must give us a sign—a new direction,'' Anacletus urged as he washed his fingers in a little clay bowl.

''He already has.'' A small, quiet voice spoke from the cubicle. Julia stepped through the door. She broke her characteristic silence. ''We have already seen our new leadership. Who took charge and secured our release?''

All eyes turned toward Stephanos. He looked up from his plate. ''What?'' he asked in consternation.

''Has not Stephanos already stepped to the center?'' Julia asked. ''Is he not the surviving remnant of Israel in our midst?''

''Just a moment.'' Stephanos put his plate down and reached for a towel hanging on the wall to wipe his hands. ''I have simply acted as anyone would under—''

''No,'' Julia disagreed. ''You have commanded as well as my husband would have. With Linus at your side, you have walked through the traps that Nero set for us. Your God has truly protected you. You are now our leader.''

''No, no.'' Stephanos shook his head. ''Peter was

our bishop and I would never assume that role. Heaven knows how hopelessly naive I am."

"My son," Mariam said from across the room, "in these days your eyes have been opened. Julia is right. You have been spared for this time. There are thousands of believers across this city. We are no small force. At least during this interim, you must lead our people. You came to Rome for this hour."

"I agree." Linus spoke forcefully. "Titles are not important, but the fact that you are a Ben Aaron from Israel is more than enough. We await your guidance."

Stephanos looked pleadingly at his mother. Mariam simply nodded. He got up from the table and walked to the window. The wind had started blowing the haze out of the river bottom beneath them. Morning had fully broken over the city, and the streets were once again filling with people. Finally, he turned around.

"We cannot wait long," Stephanos concluded. "We cannot go back to any of our houses—and we must take the codex with us. For the time being we need to hide somewhere soldiers would never search. Think, friends! Where in Rome could someone disappear?"

"We can't turn to any of the believers," Epaphroditus warned. "If your trusted servant Titus was a spy, anyone could be a plant."

"The Subura had good hiding places in the slum sections, but I am sure everything is burned to the ground now," Anacletus fretted.

"I have it!" Linus snapped his fingers. "The *coemeteria!* The sleeping places! No one would look for living people in a graveyard. Near the edge of Rome in one of the depressions at the base of a hill is a group of burial caves. Because of the low entrance, the area is called the catacombs. The tunnels ramble on forever! No one could run us down in those caves, and the soldiers would do anything to avoid the place of the dead.''

''Excellent!'' Stephanos struck his palm with his fist. ''We must go there as quickly as possible. For the moment we must not let anyone know where we are except—'' Stephanos stopped. ''I don't know what has become of Priscilla.''

''Is it possible?'' Julia smiled kindly but spoke firmly. ''Could she have turned aside—or maybe been a spy all along? She has not come back.''

Stephanos stared at his mother, searching her eyes for some hint of her thoughts. But nothing he saw condemned or reflected any doubt about his judgments. Mariam simply waited, offering silent encouragement.

''No.'' Stephanos was equally firm. ''I implicitly and explicitly trust Priscilla. Her delay has been unavoidable. She must be told where we are. I will leave that task to Linus.''

''Accepted,'' Linus confirmed.

''Epaphroditus,'' Stephanos commanded, ''you must arrange your furniture so that we can tell if anyone searches your house. If the soldiers don't hunt here, we'll know you are not a suspect yet. Linus you should do the same if Anacletus can lead us to the *coemeteria*.''

''Sure, I know the way,'' Anacletus wrapped his toga around his shoulder.

''Then we can leave as soon as we gather our belongings.'' Stephanos fixed the Greek leather headband on his forehead. ''We won't look any different from the mob surging up and down the streets. We can pass through the city easily for the time being.''

Suddenly there was a knock at the door. Each person froze in place. Then the two women tiptoed back into the cubicle, and Linus dropped into a pile of blankets left from the night before. Anacletus slipped into a chair by the table while Stephanos edged toward the open window. The knock came again.

"Just a moment." Epaphroditus cleared his throat. "I'm coming." He looked carefully around the room again before he stepped to the door. "What do you want?"

"Who lives here?" a woman's voice inquired. "I'm looking for the house of Epaphroditus of Philippi."

"It's Priscilla!" Stephanos bounded for the door. "She found us!" Stephanos began unbolting the chain before Epaphroditus could lift even the first wooden brace against the door.

"Stephanos?" Priscilla called out. "Is that you?"

Stephanos pulled her through the open door. "Come in, come in." He hugged her tightly. "You're all right?"

"What's happened to you?" Priscilla stared at his face.

"I've become a Greek!" Stephanos laughed for the first time in days. "Even that little traitor, Titus, wouldn't expect me to be wearing his clothes." He stepped back and looked at her carefully. "There is a bruise on your cheek—What happened! How did you get here?"

"Perhaps I can sit down? I've been running since the middle of the night." She slumped onto a bench. "Last night was terrible. So much happened—" Priscilla clutched at her stomach and winced. "My father and I had a very heated confrontation. I renounced him as well as the rest of his class." She bit her lip.

"I'd rather die than live with them. Their door is forever closed to me."

"Oh, my child!" Mariam rushed to Priscilla. Pulling the young woman's head to her breast, she held her tightly. "I'm sorry, so sorry."

Priscilla began to shake as she wept silently. "I don't know how I ever got here," she sobbed. "Sometime near dawn I remembered where Stephanos had once said this place was. I had already tried every other house I could think of. I went to Linus' place first. It was so, so . . . terrifying." Priscilla began to cry again.

"We will care for you, my child." Mariam cradled Priscilla's head in her arms as she swayed back and forth. "You will be in good hands here."

Julia dipped a cloth in a bowl of water and began washing Priscilla's face. "I have misjudged you," Julia said gently. "Perhaps, only I can fully appreciate what a courageous stand you have taken. You will be an outcast in Rome. You have paid a great price this night."

"They took me before the emperor," Priscilla managed to say, "I tried to discredit Titus—but he's told them everything he knows."

"Nero!" Stephanos exclaimed. "You faced the emperor!"

"They will send the general and your father to the gladiators or the beasts," Priscilla choked. "We don't have much time. Soldiers will scour the city for us."

Linus turned away. "Nero will make a spectacle of their deaths. They will be arraigned before all of Rome"

"Yes," Stephanos said. Reaching down to help Priscilla to her feet, he mumbled, "Time is running out."

Unable to talk further, he held Priscilla close as they started for the door.

Stephanos was right. The streets were filled with confused, surly people too preoccupied with their own problems to pay any attention to his band of ex-patriates. Many citizens were still confused about where to go, and the crowds seemed close to panic. The six exiles quickly wound their way up the river bank and then cut across the city toward the outer wall. In the Carinae area they went down Clivus Pullius street, passing the Tellus Temple erected to the worship of the Roman earth goddess. Finally the little band sat down to rest on the steps that led up to the temple.

Mariam walked halfway up the high stairway where she could see far up and down the street. Behind them was the Mons Oppius outcropping. Red terra-cotta houses lined the streets and bumped up against the great ornate marble temples. Everywhere she looked were painted columns and the amazing lifelike statues that seemed poised ready to leap from their pedestals and do combat. Mariam could also see the tall, thin cypresses and pines up and down the hillsides. Down the center of the overpowering spectacle that was Rome ran the huge blocks-wide scar left by the raging fire. Charred stumps and blackened houses with the roofs cratered were still smoking. Mariam could see where the fire had burned out at the edge of Vicus Patricii street. Fortunately the flames had not leaped across and violated the area around the Tellus Temple. Abruptly the wind changed, sending wisps of smoke toward her from behind the buildings on the north side of Clivus Pullius street.

At that moment, Mariam felt the threatening premonition that had periodically gripped her imagination in the past. The dread sensation had come before Stephanos was conceived and then again in Yerushalayim as well as by the shore at Caesarea-by-the-Sea. With an overwhelming reluctance, Mariam turned to look into the entrance of the Tellus Temple. She had last seen him at Honorius' house looking through the door at her manuscript. Now here the monster was once more.

As if feeding off the carnage of destruction, he had both grown and aged. The first time Mariam had seen him in the fields, the creature had the hair of a young man. Now he was nearly bald. Deep creases in his forehead ran up into what had once been his hairline. His nose had become more bulbous, redder and more swollen. The wrinkles running down his cheeks and neck looked like canyons. Soot and ashes were sprinkled over his entire body. His bloodshot eyes were so red, they looked on fire. Suddenly he shook his fist at Mariam, blood oozing between his tightly clutched fingers. He grabbed his cloak, swung it around himself, and was gone.

While he was more terrifying to behold than at any time in the past, Mariam felt strangely less frightened. She had not turned away or retreated from his awful stare. "You are not winning!" Mariam said aloud. She stood up slowly, very much feeling her age. "Come," she called down to the others, "we must not waste time."

The *coemeteria* was situated well beyond the outside circle of walls that ringed the city. Roman law strictly prohibited either burial or burning of the dead within the city. The opening to the particular area that Linus called the catacombs was at the bottom of a steep cliff. Nothing unusual marked the cavelike entrance. Centuries earlier, someone had simply begun digging in the soft tufa stone, and the myriad of tunnels had evolved.

Once the little band was inside, Anacletus lit a torch. "I'll light some of the oil lamps hanging from the ceiling as we go." He held the fire up high. "There's no light in here, and it's pitch black. Sometimes animals wander in, but there are no snakes."

"You've been here often?" Mariam felt the damp, powdery walls.

"Ancestors are buried here," Anacletus answered. "Never liked coming, but I have been down these corridors more times than I care to remember."

"Can we get lost?" Stephanos peered into the opaque blackness.

"At first you'll think so." Anacletus started walking forward. "But you'll discover that we are in the main tunnel that goes right down the middle of the *coemeteria*. All the other passages simply crisscross off the sides. Anyone who has never been in here will get confused immediately. The place is a natural hideout."

The group walked on slowly and quietly. The musty, stale air filled their noses and made them cough. Anacletus periodically explained the nature of the place. In the various crypts or chambers in the walls were the hollowed-out tombs. Many were sealed while others awaited use. Some were decorated with richly colored stucco. Tombstones with names covered the niches where people had been placed. Oil lamps hung from the ceilings. Here and there small openings up to the surface allowed little shafts of light to seep in. However, once the lamps were extinguished, the endless corridors were eerie and foreboding.

Linus led the group to the far end of the main passageway, where a large room opened up from where several tunnels split. The large open space made a natural gathering area where all of them could sit on the floor. The adjacent corridors offered relative privacy and sleeping areas. In a small hollowed-out space near the top of the back wall, Stephanos placed the scroll that his mother and John Mark had written. Food they had purchased along the way was stashed in similar small holes in the sides. By the time Linus returned, Stephanos and the exiles had settled into the catacombs.

"The word is spreading quickly through Rome," Linus said once the group gathered around him. "Saturday has been set as the day of reckoning. Nero himself will watch the executions. The emperor has announced a special execution in his gardens that evening." His voice echoed down the tunnels, making the whole area seem all the more empty.

"Surely there is something we can do!" Epaphroditus ran his hands through his hair. "Something?"

"No one even knows where we are." Stephanos looked down the dark tunnel in front of him. "But if the word gets out, we will surely perish. Yet we are isolated, worthless. Couldn't we have done something back in the city?" The lamps cast long shadows everywhere, shrouding every corner of the area in forbidding silhouettes of blackness.

"Nothing!" Priscilla shook her head empathetically. "Absolutely nothing. The emperor would delight in an attempt to free any of the men from the jails. Then he could claim a military revolt and say that the believers are insurrectionists. His hand would only be strengthened in the senate. Make no mistake! A legion of soldiers would find it difficult to break into the jails today."

"We are completely helpless." Epaphroditus ground his teeth. "Helpless." The stale damp air chilled him, and he shuddered.

"Rome will not stop until they have hunted down the last one of us." Linus ran his hand through his hair, leaving streaks of the gray powder from the tufa stone. His tunic was smeared and stained with chalk dust that was everywhere. The blotches made him look like a beggar on the streets. "Soldiers ended the revolt of Spartacus with slaves dying on crosses up and down the Appian Way. They will be no less persistent in pursuing us." He slumped to the ground.

"Our options have gone up in smoke." Anacletus dropped his hands. "Rome has all the power. We are inept, broken."

"No," Mariam answered resolutely. "Rome does *not* have all the power. I was there the day after the crucifixion of Yeshua,* when evil seemed invincible. And I listened during the weeks that followed as Yerushalayim was turned upside down by the discovery that a new reality had been unleashed in the world. Only the power of love is *supreme*."

Mariam got to her feet. "I was there the night they brought our first martyr in and laid his body on our living room floor. Yes, I know what it is to feel completely powerless, like an abandoned child caught in the middle of a battlefield. I know how bitter such losses are. But I learned from the mother of the Crucified One that God uses weakness to manifest His

* Jesus

power and glory. From each one of these deaths new life sprang up.''

Intense quiet settled over the room. Most of the group stared at the floor. Linus sat with his legs folded up next to his chest. His bent head nearly touched his knees. Stephanos looked down the long dark tunnel.

''If my father and husband are to be living sacrifices for our God, then I will glory in this moment. I will not desecrate this time with fear. Yes, in the days ahead I will weep by myself, and my grieving heart will know emptiness. I, of all people, understand what those dark hours in the night will mean. But this time I will not shrink back or fall victim to either fear or bitterness. If we are victims today, we will be victors tomorrow. In the end, Rome will bow before their own crosses. We hide in these caves now, but we will conquer even as Yeshua did from His cross.''

Stephanos turned and stared at his mother. Never had he seen her speak with such conviction and force. Her words lifted him and gripped his imagination. Suddenly he knew what they must do.

Stephanos rose to his feet and took Mariam's hand. He beckoned for the others to stand around them. ''The cross must be our new sign. We will paint it on these walls and wear it around our necks. We will hold up the cross until the whole world understands that even at our weakest, we are part of the greatest victory the world has ever seen. Now! I see the way, and I have a plan. God has called us for this exact moment.''

''What are you saying?'' Linus asked.

''I want you to return to the city,'' Stephanos answered quickly. ''I will tell you what to get. Someone must go back to the Porticus Margaritaria. Linus, I want you to find out if we can smuggle a message in to Honorius, to my father and grandfather. We only have two days, so we must move quickly.''

''Exactly what do you have in mind?'' Priscilla asked.

''I will tell you as we go,'' Stephanos answered. ''We will not be defeated, not even by our losses.''

''Yes!'' Mariam spoke emphatically. ''Now is not the time to retreat.''

''Before we go further, we must celebrate the victory of our faith.'' Stephanos opened one of the sacks they had brought with them from Epaphroditus' house. He took out a small wine goblet. After spreading a linen cloth on the floor, he filled the goblet with wine. ''We taste the victory before the fact.'' He tore off a piece of bread from one of the flat loaves they had purchased. Stephanos set the bread beside the cup and knelt down. The rest of the group gathered around him.

Stephanos bowed his head and prayed silently for a few moments. Gently lifting his arms, he prayed aloud, ''*Abba*, receive our offering. On the night that the Lord Jesus was betrayed, He took bread and blessed it and broke it.'' Stephanos picked up the bread and held it above his head, tearing it into two pieces. ''In the same manner, He took the cup.'' He set the bread on the cloth and held up the chalice. The glowing light from the lamp reflected from the polished gold. ''His body and His blood.'' Stephanos gave the chalice and the bread to his comrades. ''Our redemption.''

Two days later the seven believers gathered again in the large room at the end of the central tunnel. The darkness of the tunnel completely concealed the fact that it was two o'clock in the afternoon. The gray color of the tufa-stone walls further muted the light.

Stephanos spread a large cloak on the ground, and the group gathered around him, carefully avoiding casting any shadows onto the work he had been doing. His creations of the last twenty-four hours were scattered about on the cloth.

"Thirty years ago my grandfather first made such a necklace for Honorius." Stephanos held up one of the golden necklaces with a cross attached to the center. "Just before Honorius left Judea, he gave it to the general to commemorate their time standing together at the foot of the cross of Yeshua. At the time, it seemed like a strange gift to many of the brethren. After all, the cross is a hideous symbol of torture and execution. Surely a Jew would see nothing there but injustice and oppression. For us, it was only another reminder of Roman rule. No one wanted to wear such a thing. I don't believe that my grandfather ever made another one."

Mariam nodded her head, confirming the facts.

"But now that shall be changed." Stephanos put the necklace over his head. "In the last few hours I have made as many replicas of Grandfather's work as I could. We shall let all Rome know that God uses their worst to accomplish His best." We shall make the hours before us our finest moments." Stephanos began to hand out crosses to each person. "Linus has done exceedingly well in getting our friends in the Porticus Margaritaria to give us many gold chains on credit."

"When I said I needed these chains for the Ben Aaron family, merchants almost began throwing them at me. No one hesitated in giving me the materials you needed. Everyone was concerned because they had not heard from you. There are many believers in the Porticus."

"Anacletus, how have your contacts gone?" Stephanos gave him a cross.

"I have been able to talk personally with many of our key people as well as the leaders at the Great Synagogue. They were greatly encouraged to know that you escaped. They stand ready to follow your guidance. Everyone now knows that both Peter and Paul are in the Mamertine Prison. We have people who keep vigil there as well as the Lautumae jail. If there is any movement in either place, we will know immediately."

"And Saturday?" Stephanos queried.

"Our people will be everywhere around the Circus. We are spreading the word that they should wear crosses to identify each other. They will mingle in the crowd, telling the citizens the truth about the fire. By the time word gets back to the emperor, we will be gone."

"Excellent." Stephanos turned back to Linus. "And is there any way we can make contact in the prisons?"

"At this time we can't get through the guards at either prison. The fact that we got in the first time is considered a major miracle." Linus began to talk rapidly and with animation. "But when they are moved to the Circus, I have found a way that we can get a message in. The slaves that manage the animals and many of the gladiators are easily bribed. Moreover, some of our believers are employed in the upkeep of the track. We will be able to make contact. I have a plan."

"Most excellent." Stephanos patted Linus on the shoulder. "I think it will be necessary for the women to stay here tomorrow. Priscilla and Julia will be known by many people, and soldiers would be on the lookout."

"Not so," Priscilla put one of Mariam's Judean scarfs over her head. "I, too, have a plan." She pulled out a little jar filled with an ocher paste. With her fingertips she began rubbing the paste on her cheeks. Her Roman skin color quickly changed to Semitic darkness. "No one is looking for an Arab woman."

"I don't know," Stephanos objected.

"Perhaps Julia should stay concealed," Mariam answered, "but I must stand with the rest of you. The least I can do is be as close to my family as possible. I cannot stay here."

"Nor I!" Julia was uncharacteristically firm. "I can conceal myself as well. My husband's courage and integrity would not be well served by anything less than my telling people the truth. Rome knows who I am, and my lineage speaks for itself. When the gossips hear that I defied Nero, the story will become a legend. Nothing the emperor can say will be able to refute this witness in the streets."

Stephanos looked at the men for their response, but each one looked away. "And I thought I was in charge," he laughed. "Well then, we march together! Tomorrow will be another resurrection day!"

XXI

Dawn had barely broken when the soldiers opened the door to the Lautumae Prison. Without any explanation Jarius and Philip were separated from Honorius and the rest of the prisoners and taken outside in the large open area in front of the prison door. The high, abrupt hill that ran up to the edge of the Forum blocked out the rising sun. The air was once again heavy with smoke. Both men shielded their eyes momentarily from the sudden light and stinging smoke. When Philip looked around, he was astonished to see men and women kneeling before him on the ground. Some were Greek; others were Roman. They were chained together and surrounded by soldiers with spears. Most were huddled together, though some stood with ropes hanging from their necks like leashes.

"Look!" Jarius pointed at the captives. "I know some of these people. They are believers . . . friends!"

"There are seventy, eighty people." Philip gasped. "Soldiers must have spent the night rounding them up."

"We need to speak to them." Jarius shuffled forward.

282

"Don't I know you?" Philip asked a man he remembered seeing at many of their meetings.

"I am Philologus," the Greek answered. He was tall with an aristocratic bearing. His silk tunic was dirty and smeared with black stains.

"I am Philip."

"Of course," the Greek answered softly. "Everyone knows you. I am honored to stand next to you."

"What is happening?" Philip asked rapidly as the guards moved among the captives checking their manacles to make sure they were secure.

"Many of us were arrested in our beds," Philologus explained. "The emperor panicked when the fires began again."

"Again?"

"The fires burned for three days and nights before dying down. Then suddenly the fires flared up once more, even worse than before. Now the Temple of Luna is gone as well as the Temple of Jupiter Stator. Even the Shrine of Vesta is ruined. People are going crazy. They are homeless and their household gods are charcoal. The Senate is terrified of a citywide revolt. We are to be the sacrificial offering to the mob."

Philip looked over the group once more. Many were slaves and servants, but a significant number were of the higher class. Several women cradled babies in their arms, and there were a number of teenagers standing by their parents. The bedraggled group looked bewildered, tired, and worn.

"Where are they taking us?" Philip asked.

"I heard a soldier say we will be marched up to the Ager Vaticanus Hill.

"What's up there?"

"The Circus of Caligula and Nero, where the big

chariot races are always held. I fear there will be no races today.''

''What do you mean?''

''Moats with water are around the course to protect the spectators from racing accidents. It would be a good place to turn wild animals loose on us.''

''Get up!'' A guard cracked a whip in the air. ''Hurry up!'' The guard lashed a man only a few feet away from Philip. ''We're moving out.''

Suddenly Philip stiffened. To the far rear of the crowd of prisoners he saw a face that he didn't want to recognize. Everything in him repulsed the inevitable truth. ''O heavens!'' His hand came to his mouth. ''John!'' he called out before he thought. ''John Mark!''

Instantly a guard cracked Philip across the shoulders with the shaft of his spear, sending him sprawling on the ground. ''Keep your mouth shut!'' The guard kicked Philip hard in the side.

''Move it!'' another soldier barked. ''We'll drag you across the pavement if we have to.''

Philologus helped Philip stand. ''John Mark heard you,'' the Greek whispered in Philip's ear, ''but don't try that again. Don't make any contact or they'll turn on both of you.''

Philip shook his head mechanically, trying to clear his dazed mind. Jarius stood alongside him, helping him to support his weight.

''We're in for a long walk.'' Philologus spoke very softly. ''We must walk to the edge of Rome. Do your best.''

''We didn't even say goodbye to Honorius.'' Jarius looked back at the metal door in the side of the cliff.

''Perhaps it is easier this way.'' Philip trudged on. ''Stay close so I can help support your chains.''

The soldiers were in the full battle dress of the common recruits. There was none of the ornate armor and helmet plumes of the Praetorian Guard. Plain leather and metal helmets were tightly strapped down ready for combat. Some of the men had leather breastplates, and others had their chests covered with leather strips bound together in a protective vest. Many men had shields, and some carried spears, but each man had a long battle sword strapped on the right side and a dagger on the left. The contingent of soldiers looked mean and eager to strike.

The squad surrounded the prisoners as they began the march up the hill toward the Roman Forum. The ranks closed so the soldiers' shields prevented any contact with prisoners from the outside. The guard's stern warning about any conversation kept the march silent.

Once the company of prisoners and soldiers topped the hill, they turned up the narrow Vicus Tuscus street that ran toward the Basilica Julia in front of the Roman Forum area where the processions, ceremonies, and official political life were held. Philip was startled to see that the fire had swept through even the heart of the official fulcrum of Roman life. As Philologus had said, the Temple of Vesta was burned. The roof had collapsed, and the ornate grillwork was burned away.

Vicus Tuscus adjoined the large broad boulevard running down the center of the Forum. Philip was also shocked to see that the Temple of Caesar had also burned. Apparently the roof had also proven vulnerable. Tall Corinthian columns still supported the pediment at the top, but the statue of the goddess on the roof had toppled through the ceiling. The enormous doors had burned and fallen back inside the temple.

The prisoners trudged past the smoldering ruins into Via Sacra. Ahead of them they could see the over-powering temple of Venus and Rome. Once they were in the wider street, the soldiers double-timed the march through the arch of Triumph and beneath the statue of the victorious charioteer and his team of four horses. People immediately began tripping and falling.

"Watch out!" Philip put one arm under Jarius' shoulder to keep the old man on his feet. "I'm keeping you from stumbling. Look out for the people in front of us."

A family who were shackled together fell just feet ahead. "Clumsy fools!" The guard swung the butt end of his spear at them striking the man in the arm. Blood sprayed everywhere. The mother and son quickly struggled to help him up. The guard grabbed their chains and yanked them forward.

When other captives fell, they were dragged along by the sheer force of the group's forward movement. Philip kept looking for John Mark but could only periodically catch a glimpse of him walking with the vanguard.

The Via Sacra led the group out of the Forum proper and into the Porticus Margaritaria. Philip kept looking for familiar faces among the pearl vendors, but the market was nearly empty. Back near the area where the family had once practiced their jewelry business, all of the tents and awnings were burned. Counters and tables were charred and broken. The whole area looked abandoned.

The street turned abruptly into Clivus Orbus, which led away from the center of Rome. Soldiers relentlessly drove their victims on without pause for rest or care for the fallen. As the sun rose, the group's pace did not slacken.

When they finally neared the Vaticanus hill, the large entryway of the Circus came into view. Fourteen large arches with a sentry box centered on top were bordered by two-story buildings on each side. The entrance formed one end of the huge oblong racing track. On each side were high bleachers for the spectators. The prisoners were marched through the arches onto the dirt racing track. In the center was the long spina divider around which the charioteers made their racing laps. At the front end of the center island were three columns, and behind them were shrines to the god Consus and the goddess Pollentia. At the far end was an eighty-four-foot-high Egyptian obelisk that Augustus had once ordered placed there. The prisoners were herded into a large circular building behind the monument.

Roman and Greek prisoners were crammed into the bottom section, but Jarius and Philip were singled out and shuttled upstairs. Their small room was large and dusty smelling as if it had probably been used for grain storage for the animals. Six openings in the stone wall allowed a viewer to see out in any direction. From the second story it was possible even to see out above the bleachers and beyond the arched entryway.

"We have a special place for you Jews," the burly guard sneered. "The emperor wants you to be his special guests." Abruptly the guard pushed Philip and Jarius onto the floor. "Enjoy yourselves because this afternoon we're going to enjoy you." His laughter was coarse and cruel. "You're last on the menu. You might like to watch out the windows so you'll know what's waiting for you." He laughed again.

As the morning dragged on, periodically Philip looked out the second-story windows. People were milling around the bleachers and the race track. Horse-drawn carts with cages of wild dogs, boars, and a few lions lumbered into the arena. A dozen men were limbering up by practicing mock battle attacks. Several men were bare-chested with armor running only from one shoulder down the arm. They carried small circular shields. Other men had three-pronged spears and nets. Their helmets ran down the backs of their necks and had metal strips that crisscrossed their faces. The clunk and crunch of swords clashing against shields punctuated the endless roaring of the beasts. Philip surmised that they were gladiators and not soldiers.

Late in the morning servants and slaves began carrying in large stacks of raw animal skins. Other workers put up cloth banners in front of the imperial box seats. In spite of the smoke hanging heavily over the city, the Circus took on a festive atmosphere as if some great celebration were about to occur.

The men with the skins began piling the bundles at the base of the center tower. Philip heard the noise and looked down watching the workers making trips back and forth. Some men dropped the skins outside while others carried some of the bundles in. When Philip looked out the other windows, he could see that the lions and dogs were excited by the scent of the skins. The roaring and barking created a frenzied atmosphere. Soldiers kept riding in and out on horses as the bleachers started to fill. Philip could tell by the location of the sun that it was early afternoon.

"I wonder what the skins are for?" Philip kept looking out the small portholes. "Strange."

Jarius lay on the floor, propped up against the wall. He was so exhausted he couldn't respond. His skin was gray and drawn; his arms lay limp at his side, and his head hung awkwardly against his shoulder.

"They are adding more water to the moats," Philip continued, talking more to himself. "They're sealing up the archways."

A man walking across the track with a bundle of skins on his back caught Philip's eye. The servant was bent so low that his face was nearly down to his waist, but he walked with a very determined pace toward the tower in the center. Once he reached the base, Philip heard him knock for entrance. Apparently a guard had let him in. Almost immediately Philip heard steps on the stairs. To his surprise, Philip watched the man and his burden come up the stone staircase.

Without a word, the man dumped his bundle on the floor. Slowly he turned with a finger held to his lips. "*Shalom*," Linus greeted them.

"Linus!" Philip exclaimed. "Linus Decius!"

Linus quickly dropped beside Jarius and felt for his pulse. Jarius roused and blinked uncomprehendingly at the room around him. "I only have a few moments." Linus reached for a leather pouch as he talked. Jarius stared with his mouth open. "Stephanos has escaped and is now our leader," he told Philip. "We were able to rescue Mariam and Julia."

"Praise God!" Philip held his arms up. "They still haven't caught my son. My beloved wife is safe."

"The believers stand with you today," Linus whispered in Jarius' ear. "Even now we are gathering outside the Circus to make our witness. Stephanos is disguised as a Greek, but he stands just beyond the arches and prays for you. His mother is by his side. Remember this?'' Linus held up two chains.

''Years ago,'' Jarius whispered, barely able to speak, ''I made such a gift for Honorius.''

''Stephanos made these crosses for you and similar ones for all of us. We wear them today as a sign of the victory of the Christus. When the final moments come, cling to the cross, as we will. Today you will strike a mighty blow for our God. Peace be with you,'' The tribune dropped the necklace around Jarius' neck and hugged Philip, ''Peace,'' he concluded with tears in his eyes.

''What's taking so long?'' A guard barked up the stairway. ''Get back down here!''

Linus adjusted his dirty robe and reached for the skins. ''I'm separating the bundle,'' he answered.

''We'll do that,'' the soldier shouted. ''Leave those damn Jews alone!''

''Coming,'' Linus called back. He turned slowly and smiled bravely. ''Peace.''

''*Shalom aleichem.*'' Jarius waved feebly.

Philip returned to the window. After a few moments, Linus walked out of the tower toward the side entrance from which he had come. His steps were resolute, and he did not look back.

''Can you imagine?'' Philip held his chain and cross up. ''Stephanos made these for us.'' Philip sat next to Jarius. ''These chains are even a link with Honorius right now.''

Jarius felt the little gold cross with his thin, worn fingers. ''What courage for Linus to come here. We do not have much time left.'' His speech became stronger. ''Strange, I remember the afternoon that we found my poor brother Zeda in the marketplace after the Zealots' attack. I worried if he had suffered. I thought the same thing the night you and the young men came back after they had stoned Stephanos. I hoped the pain had not lingered. Now I know that it doesn't matter very much. God will be merciful, and the afternoon will pass quickly enough.''

"You have always been a brave man, *Abba.* You will be strength to me.''

Jarius patted his son-in-law's hand and smiled weakly. ''I wonder what Simeon is doing this afternoon in Yerushalayim. Perhaps he works on another such fine chain in our old jewelry shop. Maybe he is up at the Temple arguing the law. I trust that he is well.''

"As I pray the same for little Zeda and Leah,'' Philip added. ''The children will find this news very difficult to bear.''

"Who would ever have believed that we would end up here?'' Jarius looked around the dirty room. The skins that Linus carried were matted with blood and filled the room with a nauseating odor. The afternoon sun was hot, making the smell and the dusty room even more offensive.

"Oh, Simeon did.'' Philip shook his head. ''Yes, he always warned of such a fate at the hands of the Romans. I sometimes wonder if Mariam did not have a premonition in her spirit as well.''

"Was not my daughter a wondrous woman?'' Jarius tried to say more but began to cry.

Philip pulled his father-in-law close to him. He could feel the old man's body shake as he sobbed. Finally Philip wrapped both arms around Jarius, holding him like a child. Only then did Philip begin to weep.

"Perhaps, we should pray,'' Philip finally managed

to say before the tears choked off further conversation. Taking his father-in-law's hand, he silently prayed. Philip finally said aloud, "Oh Adonai, be with Stephanos!" Under his breath he petitioned, "and comfort my beloved wife." Once more he fell silent.

After several minutes Jarius spoke, "I wonder if John Mark is still downstairs."

"I suppose so." Philip stood up. "Let me see what's happening."

When Philip looked out the window, the stands were nearly full. Cages with animals were scattered around the sides of the arena. Barricades had been completely erected in front of the fourteen entry arches to keep people and animals inside the walled track. Gladiators with their pronged spears, small shields, and swords walked around the arena. People milled about the bleachers waving and talking in a festive atmosphere.

"I think they are about to begin." Philip told Jarius. "We will be slaughtered for sport before this crowd of depraved pagans."

"We may only be a diversion for them, but we are an offering to our God," Jarius answered. "For hundreds of years, our sacrifices for sin in the Temple saved the rest of the world from the righteous wrath of God." He stopped and bit his lip. Tears filled his eyes. "Now we are privileged to present our bodies as living sacrifices." His words began to fade away. "Our heavenly Father honors us today."

"I am so grateful Mariam was spared this route," Philip breathed heavily. "I gladly stand in her place. If I could just touch her fingertips right now—" He stopped abruptly. "Rome may destroy our bodies, but from this day forward our witness will continue from heaven itself. No, Father, we need not pray for ourselves. Let us pray for Stephanos and Mariam and the days that remain before them."

Jarius held Philip's hand firmly and began praying once more: *"Yit-gadal ve-yit-kadash shmei raba b'alma divra khir'utei ve-yamlikh mal-khutei e-hayei-khon uve'yomei-khon . . . ."* Jarius choked and could say no more.

"Ye-hei shmei raba meva-rakh l'alam ul'almei'almaya," Philip continued alone.

Jarius struggled to begin again. *"Uve-hayei di-khol beit yisrael be-agala u-vizman kariv v'imru amen."* Their prayers were interrupted by the roar of the crowd.

Philip jumped up as a white and gold chariot roared out of a side entrance. A soldier drove the team of six white thoroughbreds while the man at his side waved; the fat man's white toga edged in bright crimson blew in the breeze. His tunic was bordered with the same banding; in the center was a laurel wreath and in his hair was a similar golden wreath. The crowd applauded wildly. Trumpeters began blowing a salute.

"Nero is here," Philip spoke from the window. "The debacle is about to begin."

The emperor's chariot pulled in front of the royal box. Nero got out, still waving to the crowd. When the spectators quieted, a proclamation was read, but Philip made little out of what was said. Once more trumpets were blown, and the mob started stamping their feet. The first of the prisoners walked from the circular building out onto the track. Animal skins were tied to his back, arms, and legs with the raw side out. Three prisoners followed him. At the other end of the Circus, Philip watched soldiers begin opening the cages of wild dogs.

"No! No!" Philip recoiled. "Now I understand the skins!" As the dogs slowly emerged from the cages, the spectators went wild. At first, the animals seemed bewildered and frightened, but the guards began jabbing at them with long spears, herding the pack toward the skin-wrapped prisoners. Philip could see that the dogs were big and vicious, hungry, with ribs protruding; their coats were matted and dirty. Philip had been warned always to avoid the north end of Via Nomentana outside the Servian Wall where such wild packs roamed. One quick lunge and a big dog could nearly tear a man's arm off. These curs might even have been captured beyond the walls.

The mongrels began barking and snapping at the soldiers as the beasts backed toward the four men who had stopped just beyond the spina. At that moment another group of prisoners was released on the other side of the track. Once more soldiers swung open the doors on the wooden cages. A wild boar tore out onto the tracks as a long horned black bull trotted out a side door at the other end. Soldiers ran behind the bull, hitting and jabbing with spears.

Suddenly the pack of dogs got the scent of the skins and charged into the first group of prisoners. Instantly men fell backward as the crazed beasts bit at their arms and legs. A huge brown dog grabbed one of the men's throats and began dragging him across the track.

On the back side, the bull charged into the prisoners, scattering them on the ground. Other dogs began chasing the wild boar. To Philip's horror, dogs attacked both the boar and the men. When the bull reached the moat, he turned and lowered his head, charging the soldiers. They quickly retreated behind the barricades. One of the dogs sank his fangs into the bull's hindquarters. The bull snorted a fierce bellowing roar, kicking his legs straight back. On the second kick, the dog fell off and retreated. The bull swirled around several times and then charged the nearest group of prisoners. He caught one skin-covered man on his left horn and ground the prisoner into the track.

When the bull backed away, the man lay flat on his back with his stomach ripped open. His lifeless eyes stared upward at the sky. "I know him," Philip choked. "Philologus . . . the man we began the march with." Philip slumped against the wall. "He came . . . to many of our meetings."

In a matter of minutes, Philip watched all the remaining prisoners be torn to pieces. When the last prisoner was dead, soldiers came out with nets and dragged the dogs back into the corners. By then the boar was dead, and soldiers had hauled it off. The bull went limping back into the chute from which he had come. Dust began settling, but a strange, sticky smell of blood hung in the air. A horse-drawn cart pulled alongside the mutilated bodies of the believers. Slaves threw the dead on the back of the cart, and the arena was prepared for the second round.

Philip was so nauseated he had to sit down. Holding his mouth, he breathed rapidly, trying to prevent his stomach from erupting. For a long time he sat doubled up against the stone wall.

"I remember," Jarius said resolutely, breaking the ominous silence "that Peter told us not to be surprised when this time came. Paul said much the same thing. We are to rejoice because we share in the suffering of our Messiah."

"I find it impossible," Philip said, swallowing hard, "to keep from being terrified."

"I was always very concerned with justice." Jarius seemed not to hear Philip's answer. "Yes!" He sat up straight. "I once hated the Romans for all the oppressive crimes they had committed against our people. And now I will die as unjustly as did Yeshua." His eyes filled with tears but he spoke forcefully. "Philip, the Romans are going to hoist us up alongside our Lord. Our captors offer us the consummate honor. We will not be afraid."

Philip's face was colorless and his lips pale. He breathed heavily through clenched teeth. "I did not know it would be so hard."

"Don't fret," the old man comforted Philip, "when the final moment comes, you will be sufficient." Jarius pushed his way to his feet and hobbled to the window. "Somewhere out there Mariam, Stephanos, and many of the others are standing with us. We are not alone." Jarius turned back and shook his bony finger at Philip. "We will walk into that arena with boldness. When night comes, the best that even the Caesar can do is return to his palace. But this evening we will be in paradise. We will be home!"

Philip smiled faintly at his father-in-law. All the brash courage of the Ben Aarons had returned. Jarius was always physically strong. Most old men would have perished on the march up to the Circus. Even though he was worn and tired, the last vestige of Jarius' nerve and tenacity still served him. Philip felt himself buoyed up by the sight.

"Once again they are clearing the track." Jarius looked out the window. "I'm sure they will come for us shortly. There can't be many believers left downstairs."

Philip stood by Jarius, looking out over the Circus. Soldiers were forcing a lion back into a large cage.

The wild dogs still ran uncontrolled about the track, but they were being slaughtered by the soldiers. The demented pack had killed the boar before turning on the crazed bull. The frenetic attacks had not ceased until the bull's throat was torn open. Soldiers dragged the black carcass out behind several horses. Bloody skins were scattered all over the arena.

"Look!" Jarius pointed toward the middle. "They are doing something different. Poles are being stuck in the ground."

As they watched, two poles were sunk at the end of the spina island divider that formed the center of the track. Slaves began piling bundles of sticks around the poles. Not far from the poles another hole was quickly dug for a large cross, which several soldiers carried out to the center.

"All right," a guard yelled up from the bottom. "Come down here you two. Move it."

Jarius carried his chains in his hands, and Philip helped him down the stairs. "Our time has come," the old man said simply.

"Unshackle 'em," the guard in charge commanded.

The room below, which had been packed with people, was now empty of all their brothers and sisters. Only the soldiers remained with a few slaves. A man in a dirty brown tunic quickly removed their chains.

"Don't want to fish hot iron out of the ashes," the guard snarled.

Jarius looked knowingly at Philip.

"When the door opens," the soldier instructed, "you will walk straight out to the poles. Don't monkey with us. If you deviate one step, we'll be out of here on your backs before you've gone two steps. In that case, we'll peel the skin off of your bodies while we make sure you stay alive as long as possible. Got the scene?"

With calm composure, Philip turned to the man. "We are not afraid," he said quietly.

The soldier looked mystified. "Go on." He opened the door and stepped back.

Outside two soldiers in plain leather breastplates carrying spears stood with their helmets trapped down. They were young, with the demeanor of men pressed into service without any idea of what they were doing.

"Follow me," one said as the other stepped behind Philip and Jarius. The soldier led them down the track to the end of the center divider. He pointed to the two poles struck in the ground and stood back. "Over there!" He gestured toward the soldiers standing around the poles.

Jarius started walking—tall, proud, and erect. Philip quickly caught up. The summer afternoon was hot and muggy, the air was very dusty, and the sky filled with smoky clouds. Soldiers stood around the two poles beckoning them forward.

Trumpeters again blew their horns. A man in a purple robe stepped to the edge of the imperial box and began reading a proclamation. Philip and Jarius had no difficulty hearing the list of charges that were being lodged against all those who followed the Christus.

"Our noble and courageous emperor," the *prelector* shouted, "has spared no energy in bringing these seditionists to justice. Since the fire began, Caesar has labored day and night to capture these criminals. The ringleaders have been apprehended in record time by the sheer skill and persistence of our emperor. Before you are the foreigners who have invaded our land with the intention of destroying Rome." The reader stopped and the trumpets sounded once again.

Fifteen soldiers marched out of the side barricades. In their midst was a prisoner with his hands chained and a large log forcing his arms behind his back. The weight of the log nearly doubled him over. A chain was wrapped around his neck, and the two front guards held the ends of the links.

"We have apprehended their principal leader and teacher," the reader began again. "We offer to the gods of Rome these criminals. May Jupiter Optimus Maximus be appeased and satisfied! Praise to Mars and Bellona!"

"That's Peter!" Philip pointed. "That's Peter in chains!"

"Let Roman justice be satisfied," the *prelector* concluded. Drums began to roll and the crowd roared once more.

Once the soldiers reached the center of the track, they unshackled Peter and dropped the log from his back. The old man stumbled forward and collapsed on the ground. Philip rushed forward to help him.

"We're here." Philip helped Peter stand. "Father and I are with you."

Peter doubled up with a sudden muscle spasm, but Philip kept him from falling. "I'll be all right," he slowly exhaled.

"Is Paul next?" Philip asked.

"I think Paul is still in the prison." Peter swallowed hard. "They took me out this morning but left him. They are going to crucify me."

"Yes." Philip gripped his arm. "They are going to kill us at the same time."

"I told them I was unworthy to be crucified in the

same manner as the Messiah was. I asked to die upside down instead," Peter coughed. "They laughed
but said they would be glad to oblige me."

The crowds quieted as Nero stood in the center of
the royal section. He held his right arm in the air with
his hand raised. His gold-bordered toga lay draped
over his left arm. "Citizens," he called out. "Before
you are the barbarians who destroyed our homes and
damaged our beloved city. However, with great pain I
must tell you that the worst criminal was one of us.
The treasonous leader of these culprits was none
other than one of my own Praetorian Guard. I have
saved his execution for last. Tonight in the royal gardens I will personally supervise the execution of General Gaius Honorius Piso."

Instantly the crowd broke into a rumble; a muffled
roar followed.

"Yes," Nero shouted again, "I, too, was shocked by
the discovery that General Piso masterminded this
whole plot in an attempt to seize power." Nero
paused to allow the full dramatic effect to settle. "But
fear not! Your emperor has prevailed!"

When Nero's hand dropped, the drumroll began
again. At once the soldiers stripped Peter of his robe,
leaving him only in a loincloth. Peter was forced to lie
on top of the cross. Two soldiers dropped on Peter,
pinning him against the timbers while others started
binding and nailing him to the beams.

Both Jarius and Philip were immediately dragged
up on top of the bundles of sticks and pressed against
the poles. Philip could no longer look at his father-in-
law. He turned sideways and closed his eyes. Instinctively Philip raised his arms as the Jews traditionally
do in prayer. The soldiers ignored his posture as they
tied his back and legs to the pole.

Philip looked again just as Peter's cross was pushed into the hole in the track. Peter's body dangled strangely, upside down at grotesque angles. From his perch on the sticks, Philip could look out through the entry arches and see the people standing outside. Mariam and Stephanos must be somewhere in the crowd, he thought, but the distance was too great to identify anyone.

Philip let his head drop back against the rough pole and looked up into the sky. Above the murky, overcast waves of smoke, the sky was a brilliant blue. Large thunderheads filled the horizon with ever-changing mysterious shapes. The Roman sky was really no different from the heavens over Judea or Greece. As a boy, he had lain on the top of the Acropolis and watched such billowy clouds gather above Athens. Philip remembered sitting with Mariam in the fields beyond Yerushalayim, staring up at the clouds that drifted over the mountains and out to the Great Sea. It had been a long, long time since he had simply looked at the wondrous sky.

The noise of the crowd strangely faded, and a silence fell around Philip as if he had once again returned to the empty fields and vineyards just beyond the Ephraim Gate. He and Mariam had spent so many hours among the family tombs and at the place of the Great Resurrection where the hush was always ominous. Many a time had Philip watched the rain clouds gather above the rocky outcroppings that held their ancestors. Only then did he hear the crackle of the fire as the sticks began to burn; but Philip did not look down. He prayed quietly, "The heavens declare the glory of Thy firmament."

The goodness of life welled up in his heart. He could again taste roast lamb and the figs he enjoyed so much. The laughter of his small children filled his ears, and he could see Mariam's face always full of tender kindness and delight in the simplest little gift he brought her. He remembered her fascination with the bright stars at night. Never before had he realized the magnificence of the gift of life.

For a brief moment, Philip thought he saw faces in the thunderheads above him. Romans would have seen the gods of war, the Magna Mater or some such thing; but Philip saw the outline of Leah's face and maybe something of his son Zeda. Tears ran down his face well before the first wisps of smoke filled his nostrils.

At the first tinge of pain around his ankles, Philip pulled at the cross around his neck and squinted his eyes so tightly that for a moment he blocked out every other sensation. He tried to remember the story they had told so often of Yeshua's death on the cross. Jarius and Honorius had always told of the Master's quoting the twenty-second Psalm. Philip tried to lock his mind on the words:

> Be not far from Me,
> For trouble is near;
> For there is none to help . . .
> My heart is like wax;
> It has melted within Me. . . .
> My tongue clings to My jaws. . . .
> For dogs have surrounded Me . . . .
> Save me from the lion's mouth
> And from the horns of the wild oxen!

Total and complete aloneness settled around Philip. He surmised everyone must encounter a similar absolute isolation just before death. The sense of being left behind while the family went on, of being cut off from all that would follow, bewildered Philip. His intense solitude deepened until the vacuum engulfed every thought and reflection. At the exact moment that emptiness almost overpowered and suffocated all hope, Philip knew he was not alone and never had been. The words of the Psalm intruded:

> For He has not despised nor abhorred the
>   affliction of the afflicted;
> Nor has He hidden His face from Him;
> But when He cried to Him. He heard. . . . All
>   the ends of the world
> Shall remember and turn to the LORD . . .''

A magnificent light exploded behind his closed eyes. Mariam had often spoken of the light. When he looked up again, the sky had become turquoise like the best amalekite in the finest necklace he had ever created. The white thunderheads were dazzling white. The final line of the Psalm filled his mind: "They will come and declare His righteousness to a people who will be born." He did not see the flames leaping up before his face—only the majesty of creation and an awesome *shekinah* light.

XXII

And so on this Sunday we remember that a week ago we laid to rest our martyrs." Stephanos spoke loudly. "My father, grandfather, and dear friends Honorius and John Mark were sealed within these tunnels to wait for the Great Resurrection that is close at hand. Peter, our first bishop, lies in the center at the end of the central corridor. On this first day of the week, as we celebrate the victory of our Messiah, we proclaim that these loved ones have also overcome this world. All who eat of the flesh of the Master and drink of this cup shall be raised up with them at that last day."

Sunrise broke over the hills of Rome, covering the hundreds of people gathered at the entrance and around the slopes that led down into the *coemeteria*. Stephanos stood behind a small table in front of the entrance to the catacombs. Before him was a large chalice and a flat loaf of bread. Instead of wearing a Greek tunic, he was dressed as a Judean, a simple robe covered with the seamless outer cloak, embroidered with the markings of the tribe of Levi. The heat of July was already in the air, even at such an early hour. As Stephanos finished his teaching, he could

304

see other people still coming down into their gathering, swelling the ranks until it seemed that the basin would not hold them.

Stephanos looked down at his mother, who knelt on the ground before him. As Mariam bent forward, her shawl draped and covered much of her face. She held her hands up in the simple Jewish prayer posture. Priscilla knelt next to her, waiting to receive her first Communion. In contrast to Mariam, she watched Stephanos' every movement.

"We have taught you," Stephanos preached, "that baptism is entering into His death. Now you know that joining Him is truly participating in that death. Some of you have lost family and severed all ties with your past for the sake of Christ." Stephanos looked at Priscilla once more. "Each and every loss is agonizing. No one can fully extinguish the pain of our bereavement. Yet each deprivation only further establishes our participation in the kingdom of God. As we consecrate this bread and wine, we continue to receive new life in Him. Let us worship."

The top of the hill obscured the outskirts of Rome lying behind the gathering, but nothing blocked the threat the city now represented to the believers. Slaves in plain cotton tunics dropped to their knees beside Romans in bright-colored silk togas. A number of soldiers could be seen among the people who knelt to pray. The group in front began to chant in Greek, *"Uparchian en mortan Teon."* Other voices sang, *"Harpagmos eanton ekenossen mortan doulos."* The mighty chorus resounded: "He humbled Himself, He emptied Himself, becoming obedient unto death, even death on a cross."

Stephanos held the chalice above his head and prayed, "This cup is the new covenant in His blood."

He set the cup down and held the bread before them. "Take, eat. This is My body, which is broken for you. Do this in remembrance of Me."

When Stephanos broke the loaf, the crowd once more prayed in unison. "Our Father who is in heaven, may your name be holy . . ." And so the prayers continued. Linus, Clement, Anacletus, and others moved to the front of the table to receive before they assisted Stephanos in serving the people. When the prayer ended, believers began coming forward; they knelt before the table, waiting to receive. From across the hillside men and women quietly made their way forward.

Near the very back a man in a plain cotton tunic turned to a patrician in red sandals, wearing the purple-striped toga of honor. "Have you heard anything about the death of General Piso?"

"Oh yes!" The aristocrat drew himself up to his full height. "General Gaius Honorius Piso died as a Roman soldier of great valor—and as a believer who laid down his life in love. But the end was not easy." His face stiffened as if his countenance was held in place by an inner reserve, developed through years of great discipline.

"Might I ask what they did to him?"

At first the patrician looked annoyed and irritated by the question. He held his head erect and turned away for a moment before answering. "Of course you should know," he said as he turned back. "Everyone in this place should know." In an uncharacteristic gesture, the patrician put his arm around the shoulder of the commoner. "On Saturday night a week ago, Honorius was taken to the imperial gardens behind the palace. Nero invited senators and the royalty of Rome to watch. The emperor commanded that animal skins be sewn over the general's body, and Honorius was tied and nailed to a cross. Nero rode around dressed as a charioteer and mingled with the guests as if he were a great war hero. The swine has never even seen a battle.''

''Yes, yes,'' the man in the plain tunic urged, ''what followed next?''

The patrician momentarily lost his composure and didn't speak. Finally he smiled weakly. ''The skins were doused with lamp oil. At sunset they ignited the oil and the general became a human torch to light the garden.''

''Oh, no!'' the man muttered, ''No—no.''

''I want you to remember this.'' The patrician held the man's arm very tightly. ''Honorius knew exactly what was coming. Even before they lit their torches, he began to sing. Yes, the same hymn you just heard. 'He humbled Himself, He emptied himself.' As they approached his cross, he continued, 'becoming obedient unto death, even death on a cross.' Nero screamed for Honorius to stop it, but he sang even more loudly and did not stop once they set him on fire. When he finally could no longer speak, there was no cry of pain or shout of agony. Silence fell over everyone in that garden. I tell you Nero was robbed of any satisfaction in the death of this great man. Make sure the world remembers how he died. Remember!'' he shook the little man's arm.

''Of course,'' the man answered timidly, looking at the place where the patrician's fingers were pressed deeply into his skin. ''I will tell the story among our people.''

''Thank you.'' The patrician released his grip. ''Thank you.''

"My name is Junia." The man extended his hand. "I have not been a believer long."

"Welcome," the patrician smiled. "My name is Lucius Capena."

"How did you come by this information?" Junia asked.

"I once served the Praetorian Guard," Lucius answered. Abruptly the crowd moved forward, and the man named Junia was moved away from Lucius.

"Excuse me," an elderly lady said to Lucius. "I couldn't help overhearing your conversation. Is it true that a trusted family servant betrayed the general?"

"Yes." Lucius inched his way forward in the crowd.

"What has become of the traitor?"

"Rome is filled with the friends of Honorius." Lucius spoke softly to the woman, adding, "The Praetorian Guard still honors his name. I would fear to be the man who betrayed Honorius. Today he is a freed slave. Tomorrow he may well be a decaying body in some back alley. The slave traded being the servant of a kindly master for imprisonment in the perpetual bondage of fear."

People continued moving forward and kneeling until everyone had received from the cup and loaf. Those who had not yet been baptized stood in place. Finally Stephanos raised his hand and blessed the vast congregation before sending them back into the city.

As the crowd dispersed, Stephanos led his mother, Priscilla, and the leaders back into the catacombs to convene them in the large central area. Oil lamps illuminated the dark cavern. In the center of the back wall was a stone plaque that was freshly cemented in place. Across the front was one word: Peter.

The fifteen sat on the floor or on a few small wooden benches.

"Do you have a report on the status of Paul?" Stephanos asked Linus.

"Because he was already imprisoned on the old charges, Nero could not claim any connection to the fire. The jail actually saved Paul from execution," Linus explained to the group. "However, I am sure they will expedite his case, and it will surely not go well. Paul will never again be free, and we will have very limited contact with him. I am sure his days are numbered."

"Is it safe for us to return to the city?" Stephanos asked the group.

"I think so," Epaphroditus answered. "Before long the authorities will know about this place anyway. Even now we are preparing a remote but safe villa for your family. We must simply be cautious until we see how matters settle."

"And they do not settle well," Anacletus added. "Our contacts with the crowd outside of the Circus had their effect. Nero can't stop the rumor that he—not us—set the fires. There is sympathy for us and grave concern for what happened to Honorius."

"I have given a great deal of thought and prayer to what we must do next." Stephanos spoke slowly but confidently.

"Apparently the scroll of *The Gospel According to the Hebrews* was destroyed, but we saved the new codex that my mother and John Mark wrote. Even though it was damaged, I believe we must make copies at once. Perhaps my mother can add the original ending later. But we must waste no time in spreading our story through the city and across the world. We have seen what can happen if people do not know the truth about the church. Time is short. We must act quickly."

"A team of scribes is being assembled," Epaphroditus responded. "Copies of Paul's letter to the Christianios in Rome have been distributed throughout the city in years past. We can do the same with the story of the life of Jesus. We will begin at once."

"Excellent!" Stephanos affirmed. "I also have seen a written copy of a baptismal sermon that Peter wrote. In light of our persecution, I want that sermon made into a letter. We must send it abroad to such places as Pontus, Galatia, Cappadocia, and throughout Asia."

"It shall be done," Epaphroditus guaranteed.

"Now there is the matter of leadership. With Peter gone and Paul locked away, we must select another bishop."

"You are the man!" Linus called from his seat against the stone wall. "You will be Peter to us now."

"Yes, of course!" echoed around the room.

"Thank you." But Stephanos firmly shook his head. "I think not. Since I was a young boy, I admired the leadership I saw in my family. I wanted to be a *nisi* of the synagogue as was my grandfather. My uncle sat on the Great Sanhedrin. I wanted my family to be proud of my decisions and feel confidence in me. Of course, I find the suggestion that I lead the church to be most gratifying."

"You are the natural choice," old Epaphroditus added.

"No," Stephanos said again, "the church in Rome must be led by a Roman citizen who is respected throughout the city. He must be a spiritual man who is exemplary. We need a person who has already achieved some recognition within the society. Romans must direct their own congregations."

"Who then?" Linus asked. "A patrician?"

"I don't think so," Stephanos smiled. "The man must also be unassuming, significant without arrogance. He must be a disciplined man of good report."

"Yes," Linus agreed, "we have many excellent candidates of this sort. Who?"

"You."

"Me?"

I believe God has directed us to choose you, Linus, to be set aside to this office."

"Not me!"

"You are without guile and presume nothing. As a tribune *aeraii*, you are a trusted public official of proven competence. As a believer you have been since the first day an eyewitness of all that has transpired in founding the church. Your courage and faithfulness have been well demonstrated in these last days. I call you to be bishop over us."

Linus stared at Stephanos. One by one the leaders stood until Linus was surrounded by affirmation. He kept shaking his head.

"I will stand behind you," Stephanos assured him. "As Aaron was to Moses, I will be to you. But you are to be the man in front. In all the churches that Paul planted, he insisted on local leadership. We must not start a hierarchy that elevates Jewish leadership. There is no longer division or status among us because of birth or race, for we are one in Christ. Will you accept, Linus?"

"I don't know," Linus fumbled. "I a—a—had—no—idea."

"We are ready to lay hands and set you apart." Stephanos stepped directly in front of him. "The call is from God, not us."

Linus finally answered reluctantly, "If you say, but only if you say." The leaders gathered in a circle around the tribune and placed their hands on his head. Fervent prayers interceded for his well-being as they consecrated him bishop. Linus appeared more stunned than anything else. Finally Stephanos pronounced a benediction.

"I have something I want to give you." Stephanos reached within his robe and produced a leather pouch. "The day after the execution when everyone was gone, I went back to the Circus of Nero and walked out on the track where my father and grandfather died. The remains of the poles and the charred logs were still there. I knelt on the track for a while, and as I was getting up something caught my eye. When I poked in the dirt, I found this cross and the broken necklace that had fallen from my father's neck. No one saw it drop down behind the pole. I want you to have it, Linus. There is no more appropriate symbol of your office."

Linus looked at the cross. Stephanos had rebuilt the chain and polished the gold. The bottom of the shaft looked as if it had just began to melt when it dropped.

"Today is, perhaps, the most important day of my life, and I am unequal to what it has brought me. I am not worthy to wear this sacred adornment."

Mariam put her hand on Linus' shoulder and looked up into his eyes. "Nearly thirty years ago, Miryam, the mother of our Messiah, put her hand on my shoulder and told me what was to come. She told me that I would stand in the streets of Rome and proclaim the glory of our God. Miryam told me that my words would go across the world and be given to generations not yet born. At that time such an idea seemed completely and totally inconceivable to a little Jewish girl who had never ventured far beyond the walls of Yerushalayim. And yet it has all been so. Now I give to you the rest of the prophetic message she gave me that afternoon. 'Proud rulers shall fall from their thrones, and the humble be raised up. The People of the Covenant will grow and increase until the empire sits in our shadow. We will see the day when Rome will be in awe of the church and our Messiah.' Go forward, Linus, with confidence that even now a church is rising up out of these ashes.''

Linus held the chain and cross in the air. ''We will tell our story to every slave and plebeian as well as every patrician who will listen. More will come from the deaths of our friends than even from what they might have done if they had lived. The city will know that the truth for which they died prevails over all lies. When Rome beholds our honor and integrity, the citizens will know that the Christ we profess is not another aberration from Egypt or a fertility cult from Mesopotamia. We offer bread to a spiritually starving populace.''

Linus bowed his head and clutched the cross.

Stephanos ended the meeting: ''And some day we will erect a building for a church on the Ager Vaticanus over the exact place where they died. Go forth in faith and confidence.'' The group continued to stand around Linus for several minutes.

Stephanos and Priscilla watched the leaders' departure. Mariam stood by them as Linus and the other leaders walked back down the long dark corridors to the entrance.

"Sit down, my children," Mariam spoke gently. "I must say several things."

"Of course." Stephanos and Priscilla settled onto one of the little benches. "Your wisdom is always a gift."

"You have received the blessing of your father and grandfather. Now you are the patriarch of our family. I bow to you, my son."

"Oh no, Mother," Stephanos objected, "You are—"

"No," Mariam stopped him, "such has always been our way. Even though Simeon is still alive in Yerushalayim, the blessing has gone to you. But even more, I have seen you grow into God's mission for your life. Your future is here in this land and with Priscilla. Evil would have meant it otherwise, but the Holy One has prevailed. Your insight will be the real guidance that directs the church in Rome. I am not sure of what I am to do but I know your path and I rejoice in it."

"The times will be very difficult." Stephanos rubbed his face. "We will be the target of every evil intent and the scapegoats for the empire. I am just beginning to feel how great our personal loss is. I long to see *Abba* and hear Grandfather's voice."

"Our family has been at this empty place many times," Mariam warned. "Death can creep into a soul and live by sucking the joy of life from your very bones. You must rejoice in the resurrection and trust God to bring His justice in due time."

"I have not yet let myself think about the monstrous deed the emperor has done to us, Mother. While we marched bravely on the Circus, I could push the questions aside. In this dark, lonely cave, justice does not seem so easily served. I wanted

Father, Grandfather, Peter, John Mark—all of them—to escape."

"Yes." Mariam smiled sadly. "I, too, wished that the Red Sea would part one more time, but it didn't."

"I don't want to leave these catacombs." Stephanos dropped Priscilla's hand. "I want to retreat into these tunnels and the memories we have sealed behind their grave markers." After a long pause, he added, "but I know I can't."

"We must not come here too often," Mariam counseled. "I know. We will honor them, but we must go on."

"Your wisdom will be our salvation." Stephanos stood up and kissed his mother on the cheek. "Thank you for your guidance."

"Come here, Priscilla," Mariam beckoned. "I want you to have my blessing as well. In the beginning, I worried about the influence you might have on my son. I admit I was deeply disturbed that you were not Jewish."

"We went to see Paul," Stephanos interrupted her.

Mariam smiled. "Yes, and I also went to see Paul. He reminded me that Ruth the Moabitess was the grandmother of David. He spoke well of you, my child."

"You went to Paul!" Stephanos said in shock. "You never told me."

"I took my own medicine, and it was good for me. I see great strength and goodness in you, Priscilla. I believe the hand of God has joined your life together with my son's. As you stand beside Stephanos, your counsel will be invaluable. I only ask that you observe our dietary laws and keep the ways that Moses gave us long ago."

"I have much to learn." Priscilla took Mariam's hand. "If you will teach me your ways, I will gladly follow."

"Then I gladly give you my blessing." Mariam put Priscilla's hand in Stephanos'.

"May the Lord bless and keep you." Mariam looked upward. "May He keep you safe and always number you among the righteous and the pure. In return for all you have given up, may Adonai multiply and supply His bounty, prospering you in His sight. May He make your life full and satisfy the longings of your heart. Amen and so be it."

Priscilla hugged Mariam.

"Now, my children," Mariam said, patting Priscilla's cheek, "I want to walk back to the city by myself. I have much to consider. I will not be alone. I will meet you at the Villa of Epaphroditus."

Stephanos put his arm around Priscilla's shoulder as he watched his mother disappear out of the tunnel. "It is right that we leave here and live in the city again," he finally observed. "Our future is not in a graveyard."

"You laid down your life today," Priscilla said. "I knew the decision was hard. You are even more of a man than I thought."

"I prayed very long until I knew that Linus was the right one. He will know how to lead our people in this place. I am only a stranger here."

"And I have become no less an exile." Priscilla smiled. "An ancient king of Rome is numbered among my ancestors, and I am no longer even acknowledged by my own father. The paterfamilias laws give him absolute legal authority to do to me what he pleases. Once you and I are married, his displeasure will extend itself to complete excommunication from the family. In the meantime, he must not be able to find me."

"You have indeed laid your life down." Stephanos kissed her lightly on the forehead. "I cannot calculate what your decision will cost you."

"Like every young Roman girl, I dreamed of being married in the *confarretio* ceremony reserved for the patricians. I would have woven a grass crown for you. My father's holdings would someday have ensured me of the best privileges of Rome. Now all I have is adventure, significance, purpose, a life that counts!" Priscilla laughed at her own joke. "I have you and all of the tomorrows in the world."

Stephanos hugged her. "God has brought us together even as He sent my family on this journey from our homeland. We are not out of the night yet, but the dawn lies before us. I know the emperor will continue to hunt for us, but we have already suffered the worst Nero has to offer. Peter spoke of the sacrifice of Jesus as being the stone rejected by the builders, which became the cornerstone. If the Lord tarries, what we offered may prove to be another such a piece of granite."

"We can do it—" Priscilla took his hand, and they walked toward the entrance to return to Rome, "—together."

XXIII

DECEMBER A.D. 66

Winter came again to Rome. Over a year had passed since Nero ordered his wife Poppea Sabina to commit suicide. Other rumors persisted that the emperor had actually kicked her to death. Nearly two years had elapsed since Stephanos and Priscilla married. Time waited for no one.

The usually pleasant days of fall gave way to the colder days of gray. Fog settled over the city in the mornings and often stayed for hours. Although the temperature virtually never reached freezing, the nights were biting. Time and the season inched inevitably onward in the ancient city.

Gaul was quiet and the tribes of Germania were not on the move. Rome's northern frontiers were secure and life was routine in Hispania. Britannia and Hibernia were under control and of no major concern. Problems of an earlier century in Mauretania and Numicia had been sorted out, and the areas remained well regulated. Unfortunately, rumbles and rumors came from Syria. The Judean province remained a festering sore, threatening to explode at any moment and infect the surrounding region. Nothing seemed to pacify nor intimidate the unruly and unmanageable Jews at the other end of the great Mare Internum. Sooner or later the boil on the skin covering the great Arabian desert would have to be lanced. The Judeans were asking for attention, and Rome would soon give it to them. Time was running out for Israel.

Legal due process had ground slowly, preventing Paul from being swept along with the first persecution, but in time the sinister intentions of Nero were fulfilled. Just three months earlier Paul had been put to death on the Ostian Way just beyond the *pomerium*. Although he had not been outside the Mamertine Prison in two years, that time was filled with writing letters. For limited periods, Paul was allowed visitors, but near the end he was totally sequestered. His letters were still smuggled out, copied, and dispatched across the empire. Nothing stopped or stifled the work of the People of the Covenant.

The persecuted fledgling church continued its steady expansion. In spite of gossip, innuendo, and direct assault, increasing numbers of small cell groups met in private homes across the city. Each Sunday a large gathering assembled at dawn before the catacombs to receive the Lord's Supper. Their moral purity and integrity was obvious in a world of intrigue and decadence and a city filled with disillusioned citizens, disenfranchised slaves, and servants. Romans came to explore the faith of those who died so fearlessly. Time was clearly on their side.

Linus quickly became publicly identified as the new bishop of the Christianios. Once the new role of the tribune was known, he was denounced by senators and plebs alike. Linus' duties at the treasury came to an end. Nevertheless, his connections with the upper echelons of Roman society remained intact and allowed his spiritual influence to penetrate the highest level of affluence and power. At the same time, the poor and the dispossessed found an important place among the believers who gladly followed Linus.

Although Linus retained his residence, he lived elsewhere most of the time. Epaphroditus' house had amazingly escaped identification with the movement and was never investigated, so it remained a good meeting point near the center of Rome. Finally a villa was obtained for the Ben Aarons outside the Servian Walls of the city. The large house was beyond the *pomerium*, the sacred boundary of the city. Inside Roman territory technically but not in the capitol itself, their villa was close enough to the *cippi*, the stones that marked the boundaries, so access to the inner city was relatively quick. At the same time, the grounds around the house were open so soldiers could not sneak up without being observed. Often the trek into the city provided time for thought and reflection.

Priscilla particularly enjoyed her walks back to the villa with Stephanos. Often they shopped along the way, talking of what was happening with their rapidly expanding movement. "There's a little market ahead," she mentioned, pointing to a large temple in front of them. "Let's stop."

"It's behind the Temple Semo Sancus Dius Fidius," Stephanos pulled his toga more closely around his neck to shield himself from the cold. "They sign oaths and make treaties in there."

"Let's rest in one of the stalls and warm up a bit." Priscilla nestled close to her husband. "I'm a little chilled."

"Me too," Stephanos wrapped his arm around her. "The shelter will help."

Once they passed the stairs going up to the temple, the market sprawled out on the back side of the large marble building. One whole section was under a tent covering.

"Let's sit down on something." Priscilla breathed deeply.

Two large sacks of beans were leaning against a heavy timber that served as a tent pole for the large canvas extending over the section of grain displays. Stephanos and Priscilla settled down on the sacks and leaned against the pole. They watched servants, housewives, women, and men foraging through piles of fruits and vegetables. Not far away a spice merchant had his dried peppers, roots, leaves, and plant stocks piled on a covering on the ground. Sacks of ground spices sat around the edge, sending their pungent aromas across the market. Vats of honey were lined up next to wooden baskets filled with eggs. The smell of raisins and figs added a sticky sweetness to the wildly diverse scents floating through the market.

"I don't think I can stand this place much longer," Stephanos complained.

"Now, now," Priscilla pulled on his robe. "Don't look for some excuse to tear out of here. A few lost minutes won't make any difference."

"Oh, all right." Stephanos relaxed. He watched the shoppers for a moment and then turned his attention to the temple where oaths and agreements were sealed. As he observed businessmen coming and going from the Semo Sancus Dius Fidius, Stephanos saw a slight man rush out and start down the stairs. He stopped and looked around nervously. Almost identical in size and appearance with Stephanos, the man wore the little beanie cap of freed men, which identified him as a slave released from bondage. The freed man continued on his way, coming in the general direction of the market, but he stopped abruptly and turned away as two soldiers passed. Then the jittery ex-slave ducked nervously into the shopping area. Without saying a word, Stephanos reached for Priscilla's arm with one hand and pointed at the man with the other.

"Titus!" Priscilla choked. "It's him!"

She instinctively reached for her veil, pulling the covering across her eyes. Stephanos brought his hand up to his forehead, shading his eyes.

Titus looked up and down the street again. Once more he glanced over his shoulder before rummaging through a display of broccoli piled up in the entrance. Titus began walking slowly among the vendors. Here and there, he stopped and looked at some of the fruit as he wound his way into the tent-covered area. His eyes only briefly saw the displays and the stacks on the ground because he kept glancing uneasily at the street.

Stephanos and Priscilla sat like statues, watching their betrayer inch his way ever closer to them. An ugly scar ran from Titus' forehead down the side of his face. He looked worn and tired. When Titus was about six feet from them, Stephanos reached over and pushed Priscilla's scarf back on her head. He dropped his hand from his face and crossed his arms across his chest. Stephanos stared defiantly at his former friend.

Titus picked up two cabbages and bounced them in his hand for several moments before putting them back and turning to the grain vendor's sacks of wheat and barley. Only then did he look up at the two people sitting right in front of him. Titus glanced at Stephanos, but there was no recognition of the beardless Jew. Suddenly Titus froze and looked again. He batted his eyes frantically. His head moved mechanically back and forth from Priscilla to Stephanos as if his senses had ceased to function.

Stephanos and his wife didn't flinch nor move as they watched the color drain from the Greek's face. His mouth dropped, but no sound came out. His hand came to his heart, and he bent forward as a slight gasp slipped from his lips. He could barely step backward. His eyes kept blinking rapidly.

"You wear your freedom like a ponderous weight around your neck." Stephanos' voice was flat and emotionless.

"Oh, my God!" Titus exhaled and whirled backward, plunging into a sack of barley. He went flying over the top, crashing to the ground between other grain sacks. Several bags fell on him, making it difficult to get back to his feet. When he did stand, Titus stumbled sideways leaving his freedman's cap lying on the ground. Without looking back, he ran into the street as fast he could.

Stephanos picked up the little beanie and threw it aside. "Free indeed!" He spit the words out. "Titus will be paying for his ill-bought freedom until he rots."

"He was terrified of you, Stephanos. His eyes were like an animal's."

"And I am one of the few men in this city of whom he has no reason to be afraid. He can't even receive my forgiveness. His is the worst exile of all. Titus has no place in this world or in the next."

"We need to get out of here." Priscilla pulled at his sleeve. "I am ready."

The vendors watched Titus run up the street and then eyed the couple suspiciously as they left Titus' mess behind. Stephanos shrugged and held up his arms as if he had no idea why the strange freed man had created such a disaster.

They walked on toward the Mons Pincius hill that they knew would lead them to their villa, talking of their astonishing experience with Titus. Here and there they passed carpenters and builders restoring the many burned-out buildings that still awaited repair. Time had not healed all of the wounds left by the great fire.

During the past two years, Nero had worked feverishly to rebuild the burned-out city. However, the rich only became richer while the poor foraged through the ruins, trying to find places of shelter. The destroyed areas were cleared, and Nero's new buildings became the latest monuments to the glory of Rome. Marble and granite replaced what had been wood and terra-cotta. Although Nero could raise up new buildings, he could not put down the persistent rumors of his complicity in creating the misery that afflicted thousands and thousands of the citizens.

A week after Stephanos and Priscilla stumbled onto Titus, they met with other believers at the villa of Epaphroditus. The couple told the story of their encounter to a very attentive audience. When the old man heard their story, he smiled sadly and shook his head.

The meeting was nearly through when a runner came with an urgent message that Mariam was calling for them to return to the villa beyond the Servian wall. They excused themselves and quickly went north up the banks of the Tiber River. At Via Aurelia, they turned up Vicus Triumphalis, crossing the wall and continuing on toward their quarters.

"Are you sure you understood?" Stephanos asked again.

"Yes." Priscilla sounded irritated. "For the last time, no one has been hurt or is in trouble. The servant said your mother must see us at once. That's all. Some stranger has come with a message for your family. Linus Decius is also going to be there. Nothing else is wrong."

"Strange . . ." Stephanos pulled at his headband and continued his brisk pace. Still concealing his identity, he shaved his beard and kept his hair cut in a Greek style. The head band and distinctive multicolored Greek robe served him well. "All I know is that we were to come at once but not to worry."

Priscilla hurried to keep up. Her elegant dresses of fine wool and silk had long since been exchanged for the more common linen and cotton drapes. She wore ordinary *crepida* sandals rather than the high corked heels or bright-colored leather footwear of the aristocrats. Priscilla kept Mariam's Judean cloak with a hood close to her face. When she walked through crowded areas, she often tried to keep her face covered, but nothing could conceal her magnificent violet-tinted eyes.

"I suppose I overreact," Stephanos confessed, "but we have been through so much that I quake and tremble every time the word *emergency* is mentioned."

"I understand." Priscilla put her arm in his. "But you are walking awfully fast for a woman who is four months pregnant."

"I'm sorry." Stephanos slowed down immediately. "We're not far from the market where we last saw Titus. We could stop again."

"No, no, I think not," Priscilla laughed. "The merchants certainly will remember us. Just walk a little slower. Everything is going to be all right."

"Sure." Stephanos realized that the tragic deaths in his family had left a permanent mark. Any naive tendency to believe that things always worked out for the best was gone. The worst was *always* possible.

"You can set it down." Priscilla squeezed his arm.

"What?"

"That weight you've been carrying ever since we left the meeting."

"I'm so obvious?"

"In a very nice way," Priscilla smiled.

"I'll try." Stephanos silently reminded himself to slow down again.

The rest of the way he said little. He tried to act casual but realized that his arms were tense and his face was set like a flint toward their house. They soon left the crowded streets and the *insulae* behind crossing across the open field.

The villa was surrounded by tall, spindly cypress trees that lined many of the roads around Rome. Tucked into a wooded area, the house was not easily observed, but its second story made a good vantage point from which to survey the road.

Inside the front door an open-air atrium ran the length of the villa. As was true of Honorius' house, a peristyle garden and pool were just inside the front door while a larger *impluvium* reflecting pond was in the back. Stephanos could see his mother sitting by the *impluvium* pond talking to Linus and a man who was seated with his back to them. Stephanos walked so quickly that he left Priscilla behind.

"Mother, are you safe?" he called out.

''Ah, Stephanos. I'm glad they found you so quickly.''

''We came at once.'' Stephanos extended his hand to Linus before turning to the stranger.

A smile covered Mariam's face. ''Have you forgotten your little brother?'' Mariam beamed.

Zeda stood at once.

XXIV

Stephanos looked at the young man who stood before him. He was slightly taller than Stephanos and more muscular. In contrast to Stephanos' Greek appearance, he had a full black beard and hair that hung down to his shoulders and back. "Zeda?" Stephanos' mouth dropped. "Zeda? Can it be?"

Stephanos threw his arms around his younger brother, hugging him as tightly as he could before Zeda could even speak. Swept away by emotion, they rocked back and forth.

"Let me see you!" Stephanos stepped back. "It's been six years! You've changed!"

"I've changed?" Zeda threw his head back and laughed just as his namesake uncle would have done. "I still look like a Jew and you've become a Greek! I wouldn't have recognized *you* if we'd passed each other on the street!"

"What a big man you've become, Zeda. And little Leah? How is my little sister?"

"Pregnant again!" Zeda laughed once more. "She is populating Yerushalayim on behalf of the Ben Aaron family." He giggled at his own joke.

328

"Oh, Zeda!" Mariam hugged her younger son. "You are so much like your uncle that it brings tears to my eyes. You were always the happy child."

"And who is this charming lady?" Zeda turned to Priscilla.

"Please meet my wife, Priscilla."

"You are as beautiful as Mother said." Zeda extended his hand and bowed at the waist.

Priscilla went past his hand and hugged her brother-in-law, kissing him on each cheek. "Welcome to Rome."

"And you must be married by now," Stephanos chided. "Heaven knows you surely gave up on getting our approval to complete the betrothal.

Zeda stiffened and smiled weakly. "No," he said faintly, "the future did not unfold as we might have planned."

"Zeda comes with very bad news." Mariam took Stephanos' arm. "Please sit down. We have been talking for hours, and you have missed all the details."

"What happened?" Stephanos reached for his brothers arm. "Spare the details. Just the main facts."

"We thought maybe you were dead." Zeda sank into his chair. "No one has heard from you in over two years. We did hear of Nero's persecutions and Peter's death. I came because we could no longer tolerate the unknown."

"We couldn't send a letter," Stephanos quickly apologized. "After Honorius' death, we no longer had access to the military ships, and we feared identifying ourselves."

"Yes, yes." Zeda shrugged. "Mother has explained everything." He drew a deep breath. "My betrothed's family were arrested by the Romans on some trumped-up charges. They simply disappeared and are all presumed dead. I still don't believe it, but they have vanished."

"No!" Stephanos recoiled. "Not you, Zeda. Not again."

"Uncle Simeon was attacked by two *sicarii* and seriously injured," Zeda continued. "But he has survived and should be completely recovered by now. After the knifing, he was the one who demanded that I come to find out if you were still alive. We had to know what was left of our family."

"At least," Stephanos sighed and held his hands up to heaven, "Simeon lives."

Zeda shook his head and looked away. "I was prepared for all of you to have perished." He looked out over the courtyard. Zeda had taken on the familiar family profile. Although he was four years younger than his brother, Zeda's beard made him look even older than Stephanos. He stroked his beard with his long, thin fingers, which were another hallmark of their family. His hands were so thin-skinned that the veins protruded, giving an unusually artistic and creative appearance. "Of course, I am comforted that at least the two of you have survived. And yet—" He stopped.

"The pain of loss never quite leaves." Stephanos broke the silence. "Some days, the grief is more easily carried than others. But—" he paused. "But they died with great dignity and courage."

Zeda reached out and squeezed his brother's hand. "Leah has a wonderful little boy who is almost two years old. He is called Yitzchak."*

* Isaac

"A son!" Stephanos exclaimed. "*Mazel tov*† to me!
Better to learn late than never." Their laughter broke
the painful tension in the air.

"This is a time for discoveries." Stephanos turned
to Linus. "A week ago we saw Titus, Honorius' slave.
Ran into him in a market."

"The traitor?" Linus exclaimed.

"Titus ran like a frightened dog," Priscilla added.
"He was terrified of us."

"I thought that one of the soldiers killed him," Linus said. "I heard they chased him out of the palace
with drawn swords."

"Someone sliced him." Stephanos pointed to his
own forehead and check. "He looked like he had
aged twenty years in the last two."

Priscilla added, "The man is horrified of his own
shadow. He'd best fear more than men."

"He should!" Linus answered indignantly.

"What Titus meant for evil," Mariam observed solemnly, "God has used for His glory. We must remember to pray for Titus tonight."

"But we will celebrate now." Stephanos hugged his
brother again. "Let us prepare for a great feast tonight. We have been reunited with my brother! Who
could be of more help to us in Rome than you, my
happy brother?"

"I cannot stay." Zeda shook his head. "In fact, I
must return as quickly as possible."

"N—o—o—o!" Stephanos strongly objected. "You
can take Father's place and teach the—"

"You have not heard all Zeda has to say," Mariam
interrupted. "Zeda also came for another reason."

† Congratulations

"There is more?" Stephanos ask hesitantly.

"I am afraid so," Zeda replied. "Sit down and I will tell you more of my long journey."

Stephanos sat down slowly. "It seems there is always more."

"War has begun," Zeda continued. "Riots broke out in Caesarea this fall. The Romans violated the Sabbath, and a protest was sent to Florus, the new procurator. He contemptuously turned the delegation away. When the word reached Yerushalayim, people were very upset. For some crazy reason, Florus chose that moment to stage a raid on the Temple treasury. People protested and revolted. Florus sent soldiers into the upper marketplace, and over 3,600 of our people were killed. Simeon was slightly injured in that attack."

"—and the clash ignited a wild fire." Stephanos knowingly shook his head back and forth. "It always happens the same way."

"People hurled rocks from the roofs and blocked the streets with their bodies." Zeda added. "Finally the troops were forced out of the city and Florus was humiliated. Zealots took the fortress at Masada on the south side of the Dead Sea, killing every Roman in sight. The high priest tried to take control of the upper city but the Zealots took the Temple compound and burned the house of the high priest. Madness reigned supreme, and the whole city became a battleground. Many have left for other cities."

"The end is at hand," Mariam said quietly. "The Day of the Lord is about to break in the Holy City."

"You wrote of this," Stephanos said to his mother. "In the first book you and Mattiyahu* compiled, you wrote that Yeshua prophesied such a day."

* Matthew

Zeda continued, "The governor of Syria, Cestius Gallus, brought in a whole legion to quell the riots. Zealots trapped him in a mountain pass near Beth-horon between Lod and Yerushalayim. He lost at least five thousand infantrymen and hundreds of his cavalry. Even the siege equipment was abandoned. Suddenly everyone was talking of the victories of the Maccabees. The defeat of an entire legion fueled the rebellion. Our country is now at war with Rome."

"Can we succeed?" Stephanos asked skeptically.

"I think not," Linus answered. "I have just received word that the senate has dispatched Flavius Vespasianus to Palestine. He is the best general we have and is being sent with three legions. Actually, I came today to share this grim news. I can see no hope for your people save the return of the Christus."

"And so I came," Zeda continued, "because we feared that this might be our last opportunity to maintain contact if you were still alive. I am sure that we will be scattered everywhere if a full-scale war follows."

"Uncle Simeon always feared this day would come." Stephanos lowered his head into his hands and stared at the floor. "He foresaw what the Roman legions would do if fully provoked. I am sure he is filled with despair."

"So you can see why I must not tarry." Zeda threw up his hands. "I had no idea of what Bishop Linus has just reported, but this news makes my return all the more urgent. I must arrive before the legions to warn our family—and the believers. I am determined to search until I find out what has become of my betrothed."

"I understand." Stephanos slumped back in his chair. "But we must also rejoice that you are here. Tonight we will carve out a space in this chaotic world and let nothing dilute the joy of our reunion. I will make sure that our best is set before you. We have servants who are believers. They will be very pleased to meet and serve you. Enough of this heavy talk for now. Let us make the preparations for a great celebration.''

Linus departed while Stephanos and Zeda continued to share tidbits of family gossip. Priscilla and Mariam left to give instruction to the servants for preparing the evening feast.

Inside the *triclinium,* fires were built in the hearth as a hedge against the inevitable evening chill. By the time the sun had set, the festive preparations were complete. The family dining room was arranged in the typical Roman style with three couches pushed together to form a U-shape. The couches were very broad and twice as long. Narrow shelves inside the U were serving tables where the food was placed. Roman men ate while reclining, but the women sat on chairs inside the U, eating from narrow tables.

The boards were already filled with food when the Ben Aaron family took their places. While the meal was kosher, there was an overflowing abundance of salads, sweetmeats, and dried fruits. The fresh fruits of the season sat next to the roast lamb. A special Roman garlic and oil sauce had been carefully prepared for the evening.

In the traditional way, Stephanos said the prayers and broke the bread. Immediately Zeda told a funny story, making everyone laugh. Stephanos' serious demeanor disappeared, and he became like a little boy arguing with and teasing his younger brother. Zeda in turn countered with his own family anecdotes, which poked fun at Stephanos' stories. The two brothers laughed so much that they hardly ate the sumptuous meal set before them. They talked of the pranks they played on each other as children and remembered their good times, chasing each other through the family jewelry shop.

"And the building remains in the shadow of the great wall?" Stephanos inquired.

"Nothing has changed," Zeda assured him. "Everything is just as you last saw it. Up until the riots, our business remained very good."

"Uncle Simeon still works the trade?"

"Not so much." Zeda pushed his empty plate away and washed his hands in a finger pad. "Yochanan Ben Zakkai has become a highly respected rabbi in these last few years. He is the only sane voice to be heard among the leaders. The high priest knows that our Uncle Simeon is a force with which he must reckon. When he has wounded in the riot, there was grave concern all over the city for his well-being. No, he does not have much time for the business, and that is one more reason why I must return quickly. I have become the major source of production for our support."

"But can the business continue if there is a war?" Priscilla finished eating.

Zeda's face fell. All laughter washed from his eyes and his jaw set tightly. "If there is an attack on Yerushalayim itself, the question will be whether anything can continue."

The last morsels of food were consumed in silence. A servant came in to build up the fire in the corner hearth. The flames broke the night chill, but they appeared more menacingly dangerous than ever.

"Events will move swiftly." Mariam spoke for the first time. "And the time is short. We are at the end of a great era."

"Mother," Zeda asked, "you understand these matters as does no one else. Is this the final end?"

"I do not know, Zeda. I do know that an entire way of life will disappear. Yeshua predicted it would be so."

"Then what are we to do?" Zeda reached for Mariam's hand. "We need guidance. Our people need your insight."

"Yes, son. Particularly the believers in Yerushalayim must understand. The matter is urgent. Since the death of your father and grandfather, I have thought and prayed about this subject." Mariam turned to Stephanos. "Your future lies here in Rome with Priscilla at your side. God has given you this mantle of leadership. But my place is not here. I must return home."

"No!" Stephanos set up on his couch and vigorously shook his head. "Mother, don't even think such a thing."

"For many weeks I knelt in the catacombs before our family graves and prayed my solitary prayers. Finally I realized that my purpose in coming here was completed, and I began to sense a call back to our land. Zeda's coming only confirms what my heart has already been saying for many months."

"Please, Mother," Stephanos looked down into his empty cup. "Don't, not now . . . at least not for a while."

"We had to face a great battle with evil in this city," Mariam answered. "We paid the ultimate price and did not retreat. Death did not deter your father and grandfather. But that battle is behind us. A new conflict is about to begin. I must be there."

"You have never been apart from us." Stephanos suddenly stood up. "You might never be able to return to Rome or we to follow you. You can't leave!"

"Remember," Mariam answered. "We're exiles. We will always be. We hear the sounds of eternity. We can't be attached to any place or situation for long. There is no other alternative for us. Each of us must be true to our call."

"But the journey!" Priscilla reached out to her mother-in-law. "I fear for you. Danger lurks everywhere."

"Thank you, child, but do not let concern become fear. The only effective weapon the Evil One has left is fear. He has nothing left but intimidation."

"I don't understand," Priscilla puzzled.

"The world can be a very frightening place." Mariam looked into the fireplace. The flames leaped over the logs and the burning embers crackled and popped. "When people start living by fear, the Evil One orchestrates their anxiety until finally they are controlled by anything that intimidates them." Mariam straightened and spoke more forcefully. "But love has taught us to stand bravely above the confusion. We don't even have to fear death. No one wants pain, but I have no apprehension about walking into this final battlefield."

"You will miss the birth of our child!" Stephanos objected again.

"I seem to miss all the births," Mariam laughed. "Maybe I will make Leah's next delivery." Mariam suddenly became pensive. "My heart breaks when I think of leaving the two of you, but I must not second-guess the future. I can only go forward in faith.''

''Mother, no one could ever accuse you of doing anything less.'' Stephanos paced and shook his hands. ''But I know that when your mind is made up nothing can deter your course. I just wish—'' He threw his hands up in the air again.

''We will have to travel by boat.'' Zeda didn't look at Stephanos. ''Any other way is too slow.''

''I remember the last boat trip well.'' Stephanos said wryly.

''Your poor grandfather!'' Mariam laughed. ''He never ceased to tell us that Jews were made for the land and only fish were created for the sea.''

''Zeda,'' Stephanos sighed, ''you never saw anything like the trip over. It was terrifying!''

While Stephanos told the story of their voyage, Priscilla helped the servants clear the tables. The family laughed and talked so long that the fire had to be restoked twice. The cold winter night air poured in until each one had to cover up with a wool toga. Finally the oil lamps burned low, and the evening took its final toll.

''It seems like only last night since you came.'' Priscilla hugged Zeda.

''The week has gone in the wink of any eye.'' Zeda kissed her on both cheeks. ''We have poured a lifetime into these last few days.'' He swallowed hard. ''So much to say and so little time.'' His voice trailed away.

Stephanos pulled on the ropes that held the bundles on the donkeys' backs one last time. ''I'm sure everything is secure. The distance to the port at Puteoli isn't far enough to create any slack."

"The servant who is going with you to the boat will know the shortest route," Priscilla added. "He will take you around the city to avoid any trouble."

Mariam reached out and put her hand on Priscilla's stomach. "You are going to have a wonderful boy. I just know it in my spirit—a boy! I will so miss being here."

"You don't have to go, Mother." Stephanos immediately reached for her hand. "Not quite yet."

"I know," Mariam sighed, "but boats don't wait. And those old familiar words keep coming to me at night. My task in life has been defined by them ever since He summoned me. They called me forth again last night."

"What words?" Priscilla ask.

"*Talitha cumi.*"

"I don't understand." Priscilla frowned.

"That's Hebrew," Stephanos answered. "It means, 'Stand up, little girl.'"

"The Master called me back from the abode of the dead with those exact words," Mariam explained to her. "And He has sent me forth ever since with the same command. Sometimes I have been sad and other times afraid. In my darkest moments, His voice has spoken the same call, and when it came I knew the hour had come to journey on. Each time I was called to leave death behind and look for new life ahead. It has never been easy, but the way has always been right."

Suddenly Stephanos threw his arms around his mother's neck and hugged her as tightly as he dared. "Why can't we just go back to the way we were, when we all lived and worked in the shadow of the great wall in our little shop in Yerushalayim?" The words barely came as he wept uncontrollably. "Father and grandfather made their beautiful creations. We lived simply, happily. Life was so good."

"The Holy One of Israel graciously chose us to be part of a great plan." Mariam kissed him tenderly on the cheek. "He did not give our family an easy task, but He allowed us to be part of a wonderful purpose. He made our lives count for all time and eternity. We have been given the better way."

"You have become my mother." Priscilla bit her lip and tried to look away. "You are the family I lost." Then she leaned her head on Mariam's shoulder. "Now I am about to lose you forever." Her body shook as she silently sobbed.

"*Talitha cumi,*" Mariam whispered in her daughter-in-law's ear. "We are at the beginning and not the end. I could never have chosen a finer, more courageous wife for my son. I will tell Leah and my grandchildren of your courage when you stood with me the day Philip and Jarius died. I will tell them how my Roman daughter stood on the edge of the Circus and held her hand to the sky lifting up the cross. I will always remember you walking in the midst of your Roman friends fearlessly proclaiming the righteousness of Peter and my family. You helped me walk that overwhelming journey back into the city, and I loved you for weeping with me when we knelt together in the catacombs. You will forever be in my heart." Mariam rocked back and forth as she cradled Priscilla.

Stephanos turned to his brother. "Oh, Zeda, protect her well on that long voyage across the sea. I have something for you—just in case of any trouble." Stephanos picked up a pair of sandals and pressed them into his hand. "Uncle Simeon taught me a little trick that saved Mother's life. In the heel of these thick sandals a jewel is carefully concealed inside the leather. Tell Simeon his treasured ruby ransomed mother from prison! I put a priceless black pearl in its place. The day may come when the gem will buy another release. If all goes well, just give the sandals back to Simeon as my gift."

Zeda silently kissed his brother on both cheeks.

Stephanos and Priscilla locked arms as Mariam and Zeda joined the servant who was waiting to lead the donkey. Silently the trio walked down the path away from the villa. They stopped just as the path turned into the cypress trees. Mother and son waved a final farewell.

"Perhaps," Stephanos called one last time, "next year . . . at Passover . . . in Yerushalayim."

APPENDIX

THE FIRST BISHOPS OF ROME

Peter	Died A.D. 64
Linus	A.D. 64–76
Anacletus	A.D. 76–88
Clement	A.D. 88–97
Evaristus	A.D. 97–105
Alexander	A.D. 105–115

Glossary of Hebrew

Adonai—Lord, Name of Jehovah God
Akeda—Denotes the binding of Issac for sacrifice. The idea refers to the ultimate test of faith.

Bar Nabba—Barnabus
Bar Sabbas—Son of Shabbat
Ben Aaron Family:
   Jarius—Ruler of a Jerusalem Synagogue
   Mariam—Jarius' daughter
   Rachael—Wife of Zeda
   Simeon—The younger brother and member of the Sanhedrin
   Zeda—The eldest brother
     The children of Philip and Mariam:

Stephanos
Leah
Zeda
Dammesek—Damascus
Eliyahu—Elijah
Gaba'im—Deacons, men who conducted acts of
    mercy and charity, sometimes called Tze-
    dakah
Gennesaret—Sea of Galilee
Gey-Hinnom—Jerusalem's garbage dump, origin of
    the idea and word for hell

Ha Elyon—The Most High God
Ha Mashiach—The Messiah

Keffiyeh—Arab headdress
K'far Nachum—Capernaum

Marta—Martha
Mattiyahu—Matthew
Mezuzah—Ornament on doorways with scroll in-
    side, touched as a sacred remembrance
Mizpah—A covenant of departure invoking God's
    blessing.
Morgen David—Star of David

Pesach—Passover

Ramatayim—Arimathea
Rudach Ha Kodesh—The Holy Spirit

Sheol—The place of death
Shimon Kefa—Simon Peter, leader of the twelve apos-
    tles
Sukkot—Feast of Tabernacles

Tefillin—Leather straps that hold boxes containing written prayers that are bound to the body during worship.

Tzedakah—Agents of charity of the Synagogue, Hebrew for *deacon*

Tziyon—Mt. Zion

Ya'akov—James, referred to as the brother of Jesus. Actually they may have been first cousins.

Yerushalayim Dedaheba—Elegant woman's gold headdress made in Jerusalem

Yeshua—Hebrew for "He shall save his people from their sin"—name of Jesus. Yeshu is the affectionate familiar form of Yeshua

Yesha'yahu—Isaiah

Yochanan—The apostle John

Yosef—Joseph

Zealots—Fierce extreme patriots

Zekenim—Spiritual leaders in the Synagogue, Elders in church

The Jewish Calendar
   Tishri: September to October
   Heshvan: October to November
   Chislev: November to December
   Tebeth: December to January
   Shebat: January to February
   Adar: February to March
   Nisan: March to April
   Iyar: April to May
   Sivan: May to June
   Tammuz: June to July

Ab: July to August
Elul: August to September

The Jewish Day
First Hour: Sunrise to 9:00 A.M.
Third Hour: 9:00 A.M. to 12:00 noon
Sixth Hour: 12:00 noon to 3:00 P.M.
Ninth Hour: 3:00 P.M. to sunset

ABOUT THE AUTHOR

Author of ten books, including *When the Night Is Too Long, Where There Is No Miracle,* and *The Dawning,* Robert L. Wise, Ph.D., is a long-time student of the Hebrew language and of Jewish culture. He has traveled extensively in the Holy Land, as well as across the world.

Robert lives in Oklahoma City with his wife, Margueritte.